Rural

Harmony

JEAN CARTER

VANTAGE PRESS

NEW YORK   WASHINGTON   HOLLYWOOD

FIRST EDITION

Published by Vantage Press, Inc.
120 West 31st Street, New York, N. Y. 10001

Manufactured in the United States of America

To

"YOU ALL"

(especially the real Rob, Doug, Don, and Mari)

Whenever I've seen your worried, tired, or unhappy faces in the cities, I've yearned to rent a little store and place an ad in the window:

"Are you lonely, broke, tired, unhappy? The world too much against you?
"Won't you come in?
"I've found a secret I'll share with you. If you will work with it, you can erase your problems like magic. It's not a new secret. I didn't even find it. Someone gave it to me. I'd like to share it with you."

It is my deep conviction that religion and science teach the same principles, each using its own vocabulary. Mostly I'll use the religious because they are musical. So whether I say "God" or "Power" or "Cosmic Intelligence" they are synonymous terms. This Power to which we pray and in which we live will not solve your problems for you but it works *through* you. No basket of vegetables through your kitchen ceiling . . . although it might be a kind neighbor or a friend with his surplus at your back door at some stages of your consciousness.

When you let Him work His miracles through you, you would have it no other way. It is the difference of maturity, the transition from "child of God" consciousness to "son of God" consciousness.

"Miracles" to me are not abrogation of law but rather the working with silent, invisible laws. They work so quietly and so wondrously, with only good to everyone in an ever widening sphere, that they seem magic.

The real foursome (Rob, Doug, Don, and Mari) may recognize

some of these stories. Many may have been lost in their memories during the business of growing up. Or they may have retained the details so keenly they missed the significance of the attitudes expressed by the actors in the drama of life. I hope the principle involved is not lost in the chuckle—yet I would not wish the chuckle ignored. I believe God has a great sense of humor and often there is a smile or a laugh or sheer joy in the lovely divine way a problem is solved.

In a sense this story is a parable. But its main reason for being is that it is my gift to you. With all my heart I hope it amuses and delights you as well as encourages you to use this panacea: placing your hand in His and walking with Him. There is nothing too small nor too big, from your social life or your daily responsibilities to your business ventures, to talk over with Him.

I hope it doesn't sound preachy. I hope it sounds practical and inspiring, that the episodes subtly invite you to experiment, and then use this scientific way of living.

So, come with me through this story of Faith and John Wells. This is their story as accurately and truly as I can put together the details. From an individual Song of Life, and then a duet arrangement, they learned to be part of the Divine Symphony. They discovered rocks do sing as do the colors of the beautiful world, that there is an intrinsic harmony in the universe—perhaps more easily heard in the country.

Jean Carter

RURAL HARMONY

Only the occasional song of the birds interrupted the stillness, the predawn symphony finished. All was quiet. The August morning refreshing, slightly foggy with a hint of Jersey humidity to follow. Night wetness draped the garden. The neighborhood and the Wells household slept while Faith Wells, kneeling among the beets, carefully removed the few daring weeds, her attitude one of reverence in this lush growth.

Faith inched down the long row, moving along on her knees. This wonderful garden kept the four of them well fed for nine months, canning and freezing supplementing the actual growing season. Her busy fingers worked from the beets to the string bean department while her thoughts kept pace with her movements. John's and her plans, their desire for a farm—"a place to grow the children and to build to a going farm so that John could retire early"—these visions occupied her often.

In her garden she felt close to God. Formerly she knew Him as the Creator she worshipped on Sunday or turned to in distress. Now she knew Him as constant Father and Friend. During these early morning togethernesses she sensed His inspiration and guidance, sometimes for the day, sometimes for a long-range program. What a difference knowing Him made!

She smiled whimsically. She thought she'd "always been religious." Mere belief in a Creator or church attendance are only cornerstones, she reflected. This walking-talking with Him—this is the building. This manner of attunement she had to teach herself. Deliberately construct new habits of thought, employing words as bricks and singing affirmations while housekeeping. Prayerfully erasing former attitudes from her consciousness to make room for the new. It was work. Some of it was lessons by rote, cleansing away old thought habits, forming new roads in the brain.

Funny, the long chain of circumstances. "Coincidences" the world named them. That was really very inaccurate. Surely not Fate either. No. Man has free will. One always has the power to reply negatively or affirmatively to God. But surely if dogged by bad luck or ill health—cosmic prods—one becomes increasingly willing to turn

9

Godward! Perhaps it is akin to the lone pine tree atop the windy hill. Buffeted and racked by winds, drought or poor rocky soil, it becomes stronger and more beautiful than its sister in the lush, protected valley; it develops character . . . so with Faith Sanford Wells. The stormy childhood predating her mother's suicide and the turbulent teens compelled her spiritual roots to stretch far down even as her soul and body reached upward.

Surely, too, there is a Divine Hand guiding life. For the first time in many years she resaw herself, the young child standing in the attic windowledge, vainly summoning courage to fling herself down. She had sensed a measure of restraint! Odd that scene should well up within her now. She had not consciously remembered it for many years. It brought other scenes in its wake: the ten-year-old backed against the school wall with the taunting children in a circle. "Yeah, your mother was crazy. You must be crazy too."

There had been a stream of many years before she could be objective about some of those scenes. She had deliberately covered them. Now, unreservedly she could forgive them, bless them. They had known no better. They had parroted their families' dinnner talk. Truly she must be most careful to judge her own ideas and speech before her children!

Her recurrent dream was surely a cosmic prod! A dream a coincidence? Hardly. Even before she comprehended some of the hidden truths of the universe she sensed this dream held special signifiance for her. Many times in the fragile moment between sleep and complete wakefulness she held the slender thread of consciousness delicately, arose, wrote the words. English words from the purple-bound, gold-printed book she read while in the green leather chair in the living room. She could read them perfectly—but she could not comprehend their meaning. They conveyed absolutely nothing to her. Weeks elapsed while she pondered. Then, when she lost interest in the puzzle, the rerun appeared.

Two years now since the little book came to her. No, it wasn't purple nor printed in gold. Those were only God's symbols to her. Not once did the dream reappear after she discovered Emmet Fox's *Sermon on the Mount.*

Sometimes she wondered about her sanity—this business of prophetic dreams. Comfortingly she recalled many folks in the Old Testament days were guided by dreams. Gradually she was able to differentiate the prophetic dreams from the subconscious junk welling up in need of spiritual cleansing. Tugging gently at the small weeds around the tomatoes a smile of love and joy lighted her eyes and lips. Truly the recurrent vision prepared her, hounded her, was her cosmic prod just as the invisible restraining force that held her to the windowledge.

"You have no right to hates or resentments. . . . If God being Spirit is within everyone how can you say you love God while hating one of His children? If you are hating someone, you are hating part of God. . . . You are not required to *like* everyone but you are required to *love* everyone . . ." said Fox.

That was the stopper! For the first time in her life she had looked into her soul. She could not remember complete freedom from either emotion. She had been positively promiscuous in her attitude or words of condemnation, sweeping criticisms and judgments on the world and all its people. Tolerant, she? Merciful? Living by the Christ law of Divine Love? Yet she had thought of herself as a pretty nice person, a religious person!

"Ye tithe mint and anise and cummin yet neglect the weightier matters of the law. Justice, mercy, and love. These ye should do without leaving the other undone. . . . If any one hath aught against thee, leave thy gift at the altar. Go and be reconciled with thy brother and then come offer thy gift."

She could rationalize the matter. She could shrug and mutter she grew up in an atmosphere of hate and get-even climate. Through the example of Dad Sanford she absorbed family hates and resentments as a young child inhales family traditions and patterns—unquestioningly. But those were passive hates, acquired like handmedown dresses one puts in the closet, worn because one has nothing else. So absorbed attitudes too can be a poverty of soul. But now, at maturity, she had the right—the very responsibility—to discard the inherited errors.

The resentments she held against her Dad were different. They were like the undies in her drawers, away from the casual glance, but purchased by herself from the inheritance of retaliation and resentment, demanding an exorbitant interest. In the light of worldly logic she had a justifiable case. The list of his effronteries was

11

lengthy. His drinking up the funds for her college education. His demand of her savings on several occasions. The roughshod manner in the demand because he was in a jam. His whisking her to the lawyer's office the morning of her twenty-first birthday to sign a statement waiving even rights to question his misappropriation of her inheritance. It wasn't the point of his absorbing the estate—but that he would think her likely to stoop to such a gesture and take worldly means to preclude such a thing! No, he never whipped her after puberty but there are other indignities that crash on the feelings.

Later, experienced in the pseudoluxury of resentment, her personal list of the hated grew, including nameless people encountered in public, in stores, public conveyances, on the streets—fragmentary rudeness or thoughtlessness the only reason. Probably the inner meaning of the Second Commandment Moses furnished, this absorption of family climate and atmosphere, Faith thought to herself.

That was the challenge! That business of looking into one's heart and eliminating the junk. It is so easy to breathe and eat the family attitudes, and who on reaching his majority questions this inheritance? It was easy for her to cast off the "hate George" and "hate Gertrude" inheritance Dad gave. They never hurt or impeded; those hates were not personalized.

But the complete forgiveness of Dad was a long campaign. Fox's little book on her lap and his teaching fresh in her heart, she knew she had to forgive Dad. Her first step on the ladder to complete forgiveness of him was perhaps one of condescension, a holier-than-he thing or poor-guy-didn't-know-any-better. But it was the first rung on that ladder. The top step required months of valiant endeavor, for little memories nagged at her heels. Childhood scenes periodically appeared before her conscious mind and demanded of her. But one day there was the top rung within her grasp, and that day she reasoned within herself, "If I believe reincarnation is the logic of the universe, then everything Dad ever did to me was my boomerang and now the score is clean. I can pray for him in all sincerity for I know that he has set up boomerang stuff for himself. . . ."

The victory! The sense of freedom after the conquest of her lesser self. She'd been like Atlas, the cares of the world across her shoulders. Now the world extended and grew with this new freedom.

Memories washed over her gently. Bless him, it was John who

cast the first ray of wholesomeness in her life, back in the going-steady days. His shrugging comment, "So? It was your mother's life to do with as she wished." (It wasn't, of course. One's life is God's and one is entrusted with its purpose and responsibility.) But John's healthy comment of light rather than gloom was refreshing. He held no ominous bondages of "taint in the blood" or "insanity" over her. No wonder she loved him! All those jigsaw pieces in her puzzle of life. John's understanding, his gentle consideration, the very framework.

Faith vividly recalled her sincere prayer that spring day, Fox's little book in her lap, the afternoon sunlight spilling on her in the green leather chair. Every mind-etched word returned to her now, "God, I'm sorry. Forgive my inner attitude toward each and everyone I once hated. Even Dad. Help me really mean this prayer every day, not merely today. Help me love enough to atone for my errors of understanding . . . amen."

He had helped! She could still mean this prayer. Now she could honestly say she loved everyone. Not liked, but loved. She had not arrived. Occasional weeds sprouted in her soul-mental garden but instant attention to them kept the garden beautiful.

That spring produced its miracle in her too. She never quite pinpointed when it occurred, whether that day in the green leather chair, or if it were a gradual miracle covering weeks. Instantly though in that moment she had sensed relief. Vindictiveness dropped from her as petals from a faded flower. Her world prettied itself even as she left the green leather chair to go about the day's needs with the children and so forth. The very universe glistened new and fresh. Flowers were more brilliant and fragrant. Morning bird songs awakening . . . when had she heard with such perception! She began to see the inner beauty in all the world and all its people. And down within her body her heart healed. Once so loaded with resentments it functioned improperly, like gears not quite meshing. Now her heart held rapturous joy of living, beating in harmony with the rhythm and music of the universe. How free she felt! She would never return to the Atlas consciousness. She even walked with more spring in her step.

True, she had to continually and incessantly watch her thoughts. Old patterns in the brain were strong but self-discipline strengthened the new patterns. As the muscles of the body so the muscles of thinking. Each day it was easier to build the new thinking, develop

13

the habit of walking and talking with her inner Lord in every phrase of her living.

Yes, that spring was the turning point in their lives. She and John were happy together from the beginning of their marriage, the home harmonious. Their life goals the same as well as equal maturity in working toward those goals. Somehow, indescribably and wondrously, life together was now more beautiful, more enjoyable, and more fun. Surely God brought them a long way—and in many ways. Even money stretched further than formerly!

In the silence of her inner cathedral, while kneeling in the garden, Faith prayed. Intermittent phrases and clauses put themselves together. "Father, You've remade me—and all my life. Now John and I want a farm. Want it very much . . . so much it must be Your idea for us. . . . Please help us find the right farm, under all right conditions . . grace, You know. . . . Here and now, I pledge our tithe on all the farm income. I know John will want to also. . . . We'd like a big old place to fix up. We'd like to move in time for spring planting. Someone to do the farming until we can do it ourselves. A fireplace. Brook. Land across from the house so we can control the view. A view too! . . . And, please, I'd like a split sink in the kitchen; it's so handy washing spinach and garden harvests. . . ." She reflected thoroughly before expressing the amen. Yes, this covered all their hopes and dreams. "Amen," she whispered into the lettuce.

In the stillness Faith's busy fingers continued to work. Thoughtfully she reflected on her prayer. Within her heart she had the comfortable feeling her prayer already stretched into the universe to begin its work. She imagined a little white thread of radar groping forth like a butterfly antenna to find "the right place under right conditions" and she smiled. She thought too of the tithe pledge. John would agree with her, she knew. Furthermore it made sense.

"Give and it shall be given unto you . . ."

Now, time to awaken John, prepare breakfast, commence the day with the children.

Spring—Well, Almost—And Spring

With the mercury low in the thermometer and pavements icy in early February, it is not the ideal time to move a family. But this was not merely moving day. This was the Wells' day of fulfillment.

The huge van, parked at an angle to the long walk from the front door of the colonial suburban home, was gradually being filled with household effects. Three brawny men and one slight chap slowly picked their way. Back and forth. Countless trips. Noses flattened against the living room window Rob and Doug observed, Doug squeezing a large brown paper bag of small toys.

Interrupting his own busyness John stopped to watch, laughingly called to Faith, "I wonder why the little fellow staggers out with the big stuff and the burly chaps move the lamps."

A shout from Rob, "Here's Gramp Landemere!"

"Open the door for him please, Robbie," called Faith from upstairs. "John, all those things in the middle of the living room go with us."

"How far does the middle extend?" teased John as Faith came running downstairs.

Preoccupied, she ignored his twitting. "Here, this pile with the Electrolux. I can do all the rooms before you or the van get there. Otherwise it's silly for us to go ahead."

Rob opened the door to Pierre who theatrically removed his hat in a sweeping bow. "Ah, my dear," he directed to Faith, "your housekeeping is a mess." His left hand patted Rob's head while his right extended to John for a hearty shake and an empathic wink included Doug. "What's the plan of attack?" of John.

"Faith wants to take these things," pointing. "Food stuff, vacuum, the dog—if you don't mind a dog in your car?" Pierre shook his head and John continued, rebuttoning his jacket the while. "I'm staying down until the movemen get through." John hefted the huge bag of foodstuffs and Pierre reached for the vacuum. In perfect timing Rob opened the door as they approached.

15

Faith glanced from the children to the remaining pile of things-to-go-immediately, decided in favor of the children. "Rob, you get into your togs. Doug, come let me help you into yours. Then each of you take out a small package for Daddy or Gramp to pack in the car. If we leave now we'll be at the farm in time for lunch." She spoke half to herself, half to the boys, then each holding a package they raced to the car.

There was much to plan. The ample frozen potpie for supper; all the things for lunch, enough to include the Landemeres. She must remind John to transfer the balance of the freezer foods to the locker until she could transfer it once they were settled at the farm. Arms loaded she moved thoughtfully to the door. She turned to look back at the dishevelled living room, only the precisely half-lowered shades an indication of homey order. Upstairs the men prepared to carry the massive mahogany bedroom suite, their noise muffled. Faith's glance traveled lovingly around the room. The Wedgewood blue walls, the antique white enamel trim she and John applied. There was still a quality of love and joy in the atmosphere. It radiated despite the present chaos. Even the empty nook that once held their most prized books and precious figurines glowed. "God, bless this house and the new owners. Give them a great deal of good here," whispered Faith.

The movers appeared at the top of the stairs with the first of the heavy pieces. Faith opened the door for herself and them, picked her way to the car. The rock salt John had spread on the ice created pockmarks now that the sun was higher. "Good morning, Lu," Faith called through the closed car window to Lucille huddled in the warmth of the car heater. "It's mighty fine of you two to do this for us." From the corner of the raised car trunk Pierre waved a mittened hand in a silencing gesture. "Boys, you get in the back seat awhile. Get in on Gramp's side so you don't disturb Grandma Lu. John, where's Tramp?"

"Isn't he in the house?"

"No. I haven't seen him since we breakfasted at Miller's." Pierre motioned Faith into the car. John whistled loudly for the black cocker. No answering bark. As Pierre settled himself into the driver's seat John commented, "I suppose he's off to pay his respects to the town. You go on. I'll bring him."

"Don't forget him," cautioned Faith lifting her face for a kiss. "Make it for lunch, Dear?"

"Not at the rate these fellows are going. It's slower packing than unpacking. We'll be along." John backed away from the car, slightly facing downstreet. A groan escaped. "Here come my bosses," as Faith giggled. Three large women minced up the middle of the street.

Faith tapped Pierre on the shoulder. "Let's roll along and stop but look as though we don't expect to linger." Sensing Pierre's query she added, "They are our mothers and my favorite aunt. They've come to help, bless them! But it's all done, so they will just scurry around and. . . ." Faith's voice trailed off as the car edged forward.

Rob and Doug busily waved to their daddy from the rear window then turned to give full attention to the oncoming trio. Faith rolled down her window. "Hi! Mothers and Auntie, the Landemeres. Landemeres, John's mother to the left and mine to the right. My very favorite aunt, Mrs. Hewitt, in the middle." Murmurs of acknowledgement, then Faith added, "We're going ahead to get ready. You'll come up with John?"

Faith's stepmother, Mrs. Sanford, and Auntie exchanged apprehensions. "How do we get home again?"

"Could you bring them to Chatham?" Faith asked of Pierre who readily nodded. "They're only chauffeuring us up," Faith explained further. "Lulu, you'll still staying up with us?"

Nose buried in her fur collar Lulu nodded wordlessly as Pierre hinted his car along, the little fellows eagerly called good-bye. At the foot of the street they turned right and headed for the highway. Lucille half turned in the front seat, resettled her laprobe and invited Faith's conversation. "Tell me, Faith—I have a right to ask, for we think of you two as our children. You could be, you know," her plain face glowed with loving interest. "What are your plans for the farm?"

Pierre mumbled something like, "Give them a chance to get settled," but Lucille waved him silent, so he gave himself over to the delights of eavesdropping and driving.

"We'll sort of feel our way, Lu. Our original desire was to get a farm and give ourselves a ten-year period to bring it into a nice, prosperous going farm so that John can retire from the business world and be a full-time farmer. He thinks he wants

17

the broiler business. I like the idea of eggs by the million. I'd like to get into the restaurant business and have the farm supply the food requirements. Anyway, we have fifty-two acres with forty-five tillable. We have room to play around, and there's a custom farmer to do the field work on a share-crop basis until we can swing our own equipment and time."

Lucille nodded understandingly. Faith adjusted Doug's snow-suit a bit, adding dreamily, "Funny thing, this farm . . . It's definitely the answer to prayer. Every single thing we wanted with all our hearts comes with it ! . . . And it's all an outgrowth of our 'farm miniature' where we learned to garden and raise chickens during the war." Lucille encouraged with her eyebrows. "We wanted land across from the house so we can preserve the scenery. We wanted a split sink as we had; it's convenient for washing garden produce, you know. We wished to move in time for spring ploughing, and by the time we are settled spring will be here. We wanted an old place to fix up, maybe sell for a big fat profit and move to one with more acreage if such are our future needs. This one's ninety-one years old. Even the someone to work the fields! We got every single wish!" Lucille's head moved from side to side, an expression of incredulity on her face.

Conversation flowed intermittently, for each youngster was busy with his own thoughts during this adventurous day, and Faith was silently praising the Lord for the Wells' day of fulfillment.

The car moved along the highway, progressing into the foot-hills of the Schooley Mountains, the scenery gradually changing from average suburban home to estate, to small farms—some of subsistence level and others of lush prosperity, huge white silos standing austerely in the winter daylight.

"Care to stop for lunch?" Pierre interrupted the silence.

"It isn't much further, and I do have everything available in your trunk," offered Faith.

"My stomach reports hunger now. How about we pull into the next nice little place, men?" Pierre pulled the boys to his side, and in anticipation they wiggled expectantly. When he parked in a short time at a small place in Chester, they bounced to the sidewalk while he assisted Lucille and Faith.

Again on their way, the day changed from bleak wintery sunshine to dull greyness, sudden sharp blasts of wind accentuating the cold. Only spotty country traffic interrupted their attention to the scenery. The highway provided patchy ice surprises to startle the unwary motorist, and the dark serious mountains in stark boldness against the monotone horizon offered a bleak backdrop. Around the turns, up and down the mountains like a geographic roller coaster, until finally at a high point the Sanatorium water tower gleamed silver in the distance, well removed in height above the naked trees, the dark green of the pines unable to mitigate the rigid lines of winter.

At Bunnvale the silver tower loomed nearer. The weird little house, painted blue and orange, served as the guidepost for their turn to Woodglen. The children loved this road, already nicknamed it 'the Dippsydoodle Road.' Gradually downgrade toward the Glen, the water tower hidden from view, the church spire served as their landmark. "Here's where we turn," Robbie shouted so enthusiastically that Pierre involuntarily jammed on his brakes. It was the first word from either boy since the luncheon spot.

"Follow this little dirt road to the crossroad, then right for a thousand feet, and we're the first place on the left," directed Faith. "In a little bit our name will be on the mailbox." The boys bobbed up and down on toes in excitement, Doug humming a little song of joy that spilled out, filling the air.

Downhill all the way, past two saggy farmhouses where even the rural mailboxes toppled in forlorn dejection, around the turns, Pierre keeping in the tire lanes of the narrow road. Abruptly each side of the road sheared off into a gully. At the foot of the hillside, Spruce Run, frozen along its edges into the rocks and fallen twigs and branches of the tree-lined shores, moved its chattering way to the distant sea. The wooden planks of the bridge contributed their song as the car rolled over, continued up the slight incline to the crossroad. Pierre travelled very slowly the last thousand feet to the Wells' driveway, his practised eye calculating the house in its surroundings. In the early February afternoon it appeared grey-white, large and handsome, well set back on the spacious lawn decorated with unruly, barren forsythia, lilacs, and other shrubs. A couple of towering firs and some generous lollypop shaped maples along with several elms lent a charm and mellowness to the house, compensating for the lack of paint or the

19

romance of spring freshness. While Faith's eyes gleamed, beholding this beautiful old place and realizing anew it now belonged
to John and her, Pierre saw the dilapidation of the outbuildings,
the unpruned shrubs, and the lack of paint. Slowly, reflectively,
he let himself out, walked stiffly around the front to assist his
wife.

"It's lovely," breathed Lucille. "Lovely! A house with possibilities."

Rob and Doug bounded out, arms windmilling, shouts punc-
tuating the quietness, their staccato duet a repetitious "we live
here! we live here!"

Arms filled with packages Faith and Lucille proceeded to the
side porch as Pierre removed things from his car trunk. "Do you
have your key?" at the front door from Lucille.

Smilingly Faith opened the door. "No, it is unlocked. Always
will be." Lucille preceded her into the living room and audibly
caught her breath as she saw the magnificent fieldstone fireplace
centered in the north wall, a window on each side inviting the up-
land view to the pasture under barren apple trees. She sped from
room to room, appraising both the room and its view, delivering
a running commentary on the seasonal changes they would appreciate from each window.

Pierre entered the living room, set the vacuum near the fireplace and departed for the outbuildings, Rob and Doug self-
appointed guides.

Faith placed her packages on the kitchen table 'they' left.
Looking out to the west field she dreamed momentarily. She'd
forgotten the details of the kitchen, for they saw the farmhouse
only once, putting down their deposit to start the legal machinery.
There were needs here. She noticed them immediately. Lots of
paint. Surely a new stove. Anyway, she didn't want everything
electric. If the rural power goes off, one has nothing: No central
heating. No cooking facilities. No water for kitchen or bathroom
needs.

Lucille joined her, eyes shining, radiant smile on her lips.
"Faith, this is a beautiful place! You have things to do, I know,
but this is charming. A house with possibilities. I am sure you will
be very happy here, and I know how much it means to you both."
Warmly, impulsively, Lucille kissed her. "Tell me what I can do to
help."

"Nothing right now. Just follow me around while I vacuum—if you don't mind projecting your voice above the noise." They entered the living room. Faith slipped the vacuum parts together as Lucille walked to the northern window.

Wistfully, "We always wanted to live on a farm, Faith." Lucille paused and Faith, looking up, thought she detected a shininess in Lucille's eyes. "We did one winter. Pierre's people had one down Bucks County way. He loved it. Wanted to buy it, keep it in the family. His sister was executor of the estate though and she wanted too much. We couldn't swing it. It needed too much. We stayed that one winter—sort of caretakers. We were just sick when it was sold. Pierre's up in your outbuildings now. I guess he's in his glory. . . . You and John are doing so many of the things Pierre and I wanted to do—your children and now this. We married late. Foolish waste of time. We missed much togetherness. The fun of a family. You and John are rich, Faith. Rich because you plan a goal—and then work toward it."

Lucille turned from the window, her direct blue eyes regarding Faith, observing her swollen pregnancy. There was no envy in the older woman. Merely a wistfulness. Her life had omissions but also fulfillments. Faith's brown eyes met hers and there was a deep understanding bond between them. Faith could think of no answer. Slowly she began the business of readying the house.

The place was not dirty. Faith meticulously did the ceilings, the walls, the floors. Painting throughout, but just now the good vacuuming would suffice. Downstairs completed, the women moved upstairs. The bedrooms, bathroom, then the master bedroom. They were in the master bedroom when Pierre wandered in. Lucille shouted over the noise of the vacuum, "What do you think of their farm!" It was an ebullience rather than a question.

Leaning against the doorframe, Pierre grimaced his answer. Tersely to Faith as she shut off the Electrolux and stored it in the bedroom closet, "You got about ten years' worth of manure."

"That's our law of retribution," she laughed merrily. "We gave away our lovely chicken manure from our 'farm miniature'. . . . You know the old law about 'give and it shall be given unto you.'"

Pierre met her merriment with a serious steady gaze. He could not answer immediately. He feared for this couple, these children, not his and Lucille's by legal or physical laws. Theirs only through the law of love and empathy. Why had these children bought so impulsively! Why hadn't they brought him along? And now, Faith definitely pregnant, two other children to care for, a husband frequently out of state on company business! How large a mountain of responsibility could she stand! Faith's brown eyes laughingly regarded him and he knew she didn't even sense his concern. Pioneer stuff! he scorned. Aloud he said, "All right if you have thirty thousand dollars to pour into it the first year—and another twenty thousand the second. By then, you'll have it about as livable as what you left."

He could not shake off the impact of those dilapidated outbuildings. The broken windows, half-hinged doors of rotting wood, the sagging pig house. The musty humidity of the house cellar and that monstrosity of an oil burner—a comic strip hilarity—except that two kids he loved were going to live with it! And between those lovely wide floorboards downstairs he could see right through to the dirt floor in the cellar! The foundation was sound enough. The roof line did not sag. Porches good. But more than sixty miles from the metropolitan zone where John worked! John to commute daily—when in state! Faith to have another baby! Pierre's head buzzed with concern and his stomach felt queasy!

Lucille, not seeing the farm through Pierre's practical trained eyes, reproved Pierre with a gesture. Her laughter rippled forth coating her words, "Oh, Faith, if I were a younger woman I would outbid you for this place. It has charming possibilities. Just charming!" She walked to the southern window of the master bedroom. Across the meadow, to Spruce Run, Lucille noticed the brook's winter turbulence, heard its frothy song. "That meadow is yours too, isn't it?" She turned to catch Faith's nod and then gazing through the leafless lawn shrubs to the patches of snow and ice dotting the steep hillside across the brook, the lifeless brown carpet accenting the patchy whiteness, "Once I read every brook has an individual song . . . like every person has a different purpose in God's plan," mused Lucille. Then swift laughter giving way to the dreaminess in her voice, "Remember, Pierre, how you teased Faith in Chatham because her drapes are the new fashion and spilled on the floor a bit? You used to say 'Are you waiting for the drapes to shrink or the house to grow?'" The laughter gurgled in her voice, lights of joy played over her not beautiful but interesting face. Suddenly she was serious, a trace of prophetic wistfulness in her manner. "I have a feeling even their drapes will fit in this place. A feeling . . . of their belonging . . . Almost like destiny. I believe they will be most happy here. Find themselves . . . in a deep sense. I believe this is a milestone for them."

So long as it's a milestone and not a millstone! thought Pierre. He shook his head dejectedly. He was engulfed with pessimism about the whole matter. "Lu, it's a big undertaking. A *big* undertaking! They know nothing about a farm. Baby coming! John away a lot!" His right arm waved dramatically and he glared at Faith. Turning back to Lucille, "And she'll probably start some stock this year!"

Although Faith could control her laughter she could not conquer the twinkle in her eyes. "We've already planned 'Quota', Pierre," quietly.

"What's 'Quota'?" he rumbled.

Laughter bubbled in her voice. "You know. Although John's not exactly a salesman he is connected with the sales department. You surely know what a salesman's quota is." Her tones were light, teasing. Pierre did not respond to her mood. Respecting him, Faith was suddenly serious. "We're planning baby number four as a playmate for number three. Planning it for eleven months after this one."

Pierre winced. Lucille laughed heartily, dabbing at moist eyes and drawing a big sigh. "We have to, Pierre," continued Faith. "We don't believe in one-child families and by the time this one is big enough to want playmates both big fellows will be off to school all day."

Pierre shook his head in consternation. Lucille, now in command of speech, stretched forth a reassuring hand, lightly touching his sleeve. Softly, "Oh, Pierre, to be young again and make big plans! Then to live them!"

Downstairs the boys came into the dirty colored den, for the late afternoon February coldness was uncomfortable. Noses pressed against the window they again watched, this time through lawn trees toward the little wooden bridge. The rumble of the heavy truck crossing coincided with their yells of "here's the van!" which ended the conversation upstairs.

The Landmeres formed a reception line at the living room door.

23

As the movers brought in each piece, they indicated its site, calling to Faith when they could not remember. Faith busily supervised all things—so it seemed. The boys watched all things—so it was.

When the truck was half unloaded John and his carful rolled into the driveway, maneuvered around the van and Pierre's car. At that moment Faith was in the kitchen while four movemen held the freezer. On paper she and John were sure it would fit when 'they' had theirs. Now in actuality it didn't. Leading the way to the dining room Faith instructed them to place it against the hall wall. "Sure you want it here, Lady?" questioned the boss. "Once we go you don't move it like a lamp."

Faith looked back. No, it didn't belong in the dining room. White enamel, it definitely was a kitchen or cellar appliance. Certainly on an uneven dirt floor this cellar was not its site. In the hurry of the moment she could think of no other place. As the movemen filed out of the living room door John and the entourage entered. Greetings exchanged John kissed Faith, handing her five loaves of bread and five boxes of salt. "My love, these are from five sets of superstitious friends for our good luck . . . I let Tramp remain in the car until the van goes." John piloted Faith to the kitchen and placed the gifts on the sink counter.

"What's the joke?" noticing the merriment in his eyes.

"All the way up the girls were batting it back and forth about big houses being unnecessary and out of date. Listen to them," nodding in the direction of the two mothers and Auntie.

"Another fireplace in here," Auntie was saying from the den. "Isn't this lovely! Such nice, airy rooms!"

"I love this room. I would make this the living room. Look how the late afternoon sunlight spills into the room," enthused Mrs. Sanford.

"I like the living room fireplace," commented Lulu.

John moved back to the group. "That was all covered for a while."

"What do you mean?" demanded Lucille facing it.

"The day we bought this place 'they' told us they discovered it." John gestured to the wall separating the living room from the kitchen. "This whole area was once the kitchen, back in the days when this house was built. It's ninety-odd years old, got a dated cornerstone in front. Well, somewhere along the line one of the owners got tired of trying to keep this fireplace in fuel, covered it with beaverboard and plaster. Perhaps this was around the time they put in central heating and utilized the den fireplace flue for the cellar heating. Then when 'they' bought the house they thought this would make a lovely living room for size as modern kitchens don't have to be dancehall size. They portioned off the present kitchen, putting up this wall. As there was only the French door on the stoop and that window near it, this room was very dark. In sounding around to find the beams and know where to put some more windows, sounds were peculiar by the fireplace. They peeled off the covering and discovered this fireplace. Then it was natural to put a window on each side. . . . And then the fun began."

"Why?" from the chorus, although Pierre stood a little apart.

"The walls are stone-filled," continued John. "Mostly little stones. Some fieldstones. As they cut through the walls, the little stones kept falling down. Old-fashioned way of insulating a house, you know."

The women exclaimed among themselves, wagging their heads and their voices over the lack of appreciation for the beauty in the stonework. When the movemen staggered in with John's massive, handmade toolchest, the visitors rearranged themselves into a longer receiving line. Lulu was at the end, slightly moving her feet for warmth as the constantly opening door let in draughts of February cold, the Landemeres nearest the door and Mrs. Sanford and Mrs. Hewitt next.

Smaller pieces began coming in now, and quickly. The movemen were filled with one desire: to finish the job and be out of "this nowhere place before dark." John and Faith laughed to themselves, overhearing their comments as they moved in and out. "Glad my ole lady don't haffa wash all them winders. Complains 'nuff now." "Let's get outta here, man!" "Yeah, man! I don't glory none for these narrow country dirt roads!" "What for does anyone move 'way out to nowhere?"

By five-thirty winter darkness and stillness settled over the countryside. The new farmers and their friends listened as the echo of the truck rumble died down. They heard the gear-shift for the high, winding hill. Among themselves they laughed at the attitude of the movers. The mothers and Auntie laughed too, an empty outward gesture for in their individual hearts they too felt John and Faith had moved "too far from things." For personal reassurance Lulu glanced up the road to the stream of light emanating from the nearest neighbor's kitchen. Lucille alone was en rapport with the new farmers.

When the Landemeres, Faith's mother and Auntie bade farewell John reminded Pierre of the turns for the highway. As the Wells couple stood at the French door watching the little car ease down the driveway into the dirt road, Lulu matter-of-factly asked, "What's for dinner?"

"A partially frozen potpie, homemade, ready to pop into the oven, Mom," answered Faith. Turning to John, "And now, my love, we are left with only ten rooms of upheaval! But we're here. This end of moving I don't mind. Now each thing done is an accomplishment toward more order."

By way of answer John hugged and kissed her while Lulu headed for the kitchen. This farm, this fulfillment of a long cherished desire! Words of joy between them were inadequate, unnecessary. Brown eyes looked deeply into brown eyes. They held communication beyond the scope of words. These two were reborn. They were another John and Faith Wells, in contrast to only yesterday. In a spiritual sense, they had lived in a desert of materialism a few years ago. Now they were reaching and growing in a new consciousness.

There was a new unity of divine harmony within them and between them. This fulfillment, this demonstration of the truth that whatever you set your heart upon and believe can manifest does "come to pass." Faith's forefinger played with John's earlobe. "You know, a long time ago—back in the summer—while I was working in the garden I made a covenant with the Lord. I bargained with Him, said that if He would find us the right farm under all right conditions I would tithe on all the farm products. Is that all right with you?" softly.

John gathered her into his arms, sealed his affirmation with a kiss.

"You know . . . after I made that pledge . . . He seemed to lead us here immediately. Remember how long we sought prior to August?"

Later, the little men abed, the three adults delighting in the colorful and noisy crackles of the fire shared the day's happenings. John laughed over the movers' receiving line while he filled his pipe. Then Lulu and Faith began a dovetailed account of their erroneous assumption that all spring water is hard. Amid laughter they described their battle of the suds. Dumping in too much detergent, suds had bubbled up and over the sink division. Suds overflowed to the floor. They had patted the suds down. Attempting to dilute them, they slowly trickled in more water. Suds multiplied in geometric procession. They had pulled out the stopper; let more water into the sink. Water flowed down the drain. Suds remained. Surreptitiously they dribbled some water. Suds revived. Glorified themselves, bubbling in various colors and sizes. Cold water. No difference. Suds rejoiced and grew, sud atoms splitting and resplitting infinitely. In desperation they had walked away from the sinkful of foam, and in silent annoyance unpacked a carton of books. Only now, hours later recounting it to John, did it assume hilarity.

Every day brought more order to the old farmhouse. Although curtains were not hung by Saturday and most of the books remained in the cartons, the windows were washed and clothing in place. A lovely bird feeding station swung from one of the maple trees on the front lawn, provisioned with peanut butter, raisins, bird seed and bacon fat. Across the driveway the Dutch oven was converted into a garden tool place. By then Lulu had many barrels emptied, dishes washed and in their places. John had tidied up his workbench and tool chest, and Lulu and Faith were almost used to the transition to electrical cooking from gas.

Sunday John had to entrain for Ohio and a business appointment. He and Faith went to the old church for services, then had a quiet dinner together. Afterward Faith began the long ride home to the farm, singing songs of affirmation and thanksgiving the forty miles. Songs of repledge of herself to Him as the good steward, songs of happiness for the new and growing life she carried under her heart. Why, with this 'Unity stuff' there are no limits! This is spiritual self-psychology, she thought. Yes, these teachings are dynamite. It's all so simple. Not easy, but simple. You just get yourself all straight with God—and then amazingly the whole world adjusts around you. I wonder why one doesn't figure it out for himself?

At last, cold and stiff from the drive she turned into the farm driveway, steering around the Dutch oven to back into the garage. Wheels spun on ice. She grimaced, got out. She wedged some empty feed bags under the rear wheels. In the car again, she eased the gears into reverse. Feed bags shot against the rear wall. She turned off the motor and went to the house, too cold to maneuver with patience. "Hi, little men," as she let herself in. "Been good for Lulu?"

"A-huh," they greeted, Doug running to hug her. Rob finished putting a few more pegs in his tinker toy model elevator, then approached for his share of hugs. "Daddy just called and we haven't any water." Faith looked over their heads to Lulu standing in the doorway between hall and living room, her glance questioning their words.

"Yes," confirmed Lulu. "Right after John called the water conked out."

Faith frowned slightly. "What do you mean 'conked out'?"

"It doesn't come out of the faucet," Lulu's voice edged with excitement. "What'll we do? We got to have water! Want me to take a bucket and go up the road to that other house for some?"

Faith pushed her hat back, shook her head a bit. What does one do without water on a farm? Be calm, she told herself. Where does one get water? 'They' said there's a pump in the cellar for the house supply and the barn supply is by gravity. A pump. Does that mean a plumber? Did the spring give up or is the fault with the pump?

Slowly, "No, let me think some more." Faith moved toward the hall. Why hadn't she checked with John about these important matters! Whom could she call? "Did something make a noise, Lulu?"

"Yes, the pump in the cellar made an awful racket. I pulled a switch."

Good Lulu, thought Faith, feeling she wouldn't have had the sense to pull a switch. "I guess we need an electrician," proceeding to the telephone in the hall. Picking up the classifieds she ran her finger down the list. The first number brought no answer. Nor the second. The third produced a busy signal. In the darkening corner of the living room Lulu muttered to herself, half aloud, "You'll never get anyone on a Sunday afternoon." Confidently Faith put through the third number again and was rewarded with an answer. She stated the problem, her name, and supplied directions to the farm. Breathing a prayer of thankfulness after disconnecting she called to "Lulu, "He'll be right out, Mom. I'll put the car away now that I've thawed. Weatherman promises sleet and ice for tomorrow." Coat rebuttoned she paused to admire Rob's construction masterpiece.

Lulu flounced out of the living room, slices of words coming from closed teeth. "Humph! 'Be right out.' Wish I could believe everything you do. Brush off, if I ever heard one!"

If Faith heard she silently rejected the negation. Quietly she let herself out the side doorway. Standing before the car a moment in the crispness she heard a car slamming over ice and stones. It was a good distance away but approaching rapidly, the hills and hollows magnifying the sounds. In her car again she reached toward the ignition as a small truck turned into the driveway. Out again, walking toward the electrician she smiled cheerfully, "My word! You flew low. Aren't you from Califon?"

"Yep." He aimed a gap-toothed grin at her and reached for his tool kit, followed her into the house. Lulu's dark eyes grew in astonishment as she speechlessly watched them disappear behind the cellar doorway, the indistinct rumble of their voices faint. "Ain't no real difficulty, Lady. Jest your belt. Ain't got one that size with me, but I kin fix y'up temporary. Be back first of the week, do a real job."

"Fine!" enthused Faith. "Well, I was about to put the car away and I imagine you can work better without my breathing down your neck," remembering Dad Sanford's dislike of the housewives who stood with one eye on the clock and the other on his movements.

Faith's car efforts were again fruitless. There was no unfrozen dirt or sand to cover the ice, nor any supply of rock salt. In quiet desperation she sat still. She had to put the car away, for the weather report haunted her. With John out of state she had many responsibilities. Taking care of their assets was one of them. The car had to be available to meet him at the Gladstone railroad station whenever he called on returning to New Jersey. "Well," half aloud, "they say God likes to be used in the little things and then we know Him better to work with in the big things. . . . Please help me, God."

Her thought was barely expressed when Hendricks came out the side door to his truck. He sized up the situation and approached her with his big hand outstretched. "No traction, eh?

Ease her in." Gently the car sought the comfort of the garage.

"Thank you," was all Faith said aloud. In her heart she marvelled at the simplicity and speed of the demonstration.

"Got yuh fixed temporary, lady," Hendricks was saying. "Be back Tuesday. Got the butcher to do Monday."

Faith's feet marked time, her limbs numb. "Do you know anything about freezers? We just came, you know, and because I couldn't think quickly where to put the freezer we had them leave it in the dining room. We want it in the playroom—at least until that room gets fixed as such. It takes four men to move it."

"Reckon I'm your man," pleasantly. Turning he spit at the pond adjacent to the Dutch oven. "Four men in my outfit."

"Come in a moment. I'll show you what needs to be done in the event I'm not here. My mother-in-law will be, though, and the doors would be open anyway. Don't believe in locks. God takes care of all our stuff."

They reentered together. Faith showed him the freezer and the place between the playroom windows to which it should be transferred. "You'll need to put in an outlet. Also check this ceiling fixture. We believe there's a short. Then you may as well put an outlet in the dining room. And—do you know anything about electric stoves?"

"Little," drily. "Got the G.E. distribution in the area."

Faith motioned him to follow her to the kitchen. He stood aback, calculating the stove. "Ought to have this in an antique shop, Lady."

Faith smiled slightly, restrained herself from commenting on the wonders of the Anderson gas stove she left in Chatham. Quietly, "These two burners don't seem to get hot."

"Need new grids."

"Oh!" Then, almost as an afterthought, "Will you check the freezer motor? They handled it carefully but I should like to be positive about it."

Wordlessly he nodded his answer, looked around for a convenient place for his tobacco overflow. Seeing none, he briefly touched his cap and hastened out.

Monday ushered in an overflow of karma as well as a dense fog rather than the predicted sleet and ice. The day began with visibility at ten feet—sometimes. Patches opened occasionally where the drippy wall seemed to hang, only to close with complete definiteness, a moist curtain of nothingness. Bustling the two little men into the car after breakfast they began the pilgrimage toward the Glen. Not knowing the precise location of Rob's school, under the railroad overpass she turned left. Going slowly along the Glen main street Faith spotted a typical school sign—on the other side of the road. The school was apparently somewhere behind them. Turned around she headed for Bell's Crossing. An opportune opening in the fog revealed the little four-room schoolhouse far below in the hollow. Now Faith was annoyed with herself. If she had asked that inner Monitor she would have been guided to the correct choice of roads! No, she had travelled along in the old trial-and-error manner of her past, even though she knew that nothing, literally nothing could ever be the same since the discovery of Fox and this "Unity stuff!" Every value had changed. All the old ways were of little—or no—value! This wasn't just intellectual knowledge. This was a whole new way of living. Every department and phase of her life would be different. She knew that—but she sometimes forgot to practice it!

Turned around she once more headed for the Glen. From this approach the turn to the schoolhouse presented a problem. Between the severe right angle turn and the ice, the little Studebaker slid, abruptly stopping at the fieldstone abutment protecting the driver from the hundred-foot drop to the brook. The motor stalled. Faith restarted it. The ice prevented a full manipulation of the car. She inched it backward, turned slightly, progressed forward. The back and forth maneuver. Tedious improvement in their predicament.

Rob commenced a running stream of negation. "Ma, I don't want to go to school today. Ma, you'll go into the river. Ma! we'll never make it. Ma, I bet there isn't any school today. I wanna go home!" The last a wail.

Doug commenced a river of optimism concurrently with Rob's stream. In a quiet, assured manner he calmed his older brother, "Hush, Robbie. We'll make it. Don't be afraid. See, each time the car turns us around a little more. All the time it's turning more and more. Soon we'll be headed down the road and crossing the bridge."

Faith was bulky in her coat. She was hot with exertion and hot with annoyance. The growing baby within her protested also, kicked uncomfortably. She was too close to the steering wheel anyway. If she hadn't been so damned pigheaded, had asked her Lord which way! Her lips firm she seethed through her teeth, "Will you two hush!"

In the school hall four teachers stood talking together when Faith and Rob arrived. Miss Muriel Tally preceded them into the first grade-kindergarten room. Rob's papers were in order. Forty children milled around during the teacher-mother conversation, Rob standing in close proximity to Faith. "Where did Rob get the school bus? Was there a charge? Are there luncheon facilities for the children? What time did the bus come along?" Those were some of Faith's questions.

"Has he had number work to one hundred by ones, twos, fives and tens? No? . . . Then he's a little behind us. We may have to cram him a little," smilingly. "I'm sure he will catch up quickly."

Rob's brown eyes regarded Miss Tally seriously. Suddenly the large roomful of children overwhelmed him. When Faith asked if he wished to come home on the school bus it was the spark to set off the emotional charge. He let out a wail of anguish, clung embarrassingly to Faith's leg while her arm comforted him. Gradually his heaving frame quieted. Over his head Miss Tally was shouting, "It's a very big event, you know." Faith's arm encircled Rob until he was completely composed and receptive, "I'll call for you, Robbie, take you and Doug for haircuts."

Over the treetops sunshafts were dissolving the fog. Open patches were larger and stretches of visibility longer. Back at the farmhouse two trucks absorbed the driveway. Faith backed up to the farmer's driveway, actually a grass lane spreading from the large lawn to the west field. Again frustrating ice. Doug chirped, "If my daddy were here, he would get it in right away." Faith's lips compressed into a straight line and her eyes flashed. Dull red slowly crept up her neck and into her face. She let the car slide forward to the dirt road, then zoomed up the ice encrusted grass. Glaring at Doug she slammed out of the car and strode toward the playroom entrance. Her anger vanished by the time she entered the house and she pleasantly greeted Hendricks with, "What are you doing here today? You said Tuesday. Oh!"

"Forgot ice melts," laughed Hendricks while he and a workman continued to bail. "Changed my mind. We checked the motor already. She's okay. Needs gas and we'll shoot it in. Two of my men will get at your outlets and one at the stove. I'll take up on the water pump. You show 'em where you want the outlets."

"Right along the wall between the dining room and the hall," Faith said to the designated workman. Turning to Hendricks again, "Will you give us an estimate for wiring the barn and the two henneries on the hillside before you go? We'll use the smaller building for a battery house, the other for a laying house."

"Any special time?"

"I'm ordering the chicks this week, scheduling their arrival for the third week of March. Can you fit in your work by then?"

"Yup."

As Faith returned to the dining room one of the workmen retrieved a drill from Doug. Quietly tactful he was saying, "Oh, no, sonny. Your folks don't want a hole in the floor."

"Thanks," Faith acknowledged to the workmen. "Doug, suppose you play outdoors. It is clear now and you'll enjoy exploring the farm. Get your wagon out of the Dutch oven but stay near the house or the outbuildings unless you tell me where you are going." Rezipping his snowsuit she herded him to the front door.

Lulu, busy in the kitchen with the last barrel of dishes, occasionally sang at her work. After exchanging a few pleasantries Faith went upstairs. She wished the house to be in complete and charming order by John's return. The noises of the men at work and their called conversations drifted to her. Outside, only the rural stillness and the noise of a three-year-old at play. By eleven the men were preparing to leave, sweeping up the dust from their drillings. Hendricks pounded on the side door. "Want the estimate in writing? I got the measurements and I'll figure it more accurate at home. If you want jest an idee, I'll say around two hundred."

"Your figure sounds fair. You can plan to do the work."

Briefly touching his cap, apparently his gesture of acceptance, Hendricks added, "We'll have you fixed in time." His four workmen single filed from the cellar doorway, each touching his cap in passing.

Mindful of the departing trucks Faith resumed her tasks. Another knock at the side door. This is like a movie, she thought. A tall blonde youth, satchel in hand, stood before her. "I've come for the phone," he explained.

Faith blinkingly regarded him. "'Come for the phone'?" Her

33

echo conveyed bewilderment. "I wrote asking to have the title— or whatever you call it—transferred to our name."

He shrugged impersonally. "Don't know nothin' about it, Ma'am. Got orders to take it out." He waved his papers.

"Suppose you call them up, ask them to look up my letter." She led the way to the hall telephone, stood against the doorway as he asked the operator for the business office, then for his supervisor to whom he explained Faith's predicament. Listening to his supervisor he stared vacantly at Faith.

"They never got it," he repeated to her.

"They must have," countered Faith. "It never came back. Furthermore, the people who sold us this place wrote their confirmation."

"She says it never came back and the other people wrote too," he repeated into the telephone. Once again to her, "They can't go by what those people say."

Resignedly, "Then I suppose you'll have to take the telephone."

Going into the dining room Faith looked at the stark trees with unseeing eyes. When he announced he had the instrument Faith neither answered nor followed him to the door. She was stunned and dejected. How could she contact John in Ohio? John would try to call. He always called several times when on a trip. It would worry him if he were unable to reach her. How would she know when and where to meet him? He had been uncertain about the day as well as the hour of his homecoming.

And what about the baby! The nearest hospital was twenty miles away. Whom could she reach in a hurry to take over with the little men? Or how could she reach John in Newark? True, she wasn't due for a couple of months yet and she wasn't afraid. Or panicky. But a telephone for them was a necessity, not a luxury. A telephone was a connection with John anywhere. A link with a country doctor. The hospital. Or a friend to take over with the boys—although right now she didn't have a friend in this new world.

Lulu's heartiness from the kitchen penetrated her thoughts. "What'll we have for lunch?"

Wearily, "I don't know, Mom. Anything."

"You got to eat and feed that baby!"

"I know . . . I'll eat. . . . But I can't think up what to eat." Faith's voice trailed off into silence. This day had been one thing after another. Constant challenges. Fog and ice. Decisions about the freezer, the outlets, the hennery wiring. Now the telephone. Comfortingly her inner monitor reminded her of the billboard in the Glen about the town taxi. Of course!

She could wire John to contact her through the town taxi. Surely for a taxi fee they would bring John's message, then she could meet his train.

Not knowing the cause of Faith's preoccupation and misunderstanding the weariness of her tone, Lulu grabbed a dish, dried it so arduously it broke in her hand. The breakage served to whet her anger. Bending to pick up the pieces, she did some strong thinking that galloped along like this: "Helluva time to move! I could have told 'em that! Not that they would have listened! Way out here in the sticks. Don't know anyone. Only one car. How the hell she gonna get outta here in a hurry when John's in Spodunk or some damn place! And what the hell she gonna do with the other two! I can't wait here for that new baby!"

Faith neither heard nor perceived Lulu's smoldering rage. She had resolved the challenge regarding the telephone and was again at peace. She turned over the balance of the problem to the Lord, knowing that in some lovely, divine way all things would be taken care of. She would hold to the thought that the age of miracles is not passed. Miracles are happenings in accordance with spiritual law. Not black magic. Deeper than that. And always good. Blessings to everyone. White magic.

Within the half hour they all sat together in the kitchen, glad to pause in the busy day. Faith recounted their adventure in getting Rob to school, his tiny new teacher, finishing with the plan of calling for Rob and taking both boys for a needed haircut. So the chatter flowed until Lulu's noisy worryings interrupted, "Any place you can call up for groceries if you're stuck?"

Faith looked long at her mother-in-law before answering, anticipating the older woman's receptivity to her story. She noticed Lulu ran to the window each time an infrequent truck or car passed, joyously exclaiming, "You're not so far out." Faith shook her head slightly. Her answer was very soft, but steady.

"No. They just took out the phone."

" 'Took it out!' " Lulu's large brown eyes widened in distress. Her round face blanched. She echoed herself in a near-screech, " 'Took it out!' "

Doug's large hazel eyes regarded her minutely. This was an interesting drama.

Since Faith had overcome the matter within herself by now, she could answer gently. "Yes. They claim they never received my letter. It did not come back to me . . . But you can't call a company a liar."

"Well, I never!" exploded Lulu. Abruptly she arose, the table bench banging noisily against the radiator, scolding vehemently the while. "They never would have taken it if I had known anything about it! Suppose you go to the hospital in a hurry! And it's miles from here. 'Took it out!' " Her explosions were like a car backfiring. Abruptly aware of Doug's presence and with magnificent regain of composure, Lulu marched from the kitchen.

Faith was acutely aware of Lulu's distress. She longed to call after the retreating figure, "Never mind, Mom. It'll work out all right. We'll put it in the hands of the Lord. He never fails." But it remained unsaid. She and Lulu did not see eye-to-eye on this "Lord business." To Lulu, God is the Big Something one worships. To Faith, God is constant Friend at her elbow, Ever-Present Partner in the big and little affairs of life. To Faith, God is Health, Harmony, Protection and Supply but to Lulu the lacks of the world are merely part of the scheme of things, and one accepts them. So each believed vastly different spiritual concepts.

Once, Faith did not know God as Supply or prosperity. Now she could understand that aspect, know and work with this blessing, know it as a blessing for everyone—not merely a chosen few. This new comprehension to her was a two-way street—she choosing to work with God and maintaining a readiness to have Him work through her—"them" rather for she thought of herself as dual and as a team with John.

She longed to go into the living room and say, "Look, Lulu, remember how you thought Hendricks was giving me the brush off? Examine my belief that God never fails and that He worked through Hendricks; Hendricks came and we had water. Hardly an hour was lost. Don't you see, Lulu, how religion can be *practical?* A usable set of rules for every day? Don't you see that we receive our expectations? So all we have to do is expect high enough? Don't you see some of this is our responsibility—mental discipline —habit?"

But in the past whenever Faith tried to "sell this Unity stuff" to Lulu there was a closed door. Faith reasoned God doesn't use a jimmy to force His entrance, therefore, she had no right to force her concepts on another. Not even on Lulu whom she loved dearly, thinking of her as John's mother rather than as mother-in-law. Then, too, blushingly she recalled the matter in the Glen— her own continuation of trial-and-error rather than decreed divine guidance.

Faith stirred about in the kitchen. Lulu, hearing the dishes, called she'd "do the mess." So the two women passed each other, Lulu stomping to the kitchen, an intense combination of fury and worry, Faith calm and unruffled but aware of her own short-comings of spiritual habit.

Beginning again at the book cartons, a heavy banging on the front door alerted Faith. A large burly chap, unshaven, a trickle of tobacco juice zipzagging from lips to chin, confronted her. Mindful of her stare, he sleeved his mouth, shouted his mission. "From the 'lectric company." Right hand shot out, palm up. "Ten dollars 'cause you ain't the owner." He turned and aimed at the newly installed bird bath. A large splat, the slow downward procession commencing. Zestfully he scratched his forehead.

"We are the owners," Faith answered mildly.

"Oops. Okay then." He backed down the steps. "See that you pay bills on time or we shut off, lady. We don't mess around none." He reached his parked car. His slammed door punctuated the admonition.

Closing the door Faith mumbled to herself. "They have the monopoly. Do they have to be rude too? Who wants to retrogress a century!" Ruffled feelings resettled, she resumed work. Re-handling all these beloved treasures stilled and quieted her. Each one brought its own memory. Running her hand lightly over the walnut bookcase, she relived John's experiences—bringing home a load of lumber in a public bus, converting it to a book-case. Seven layers of varnish, each rubbed down with love and perspiration. This was his wedding gift to Faith, put together with dream stuff and devotion.

Now Doug interrupted, thrusting his head in the side door-way, "What's today?"

"Monday," she smiled at him.

"No," earnestly. "The number of it."

"Seventh."

"No! *Number!*" insistingly.

Faith puzzled a moment. Slowly, "Do you mean what is like 'today'?" Although Doug nodded eagerly Faith answered lamely, "I don't know."

"Yes, you do. What's a letter like 'tomorrow'?"

This gets worse she thought. Aloud she said, "You mean yesterday'?"

"Yes." He was excited and triumphant. He closed the door quickly, sat on the stone porch meditating.

Faith returned to the books. Now they were dusted. She began arranging them on the shelves, allowing for various sizes, placing them according to authors and subject matter. A calculating glance at the mantle clock. Doug burst in once more. "Yesterday you said tomorrow is your birthday. Is that now?"

Faith smiled, put down the books and took the three-year old in her arms. "That's a lot of thinking, little man. You mean Lulu. Her birthday is this month. Mine isn't until November and that's a long way off."

Another pounding on the front door. Faith and Doug walked together through the center hall. "I'm the dog warden. Got a dog here?"

Superfluous question. Tramp put on the best demonstration of his life.

"That's a dollar thirty-five," his hand extended for the fee. "License'll be sent you in the mail. I'm your neighbor up the road that way," pointing to the west.

"How do you do?" acknowledged Faith while digging into her purse.

"Cocker, huh? Color—black. Sex—male. Age—about two," answering his own questions, scribbling the information as he furnished it to himself.

"No, Tramp is nine this July. He entered the regeneration when we moved here," mischievously. Faith's eyes twinkled in merriment, but there was no response from the dog warden. Methodically he scratched out his answer, inserted Faith's. Nodding curtly he ran down the steps.

Lulu called from the kitchen, "Do you suppose they all waited up the road? I've moved plenty in my day but I never saw anything like this." Lulu stood at the dining room window by now. Faith joined her and they laughed together.

Then it was time to call for Rob. Doug was glad. This was a long day, this first day without Rob as playmate. The interruptions which were beginning to sap Faith's strength were of only casual interest to Doug. In a little while they were at the school, Robbie trooping out the rear door with many other little people. The bigger children streamed out the front doorway.

Faith cruised the streets of Hampton, seeking a barbershop. They found an old-fashioned one across from the fire house, complete with dirty windows, pot-belly stove, dimly lit interior. The lanky barber blended impersonally with the establishment, his scissors clacking time with his gumchewing. High on the wall, well above a dull cuspidor a brief sign:

All haircuts 40¢
Positively no reduction for
children

Faith gently pressed the boys forward to the row of chairs, re minded them she would seek a telephone and return immediately. Specifying a "winter shortie" to the barber, she followed his finger pointing. "Phone in firehouse hall," he helped.

No satisfaction from the telephone company. The Wells' name would be added to the priority list; the installation might be April—or May—or maybe June. They would get to it as soon as possible but they could make no definite commitment. Disconnecting, Faith reminded herself she was leaving this in the hands of the Lord. 'If God be for you, who can be against you?' she re minded herself.

Scribbling on an envelope from her purse she composed a night letter. "Dear John. They've taken the phone but I'm holding the fort with the help of the Lord. Call Tony's taxi in the Glen when you are to return. I'll meet you at Happy Rock. Love, Faith." She grinned broadly. It might take John a moment to translate that 'Happy Rock' to 'Gladstone' but it would serve to remind him things were okay. He would catch her confidence across the miles.

At sight of two choppy haircuts she shuddered, silently thanked

God their hair grew quickly. Back at the farm weary Lulu dozed in a chair, unmindful of the cold house, snoring blissfully. Faith tiptoed into the den, shoved up the thermostat. No response. No comforting rumble of Itchy's motor in the cellar. She flicked the control all the way to the top. Still no answer from the cellar. Noiselessly she tiptoed through the hall, down the cellarstairs, acutely aware of icy blasts piercing the cellar dankness from cracks in the foundation stones and the broken window over the oil tank adjacent to the furnace. In the glaring cellar light she stared incredulously at Itchy. A frightened whisper escaped her lips, "Monstrosity!"

There was nothing familiar about this oil burner. It resembled no oil burner she had ever seen. It was huge, white, and squat. At odd levels and many slants, an assortment of pipes joined burner and other pipes at the cellar walls. To the left of the furnace a deep round hole appeared. As Faith surveyed all before her, her dejection deepened. Cautiously she moved to the back of the burner, hoping to see some little familiar gadget, some switch or button. There was nothing to trigger her memory.

A long, deep sigh escaped. Every speck of her being protested and sagged. Her shoulders slumped. The vigorous baby within propelled itself against her body. She was now weary beyond measure and she crumpled against Itchy, its chalky whiteness rubbing on her coat. Her whole being heaved with inner sobs, wrenchings that trembled and shook her.

"Oh, God! Ice and fog and telephone men and dog wardens and rude utility guys and horrible haircuts—and THIS! Please, God, no more today!" She bit her lip, fighting for self-control. All her metaphysical studies, the angels of the Lord, came to her aid, reminding her that to lose oneself in emotional upheavel is to lose power, to dissipate strength. It now appeared she would require an increase of fortitude. Visibly she pulled herself erect, bumping her head on an overhead pipe. It propelled her into fresh but noiseless sobs.

Compassionately her inner Lord reminded, "Remember? You are 'holding the fort with the help of the Lord'! You cannot permit yourself this pseudo-luxury."

She sniffled. The last embryonic sob quavered in her throat.

Climbing the cellar stairs she held Him close to her, "Lord, it isn't honest to pray selfishly, but please keep Lulu sleeping and unmindful of the cold house until I find a telephone and get a repairman. She loves it warm and my affirmations in Your loving protection don't comfort her."

Lulu snored evenly as Faith let herself out the sidedoor and called the boys. "I heard some roosters down the road this morning. Where there are roosters there should be hens. Let's see if we can get some eggs and a telephone."

"Why?" sang Rob, skipping between ice islands.

"Itchy isn't running and I don't know how to make it run. We'll have to get a repairman."

"Why?" as the full weight of his sturdy body jarred in a jump.

"I don't know, Robbie." The tired face that looked gently at the child held patient eyes. "We'll have to ask the Lord's guidance to the right one." The boys ran ahead in abandoned freedom. A great help, this Lord stuff! I'd never be courageous alone, she reflected.

The wind gusted across the west field, slamming down the north hillside, impeding their progress, flapping their coats, stinging noses and tingling fingertips. Racing ahead, jumping small islands of ice or sliding on those islands, as the spirit moved each laddie, the boys reached the corner place first. There was no response to their knocking. Turning from the doorway Faith glimpsed a speck of coattails disappearing into an outbuilding on the other side of the road. She and the boys walked quickly to the fence, and shortly a choreboy came out, his short thickset figure silhoutted against the building. Faith could not discern his features in the waning daylight. "Hi!" The wind tore her greeting from her. But he must have seen them, for he stood a moment. Faith cupped her hands around her mouth, shouting, "Do you have eggs for sale? How about a telephone?"

A strong, heavily accented voice surged to her on the wind. "Ain't no eggs here. I just chore. Got some my place. Take you when I finish."

"How about a telephone?"

"Half hour," he answered and disappeared within the barn. There was nothing to do but take the boys home, then return to this place. She would walk. She had had enough ice difficulties for one day. Lulu was awake now, sitting quietly in the dark when Faith let the boys in. She made no comment to Faith's explanation of a choreboy and eggs. Nor did she complain about coolness or dampness in the house. Faith hoped Lulu hadn't noticed the lack of warmth and the silence of the furnace.

The last vistages of daylight were gone now. The sporadic wind died with the sunset glow. The night was clear and crackling cold. Faith's footsteps crunched on the ice encrusted road. Down at the crossroad an obsolete flivver irritated the country silence with its unmuffled noise. She opened the car door for herself, climbed into the springless seat beside the driver. As they chugged up the hill she made conversation.

"We're the new people at the Mill. Just got in last Thursday. Everything went wrong today. They took out the telephone— although it was supposed to remain. And now the furnace won't go. It's an old coal job converted to oil. I have to get a repairman. Know any to recommend?"

Complete heavy silence.

Almost in self-defense, Faith continued, "Do you have a telephone I can use?"

If he heard, he made no response.

His driving and the car were chaotic. For a moment Faith was fearful. Perhaps she had moved too impulsively. She didn't even know this chap's name nor where he was taking her. Abruptly the car swung off the dirt road into a rutted way. Faith grabbed at the doorhandle to maintain her balance. Her deeply sunken frame in the springless seat was not dislodged, only painfully jarred. She was most uncomfortable. Even when standing she felt as though her abdomen and chin were a merging unit. This forced U-formation of her distended body was mild agony. Fists thrust behind her into the seat somewhat eased her posture. At that moment she noticed the little house, hidden among bare trees and shrubs, its light streaming down a walk. The driver yanked the brake, jolted the car to a standstill and Faith was shocked forward. He let himself out his door, quickly disappeared up the pathway.

Only the light streaming from within extended helpfulness.

Faith remained still a few moments. His behavior was peculiar, and where at one time she would have censured that quality, she now mentally excused him, shrugged her shoulders and reasoned he was probably shy. Inching herself forward in the seat, she pushed herself to the ground. Momentarily resting against the car she patted her abdomen, hushing the internal protests. Then lifting her head resolutely she followed the path of the light to the little house.

The front door flew open, and a short woman bounded out. "Hallo! Hallo! My son say you come. Come in! Come in!" Her heartiness and sincerity compensated for her son's seeming inhospitality. The light behind her glinted on her welcoming smile in a tanned, weathered face. She shooed Faith inside, following and chanting happily the one refrain, "Stevee, this is her from the big house. She come see! She come see!"

At the rear of the corridor, chair tilted against a wall, a young golden-haired man faced Faith as she entered. Not changing his position he commented, "You're good. No one who ever lived there before bothered with us."

Faith smiled, opened her lips to state her plight, but instantly realized these people were honored by her visit; to be frank at this moment would be insultingly blunt.

"Come in. Come in. Have tea," bubbled the hostess, already pouring black fluid into a large white crockery cup. Faith involuntarily shivered at sight of the dark color. "Come, sit," scraping a chair from the table. The hostess stood behind the middle chair, large knuckled hands clasped together, one above the other at her breast; hoveringly like an angel presence she watched Faith sip the brew.

Faith's chauffeur slopped across the kitchen in rundown slippers. He slumped in a chair on the other side of the large room and stared at Faith, his expression a mixture of lewdness and low intelligence. Faith shuddered, a combination of much too strong tea and uneasiness.

"Ah, you cold," sympathized the mother.

Faith let the observation pass, wondering how quickly she could get to the matter of eggs and a telephone without insulting the hospitality of the good woman and the golden-haired son. Almost as conversation she began, "Our furnace is temperamental and not running. Do you have a telephone?" She wished the chap would look elsewhere! "And—do you have some eggs I might purchase?"

"Yas. Yas," the woman eagerly nodded. "Stevee," to the golden-haired son, "You get eggs. I talk." Reluctantly Stevee relinquished his place against the wall, reached for a flashlight and an egg box.

43

The hostess seated herself beside Faith. Pointing to a place out in the darkness beyond the coalrange, "The people over there our friends. They got telephone. They name Zerwick. Me, Stashi," her gnarled hand in a clutched position, fingertips touching her bosom, she bowed her self-introduction. "They nice people. All the time they let us telephone."

Stevee was back with the eggs. "How many?" from the immediately business-like hostess. Stevee resumed his chair-tilting.

"May I have two dozen?"

"Sure. Sure," quick little vehement nods accompanying her words. "Any time," with an eye to much business. One by one the eggs were carefully nestled in their sections of the box. With a deft movement of her hands, the torn lids were firmed down. "You bring back box. Save me two cents. Want in bag?" With the back of her hand she brushed hair from her forehead.

"Just the cartons are fine," smiled Faith. "How much?"

"Fifty-eight cents. That's what I should get at market."

Faith counted the money. Mrs. Stashi scooped it up from the table in one gesture, efficiently and gracefully tossed it into an earthern pot on the stove. The coins clinked resoundingly as they hit a cushion of silver.

Faith stood up, buttoned her coat, slung her purse over her shoulder and lifted the egg boxes. Stevee put in, "The girl over at Zerwicks' has a car. Maybe she'll take you home."

The other son's stare remained unbroken.

"May I have eggs every week, Mrs. Stashi—at least until we get started on our chickens?"

"Sure. Sure. All time I have," and grinning in sheer ecstasy Mrs. Stashi preceded Faith to the doorway. Her pleasantness and the light from the little house surrounded Faith as she walked to the road, mitigating the peculiar behavior of the chauffeur-son. Faith turned and waved once before the household door closed.

Encompassed by the night and its stillness, glittering stars above and a full orange moon peeping over the horizon, Faith picked her way the quarter mile to the Zerwick place, each footfall resounding in the cold. Kindness of night hallowed the Zerwick farm, softened and romanticized the defects of the saggy porch steps. The moonlight cast a halo around neglected farm

44

equipment plopped carelessly in an adjacent field. The front stairs gave with Faith's weight as she mounted them, but her firm knock was answered immediately. An unshaded light glared behind a tall, haughty girl who stood tapping a nailfile impatiently against her left fingers. "Yes?" The voice was cold, calculated, like her too perfectly made up face.

"I am Faith Wells. We just moved in at Red Mill. The Stashis told me you have a telephone and perhaps would not mind my using it, please."

The opening widened. The girl preceded Faith through the kitchen into a parlor. She flipped on a wall switch and motioned angularly to the telephone in a corner. "Do you know an oil burner repairman?" asked Faith but the hostess shrugged wordlessly, and closed the door behind Faith.

Faith suppressed a desire to giggle. This must be Jersey hillbillism, she reasoned. Then the stench of the place hit her. Except for a magnificent television set in the corner, it was a roomful of saggy chairs surrounding a cold, dusty potbellied stove in the center of the room. And each saggy chair held a cat. As though by prearranged signal, each cat now stood up in its chair, arched its back, leaped to the floor and formed a nose-to-tail procession once around the stove. Once around, each leaped back to his chair. This is a mixture of *Alice in Wonderland* and *Tobacco Road* Faith thought, picking up the classified section. I'd better make this speedy before I heave!

The first call was satisfactory and Faith let herself out of the horrible stench to the kitchen. It was empty. She waited briefly, hopeful of expressing her appreciation. No one appeared. The blend of cat odors and general mustiness overwhelmed her. Down the saggy steps, out into the clear, clean night. Walking down the moonlit dirt road, its friendly crunch-crunch under her footfalls, she filled her lungs with deep draughts of crispness, feeling the exhilarating effects throughout her whole being. At the little wooden bridge she stepped aside while a small truck zipped by, rumbling over the planks, headlights peering through the night toward the Wells' farm. Two men, one in white uniform, were at the back of that truck, lifting out an emergency kit as she walked into the driveway. "Hi," she greeted. "You got here before I did and I had a tailwind."

They laughed pleasantly with her and the one in white cap and spotless uniform introduced himself. "I'm Whitey, your repairman. This is the boss, Jim O'Malley."

"You look like an intern or an ice cream salesman," commented Faith as they started for the side door.

"Not always," Whitey grinned. "I get pretty greasy." They entered the house and Faith flipped the cellar switch, calling out to Lulu that she was home and to please send Rob to the cellar doorway for the eggs.

In the cellar the three ringed around Itchy. Whitey methodically opened his kit, removed the motor cover. Expertly he adjusted small knobs, looked within the fire chamber, and pressed a large forefinger on a small red button. O'Malley in green fedora hat and burly black overcoat smiled reassuringly at Faith, noticed her pregnancy without seeming to.

Wagging his head for emphasis Whitey spoke, "She's a wacky burner, Mrs. Wells, but she'll see you through a while unless you want to put in a new one. See this little red button?" he invited Faith's consideration by his manner. "This is your control box. This little red button will save you plenty of two-fifty charges if you just remember it. Just put this button in so . . . and hold it." He demonstrated. "And count to thirty, real s-l-o-w . . . like this . . . one . . . two . . . three . . . Then take your finger off and in about three minutes, I think it is, she should kick over. If she don't, then you start all over again. Sometimes it takes more'n one pressin'. It's the dampness down here, Mrs. Wells. Can't do much about it. Are you goin' to cement the cellar?"

O'Malley drawled in a deep, rich voice comfortingly, "Any time you do get stuck, Mrs. Wells, you can call us. Day or night. There's always someone to help you out."

Faith shook her head, her expression a mixture of dejection and high courage. She explained the telephone dilemma, finishing with, "So-o-o I couldn't leave the children. We would have to weather it out."

"That's too bad," O'Malley's voice was full of compassion. "I'm real sorry about that. They don't get around to replacements very fast. Tell you what. Are you going to a doctor out this way? You get him to send the company a letter. Tell him to put it on real thick. That'll speed up your installation." Then to Whitey he added, "Utter nonsense they had to take it out! They just want another installation charge!"

Whitey interrupted their thoughts now, standing carefully

between the overhead pipes. "Guess this'll be okay." Itchy was ruminating, purring its peculiar song of itchy-itchy-itchy-itchy, a scratchy intermeshing of the motor gears. Whitey rebuttoned his white jacket.

O'Malley patted Whitey's shoulder, "Funniest sounding motor I ever heard."

The men mounted the stairs first. Faith paused at the foot of the cellar stairs, eyes closed, breathing her prayer of thankfulness. Itchy didn't seem so monstrous now. Its song was a perfect symphony, a comfort to her untutored ears. At the side door she let the men out into the starry night, projecting her gratitude for their immediate attention, then joined Lulu and the little men.

Hours afterward, the boys abed for the night and Lulu alternately reading the paper Faith brought from Hampton and snoring fitfully, Faith's thoughts wandered over the day's happenings. Emerson wrote about the law of retribution; surely, she reflected, this was a day wherein the interest on all her projections of tactlessness or rudeness demanded payment! But if this law is constantly at work, like gravity—even in the mind and the heart, in one's thoughts as well as words and acts—no holidays—then she must not reflect on the rudenesses and unpleasantries. Rather she must think of the good. See only the good. Mental discipline. "Keep the eye single." Like the repairmen coming so quickly, and Whitey graciously telling about the magic red button! Bless him!

Lulu chortled loudly, awakening herself. "What are you dreaming about?" she demanded of Faith, rubbing her eyes as though she merely closed them to rest a moment.

"Lots of things, Mom," softly. "I seem to have lived a whole year in this one day . . . I saw a few neighbors I might not ordinarily see. If I had seen them before we bought this farm, I might not have been so strongly in favor of it." Noting the surprise on Lulu's face she expanded, "Well, there's Mrs. Stashi. I doubt if she's more than fifty. She looks sixty-five. Gnarled, workworn hands. Two teeth left. Almost a hag. She was most kind and generous, even gave me a cup of tea . . . And the Zerwick place, full of cats, stench, and sags!" Involuntarily she shivered. "Well, we wanted democratic living for our kids. Looks like we have it."

Lulu made no answer. John and Faith had made their beds . . .

47

Faith was reflecting much further than she had spoken. They sat in silence, the two women, miles and years apart in understanding yet knit together by bonds of love for one man. In a little while Faith continued slowly, "And I was thinking of the fig tree."

"*What* fig tree!"

"The one in the Bible . . . The one He condemned and it withered and died. Even the disciples were surprised the next morning that it atrophied so quickly! Yet they had been with Him a couple years, watched Him heal, witnessed His resurrections of three others before His own, by His word.

"Once this fig tree episode was merely a story to me, perhaps a bonafide miracle, maybe only a parable. I never specifically categorized it before. Now I see the episode as principle. You know— two and two are always four. . . . Now I perceive many facts at work in this story: The tree was not producing so His act was not one of destructiveness. By His condemnation He caused it to die immediately instead of slowly." Ruminatingly, almost sounding out the logic of her ideas, she continued, "Back in Chatham, when my social life on the telephone was too strenuous I complained. I wanted to be alone with the children or the garden. I wanted to have a study or meditation time. The telephone interjected itself into my . . ." she laughed slightly, self-consciously, "cathedral time. This day I reaped my condemnation and annoyance and the telephone was removed from me. I must learn to taste my thoughts and my words. I must learn to be positive I want—or need—what I decree through criticism or complaints."

Silence ensued briefly. Faith was reflecting on the Biblical instances where He commented about the power of the spoken word. She wondered why this seemed relegated to superstition and that one didn't see it as co-creation with the Infinite.

"Love is always expansive and constructive while hate and condemnation shrink—whether people, animals, vegetables—or even circumstances," Faith mused aloud. She glanced at Lulu. Faith had lost her somewhere in the maze of words and ideas as they tumbled out even though slowly. "You've worked a lot with children. Did you ever notice how expansive and shiny their halo fits when they sense your love and understanding? Or how full of mischief when you are expecting the worst from

48

them? Do you see how we respond to sincere praise—not gush? Ever notice how shriveled up you feel when someone verbally lashes out at you?

"I guess, Mom, you would say 'God did this to punish me.' A metaphysician would say of the telephone episode that I broke the law of appreciation; also that I had erroneous expectancies and today I reaped the results of wrong seed ideas. You and the metaphysician are saying the same thing except that the metaphysician believes man is a co-creator with God, and that man has the responsibility to watch over his thoughts and attitudes."

Perhaps Lulu saw a gleam of what Faith called the Truth, this self-psychology. But there was no encouragement to continue. Just those big beautiful brown eyes silently regarded the younger woman in silence.

And Faith did not know Lulu's thinking.

Tuesday was another day of accomplishment, for each day brought further order and tidiness to the big farmhouse. Lulu completed her self-assigned task of dishes, cabinets, and shelves. All the kitchen sparkled in prettiness. Now the big old place required only the continuity of daily routine—and lots of paint.

Now that the freezer was checked Faith set this day for her return to Green Village, her pickup of all the freezer foods. Six hundred pounds of goodies—chickens, vegetables, fruits, home-made breads and coffee cakes, all the result of their own gardening endeavors. This the harvests from Farm Miniature, their campaign of self-realization that inspired the bigger farm desire on which to accomplish bigger harvests.

As Faith was bedmaking a frightening hiss penetrated the old house. At the cellar doorway Faith was stopped by a blanket of fog. She lowered the thermostat all the way. The hiss gradually diminished. She would call a plumber from Zerwicks' en route to Green Village.

For a brief moment Pierre's words haunted her . . . "it's all right if you kids have $30,000 the first year . . ." Faith swept away Pierre's suggestion of defeat. Pierre just didn't understand this farm was a bargain—indeed a covenant with God! Faith reflected again on the warm summer morning in the Chatham garden on her knees among the vegetables, her promise to Him that if He brought them to the right place, at the right time and under all right conditions they would tithe on all farm produce!

49

Why, from that very moment the machinery was set in action to bring them to this place! Therein lay the miracle. John and she had searched the farm ads, pestered the realtors for two years with no good results. Then, only a month or two after that pledge, they found this place, were now ensconsed in it. Prayer never fails! If they had asked for the "right place under all right conditions" this must be it. As distinct and definite as that! And as simple!

She almost laughed outright, reflecting if Pierre knew they had only a thousand dollars loose change he would be staggered! True, they had another five thousand but it was tied up in bonds and those bonds were earmarked for a nice vacation on maturity. Those bonds were the proverbial ace up the sleeve. Insofar as loose change was concerned, the thousand dollars was more liquid capital than they had ever had.

Plus the limitless asset—GOD! In a very real sense, they were in partnership with Him.

Yes, she reminded herself, she was finished with that old mortal way of stuffing the immeasurability of the Infinite into a pint canning jar of understanding! She had now grown to a new consciousness. And it was like in the Bible, she mused to herself. When the old timers in the Bible grew up, they "moved to a new country." Abraham did. There were others. Now John and she too were in a new country.

Also, she was going to take a lesson from Adam. When the Lord paraded things before Adam he named them, and each thing became the character Adam assigned it in the naming process. She used to think that meant cats, dogs, lizards, or whatever. But now she could comprehend this to be a metaphysical thing and it could be character. So everything that happened Faith was going to name "good," and that would establish its character. Then it would be a steppingstone to greater good.

At last, ready to leave for Green Village, she patted Doug's head and whispered, "Be a good sonshine for Lulu," kissed him and sought Lulu. "I'll get a plumber from Zerwicks', Lulu. Don't wait lunch if I'm not back."

And she was off. The rear of the Studebaker was filled with cartons in which to transport the foodstuffs.

Zerwick was coming from the house when Faith drove into his driveway. "Mind if I borrow your telephone again?" she called pleasantly. "I seem to be getting the habit, don't I?" Her manner was cheerful, but Zerwick's features remained immobile, impassive. Stonily he surveyed her. "Do you know a plumber?"

"Na. Medo." He turned to go and Faith remained motionless. "Goin. Goin!" he shouted, his heavy accent encompassing his words.

On the bench in front of the coalrange in the Zerwick kitchen five Zerwick women sat. With one accord they stared as Faith opened the door, stood before them. Five pairs of black, impersonal eyes scrutinized her. A lad of four or so played silently on the floor at their feet.

"I've come to borrow the phone again," Faith explained.

Five heads jerked downward as though on a common puppet string. Faith glanced down the row of faces endeavoring to determine which was Mrs. Zerwick. "We need a plumber this time. I do hope you don't think me too pesty. In fact," she laughed slightly, half in embarrassment and half in pleasantry, "I hope our troubles are over."

None of the onlookers proffered assistance. It was difficult to determine which might be Mrs. Zerwick. They looked so alike. Black short hair, small black eyes—impersonal and cold. They even seemed approximately the same age. They look like a family of Eskimos, Faith thought. Idly she wondered the whereabouts of the girl with the nailfile. The squalor of the place, the aroma, the relentlessness of the impersonal black eyes, the possibility of misplaced Eskimos . . . Faith wanted to giggle. The last one on the bench ever so slightly inclined her head. Apparently this was the permission she sought.

The telephone call completed satisfactorily she slipped fifty cents under the telephone. She wondered if its omission the other night was the reason for their coldness. Rebuttoning her coat she wished the lineup would vanish as the haughty girl the other night. How she hated to be stared at! Bad enough when one isn't pregnant. But now. . . .

The lineup had increased. Zerwick stood at the end, his right hand on the shoulder of the head bobber. Faith felt as though she were living a horrible nightmare. In frozen silence six pairs of black eyes watched her approach. Even the child on the floor entered the spirit of their game. He now stared.

Silence was broken by Zerwick's heavily accented English. He

51

said something. His manner indicated he expected an answer.

Faith stood still. She silently regarded him. "I beg your pardon?" It was a stall for time. She did not wish to embarrass him. Surely he couldn't help his accent. Neither did she enjoy her stupidity. As he repeated his sentence she watched him intensely. Vainly she tried to get a gleam, an inspiration from his lips, his face, his hands. Anything! She never felt so unintelligent in her whole life!

Helplessly she glanced from face to face, each impassive and glum. Surely someone in the lineup could translate for her. Mentally she reviewed the shaping of his lips as he had talked, revisualized his gestures. It was so much easier in the yard; she named the subject, could guess at his answer by gestures and attitudes. Now he chose the noun! Her mind raced in place, sending little fingers of radar to determine the subject matter.

"Timsy!" Zerwick exploded, the cords of his neck rigid, his lean angular face red with fury, inky black eyes flashing.

"Timsy," she echoed half aloud, hoping to feel his meaning with her tongue.

The row of scrutinizing faces relentlessly observed her.

Finally, boldly speaking to the most approachable face, "What is 'timsy'?"

"Timothy," in perfect English answered face number four. "What is that?"

"Hay."

"Oh. . . . What about it?"

"He wants to know what you are going to do with it."

"Do we have some?"

"Sure. They had a good timothy crop last summer. When you buy a farm you get all that goes with it."

Faith wanted to reply "not quite." "They" had removed the chimes from the front door before the Wells occupancy and they had stipulated at the closing they would be back for the farm machinery—but the valuable farm manure was left. Faith chuckled to herself. Aloud she said, "Forgive me. I have much to learn about farming. Our only experience has been with chickens. If there is hay there, Mr. Wells may want to keep it, for we hope to stock the farm."

Zerwick, face flushed and muscles flexing in tensity, nodded curtly and exited rapidly. Something rigid and relentless about his back. Faith began to thank the lineup for the use of the telephone but as one corporate body they rose, followed Zerwick through the door behind the coalrange.

Faith stood alone in the kitchen, blinking in disbelief, wondering if this were truly New Jersey circa 1950. Her sense of humor asserted itself speedily and a lovely quotation of the Quakers came to her, "All the world is queer except thee and me —and sometimes thou art a little bit."

"You are to call operator three in Sandusky, Ohio," Lulu reported upon Faith's return. "A neighbor by the name of Skinner stopped by with the message."

Faith wondered why John did not call the taxi office as her telegram suggested. She transferred all the foodstuffs from the car to the freezer, noting the whereabouts of everything on a chart so that weeks later the stored items in the sixteen-cubic foot freezer would be retrievable. It was three in the afternoon before the job was finished, and the two women had coffee together. Faith didn't relish walking the Zerwick gangplank again. She hoped they all had vanished. She hoped they found her gratuity too.

Faith and Doug walked up the hill together while she recounted the story of her trip to the lad. She had timed this walk so that they would meet Rob as he came from the school bus, on his mile-long walk downhill. This whole new world of Rob's— the school bus, the new children at school—all these things required much courage of the shy little man. A small blue truck with a huge police dog beside the driver passed them as they continued up the hill. By the time they reached the Zerwick driveway, the blue truck had returned and stopped. Zerwick, leaning on his fence, picking his teeth cautiously with a penknife blade, gave ear as the driver rolled down his window and demanded, "You Mrs. Wells?"

"Yes," evenly.

"You're supposed to call operator three in Sandusky, Ohio. They called me five times!"

Faith flashed a smile. "Thank you for your message." Such anger as his should be mitigated, and she watched it ebb gradually from his face, gray pallor replacing purple tinged redness. "I was in Green Village getting food from the freezer locker. When I returned it had to be stowed away. I had already used up much of my time-deadline by travel, you see. I'm sorry you were annoyed."

"Itsawright," slurring his words together and rolling up the window simultaneously, he zoomed to the hardtop road.

Zerwick jerked his head in the direction of the house, turned and left the scene. She sensed they found the coin. Inside the house she was alone, and she was grateful. "Operator three, Sandusky, Ohio please," she requested. Silence broken only by erratic sounds as electrical cracklings during a summer storm.

"Operator three, go ahead please."

"This is Mrs. Wells. You have a call for me?"

"Oh, Mrs. Wells! I'm so glad to have you. Mr. Wells has been trying to get you since last night and all of today. He's been so worried. Just a moment, please." Faith heard the key close. Goodness! Was this a sample of the charming midwest friendliness she heard so much about! "Oh, my dear! He's been here hours—and now he's out to lunch. Can I call you back on his return?"

She thought rapidly. Was it better to stay here at Zerwicks' or take the boys home? Had Rob come down the road while she was inside? The operator interrupted her thinking, "Do you have far to go?"

"About a mile, and all of it uphill," laughed Faith. "It is a challenge owing to my loose caboose. I guess I'll wait."

"Thank you so much. He will be relieved when he hears we have reached you. What number are you at?"

"Hampton 250."

"Thank you. I'll call the minute he comes in. Goodbye."

Faith slowly replaced the telephone. Pulling on her right glove she reflected on both the friendly warmth as well as the excellent sleuthing of the telephone company! Here they were strangers in the land, yet from Ohio to New Jersey somehow the efficiency of these people had located the nearest telephone to connect her and John across the miles.

Rob came along as she rejoined Doug, demanding to know why they were there. Scooping up a handful of snow he packed it into a ball, aimed at a passing rooster. The fowl stretched his neck forward, and simultaneously contracted his hindquarters to accompany the forepart of his body. Rob's aim missed. Both boys laughed hilariously at the antics. Faith smiled to herself

54

and reasoned the boys would have to be extremely proficient to score a hit. Encouraged by the perfect timing of the assorted roosters and cats, the boys enjoyed themselves during the half-hour wait on the telephone. The feathered and furred things defied their accuracy.

She was at the telephone by the second ring. "Hi, Darlin'!"

"Hampton 250?" a cold query.

"Yes," impatiently.

"Go ahead, sir." The impersonal New Jersey dialect invited. John's deep musical voice came to her clear and strong. "Hello, Sweetheart! Where have you been? I've been trying to get you since last night." No reproach in his voice. Just the heartwarmth and wonderfulness of him racing across the miles.

"They took out the telephone. Didn't you get my night letter?"

"No. Where did you send it?"

"The hotel name you gave me."

"Oh," casually. "We're not at that one. The men decided they liked the looks of the other hotel in the town better."

Their laughter melded together.

"Well, the other hotel is holding your mail and a night letter."

John was suddenly serious. "When will they put in a replacement?"

"Sure by June."

A pause. "Everything all right?"

"Sure!" Her tones were jubilant, bubbling with easy confidence. No need to worry him with Monday's ordeal or the present day's steam leak in the cellar. All that was history now. She wasn't going to be swept in a tide of nuisance affairs. She was going to maintain dominion in her life! Dominion! She was going to keep the eye single! If, as psychology teaches, that which one dwells on in his habitual thinking manifests in one's life, why then simply don't think of what you don't want; rather concentrate on the goodies. . . .

"I'll be back Thursday. Can you meet me at Gladstone?" John was saying.

"You mean 'Happy Rock'?"

"What?"

Giggling, "I'll be there."

"I have to return to the conference, Honey. See you Thurs-

55

day." He sounded reluctant, yet relieved. Faith was wistful. It was so warming to hear from him, sounding so close, like down in the Glen or around the corner.

Faith didn't protest John's being away, not even in the privacy of her heart. She accepted it as part of his work. Although they were spiritually close there was freedom in their relationship, the freedom and responsibility of a mature love, the strong bond of empathic work toward mutual goals. These absences were merely "spaces in their togetherness." Perhaps these spacings contributed to their complete harmony, for each was unpossessive of the other. Perhaps it is a rare thing in the world, she now reflected to herself remembering John's dad's comment to her once, "Don't you even miss John when he's away?" His tones had implied he thought she should be prostrate with grief until John's return. "Sure," she had answered, "but I don't let myself think of it," privately wondering how such lack of self-discipline would affect the children. "Well, you're sure queer!" he had hurled and walked away.

Faith grinned now to herself remembering that conversation. She had bounced around too much as a youngster to feel complete dependence on any one person—even John. Early life taught her the value of mental substitution and independence. Following down the road behind the boys, she pondered how much each of us is the result of his background and environment. Tennyson's poetic words welled up within her consciousness:

> "I am a part of all that I have met;
> Yet all experience is an arch where-through
> Gleams that untravelled world whose margin fades
> Forever and forever when I move."

Lulu left after John's return, and from then until the middle of March the Wells "were in the paint can." John did the lovely sunny den a Brunswick green, Faith enameling the trim an off-white. Each lad choose a bedroom, Rob selecting the northwest room with distinct specifications of terra-cotta walls and a hint of seacrest green in an otherwise white ceiling. Doug selected the room "they" had as nursery. Two walls pink and two walls blue with tiny white lambs gamboling over flowers. Tactfully Faith tried to retain it as a nursery; it would avoid painting one room. But the younger lad was adamant. He wanted the room "back by Wobbie" and that was that!

As Faith fastened his snowsuit one morning she urged, "You hurry along outside and play now, Honey, so I can paint the southern bedroom green."

"Dreen?" wistfully.

"Yes," matter-of-factly. In a flash she remembered green to be his favorite color, almost to the point of fixation. Could it be she could bargain after all? Could tactful persuasion avoid the chore of at least one room-painting?

"I'll sleep there," he bargained, happily slamming the door behind him as he wended his way to outdoor toys.

Rob off to school and Doug outside, Faith could whiz through things. Now was the time for vast accomplishments. Now, before the new baby arrived. After the baby was here, she wouldn't have time for more than the baby, normal housework, and stock chores. Furthermore there was Quota to plan for . . . and with two babies she would really have assignments! Now she could paint and finish off the extras.

She liked to paint. It was creative. One dusted and in a little while the dust was there again. One made beds, slept in them, then remade them. On and on. But painting, all looked fresh and clean and prettied up. There was not the feeling of transiency with painting! Stirring the paint and humming, she reflected happily on the chain of events that led them to this old place to fix up. She laughed aloud. She hadn't meant quite so old— nor quite so much fixing! But she truly got the answer to her prayer. This whole thing was a tremendous demonstration of the power of God. She could never cease to marvel at their receiving every single stipulation!

She rethought of Pierre's comment about the thirty thousand the first year. . . .

Silly stuff! They hadn't lived in a palace back in Chatham. It was a modest six-room house sitting on one lot, and the garden on another lot right beside it. Of course, everything was brand new, very modern and she already knew it would be expensive and time-consuming to fix up an old place. But she wasn't going to let Pierre's negative suggestion take root. She wasn't going to empower the negatives by arguing with them nor contemplating them, surely not through worrying about the possibility of their seeming factual.

No! she would think about God! The Good! Always present. The only Power and Presence! "God is always Good. In fact, His very name means good. Just as the sun can only shine, so God only sends good. All the error you see, Faith, is of man's doing."

The words from a loved dominie in her teens returned to her now and enlightened her. Long ago she understood it as meaning God doesn't send wars and famines nor condemn people to live in slums or create abnormal babies. As a teenager she reasoned man brings on these conditions among men through greed and other errors of understanding, and that sometimes they carry over into another lifetime—thus the logic of reincarnation. Now Faith comprehended the science of thought—that through the higher self, the Christ self, one can erase his past errors with the aid of Divine Love and Wisdom.

Ideas in her mind demanded her attention as she stirred the paint. (Ten minutes by the clock. John always said most people have paint problems because they are too impatient to stir sufficiently.) Peculiar, how paths cross in life. The "law of attraction" some call it. "Like attracts like." True on all levels. She and John belonged together. Each complemented the other. She and John were very alike. Yet very unlike. While they wanted the same things from life, they also both wanted to give the same things to life. Wonderful John with his multi-faceted abilities —his mechanical know-how, outgoing personality, social and spiritual sensitivity that enabled him to say or do the right thing in the right way, putting others at ease without any sacrifice to his principles or sincerity. She didn't have that talent. Living with John all these years she was learning some. Not that he harangued her. Rather by osmosis.

Even their mutual desire for a farm. John desired it as a long-range program, possible early retirement from the business world to a "going" prosperous farm. Faith yearned for the farm because of a strong desire for solitude and study, the wife part of her willing to do the farm work to get into the "going" classification.

Behind the wife aspect of herself was the personal, intense need to study metaphysics. Live in her ivory tower, going out into the world only on demand. Duties like PTA or hospitality for the children, whatever the children required to round out their young lives. The inner woman yearned to know God face-to-face, saw the immense possibilities of these teachings, the panacea for the world!

How was it Fillmore put it? Something like "Jesus was a carpenter, a builder. You are a builder of your consciousness by your thoughts. Your words. Use your thoughts, your words, to build a life you really want."

This self-psychology! Psychology is not a lever to apply on others. It is the scalpel the individual must use on his own soul!
She was astounded by her own conclusion.

Stirring most slowly, she resolved again that every day, living in the quietness of the farm, she would take a phrase, meditate upon it, build it into her consciousness. Her world. This was what the farm meant to her. Seclusion from the world. Quietness to probe the depths of life itself, the laws behind life. Hear her inner guidance, and then go forth into the world only as she felt guided or needed. Silence to study and comprehend the vastness of the Infinite and its Wisdom!

"Omnipresence" for instance. Long ago she sought in the dictionary for that word. Then she understood its meaning only in an intellectual sense. Now she comprehended. The Orient called it realization, a kind of spiritual understanding, not always translatable into words, perhaps better depicted in symbols. Like the circle for eternity which means the egg, continuity of life, the never-endingness of the Infinite, constant creativity, evolution. . . .

This was the evolution from the personal God to the universal concept, from the divine Santa Claus to Cosmic Consciousness. When she was little she stood at the window watching the stars twinkle into perceptability. "God is out there somehow, somewhere," she mused. Once, when she was eleven, she went through her Bible and whenever it referred to God as "which" she crossed it out and inserted "who." She smiled at the memory. Now, at another level of understanding, she knew God to be both indwelling and everywhere evenly present.

Omnipresence.

Different aspects of God. Divine Order that keeps the stars and planets in their orbits. Life and Love and Wisdom, the spark within every living thing. Law, impersonal, but constant. Like gravity, holding the universe together. And all this the combination that gives man his free will, the very substance of the universe that loves man, all men—even when they err.

Yes, Nicodemus had only intellectual knowledge even though he was a teacher in Israel. She wanted the full light! No travelling around in the dark of night for her!

She lifted the paint paddle, letting the paint flow off into the can. Consulted the clock. Another two minutes to stir.

Odd, how all her life this feeling stirred within her heart. This magnetism of metaphysics. Years ago in the big city library, when she passed the shelves labelled metaphysics she felt irresistibly drawn to them. Time and again she stood beside those shelves, selecting a fat book or two, handling them. Chapter headings puzzled her. Their verbiage was obtuse. Never had a book or chapter demanded her. None until Emmet Fox and Charles Fillmore blazed into her consciousnes. They were her hounds of heaven. Now all the pieces of the universal jigsaw fell into place and she understood.

Peculiarly since first reading Fox's *Sermon on the Mount* she did not experience the recurrent dream. It did not return for four years. When it did, it came as a sequel: A golden key lay in the palm of her hand as she closed the little purple book, and she understood all the words in their sequence.

Right then, stirring the paint and preparing to apply green to the southern bedroom walls, Faith mulled both the events of her life and the studies. She resaw herself as a youngster, a fortune-telling slip of paper in her hand that read "those born under this sign have tremendous capacity to be exceptionally good or extremely bad . . . when good these people frequently practice their benevolences under another name, not letting the left hand know the doings of the right." She recalled determining that day to cast her net on the right side, the side of the exceptionally good.

Could this inner pledge as a child have been one of the angels that kept her on the ledge of the attic window, rooted to the spot instead of wantonly pitching herself headlong to the city sidewalk when all her world was so black after her mother's suicide? Lonely and wretched, her inner being crushed by tauntings of schoolmates, yet *something* kept her glued to the windowledge.

Later, in high school, George Eliot's poetry about joining the choir invisible. Faith could still recall the inner glow the little

60

poem fanned. This also was for her—to leave the world better than she found it.

Surely she could not subscribe to the idea of fate or predestination! It was not fate that kept her on the windowledge. Perhaps the truth is a combination of what the Orient calls karma or the boomerang law—a combination of that and free will. If that is so, then rebirth or reincarnation is the law of opportunity for growth toward Christhood, and karma is the law of reaping, or retribution, either in one lifetime or when propitious for the soul's education as well as the paying off of old debts, the eye for an eye bit of Moses' teaching. Jesus expanded that teaching to "as ye sow ye shall reap." Also, He gave the precept of making only good karma for oneself by living the golden rule—in mind as well as in act. Perhaps progress is effected by what could be called divine challenges, cosmic prods, invitations to use one's talents for selfless helpfulness to others—more than just the family and the neighbors.

Faith began to paint. It was pully—John's word for it. Some turps. She stirred thoroughly, resumed painting. Good. The brush moved rhythmically.

Rhythmically. Yes, since they found this "Unity stuff" the whole universe moved rhythmically and harmony was present. Events made sense. Faith could now perceive a divine logic behind seeming inequalities.

This impelling force that pulled her to study Unity teachings would not quell. Night after night, she pored over the little Fillmore books, so much so that a few nights ago John remarked—a little caustically for him—"What are you cramming for? Going to be a minister?" His tones were half teasing, half serious.

Faith had not answered immediately. She didn't know how to answer, for she had not examined the underlying reason. When she ultimately acknowledged his question, her tone was full of thoughtfulness. "No. . . . I don't think that. I really don't know the final goal. . . . All I know is that I want to know *all* the Law. I want to be able to work with Principle. I see this—these teachings —as a recipe, a formula, to help the whole world. Not just us, John, *everyone*. I see this as the second coming of Christ—in a universal sense. This Christ Self awakens in each of us individually, and like Dr. Schweitzer I believe the world is readying for this tremendous step forward. This is one of the ways to help it. . . . I don't think I want to be a minister. I don't believe He wants me to.

"But neither do I know right now what He wants me to do or be. . . ." Her voice trailed off, and John returned to his evening papers. But John's question planted a seed in Faith's mind.

Applying the paint now in the sunny room, she brought herself up short. All this ruminating of memories was not concentrating on God. Thinking about God was her dedication. All these thoughts were merely reviews of fragments in her own life, fitting her jigsaw puzzle together as cause and effect. The brush moved evenly. The room gradually made the transition from yellow to green.

"Here and now I am in Your Holy Presence . . . here and now . . . always . . . like Jonah there is nowhere I can go where You are absent! . . . I wonder why we have to deliberately cultivate this awareness? Personal ego, I suppose; this is the 'satan' that needs to be overcome. . . . Most of us don't wish to relinquish the personal ego for the Divine Ego, letting the Father channel through us. . . ."

With a burst of enthusiasm, "Oh, God, I do love You and I love all Your people everywhere. There *are* no exceptions! I am so happy I can sincerely say that! I feel so relieved from the old burdens of hate and condemnation! I am truly at peace with all Your people. And I love You with all my heart, mind, soul, and strength! I love You and I am willing to serve you, humbly and well. . . ."

In the morning light of the third day John and Faith stood arm-in-arm in the doorway, admiring their handiwork. The green was just the right shade for this southern exposure, light enough for winter, dark enough to be restful and cool in the summer. The windows, neat and clean, were framed in their sparkling white enamel. John's antique oak floor finish Faith thought a trifle too orange, but John explained it would darken with age. The boys joined them, ducking under their arms. Doug chirped, "This looks pretty. Now I'll sleep here while you do my room dreen."

Evenly Faith replied, "Honey, you said you would take this room for your bedroom."

"No, I didn't," he countered firmly, his voice intense with feeling. "I said I would sleep here 'til you do my room."

That was it. John and Faith had joked about "buying a houseful of yellow." Slowly it was being transformed to a houseful of green.

Early March brought a light snow, enough to embarrass a Studebaker on the winding, steep hills, to provide John with an honest reason to remain home. School closed too; the boys and John trudged the farm together. They checked the new wiring job in the barn and henneries, puttered around the five-story battery set up to house the first arrival of chicks. Then, far up in the north field they spotted three wild geese amid the winter wheat and snow. John aimed his .22. Later he laughingly told Faith "either they're bullet proof or my sight is wacky."

Lunch over, John hitched the boys' sleds together and Faith stationed herself at the curve close to the little bridge. Wrapped in her grey and black tweed coat she watched Spruce Run, fascinated by the brook's deepening tones of blues and violets along the icy edges. At times her gaze lifted to the large fluffy clouds scooting across the sky. Whenever the sleds flew by a noisy "hi" penetrated her thoughts.

From afar Faith saw a lone woman in leather jacket, jeans, cuffed white socks over the tops of hiking boots, snowhood and a knobby walking stick completing the ensemble. The woman walked with enthusiasm, employing her stick with ease and familiarity. On the hillside John noticed Faith's attitude and called for a clearance. Faith waved them on. They ditched themselves harmlessly, enwrapped in snow and laughter. Faith's attention returned to the approaching figure.

A radiantly flashing smile and a charmingly modulated voice inquired, "Hello. Aren't you Mrs. Wells?"

"Yes." Faith's tone betrayed a who-are-you inflection.

"I'm Mary Banners. We are your nearest all-year neighbors to the east. I heard you moved in. How do you like the country?"

"Love it! Wish we found it ten years ago!"

"Well?" laughingly.

"Didn't know we wanted a farm ten years ago."

"Oh, had to get old to appreciate farm possibilities." Mary Banners' grin was disarming.

A windtorn "hi" again as the three figures zipped by on sleds.

"Are those your three sons?"

A mischievous light appeared in Faith's eyes, a pucker played at the corners of her mouth. Quietly, "Two of them are. The big one's my husband." A sly look at her conversationalist. Simultaneously

63

they burst into laughter. "It's the bulk of pregnancy under the strained coat makes me seem old and fat—I hope," explained Faith.

Together they watched the sled coast to a standstill at the crossroad.

"Are you going to Warren Hospital?" Faith silently nodded her answer. Tenderly, "If you need anyone to stay with the boys while you go—especially if you go late at night—and babies seem to start coming then—I'll be glad to stay. I'm a registered nurse. Only your husband will have to come for me. We don't have a phone yet."

Faith turned to look long and deeply into the green-gray eyes of this new-found friend. Already God had answered her prayer for the friend in need, and in the silence of her heart she thanked Him. Aloud she accepted the offer, her voice vibrant, betraying sensitive response to this generosity. In the next moment she quipped, "Perhaps most of them start in the night because most of them are begot in the night."

When the fluffy balls of yellow arrived one Saturday in March, their very appearance seemed to signal the acceleration of all farm plans. Suddenly John felt the terrific urge to be a complete farmer immediately, junk the long-range plans. Putting the farm into the "going" classification, fixing up the farm house and the outbuildings, his many plans constituted John's whole dream and conversation. And Faith shared the goal.

Their brief note to the County Agricultural Agent brought him within a week. Generously he gave of his experience. Also he mentioned the former owners; they called him in years ago. They thought of the farm as a subsistence affair. "On fifty-two acres no farmer could swing into a going classification merely on grains. They would need to fill out the farm activities. Diversify. Chickens? Since they had experience with chickens, good. They would require at least two thousand to produce any kind of family income. No other experience? Sheep were a good supplement, would keep the 'backyard' in order, easily manageable too. Mr. Dan, up Allamuchy way, a most reputable chap, had good stock too. . . ." So went his tactful guidance.

So a note to Mr. Dan, asking about "live lawnmowers" and specifying two two-year-old ewes and a ram. "Old hands at delivery time," the County Agent had advised, thus preferable to yearlings.

Early one March afternoon the Landemeres dropped in. "Spring-like down our way," Lucille giggled at sight of Faith's surprised expression. "So we packed a picnic lunch and here we are. We'll take a cup of your delicious coffee."

Laughing like a schoolboy, Pierre kissed Faith with warm paternity. Alternately flaying their arms and rubbing their hands, they took a stand before the warm hall radiator. "Glad that burner's working all right!" Pierre enthused to Faith. Their glances met and held momently.

"Itchy's a blessed burner," Faith commented. Her tone contained a finality which did not invite further comments about Itchy.

As Faith readied the coffee, they chatted about this and that, calling their tidbits of conversation back and forth from the center hall to the kitchen. When the Landemeres thawed, everyone moved to the living room, Faith having lit the fireplace for their comfort. Folding his chubby legs, Doug squatted before the old gentleman, staring up at the kind face as the elders talked. During a lull the lad interjected, "Gramp, do you hear that knocker out there? What's he doing this time of year?"

Pierre's one jet eyebrow shot upward questioningly and Faith laughed aloud at him. He smiled easily and looked to her for interpretation. "There's a woodpecker working on the tree. Do you hear him?"

Pierre rose from his comfortable seat near the fireplace, and hand-in-hand the old man and the young man viewed the bird from the window. After coffee was relished they ambled out to visit the farm accomplishments while the women settled to a gab-fest, interrupted by Faith's persuasion to stay for dinner, over-riding Lucille's gentle demures.

March lost her tentative fingertips on Spring early that afternoon. Abruptly the day was grey, somewhat sullen. The wind began to whip up, a raw feel to it, snow in the air. The change brought Pierre and Doug scurrying indoors about the time Rob came from school. Faith turned over the hosting responsibilities to the lads while she chored and later, humming gaily to herself in the kitchen, she prepared dinner for the boys. Lucille joined her, standing in the doorway between the kitchen and the dining

65

room. Arms folded across her chest she furnished Faith the remainder of the Chatham doings, not quite definable as gossip, a little more substantial than mere chatter.

And John's enthusiastic greeting to the Landemeres, "This is a handsome surprise! We thought most of our company wouldn't venture out until this summer. Glad you remember the route! How's the old town, Pierre? Lu, you're looking beautiful!"

Lucille's plain face wreathed a glowing response. She knew she wasn't beautiful but she also knew John's comment to be sincere, and that plainness in a woman becomes beauty through admiration and love.

"We were tricked into this," Pierre explained. "It was spring in Chatham—or just enough so to get us picnic-minded and on the road. It is much colder in your hills though, and when we were here awhile spring vanished. Poof!"

Dinner over for the adults, the boys abed and the dishes done, the foursome sat before the crackling fire. Each of the men relaxed with a pipe, alternately puffing and lighting matches, as conversation flowed. It was Pierre who switched from politics and world events with, "Well, John, you've been commuting almost two months. You've had a good taste of country living in the hardest part of the year. How do you like it for the long haul? Want to continue your far flung plans?"

John removed his pipe, shook out the dead ashes against the ash tray at his side, carefully laid the pipe on the arm of his chair before making an answer. "There's nothing I want so much as to be a prosperous farmer on this place. We belong here, friend. In going through the legal machinery, selling the suburban house, everything opened to us miraculously. The Chatham house even sold during the Christmas holidays—all the realtors informed us nothing moves then, you know."

Pierre nodded silently, confident a man of John's caliber doesn't dedicate his life on the superstition of legal machinery moving smoothly.

Faith interrupted, placed her hand on John's sleeve. "We do belong here, Pierre. We're doing it on prayer and a song. Some of our plans depend on a raise for John until we manage a comfortable backlog."

" 'Don't count your chicks before they're hatched' is still a safe motto," tersely.

John laughed slightly, left his chair. Going from lamp to lamp he extinguished them as he spoke, "The original idea was the ten-year plan, me to commute that long. This place calls me. I don't think I shall take the long road." At the northern windows, he parted the drapes and invited them. "Come! The poet in me exclaims 'behold the starry vault!' Where in the city, or even the suburbs, do you see such beauty? Where can one feel the Presence of God?"

Looking up the hillside, the stars were as light decorations atop the trees, the scintillating ornaments, twinkling in the keen sharpness of the March night. "I know God is in the cities—in spite of their smells and noise and rush. The freshness and cleanness out here inspires me, lifts me up physically as well as spiritually. 'I will lift up mine eyes unto the hills,'" he quoted putting his arm around Faith.

"You are thinking me foolish, I know. A man with a wife and two and a half children. Planning a fourth." John's voice was warm and mellow. Gently he added, "There was a time we thought one got somewhere—success—only by dint of his personal efforts and determination—or by knowing key people. That was before we found this working religion, the untapped and scientific power in prayer. Where once we lived in the shallows of mortal strength, we now understand that even strength is from God. Pierre, it is not only comfort knowing this and working with it; it is also inspiration and joy undiminishing. And—do you know—it is magic! The more one uses this practical religion the more one has it to use. It keeps growing—atomically."

Only the heavenly stars furnished light. Even as the foursome stood in the darkened living room at the window, the stars seemed to wane. The fire shot forth its red, green, blue and amber tongues of light. Pierre, looking penetratingly at the younger man, saw only the darkness of the room, the stupendousness of the project, the diminishing starlight. He turned from the group, resumed his seat. John reached to a lamp, lit it as Pierre resettled himself, stretching out his legs, crossing them at the ankles. Reaching his arms upward, cushioning his head on his hands, he offered, "I see you've made some changes. Doug and I toured this afternoon. What I might have overlooked he pointed out." His tone was matter-of-fact. John concealed a smile at the absurdity of Pierre's missing anything. "Noticed you have electricity in the barn and the little building on the hillside. What's that?"

"The battery house. We have a hundred chicks started. Another batch comes in April, coinciding with moving day from the battery to the hennery for this group. Graduation day, you know." John's eyes crinkled at the corners. "Had the barn done at the same time so we can get going."

"Cows?"

"No. We're playing with the idea of sheep. Ordered three live lawnmowers. Our second crop could well be sheep. Won't be cows."

"How do you commute?"

"From Gladstone by Lackawanna. Eighteen-plus miles from here to there. Around lots of curves. Up and down beautiful mountains. Some of the loveliest scenery in N.J. Frequently the beautiful mountains are sheets of ice or sleet instead of rain or snow. From Gladstone it's a fifty-minute express ride to Newark. I read, relax. When I am on the road Faith is complete manager here."

Pierre silently evaluated John's words. "There seems so much to do here, John. It bothers me because I know you kids don't have the capital. If I were assured you had a limitless supply I wouldn't care. I know none of this is my business. Forgive me for intruding. But I've known you a long time, feel a paternal interest." His voice trailed off, whittled at by his well meaning emotions. "Perhaps that is why it bothers me. You could be our children. . . . Well, I wish you the best and most of luck if you are determined to stay. You could resell easily. The real estate market is still good."

"Oh, Pierre!" interjected Lucille. "This is a beautiful place. Just beautiful! If I were only younger," she sighed and laughingly admonished Faith. "I said it before. If I were younger you would never have this place. I would have outbid you!" Lucille got up and wandered about the room. Her mien was almost reverent. Softly she exclaimed, "I know what John means. It does smell clean here. Pierre, they'll make a go of it. One can't measure everything with the dollar yardstick. In every real home there is a great deal of the people, the essence of their character, that goes into the house, into the very atmosphere. I feel it in this house. It isn't merely the painting they've done. It is the weaving—and the wearing or the living—of their philosophy. You know these things, Dear. Let us encourage them—not tell them to move out." She sat down next to Pierre, patted his knee reassuringly. Unconvinced he wagged his head articulately.

Faith spoke, slowly, her words coming forth with spaces between them. There are spiritual understandings beyond the scope of mundane intelligence. They come from the heart and frequently there are no tailored words to convey such revelations to another. Sincerity demands that one try, however. "You know, the most amazing things happen to us lately. Miracles. Ever since that Emmet Fox book our lives have been revolutionized!"

Suddenly her words came in a rush of coherency. "We sold the Chatham house during Christmas holidays. John told you that. We had the miracle of the buyer upping his own offer. We had the miracle of procuring a certified bank check from the cashier of a large city bank when we had two strikes against us: our buyer's checks had not cleared his bank yet, and I didn't have our passbook; it was somewhere in the mail between Newark and Chatham. You already know we experienced the miracle of receiving every qualification we desired—the split sink, custom farmer, property across from the farmhouse, the fireplace, the brook, you know all these things. . . ."

Faith's words limped to a finish. She experienced a queer tingling sensation at the back of her head and she sensed rather than felt a great light encompassing her. She put her hand to the nape of her neck, readjusted the pins in her bun. The sensation was a little higher. It feels like a misplaced electric pad, she thought, and suppressed a giggle desire. The sensation diminished while great, surging music swept through her whole being. Words to the music uplifted her, even as they filled her with humility and awe. "I am your Christ light. Heed me. Use me. I will lead you in the way you should go."

She looked from one face to another. Each of the three facing her waited expectantly. The Landemeres smiled encouragingly in her direction. John firmed down the tobacco in his pipe. They don't hear it, Faith thought. Faith felt as though light within her being were merging with this luminescence surrounding her. It was not as a searchlight glaring into dark places but rather it was a comfortable, glowing warmth, an effulgence. Through the days and years ahead it would increase in brilliance, a full-length, walking halo. A light upon her pathway, penetrating all around her. At this moment of the Aura's birth Faith knew the old way had passed. No longer could she wrap up Fox's little book or the Unity stuff and send them forth surreptitiously like dawn stealing over the eastern horizon. This was noonday light. This was for the world. Quietly. And Faith would be identified with it. Not just their families, their friends, their neighbors. All of their world and beyond to multitudes.

Where once her Song of Life chorded with Infinite Harmony, now a comprehension of the Divine Symphony manifested. Now there were great sweeping, inspiring melodies blending tenderly and inspiringly with surging harmonies. Faith's Song was not lost amid the greater chords. Rather her Song was complemented, strengthened and beautified. Whispering concurrently, weaving melodically with the great chords, there came intuitive assurance deep within the recesses of her soul that Faith Sanford Wells had work to do. A divine assignment. Or assignments. No hint of the specifics. Just the conviction of greater purposefulness in life.

The trio waited for her to finish her thought. It seemed an aeon ago. She could not remember the subject nor her words. A swelling inner chorus rose to crescendo. "Divine assignment" . . . "divine assignment" . . . "divine assignment." The very theme hounded her.

"They say," Faith murmured, "the Bible means 'good thoughts' wherever it reads angels. The only place we can meet God is in the realm of Mind, so this must be true." Faith's tone held warm resonance but her words seemed to flow unevenly. The Landemeres attributed the meanderings to the lateness of the hour. "Did it ever occur to you what John—the Gospel, you know—means where it says. . . ."

She stared into space momently, then seemed to read from the very atmosphere, " 'There was the true light, even the light which lighteth every man coming into the world.' Notice the emphasis on 'every'? Jesus did that too. Kept telling His followers they were as special as He! Remember?" wistfully, " 'I said ye are gods and all of you Sons of the Most High.' "

At times Faith's words tumbled out in quick profusion, and at other moments they were labored as she groped for a particular frame for her thought or looked silently from face to face. Her voice became stronger, less tentative. She took a big breath, her eyes narrowed in concentration, her chin tilted upward and almost as though spoken through rather than speaking from her own thoughts she said, "I think John meant . . . everyone is born with a rich aura. This is one's divinity. This is the higher Self the psychologist refers to. It is his constant Inspiration. Supply. All-Sufficiency . . . like the plants, tulips for example, can move to

70

another location when dissatisfied with the present one. Like plants know how to utilize the soil and the weather. So inborn in each of us is the very substance or intelligence . . . talent . . . he requires for fulfillment. It is individual. No two precisely alike. If each snowflake is individualized so is each human being. God doesn't need two Tom Edisons nor two Albert Schweitzers, for the world is still evolving. Evolution is constantly continuous.

"It is the very self-expression of God. Each of us can enlargen his gift. Some of us don't. You know, the parable of the talents! The aura I spoken of—that is God's Presence—yet also indwelling. God is always with us—even if we are atheists—but where we invite Him to work through us, consciously cocreate with Him . . . He can work more perfectly, for then we are His hands and feet . . . and then we grow too . . . and can be bigger and more perfect channels . . . or something."

With a rush, almost a gulp of air, she continued, "Like the unborn children in Maeterlinck's play *Blue Bird*. Each of us does come to life with a divine assignment." Her voice faded to a barely audible wistfulness. Silent a moment she wondered about hers. There were no orders. No memory welled up within her. Merely that now she had this unquenchable inner conviction she would continue preparation, that she had a divine assignment.

No one spoke. John puffed his pipe. The Landemeres smiled politely. Odd, the impasse, thought Faith. So many people seem almost embarrassed by talk about God. It was as though most people—even wonderful people like the Landemeres—kept Him on a shelf, somewhere beside a prized heirloom. Or in a medicine cabinet with instructions to be taken upon retiring.

The Landemeres were merely being courteous. It was quite evident they thought her a little God-intoxicated. Pierre did. Faith could practically hear his thoughts. But she could not ignore this inner compulsion. It would not hush. Somewhere, somehow, in this farm country there was something special Faith was to do for Him.

In the silence that ensued after Faith's unusual theme the guests were aware of sporadic pinging on the windows. Pierre went to the sideporch and looked into the night as Lucille matter-of-factly asked, "When do you expect your baby?"

"I wish I knew precisely," Faith's tones were rueful. Then she burst into a radiant smile. "But the Lord has sent me a friend.

71

They live up the road a mile or so, and she has offered to stay with the little men if I go suddenly. It's twenty miles to the hospital, you know."

"Yes," moaned John. "And there's a railroad track near it—and the freights do all their heavy moving at night." They greeted his concern with laughter.

John brought out a chess board from the den closet, and seeing it Lucille protested hastily. "Oh, boys, I don't like to wet blanket your fun but I think we should head for home. That's sleet, dear, isn't it?"

"You could stay over," warmly offered Faith. "We haven't the guest room prettied up but you can take our room. John and I can settle on the daybed in the den. It opens into twin beds and is most comfrotable."

"No," Lucille instantly refused. "I think we should get along."

Pierre had risen too, preparing for their long trip by a generous helping of John's tobacco. John brought their coats and scarves, which seemed to signal both Landemeres into a duet of conversation. Both assured the hosts they would return when Spring actually entrenched. Lucille cooed, "Good-bye, dear. Your dinner was delicious as usual." Then in an impulsive gesture she enveloped Faith to herself and whispered, "God bless your big plans, you wonderful children! Don't ever let anyone blow out your candle!"

Carefully the Landemeres stepped down the stone porch and gingerly reached their car. Slowly, cautiously, Pierre maneuvered it out of the driveway and up the dirt road. Snow silenced the rumble over the wooden bridge.

At the doorway John snapped out the light, tenderly nestled Faith in his arms, kissing her ear and brushing her hair with his lips. "Everyone seems to think we are so unusually brave to live in the country. My office associates. Our friends." They giggled together at so bizarre an idea. "You're a wonderful wife for a man, Faith. I'm proud of you."

"Me too," her face upturned, eyes laughing at him.

Abruptly she was serious. A wistfulness crept over her countenance. "Honey, it was the queerest thing tonight. While we were talking about lights and auras and things. . . ."

"Yes, I know. I sensed it too." He kissed her again, fingering the curve of her ear, his lips warm on hers.

72

She tried to speak but his lips muffled her. Teasingly he pressed, stifling her speech. She pushed him away. "John, did you hear a . . . kind of crackling . . . like static on the radio?"

"No. I thought I heard a small clap of thunder in the distance."

"John, I'm serious."

"So am I."

"You are not. You are teasing."

"You aren't kissing me. In fact, you pushed me away." Faith kissed him in a preoccupied fashion. "You are not kissing me properly. That was most perfunctory. Kiss me again."

"Do I look any different?" ignoring his complaints.

"You are always beautiful to me, yet somehow each day you improve on the previous day's beauty. I have never determined how you manage it."

"Oh, slush." Faith struggled to suppress a yawn but its fringes appeared. "Come to bed. I'm sleeping for two as well as eating for two. Somehow the five-thirty alarm seems too early for one of me."

John grinned as he made his way to turn off the living room lights. "You used to be the family night owl."

"Hmmm," she agreed sleepily, giving vent to a full mouthed yawning luxury. "It's getting to the point where I have to pray, 'Dear Lord, give me the quality of eight hours' sleep in the quantity of six.'" She did not flip on the hall light but rather felt her way up the bannister.

In the new way of life there was time. True, there was much to accomplish: The baby chicks had to be checked every two hours; their temperature must be just right, must be decreased weekly by five degrees until the sixth week. By that time they were able to dispense with heat entirely. The medium by which it was determined if the chicks were "just right" was their social attitude. If they huddled together they were too cold, and could crush one another, zooming the mortality rate. If they flopped around in lonely little isles of yellow fuzz, they were too hot, would refuse food, starve to death. But if they ran about in happy little cheeping scurryings they were just right. This was the aim. So faithfully, every two hours, each day of the week and until retiring at night, the chicks were inspected. Their social attitudes, heat, water, feed —each item was noted.

Yes, there was also much to do in the big old house. Painting was the biggest need. When funds permitted there was the gargantuan job of restoration, but surely the place was liveable. John had replaced whatever panes of glass were required in the house cellar, rebuilt a few doors, lessened the sagging features wherever possible.

Despite all the demands, this new way of life gave them time. Time to notice the beauty of the world about them. Time to look up at the nightly stars. Time to watch the hillsides daily. Time to observe the beauty of the silver rain as it blessed the fields and meadows, infiltrated to the little singing brook, Spruce Run. Time to witness the handiwork of the Lord. Time to really see and hear the world in all its beautiful manifestations.

Time to be with each other, to be quiet and serene together, to have family fun. Time to have family reads, for they had withstood the pressures to own a television set. In the family reads they absorbed the beauty of ideas and words, the singing beauty of some authors, and family oneness followed.

Too, they developed a ritual for weekends. John and Faith with the children sought the highest spot of the farmland, stood hand-in-hand overlooking their land to the breadth of the horizon. Being youngsters, the lads did not linger too long to immerse themselves in the beauty of the color-swept hills, the changing skyline, but their souls were stretched to appreciate the color harmony of each sublime moment, the pastoral joys.

"God must yearn for our appreciation of His beauties or He wouldn't give us bird songs to hear, glorious sunsets to see, or any of the myriad kinds of the beautiful—or inspire man to write about it, sing about it, or paint it. . . ." Faith would comment to the boys.

Once Faith interrupted the silence of the hillside by saying to John, "Did you ever notice how a winter sunset goes through all the color seasons? Commencing with the bleakness of winter, color hints of early spring evolve. Then hints crescendo into flaming shades, the passions of summer and the exotic displays of autumn. After the last glow it's back to the austerity of winter when twilight sets in, before the stars gleam."

John silently continued observing the horizon.

"Have you ever?" persistently.

"Yes."

"Why didn't you share it with me?" teasingly.

74

Gently, almost reverently he answered, "The deeps we ponder ourselves we have forever."

Would she ever tap the depths of John! Sometimes before marriage she wondered if they had sufficient mental mutualities? How smug could she have been! In many little things—like this now— John's deep understandings and appreciations came to light. She was the one who had to cram child psychology, now this Unity stuff. John inevitably knew from within himself. In her heart she whispered, "Thank You, God, for giving me this man in marriage —not to possess—but to blend with and to grow with."

So they lived their new way of life. Occasionally someone wished to explore their new way, and accordingly one weekend John's dad, Pete, met the same train in Newark and they came together on the commuter express, rollercoasting the Califon mountains to the farm. Only the car headlights bobbed along in the inky blackness the long way from the railroad station to Red Mill. Infrequent barn lights or farmhouse lights gave Pete little comfort through the distance. "How the hell you know where you're going!" Pete finally exclaimed. "No highway lights. Nothin'! We should be in Ohio by now."

John chuckled pleasantly, "Not much further, Dad. Hungry? Faith has it ready for us."

Pete lapsed into silence. Several more miles were covered. John slowed at the beginning of the curve and the steep downgrade into Califon; Pete leaned forward eagerly in his seat. The little town lay nestled many feet below, house lights twinkling in the crispness; it reposed as a child's toy village. The car continued down, its tires singing over the steel bridge, up the other incline to the highway. More mountains and curves, the lights of the town well behind them. Pete slumped in his seat again. He had warmed to the aspect of civilization. In the blackness of the car he cast a despairing glance at John.

"Not much further, Dad."

"You're crazy, commuting this distance every day!"

"Wait 'til you see the farm!"

Pete remained unsold, but the warmth of conversation stirred him. "Goin' to work it?"

"It's like I told the mailman. He asked that too, the first day he saw me. I told him, 'Reckon you got to get your feet wet before you can swim!'"

75

"Helluva answer."

John grinned disarmingly. "I told Faith my retort and she shot back, " 'Oh, no, you don't. You can always dive in.' " Tomorrow, after Pete saw the place, would be time enough to tell him the plans. Right now John knew he was tired and hungry, any dreams of theirs would create antagonism.

A few miles later John brought the car to a standstill in the driveway. As though by a magic signal the sideporch light beamed its welcome. Two little men danced and squealed delightedly on seeing Pete, and in his response to their enthusiasm Pete almost forgot the long cold miles from Gladstone to Red Mill before dinner. But all that evening he could not bring himself to look directly at Faith. He was certain she was wholly responsible for this silly farm idea, saddling his son with too heavy a burden of commutation and probably mortgage too. He felt only animosity for her.

John and Pete toured the farm early the next morning, and Pete's expansiveness mounted as the day and its inspection progressed. In an ebullient moment he promised that he personally would apply all the paint required, wherever required. With all this room they should contemplate horses and cows too. Just chickens and sheep would not suffice.

At noon, waiting for Faith to place the lunch on the table, Pete idled at the southern window overlooking the meadow to the brook. Faith joined him. "I mean to watch spring come to that hillside. There's no little peep of green yet, but I am sure if I watch constantly I'll see the first hint. Hear the cadence of Spruce Run? It sings, doesn't it? Sometimes in the quiet of the night, after stormy rains and the downpourings from the hills from which it comes, it pretends it is part of the ocean already and it puts on quite a roar. In its turbulence it churns and tosses some of the lighter rocks."

Pete nodded. He thought it pretty too but his mind was on other things. "Wish we could get those geese for you. Be mighty nice for your freezer. Dang it! They don't even jump when the bullets whiz by. I ought to be able to just walk out there and talk them into your freezer." Faith returned to the kitchen quickly to hide her laughter. Secretly she was delighted with Pete's and John's failure.

There was no indication of daylight yet Monday morning when

76

John and Faith were awakened by a terrific din. Reverberating echoes bounced from the hills, intermingling with new noises. Each note interspliced dying echoes. There seemed to be a metallic quality about the noise. Shaking sleepiness from himself John rose to investigate. Returning to the bedroom his countenance registered a combination of apology and anger. "That's my pop! Heard me say I'm going to remove the tin garage. He has a nice early start for a noisy job!"

Then, many hours later at dinner, amid delighted chuckles from the youngsters Pete divulged his goose story. "Just got tired of target practice. Just thought I could walk right up to them. So I did. I kept saying 'shoo shoo' and they paraded right straight ahead of me. I aimed them into your big building back there, where you're going to have the chickens. Light as a feather, Faith. No food in weeks," he summed up.

The boys named the geese Henry, Henrietta, and Harriet, fed them leftover duck pellets brought along from Farm Miniature of Chatham days.

Before the month was finished, Faith's dad made the pilgrimage. Dad Sanford appeared with an entourage of women—Mom, Auntie, and a couple of cousins, Polly and Dot. They would only have coffee and dessert, for they had lunched en route. Only Doug was home to escort Dad Sanford around the farm, Rob being in school, but they meandered around the farm as Dot flitted from window to window within the farmhouse, enthusing over the china window knobs and the other antique features of the lovely spacious house. Polly kept interrupting Dot's enthusiasms with questions about over-all purposes while Mom and Auntie formed the confident, beaming background.

Returning from his stroll with Doug, Dad Sanford was strangely silent. Faith interpreted his taciturnity to indicate complete approval, perhaps even a touch of nostalgia. She hadn't thought about it before, but now she remembered the property he had held near Hackettstown when she was a child. Memories of it high above the Musconnectong River came vividly to her mind. She recalled the rocks she and her younger brother stacked in places and that the family dream was to build a fieldstone house sometime. It never materialized, of course. Faith's mother, Elizabeth, committed suicide and when Dad married Mom—well, she didn't like the country and bugs and things. Dad Sanford sold

77

the property. He remembers those dreams, Faith thought, and is reminiscent because John and I are doing the things he and Elizabeth planned—but didn't do.

Perhaps there was a measure of nostalgia in Dad Sanford's thinking on that first visit to the Red Mill farm. If so, it was a very slender thread. He too noticed the broken windows of the outbuildings, the need for nails, cement, new wood; the accumulation of manure; the wildly overgrown orchard in desperate need of pruning; the dirt cellar floor—and that antiquated, converted oil burner! Slender cracks in the house flooring between the old-fashioned boards that permitted one to see right through to that dirt flooring. His soul groaned.

The stream of little Doug's conversation had fallen on deaf ears as Dad pondered. He had sat outside briefly in the sunlight reflecting on it all. He wondered if John remembered the only caution he extended. Right at their wedding he had offered the advice, after the ceremony in the church vestibule. Tactless. Inappropriate. But there had been much inharmony and misunderstanding between the generations. And it was just one of those things; he thought of it then and so he said it then.

He had always thought Faith very much like Elizabeth. Not in looks. Faith seemed to look like herself, resembled no one on his side of the family or Elizabeth's. But in coloring and surely in talents Faith was like Elizabeth. Not exactly alike in temperament, but there was the same kind of. . . . He sought within himself to categorize it accurately. Romanticism, yes. Also, could one say determination? Whatever Elizabeth contemplated she executed. Faith had that quality. Perhaps it was persistence. But mostly he thought of Elizabeth—and Faith—as being too romantic and when problems arose Elizabeth resolved them through suicide.

Sometimes he thought Faith evidenced an emotional instability like Elizabeth. A desire to flee the world. The world wasn't quite perfect enough for their sensitivities. That often worried him about her. One has to be a realist, face facts. He recalled a summer evening long ago when Faith was in her teens. The whole family was at the dining room table, and from her place at the table Faith noticed a youth walk peculiarly up the street. Something about his walk prompted her question. Tillie wisely used it as an example of what happens to the physical body as a result of lust and boiling passions. He remembered those were Tillie's words. Faith was horrified. She recoiled. Tillie sought to mitigate it with a gentle, "That's life, dear." But Faith had fled from the table, hurling a distressed, "Then I want no part of it!" behind her.

Possibly Faith lived in a dream world and sometimes he wondered if Faith lacked the stamina life occasionally requires. Now in the sunshine of the farm he wondered if John remembered his caution in the church vestibule. He could hear his words. He saw himself holding the young man by the lapel. He had fought against his emotions throughout the whole ceremony. Around and through those emotions the words had come, clearly and brusquely, "Watch her, Young Man. Especially if the going gets tough. She's like the animals. Goes off by herself to stand her pain in solitude or lick her wounds—or die. She never cried as a kid."

Yes. He well remembered. Faith never cried. Not through childhood spankings. Not even when Elizabeth and the boy lay in their caskets in the living room, all the dark shades drawn. He couldn't recall Faith crying in anger either. It didn't seem normal. Here he was fighting to avoid tears himself, yet the only time Faith cried was over books or in the movies. But not in life. Needs a safety valve, he worried half aloud.

Dad Sanford kissed Faith most tenderly when he and the women left that March day. His eyes brimmed with unshed tears and he averted his face from the women. This was the only surviving child of the six he and Elizabeth created. There was nothing he could do. She was not his now; she was married. Furthermore, at sixty-four he was still mortgaged to the hilt and his age was showing. He probably didn't have too many more years himself. To just talk to John or Faith, advise them to move out . . . Faith would hush that up!

The women chattered the long way back to the city, but Sanford's worries juggled in his mind. Would this remaining child of his be required to face duplicate problems as he and Elizabeth? Could she stand the stress? Was her romantic quality fortified by practicality? Was that "working religion" she talked about, was it sturdy enough to see her through? Was this a case of "the sins of the fathers unto the third and fourth generations?"

Each revolution of the car wheels monotonously dirged its refrain: the sins of the fathers.

79

April appeared.

Faith did not witness the first thrust of green in the hillside's brown carpet. As by a mystic wand, it surreptiously stole over the entire hillside in the dark of night. Pasture lands hinted of emerald dyes in the morning light. Gently trees put forth their delicate unfoldings of chartreuse.

From the high places the whole countryside wore new rainment, lending the checkerboard effect to the hills and hollows. Each day the full-throated song of farmer busyness filled the world. The noise of the tractors was heard in the land from early morning until late at night, their headlights gleaming and bobbing along the horizons and fresh brown earth appearing in the wake of the singing ploughs.

In the wet places, along some marshiness of the brook, twilight seranades sponsored by a new generation of peepers began about four o'clock. Usually a signal by the soloist pierced the stillness. At his pitch note the whole chorus joined in, trilling in bewitched abandon until nearly dawn.

Then, the precious hour of complete silence until the feathered world stirred.

By day the cardinals disappeared from sight, protected by spring-summer garments, their penetratingly clear whistle the only reminder of their presence, invisible to all but the experienced eye. Robins' gay spring cheerios relieved the monotonous mournfulness of the dove's single noted complaint. One day a whole flock of startlingly resplendent bluebirds perched atop the meadowland fence across from the farmhouse. Hearing their unfamiliar song Doug excitedly demanded Faith come with him to watch the spectacle. Together they beheld the blueness flit in and out of the leafing mock orange shrub and the dowdiness of the fading forsythia, their glorious blue irradiant against he drabbing yellow.

Nightly frosts were kind and gentle, disappearing quickly in the morning sunlight. Bits of green popped up in the extensive lawn, transforming quickly into tiny wild, purple-blue hyacinths, dainty and fragrant. Beyond the retaining wall at the foot of the backyard orchard daffodils danced and tulips thrust through the earth. The whole world about them moved in rhythmic syncopation to the melody of spring birds, the song of the Spruce Run, and the caress of fragrant breezes.

When the buds on the small magnolia tree at the end of the garden and the lone dogwood tree readied itself for the spring festival, the former owner appeared. With an air of loving devotion he escorted John throughout the whole farm, naming specific apple trees, the two peach trees, the plum and the pear. With misty eyes he showed them the asparagus site between the raspberry rows, waved his massive arm in the general direction of the hay field by the old well, indicating the old asparagus site. Thumping John's breast with the back of his hand, in a tremulous voice he confided, "Young man, I hated to sell this place. I love every inch of it. It was nothing when I got it. I made it. I planted every shrub and tree and berry with my own two hands." He held them up for John's inspection. Great massive hands with blunted fingers and gross knuckles.

"You got strawberries by your laundry there. And up in the back are five acres of trees. Loblolly pines." He found his handkerchief, blew noisily. "Yes, the Lord and I planted every bit of it. Prayed over it. Loved it. . . . When we had to sell I prayed someone would come who would love it as I did. . . . I had to see if my prayer was answered. It was." Abruptly he lumbered to his car, concealing his emotions by escape.

About three weeks after goose eggs appeared regularly, Faith experienced one of her prophetic dreams: In her dream Chatham neighbors formally called on them, sitting rigidly in their chairs like a Victorian painting. Part of Faith seemed to be standing aside during the dream, laughing at the whole episode and remembering that in the Chatham days they were on a first-name basis. Almost at the end of the visit the gentleman said rather stiffly, "We've come for our geese, Mrs. Wells. You have them. We want them returned."

Faith awoke laughing. Silly stuff. They had ducks, not geese. Anyway, they ate them.

That afternoon while Faith and Doug were busy in the hennery with the chicks and the geese a yellow Jeepster pulled into the driveway. Doug spotted it first. Thrusting the goose egg into Faith's hand he whooped down the hillside to the visitors. Now great with child Faith followed more leisurely.

A petite, dark haired woman stood in the driveway surrounded by her four children, the youngest in her arms, the other three holding to her skirt. Her air was charmingly friendly and she smiled readily at Faith, "I've been trying to visit you since you came, welcome you to the neighborhood. This is my first chance though. I'm Evelyn Farnsworth and I live right in back of you. Our front yard joins your backyard."

In a flash the dream sequence was before Faith. "Did you lose three geese?"

"Why, how do you know? They've been gone long before you moved here."

Faith led the way to the lawnchairs near the laundry. It would surely sound ridiculous to claim the Lord told her in a dream. Within herself she marvelled, awed and humble, but aloud she explained, "We kept them well for you." No need to tell her both John and Pete had target practised on them! "We have been rewarded by four eggs weekly." She grinned a little, "The children even named them for you: Henry, Henrietta, and Harriet—only Harriet should be Harry."

Mrs. Farnsworth burst into gales of laughter, her children looking wonderingly from her to Faith and Doug who stood by silently watching everything. Between bursts she gasped, "My husband's name is Henry. He'll be charmed to have a goose named for him." She pealed into fresh mirth.

After the Farnsworths left, Faith busied herself preparing a pudding for dinner. She was still prayerful, awed by the coincidence of the dream and the reality. Surely this proves all dreams don't have sex significance! How is it Fillmore expresses it, she wondered? Something like. "During sleep the Lord paints upon the canvas of the conscious mind . . ." Yes, that is it. Faith also acknowledged to herself, though, that until she became accustomed to the prophetic dreams she sometimes wondered about her sanity. But little by little it came to her that in the Biblical days those dedicated people always received their guidance through visions in the night.

Now, while busy in the kitchen, Faith was given wisdom from deep within the recesses of her inner cathedral. It did not come in precise words but rather through intuition. It could be expressed this way, "The light you acknowledged the night the Landemeres visited is growing. You have been encouraging this unconsuming flame, this Aura, through your prayer and meditation periods, by your concentration on what you facetiously call 'the Unity stuff.' By your choice you are growing to God's noble purposes This is the inner Christ light in you that never slumbers nor sleeps, leads you into all good. . . . Can you now remember that as a girl you had prophetic dreams? But you got away from the Lord for awhile, became immersed in materiality. You have reopened the door to Him. You are growing in grace and understanding."

Humbly Faith responded to this idea. She was supremely happy, in harmony with God and all His world. Although their marriage was a "made in heaven" variety, they were somehow happier than formerly. But this new spiritual consciousness was like new shoes, a little stiff; she had to deliberately build the new habits and reflexes. Where previously she lived in the intellect and personality part of herself, she now strove to spiritualize every thought and every feeling.

There was no inkling yet of God's higher purpose for her life. Daily the conviction of that idea, however, grew. With her lay the responsibility of continuing steadfast in the constancy of prayer and study. "Pray without ceasing," St. Paul had admonished and she understood that to mean not constant importuning but rather a constant awareness of God as Presence, Intelligence and Power. Often she reminded herself through the days of this fabulous Partnership, working with Him in Love.

He would tell her when she was ready. She would do wonderful things for Him. In fact, He would do them through her but her part was to develop the constant awareness of Him. She could not guess what form her divine assignment would take. Perhaps even Jesus had not known in the beginning, maybe just a faint glimmer in the temple at twelve. Surely Jesus quietly practised carpentry during the long years while he perhaps studied too and certainly prayed until He felt guided to be baptised and go forth. . . .

In a week or so Mr. Dan telephoned to be assured they had fencing for the sheep and "a place they could run into if a cold rain came up." Faith was delighted this modern shepherd cared about his stock even though they would no longer be his! It seemed only a few hours after the telephone call that a short, compactly built little old man stood at her side door. In the driveway a small pickup truck held their sheep. The boys and she flew to the tailgate. Standing so close she had momentary misgivings.

They were much larger than she expected. She had never seen live sheep. She wondered how one handled them.

Mr. Dan reached her side, heard her exclamation, "They are lovely. But so awfully large." A thread of reason comforted her. She was much taller than Mr. Dan. Right now, in her pregnancy. she was also much larger. If he could manage those huge animals, so could she!

"They are purebred Hampshires but they are not registered," Mr. Dan explained. "Where do you want them?"

Many thoughts raced through her mind. She remembered an experience on Farm Miniature with the first baby chicks. No books informed them to transfer chicks to the new *house*. John and she had transferred them to the new chickyard, believing the little things had enough intelligence to wander into the house. But the little things didn't. So for two weeks, every evening Faith and John had to scoop up the little things from the ground or the fencing or whatever and put each of the 200 individually into the chick house. Looking at the size of the sheep, Faith didn't want to have to scoop up those huge things!

"Where do you want them?" Mr. Dan repeated.

"Up here," as she led the way to the orchard pasture. "Can you back up to that door?" pointing to the small door on the upper level of the barn. "Then they'll know where their shelter is."

"They will find it all right," and he started for his truck.

"How much do they weigh?" She was still comparing them to little chicks.

He paused and turned around. "I couldn't bring you two two-year old ewes as you asked. The smaller one is a yearling, goes about a hundred fifty. The two-year old is probably two hundred, and the ram about two-fifty. These are a heavy breed, you know. By the way, the yearling may be pregnant. We don't generally breed them so early but we had an accident. She might be. Kinda hard to tell with sheep. They're small, you know—the lambs. If she is, it's all to the good."

Faith giggled. She imagined John on delivery night, torn between helping a yearling ewe or taking Faith to the hospital. "If she is, when will she deliver?"

"Mid-April or early May."

This time he continued on to his truck. When he lowered the tailgate in the pasture, three sheep jumped down. Immediately they began to graze. "You got a nice place here for them. I'm glad you have good fencing. They keep wandering. Just be sure to keep water before them and salt. I used the loose salt with pyrotheozene, but you can get the cake salt if you wish." He made a movement toward his truck but sensed her concern about the lambing matter. "You won't have any trouble at lambing time, Mrs. Wells. You have at least two acres up here. They keep moving; get plenty of exercise. She'll do all right."

"Thank you," smiled Faith. "What about shearing?"

"They're taken care of this year. They get shorn only once a year. When you need it next spring, drop me a card. We keep Sundays to help out you folks who have just a few sheep." His blue eyes twinkled from under his hat brim. He was in his truck by now; he let it roll, starting the engine with the momentum.

The boys and Faith remained at the gate watching the flock beginnings. "Now we're real farmers, fellows. Chicks. Sheep. And our dirt farmers ought to be here any day."

"They're big," in unison, was the only comment from the boys.

At dusk the boys and Faith endeavored to herd the sheep to the barn, toward the man-size door on the northern upper level. Accurately they anticipated her, maintaining a twenty-foot distance between her and themselves. When she walked so did they. If she ran, they ran. If her movement were sudden, they fled in terror. When she quietly paced, they quietly paced. The boys were no help. They were dubious, cautiously remained well in the rear. After an hour Faith relinquished the program. It was time to get dinner for the little men. She and John would have to resume the project later. And they would have to! There was to be a full eclipse that night and she reflected that weather is often eerie during such an event. Also, while walking a few weeks earlier, she and Doug had seen a fox run along the brook. It seemed to her many children's tales revolved around foxes stealing sheep. Why hadn't Mr. Dan backed up to the little doorway as she suggested!

The little men in bed and dinner over for John and Faith, they repaired to the pasture. Faith carried a flashlight, although it seemed superfluous. The moon cast a golden glow into all the spaces beneath the apple trees. Each star in the universe shone clearly. Every stone in the pasture loomed large and distinct.

But the small barndoor was in darkness, its northern exposure beyond the reaching fingers of moonlight.

Three sheep simultaneously raised their heads on hearing John and Faith approach. They retreated beneath the largest apple tree. John and Faith walked quietly, John speaking in reassuring tones as they approached. Heads up, ears forward the sheep stood. When John reached a distance of twenty feet, matching his pace, they moved away.

"The sheep know my voice and obey me. The voice of the stranger they know not," remembered Faith.

Patiently John and Faith kept at the program. Overhead the moon ascended higher. An hour elapsed. Sometimes the sheep bolted, splitting in three different directions. Once or twice they panicked as one, fled headlong in a single direction, their sides heaving in fright. A pasture stalemate. John became visibly discouraged. He wanted to settle in a chair, remove his shoes, have a leisurely pipe over the evening papers. It was a long day, this early arising and trekking sixty miles to the city. Faith detected a slightly harsh note in John's voice. It was then the sheep got behind the hennery and John shouted across the orchard. "Don't let them get in there! They'll find where the fence isn't!"

Faith remained motionless. "What shall I do?"

John reached her side, breathing hard. "Do you mind getting behind there and shooing them out?" His tones again gentle and considerate. If he was weary, hot and tired, how much more so she must be—unable to move easily, burdened by extra weight and unexpected abdominal movements. Yet she had kept pace with his activities. "I'll get a lasso ready. If I can get one sheep, perhaps the others will follow," quietly reassuring.

Pressing down the leftover growth from many years and mindful of her footing amid unfamiliar stones, Faith carefully made her way behind the hennery. This building too screened out the moonlight. She glanced at the heavens. The moon was sailing in a cloudless sky. It wouldn't be covered for another hour. John called softly that he was ready. She clapped her hands noisily and the sheep dashed madly down the alley between the hennery and a hedgerow composed of dense sumac and grapevine shrubgrowth.

"Damn!" explosively from John.

John was recoiling the rope in front of the hennery. It was

thick enough to anchor a ship. Faith wanted to shout with laughter. She didn't dare. John was angry clear through. She had never seen him like this. "They can stay out all night," between clenched teeth. Perspiration poured down his face, glistening in the night light.

"Oh, no! Mr. Dan wouldn't like that. 'Cause they've been shorn. And Doug and I saw a fox!"

"To hell with Mr. Dan! Anything as dumb as they can get chewed up and I won't care!" John strode down the hillside.

Usually John was more patient than she. A gust of wind rattled a hennery pane. The change was sudden. Clouds scuttled across the sky from the horizon. The air had a queer feel to it. She'd better check on the chicks, be sure that rattling window permitted no drafts. Inside the hennery she tapped the window with the heel of her hand, firmed it into the frame. She stood watching the fast moving clouds a few minutes.

How could she pray about the sheep? There is a divine spark in animals. God creates everything, so all life is divine. But how does one appeal to the divine in animals? Get them to obey? Vaguely she was aware of baa-ing. The sheep had not bleated since they came, not even when frightened by John's and her attempts at herding. Was it the sheep? Or was it John with his clever mimicry? She listened intently. She could not determine.

Quietly she stepped outside. John was slowly herding the sheep away from the apple trees toward the large barn door, the little door invisible in the shadows and just beyond the large tractor doorway. The sheep moved placidly. Spacing his baas between words, "Don't . . . move . . . or . . . they . . . might . . . bolt."

Three sheep stopped where the barn shadow fell. John stopped behind them. Now what? thought Faith. On her inner ear fell the words, "Simple, Dearie. Beam your flashlight on the obscure doorway."

"Oh!" she ejaculated aloud.

Three sheep moved forward rhythmically, confidently, passing within the barn as the small ray concentrated on the little door. John followed, closed the door after them.

Arm-in-arm John and Faith swung down the hillside together. The moon was now a quarter obscured.

As days slid along, the multicolored glory of established spring replaced winter's silhouette. Winds gently monologued, caressing each bit of God's reawakening manifestations. The sun shone warmly, drawing forth all frost depths, magnifying all greens over the earth. Rob's long uphill walk to the school bus was under a canopy of pink and white wild apple blossoms until he reached the little bridge. Delicately fragrant breezes. Within a week the canopy of pink and white was a mud-besplattered carpet, and his umbrella a continuous dainty misty green.

From the high places and as far as one could see, patches of white interspliced the countryside's green. Dogwood blossoms were luxuriant amid farm hedgerows or on the hillsides amid the pines, along the roadsides, vying for beauty honors with blossoms of wild cherry, gradually relinquishing to the delicate pinks of peach blossoms. Daily the atmosphere was filled with their tantalizing perfumes, subtle and ever changing, blending artfully with one another, wafting with the breezes.

In the Wells' garden the first ruby shoots of rhubarb thrust upward. Encouraged by midday warmth they exploded to lush redness, elongating from dark green leaves. Wee shoots of asparagus tentatively thrust for light. At the end of the lower lawn the full-blown magnolia filled the air with its heavy fragrance while the driveway lilacs readied their charms.

Indoors late one afternoon Faith unpotted the windowledge daffodils which she had brought up from the Chatham garden. The boys watched her while they ate their supper. She returned the earth to the garden, set the bulbs on the window sill to dry. "Mom, what do flowers come from?" wistfully from Robbie.

"Depends on what kind of flowers, son. Some grow from seeds, some from bulbs, some from eyes. What kind do you mean?"

"Those," nodding at the daffodils.

"They are bulbs. They produced the lovely yellow blooms we had. Weren't they like spring sunshine?"

Munching his cookie reflectively he ignored her question, then asked one of his own, "Old electric light bulbs?"

With spring entrenched and Faith's delivery not due for another month John travelled during the weeks, but was always home weekends. Faith was not lonely. Many things occupied her day. Chores with the growing chicks, both colonies of them. Letting the sheep out in the morning, calling them in at night, for now they obeyed her voice. Their confidence in her was a daily thrill. And, of course, there were the needs of the little men to be met.

Always there were the self-impelling demands of the metaphysical study, wedged between chores of the day and long periods at night when the boys were in bed. Prayer. And study. Faith's growing cosmic consciousness. Her accelerating dedication to live harmoniously in conscious awareness of the Creator.

These were surging moments of high exultation. These she did not share with John. They did not fit into words. They were unconfinable. They were more a mystical but continuing emotion than thoughts. They were forceful, beautiful stirrings within her heart. They were the strengthening conviction she was to be divinely used for more than wifehood and motherhood.

On weekends they made their pilgrimage to the high place in the first east field. Standing hand in hand they gazed at the horizons together. Often they stood in silence, occasionally there was communication, as the time John burst forth with, "I love this place! I never want to leave it!"

Faith was a bit startled, made no immediate answer. After a bit she said gently, "You must always leave yourself free, John. . . . Free to go wherever you believe He is directing you. Free to do whatever you know He wishes . . . I believe this is the right place for us now . . . Sometimes later He might have another place and purpose for us."

Sometimes she felt tempted to coerce John into metaphysical studies too. She yearned to suggest he omit reading newspapers. She wanted to explain about the law of attraction, that what we permit to saturate our consciousness we reap in our lives. One should by-pass the auto accidents, the rapes, the murders. She wanted to say "I am building a purer consciousness this way. I need to—and I want to. Won't you come with me?"

She couldn't say that. It sounded so holier-than-he. John was so fine and noble. She loved him. Dearly. Not just having his babies. They inspired each other. They buoyed each other, complemented each other in a rare manner. Profoundly. She realized their love for each other was unpossessive, each allowing the other to stretch spiritually, mentally, socially—or whatever. So then she would have to let him find these truths for himself!

Waves of love and understanding broke over her as though she stood in the breakwaters on a moonlit beach. Not that their life together had been devoid of problems. They had sweated through John's salary freeze when inflation shrank their funds. They had experienced the miscarriage between Rob and Doug and her "ticker" misbehavior. She recognized she had been almost abnormal emotionally during the trying time after the miscarriage. John had called her on the telephone every day, at odd hours. She wondered if he had worried about possible suicide attempts on her part . . . that silly thing Dad had said to John in the church right after their marriage!

From within her heart welled up "Whoever puts his hand to the plough and looks back," and "forsake father, mother, brother, sister, lands for My sake. . . ."

Did it say anything about a husband?

Surely God and the love of doing His work would never come between a couple!

An almost imperceptible whisper within. No! Hadn't He also said "what God hath joined together . . ." Well, if man is not supposed to separate that joining, surely God wouldn't! She hushed the tiny whisper with her intellect. Each of us has a divine growth rate just as each has a physical and mental and emotional growth rate. Because it is divine it is always right. Perfect for each individual. She must not force the flowering in John's consciousness. Forcing would be like the florists' work for the Easter demands—the ruin of a plant for many years.

John would grow with her at the right rate for him. If she but held her light high enough, because incandescent with Christ, she would inspire John to want these truths too. Her assignment was to follow the leading of her Christ light, her Aura, and glorify God. That would keep her plenteously busy! Humbly she was well aware of the gigantic work in keeping the constant stream of her thoughts pure and clear, charitable and kind, free from the scum of mass negatives.

April's obsolete page fell from the calendar.

May!

Faith's last month of pregnancy, for the baby was due Decoration Day. Faith hoped it would come early. Rob and Doug had. She was wearying of lugging the extra weight, the steady plodding through chores. The hillside to the hennery seemed like the Alps. She was so heavy with child. "Low slung," John teased. Down inside she was *so* tired!

When tiredness came upon her that completely, she took strength in words. "I can do all things through the Christ in me." Doggedly continuing the chores, reiterating the phrase as she worked, she obtained strength and nourishment from them. Emptying heavy feedbags, lugging water when necessary much to John's fury. But when he was away who else was there to do it?

One still night early in May while John was away on the last of his business trips prior to the baby's arrival, Faith slowly came down the hillside, rested against the fence, the stars her canopy. The boys were long since asleep. This was her last trip before her own bedtime, for the first crop of chicks were feathering nicely, the cockerels from this group would be ready for the market in a few weeks.

In the stillness of the night some of the shackles of limit and weariness slipped from her. She stood straighter. Minutes passed. The quietness of the country saturated her. No sound issued from her lips but her soul sang lilting music. She could hear great depths of music like the swelling voices of a gigantic chorale. One solo voice rose sweetly above the others. With new meaning words came to her, "This is the night the Lord hath made . . . my inner Lord, the part of me that co-creates with God . . . How wondrous and right are thy works, O God . . . beautiful, beautiful universe. All of its ours to live in, be in. . . . This is the God in which we live and move and have our being . . . 'All that is thine is mine' . . ."

The rich contralto solo within her heart ceased. The orchestral music ceased also. She pulmeted downward like an injured eagle. Suddenly, violently the human part of her imposed demands that would not hush. Two thoughts demanded her attention: The vision of John on the hillside wishing aloud to live out his days here, expedite their farming program. Concurrently the vision of herself kneeling among the beets in the Chatham garden, covenanting the tithe, flashed before her mind.

Shortly the first produce, the cockerels, would be ready for their part of the covenant. God had surely done His part, found them the farm! But—all their loose change was gone. The thousand dollars which constituted their backlog to get the farm rolling had disappeared in Itchy's monthly guzzlings of oil. The simple bedroom suites for the boys had not been extravagant. Drapes for three living room windows. No, she had not dissipated the backlog. She had not betrayed John's trust by mismanagement. The mortgage payments were too high! The oil bill was far beyond what they were led to believe! The loose change had vanished!

They had the bonds yet, although they didn't mature for another four years. And John's salary coming in so regularly. But not necessary loose change to manage chick feed bills and the bit of grain the sheep required daily. She put her head on her folded arms atop the fencing, and a drawn out, slow sigh escaped.

"O, God! There's a little part of me scared silly when I think about Itchy's big drinks. $85 for the month of February. The same in March. April's bill didn't reduce by much. And we need Itchy for hot water all year. John doesn't know all the change is gone . . . But You and I do. I'm trying, Father, to remember You are our supply, our security—not bonds, not John's salary, not a bank account. The teachings tell me those are only channels, but my heart whirls. It's a little like 'Lord, I believe; help Thou mine unbelief.'"

She was whispering into the night stillness.

"Father, before You led us here I promised You a tithe on the farm stuff. Like Robbie said in his prayers when we found this place. 'Dear God, thank You for the farm. We'll take good care of it for You.'. . . Me too, Father . . . But now the way seems a little rocky. Itchy's big drinks are so gargantuan. The chick feed bills so high. The sheep weren't expensive, only a hundred dollars for the three of them. They eat mostly grass, just a little grain. And Oh I love them!

"But, Father, Itchy and that high mortgage. . . . I'm scared. There just isn't enough left of John's salary. Now it's spring planting time. The farmers will be here and the contract is that we pay for the seeds and fertilizers and they contribute with machinery and their work . . ."

She could not word any more of the problem. It was a towering, swaggering Goliath that she had succeeded in not hearing for many days and nights. This night it was a swashbuckling, raging giant commanding her attention. This night she seemed weaker, less courageous than the little shepherd boy of slingshot fame.

"Help me, Father. Help me keep up my courage and faith. And give me the wisdom to make right decisions."

Looking at the appearance, Faith's confidence had sunk like mercury in a winter thermometer. After her outpouring a new lightness appeared, the comforting glow of Aura. She knew she could not afford the contemplation of appearances. She must remain steadfast to the goal. Peter sank when he contemplated the height of the waves, the wetness of the water, the strength of the winds. She too must keep her vision on the Christ way!

In the west an early retiring crescent moon hung low on the horizon. Although she had waddled up the hillside, she now left the gate with an almost swinging stride downhill, a spring in her step born during the communion with the Lord. The sliver of moon was ready to slide beneath the hills.

May's milder weather augmented Itchy's temperamentality. The ideal arrangement was to operate the burner from the thermostatic control in the den. In theory, a morning and an evening run would produce sufficient hot water for laundry and baths, take the chill off the stone-filled walls. Itchy held no respect for theories. Faith's trips to the magic red button in the cellar increased. One morning the stairs' toll was twelve. Even on the twelfth count, Itchy grumbled shortly—and stopped. Faith reached a point of tense patience. Aura cautioned instantly, "Turn the other cheek, Faith. Do not give this power by your annoyance or anger."

"Yes, I know," Faith answered her Self. "But the *me* of I gets weary sometimes!"

"Remember the old hymn 'I'll go all the way . . . all the way with . . .'"

Faith's good natured laugh rippled forth. "Don't preach, Aura. If anyone overheard us he'd be astounded or pity my wonderful Johnny Truthseed for being saddled with me."

Solemnly she addressed Itchy, "I just bet my Mr. Fixit can take care of you, Itchy . . . 'Fixit!' 'Fixit?' . . . Maybe that's my problem. I was going to name everything 'good' and instead we've dubbed John 'Mr. Fixit' and we've been expecting to fix things. Thank you, Lord, for inspiring me with this 'Johnny Truthseed' name. From now on John is Johnny Truthseed."

As she worked during the day she weighed truth in her mind and heart. Itchy's misbehavior had brightened her vision of truth. John had not gone "whole hog," as he put it, on this Unity stuff but he was expanding. Sometimes he amazed her with his perceptivity. If she now thought of him as Johnny Truthseed perhaps it would help him, lift him along with herself. Was that what He meant in "And I, if I be lifted up, will bring all men unto Myself." He wasn't merely predicting the crucifixion. He also meant inspiration, the helping hand extended to another. Perhaps this helping hand could be on the spiritual-mental plane rather than the physical.

John often understood what was in her heart without their

conversing. It was as though there were waves of light, waves of intelligent communication between them as well as from the Creator to them—and back again. After all, the whole matter of God is like a two-way radio. Faith's only error was in her former belief it was one-way, a personal sending station rather than a built-in reception center also.

Funny, John had a way of stumbling into things too, a way of discovering her left-hand deeds. It seemed to be intuitive on his part rather than someone betraying a confidence. Pure knowing, uncomplicated by human speech.

She was aware of the differences in John too. In his own way he also was using these principles, working with them, selling them to others. New doors of contact were opening to him. John didn't word things her way, he said things like business letters or sales campaigns. John would never use a phrase like, "As I opened the door I thought to my Self 'Divinity in me bows to Divinity in you!'" But John's wording meant the same thing, merely the implements of speech were not in the music of scriptures.

Now looking at John afresh in the realm of her heart she realized John had a different air about him, a new confidence. He always walked with personal assurance, an attitude of knowing his destination. He was different lately. His self-confidence is deeper, she thought, yet there is a wondrous humility in it. The old haunted expression, the expression they both wore while in the Atlas consciousness trapped between the frozen salary and increased living costs, is gone. Now each of them had the growing awareness of God as the Source, the Supply itself. They had not arrived—but they were on the highway to the new consciousness.

It was wonderful having this new assurance of their good, of their prosperity. Just the realization that their growing abundance would and could grow on spiritual foundations was blessed. The knowing, deep down in the subconsciousness, that God's prosperity is rich and abundant for all, that He never subtracts or withholds from one child of His to bestow more richly on another! Anything God does is always perfect, a blessing to everyone. Why, she read recently it would take only one bushel of cornseed for a whole ten-acre field! And from that they would reap tons and tons of corn!

"Consider the lilies of the field how they grow; they toil not, neither do they spin, yet Solomon in all his glory was not arrayed as one of these."

Almost overwhelmingly it came to her that the full meaning of this poetry meant the divine intelligence in the lily. It knows how to utilize the qualities of the soil and the sunshine. With people it was that each has talents to supplement the divine spark with which to work, let Him work through, attain fulfillment. . . .

The farmers called that evening shortly after John got in. The big good-looking chap leaned against one of the kitchen doors while the shorter, one, Jim, silently scrutinized both John and Faith. He embarrassed Faith by his impersonal x-ray expression, and in her embarrassment she talked a good deal, enthusing about the wonderful results they had on Farm Miniature in Chatham. She rambled about the soil rebuilding they had achieved, dramatically changing the very texture of it. Orville, leaning against the door, grinned. Possibly he knew the workings of Jim's mind. Jim's blue eyes narrowed; there was an unyielding, almost suspicious expression in them.

"You'll have a good chance here, Mrs. Wells. Most of the farm needs soil reclaiming. It's been farmed out. Winter wheat in your north field looks sick. Color's off. The big east field never was much good. After ten years of heavy working it needs plenty." Cold, terse, emphatic statements.

Faith made no answer. Silently she returned his look. Determined thoughts marched in her heart. We'll demonstrate to you. We'll show you how God works if you need proof, that if you bless and pray even the grasses of the field respond. We'll work it materially too. We'll cut the hay twice, leaving one cutting to bless and rebuild the field and the other to gather in. We'll lug chicken manure and the sheep stuff and what's left in the barn in a wheelbarrow if we have to! Just you wait 'til we get rolling!

During the weekend John busied himself with Itchy's temperamental requirements, taking the whole burner apart, laying down each screw, nut, bolt in a straight line, cleaning and puttering over the parts to his heart's delight. Once Faith looked in on him in the dark cellar, hastily retreated less her mental misgivings flow to John and permeate the situation. Faith noisily sang during the domestic chores, more to hush the misgivings in her heart than because she was joyful.

Noon mail brought a letter from Jerry. They hadn't seen or heard from Jerry in ages! Once when John and Jerry worked together on the Boy Scout program in Newark they were inseparable, but during the war Jerry was overseas and now the Wellses lived rather a distance from Newark.

Faith tore open the letter addressed to them. She scanned it quickly. Then seating herself, she reread it slowly. Jerry surely got to the point! ". . . an investment possibility has come to me. I thought of you two. It should pay off well and rather quickly. Perhaps as soon as October or November. Surely within a year! If you have about $3000 to invest it should make it well worth your while . . ."

Faith closed her eyes. "God, how quickly You answer my prayer!" Refolding the letter she silently contemplated her backyard prayer over the gate only a few nights earlier. In the kitchen she put Jerry's letter at John's place so that he would see it at lunch.

They did not have the opportunity to discuss Jerry's proposal that noon. Two carloads of city friends descended. But that evening John and Faith reached agreement. John would take out a note in the city bank for five thousand, using their bonds as collateral. This would give them ample for seeds and fertilizer on the farm program plus Jerry's proposal, a catch-up program for the chick feed bills and Itchy's big guzzlings of oil.

They talked too of the children that evening. Faith mentioned her spur-of-the-moment invitation to some of the guests' children to come out for a vacation that summer. John looked askance momentarily, feeling Faith would have enough to do with a new baby. "It's just that Rob and Doug looked so delighted when I suggested it. I think they're a bit lonesome."

Even as she briefed John she was aware of an inner dissatisfaction. "Why waste recuperative strength on city kids who have everything? Or whose parents can supply advantages?" Aura was demanding.

"How?" Faith asked in return.

"Your every need is met." Faith was content with that. The divine law of supply and demand would be met.

While John negotiated with the bank on Monday Faith was readying ingredients for homemade bread. Casually she flipped on the radio. A spot announcement came in clearly:

96

"If you have room in your heart and your home, why not take a city boy or girl from the hot streets this summer? For details, write or call the Herald Tribune Fresh Air Fund."

"This is it!" shouted Aura.

Of course! Why not? She could take two boys, one for each of the little men. Every cell in her brain seemed to be whirling with delight, so great was her enthusiasm. Bread could wait. She wiped her hands, dashed off a note to the newspaper immediately.

She was thrilled with the possibility. Busy with ideas about it. Where to put the boys, when to have them come. It would be fair to wait until she was peppy again, say when the baby would be six weeks old. Wouldn't be fair to saddle Lulu with the care of two extra children and a new baby. This was not Lulu's commitment. This was Faith's.

In the midst of her enthusiasm she thought of John. He wouldn't like the idea at all. He would find all sorts of objections, mostly because of the new baby. In her heart Aura whispered, "John will reflect your expectancies. . . . Raise your attitude, your expectations of his reactions. . . ."

Faith puzzled over that. Sometimes Aura startled Faith, offering end-result rather than step-by-step teaching. Sometimes Faith had to ponder the message. Well, the note was written and she would wait until she had all the data to furnish John before she mentioned it. Anyway, she wanted to do it. This would be a kind of tithe. A physical tithe. One can't just send off checks. One must give of oneself too. This would be a way to prove their good stewardship.

Within a few days everything was coordinated. The short-term note was arranged at the bank, the money in their account, the bonds with the bank and three thousand dollars transferred to Jerry for the investment. Also Faith had the Fresh Air Fund information. All she required was the propitious moment.

It rained the following Sunday morning. Faith was happy about the May showers. It kept the steadily increasing stream of city company away. John and she had so little time together that such constant weekend company was something of an intrusion. When the showers stopped about midafternoon, the Wells family

97

moved outdoors, drying off the lawn chairs and relaxing. They breathed deeply of the clean, washed air, looked to the hills, sharp in their coloring. All the world seemed bursting with life, beads of rain on foliage scintillated in the sunlight. The boys played on their bikes or with model construction equipment in the garden. An open book lay on John's lap while he rested in the deckchair, curly hair blowing a bit on his interlocked fingers behind his head, eyes closed, slow pipe puffs rising.

It seemed the moment. "John?" softly.

"Yes."

"There's something I want to do very much . . . even if you disapprove," with a little laugh.

"Sounds ominous," around his pipe.

"It isn't—not really." Her voice was quiet but there was a quality of deep emotion in it, an undercurrent. She looked across at John, squinting a bit in the strong sunlight, searching his kind, passive face. She couldn't tell his thoughts, not even psychically, but she knew he trusted her. "It's . . . well, an outgrowth of a search in myself. And it seems almost coincidence how I got the answer."

He turned slightly and faced her. "What's it all about?"

"We're inviting two city lads, underprivileged boys—for a couple weeks in August. If they like it and us, we'll keep them three weeks."

There was no immediate answer. John was always that way. When she first knew him it maddened her. Gradually she came to understand he looked at a situation from all angles before reaching a decision. She learned to trust that quality in him. Calmly, "That's a big responsibility. Someone's else children. Suppose they get ill."

"They won't. This air will give them whopping appetites and if they eat well they won't be ill."

"Suppose they bring something with them? Why expose our youngsters to whatever they might bring?"

Faith's laughter rippled forth. "I don't believe in bugs any more. You know, sort of like Peter Pan. Remember when he told Wendy that every time someone says 'I don't believe in fairies any more' a fairy somewhere drops down dead?" Faith's eyes twinkled and matched the laughter in her heart. "Perhaps Barrie was playful. Perhaps he was metaphysical. Anyway, I go

98

about shouting to myself 'I don't believe in germs. I believe in God!' And I think I am slaying the bugs right and left."

"You're coocoo but I love you." John joined in her laughter.

Seriously she added, "On the practical side the children are examined by a doctor before they are entrained."

No comment.

Faith began her sales campaign. "We can do it nicely. I think we should. The Lord has surely given us our dreams. This wonderful place with beautiful scenery, glorious pure air, a place for a garden, chickens, their potential eggs. The cockerel crop soon. Sheep. To say nothing of health—all of us!—our health. Surely we can take on an extra milk bill. I think we could call it physical tithing.

"And in all honesty I must admit a selfish motive, dear. Our lads have no one to play with. To learn how to get along with people one has to practice on people. The boys may not wish to hibernate, be farmers. There are precious few vocations in life one can choose that do not include dealing with people. We are not only giving a vacation to two city lads from a hot, smelly city, we are also giving playmates and a social education to our lads."

"What age boys have you requested?"

"Anything from six to nine. I asked for brothers, thinking they would be happiest in a strange place with a kind of union between them. I left it open insofar as religion is concerned, promising to eat fish on Friday if necessary."

Kindly but with conviction, "I think you're crazy with the baby. You'll have enough to do without two additional children to bother about. You know that every friend from here to Spodunk will visit us between now and the first frost."

"I'll manage," with quiet determination. She was thinking of the wearying trips to the hennery with only sustenance from the words "I can do all things through the Christ in me" to re-strengthen and encourage herself. By summer the baby would be here, she could see her feet, she could romp, this excess weight and bulky shape would be a thing of the past!

John knocked the ashes from his pipe against the heel of his shoe. Grinning at her, "If you have already decided there's nothing for me to say, is there?"

She glanced up into his smiling face. "No." Her dad would

have shot through the roof. John answered with calm politeness. What a man! Always considerate but surely no pushover.

Dreamily she contemplated the hills behind him. "Honey, I don't mean to seem so autocratic but Rob has been so shy. He is gradually coming out of his shell. It hasn't been easy, adjusting from suburban living to country stuff. The noisy school bus has been an ordeal for him. The advanced curriculum has been another challenge. Doug and I have walked to the school bus many mornings, lessening it gradually before the baby comes when I can't go with him. . . . Sometimes we've met him in the afternoon. Let's help his self-confidence in meeting new people, new personalities, new situations . . .

"And—let's prevent Doug's getting to such a personality predicament. He has felt the change too in his way. You haven't noticed because you aren't home during the week while he's alone. All day he waits eagerly for Rob's return. Sometimes when Rob gets in, he is so impressed with being almost-seven, he won't play with the preschooler! I ache when I see the expression on Doug's face at being rejected after that all-day wait.

"We owe more to the children than mere necessities and an education. We owe them a healthy outlook on the world, an understanding of other people. This experience with city kids will be an education for them, something we could never buy.

"And spiritually we should teach by example rather than preaching—even though I'm preaching at you." She laughed a little self-consciously. "Aura told me the inner meaning of 'To him that hath shall be given and to him that hath not, even that which he hath shall be taken away.'" John looked up quickly, searching her face. "The world translates it as 'them that has it gets'." She grinned disarmingly. "Aura says the 'hath' is the key word. It should be interpreted 'spiritual consciousness' and it means one has to live the life—just holding the theories isn't enough." She looked keenly into his brown eyes. "I know we have both come a long way. It's only lately I have any real understanding—the acknowledgement of God in all departments of our living. We can't give that to anyone, not even bequeath it to the youngsters. But we can surely live so that they may catch it. I imagine it could be more contagious than measles!

"We must be good stewards of God's gifts." Her voice lessened to a mere whisper. "Who knows? We may even plant a seed of hope or spiritual upliftment in the hearts of the little people who come? Unless one touches the heart the individual stays bound, sometimes even falsely believing a Just, Wonderful, Loving Creator would send them limits of health or finances. A chosen people doesn't mean God selected them above all others but rather that they also chose Him!

"These things aren't theory with us, John. We're working with them. Applying them in every step of our onwardness. They are practical, useable. I only wonder why we didn't see it ourselves? We had to read it in *Sermon on the Mount*. It seems so apparent. Lets share it."

Her voice was vibrant with emotion, her eyes misty. John made no answer for a long time. Faith did not press him. She had used her whole sales pitch, but every idea she believed in with all her being.

At long last, "Whom are you using for reference?"

"I have used the Dominie's name from Summit. They also want two of our new neighbors. I asked Mary Banners and Dottie Saunders. They are the only folks we know well enough around here."

John nodded slightly. He was still digesting Faith's plea. He lightly kissed her hair as he passed behind her chair and joined the little men, whistling as he covered the distance to them. Soon their noisy laughter interrupted the country stillness.

Birds began their twilight serenade long before daylight dimmed. Listening to the feathered world, the boys' spontaneous joyous whoops began to dim as Faith succumbed to drowsiness. A slight smile on her lips faded as she slipped into a restful slumber. John had been sold. She awoke to John's nose-rubbing and gentle kisses on her lips and eyelids. "Don't we eat Sunday supper any more, Sweetheart?" he whispered.

As Faith and Doug waved Rob down the road one mid-May morning, Faith calculated her day. It was Rob's seventh birthday. She planned the cake and its trimmings, his favorite meal for the family birthday party. While these plans occupied her thoughts Doug observed a mother robin in the tree, feeding her noisily hungry family. "Hers came 'fore ours, huh?" staring at his mother's largeness.

An anguished bleat from the orchard pasture! The fox!

They fairly flew to the barn, Doug well ahead. In front of the

101

wagon house Henry and Harriet contently grazed, looked up briefly as Doug zipped by, Faith trailing afterward. Can't be the fox, reasoned Faith, observing their behavior. Doug at the barn-door stood speechless, hazel eyes wide in wonderment as Faith arrived.

At the open doorway they stood hand-in-hand-watching Henrietta ready her firstborn. Efficiently, with great ardor, she licked his black kinky wool dry, his sturdy little body giving a little on wobbly legs with each determined lick. Once he baa-ed his protest and Henrietta murmured throaty conversation, reassuring him this grooming was for his good. Doug looked up at Faith, swallowed hard, whispered, "Did her just lay it?"

"Yes."

Faith's emotion and reverence was as great as Doug's. She was thinking of the profundity of instinct, a yearling knowing precisely how to care for her first baby. "Doug, chickens 'lay' eggs but sheep either 'lamb' or 'deliver' lambs," correcting his farm lore.

"Ooooh. Deliber?" meditatively feeling the word in his mouth.

It was many minutes later that they departed from the loveliness of the nursery. When they came down the hilliness the whole world seemed to be celebrating the event. A pair of bluebirds rose before them in their love ecstasy and some goldfinch flew so close that Faith dodged involuntarily.

All that long day Henry and Harriet made frequent trips, standing in the barn doorway, noisily requesting their friend to join them. Henrietta ignored them entirely, not even answering their entreaties. Only once in the late afternoon did she leave the newborn as he slept, obtaining a drink and a quickie lunch, galloping to his side on his waking bleat. Henrietta was a mother now. Life held new responsibilities for her. She had forsaken the ways of the fickle crowd.

The next day's weather alternately drizzled and rained, the earth soaking up the wetness. That day Henrietta introduced her son to the great outdoors. In vain Faith and Doug tried to herd the mother and the little frisky lamb into the barn, luring Henrietta with hay and grain. This was not as the first night when the sheep fled before them in distrust and fear. Rather this was a determined mother ewe, instinctively knowing the warm May showers would have no adverse affect on her child, would not even penetrate his lanolin. Standing before Faith she stamped her right foreleg, an annoyed expression on her usually serene face, anger in her resonant bleat. Faith did not comprehend. However, winded and weary she reluctantly gave up. "Come on, Doug. We'll have to ask God to tell her what to do. I just can't run—or even walk another step."

Doug ran up beside his mother. "How does God tell her what to do?" He was intrigued.

"He told her mother and her mother told her."

"How did He tell her mother? Where is her mother?"

"Way back with the very first sheep He gave them instinct. So animals always know what to do. The Bible puts it this way: 'God said I will write my law on their inward parts; in their hearts I will write it'." Faith glanced at the sturdy lad beside her, striding along to match her step. "Oh, for goodness sake! He did tell her—and she tried to tell dopey me. The spring rain is warm and it won't bother the baby. It isn't a baby chick needing to keep warm at 98°! It's a lamb with kinky wool and lots of lanolin that rain can't penetrate!"

Looking at Doug she continued, "You know that God is in everything, through everything, and all about everything. In people, animals, brooks, rocks, trees. Even the law of gravity is part of God." Usually when Faith or John reached this point the boys would test with, 'In the house? In tables and chairs and things?' And Faith and John would answer 'Yes, because God gave the idea for their invention to someone.' But right now Doug was very earnest. He made no little questions, nor any teasings. "Literally everything, Doug, and God loves all that He makes. Sometimes His love shows as care for something or someone through a person and that individual is God's hands and feet. Sometimes it is through mysterious ways that we cannot see. But it is always perfect. We can't see God or know Him through our senses, but we constantly witness the effect of His work."

"Ye-es," he turned his happy face upwards and beamed his answering joy. "Am I getting freckles?"

Faith squeezed his hand, nodded her confirmation of his hope.

Up in the wetness of the May pasture baby Claude kept side by side with his young mother. In the days that followed, he waxed strong and beautiful, an only child, an only nephew, sedate and serious in his ways.

By the third week of May the family vegetable garden began to show the loving work of Faith and Doug. Wobbly rows of tiny greens affirmed that love. Between rows of seedlings a foot-thick mulch of barn stuff replenished the earth. An hour a day for many weeks Faith had wheelbarrowed that barn stuff to the garden, working consistently until the point of tiredness. The straw would break up with each footfall upon it, disintegrate into the soil, transmute the quality from its present hard, clay-like composition. Under her loving work, it would become as the soil of Farm Miniature, pliable, warm and rich. Now that the heavy work was accomplished it was good to walk among the rows. Back in the Chatham days, before finding Fox's books and the Unity stuff, Faith's garden was an almost frantic effort to save on living expenses. In those days and nights Faith canned or froze vegetables until exhaustion, whipped by the penuriousness of her personality. She smiled wanly to herself now, contemplating those days. She had truly come a long way, brought along the highway by her good Lord. True, she worked hard now too, but it was easier with her vision uplifted and the knowledge that He worked through her. There was no longer the urgency to fight increasing living costs. Now it was the joy of sharing their plenty. She might still can and freeze vegetables, or make jam until late in the night, but it was the delight to have foods or preserves at peak flavor rather than to tight-fistedly hold money.

Sharing their plenty. Wondrous to think about. The tithe on the farm produce. The physical tithe with the little city men who would come to them. And as the days and years passed, there would be an increase they could share.

There was time to live here on the farm. Really live. The surrounding world did not encroach as it did back in Chatham with neighbors dropping in to chat or waste time. Here the neighbors were too far apart. Also, in all honesty, Faith admitted she didn't know very many of them yet. But here there was time to think, study and work with the Unity teachings, make them part of her daily living, her climate of mind and soul.

Here there was time to talk and walk with the children, marvel at the usual miracles of returning spring, the way a bird builds the nest, the artistry of a spider spinning his web or "canning a fly" as the boys put it. There was time to notice the dew spangled web in the early morning sunlight, beads of moisture iridescent in early light. Time to hear the symphony of the neighbors' stock mingle their songs with the Wells' stock. Time to observe the constantly changing color transition of the hills.

The hills; Faith loved them. They were not as high as those in New Hampshire when John and Faith tripped through them years before. Nor the Smokies of Tennessee when they toured those. These were lower, cosier, not so grand or austere. These were friendly, seemed to cup her very world in their hollows of protection, holding the earth in color ecstasies. The blue-purple shades of evening enveloped them completely, tenderly each night. That was the only color recurring daily—blue-purple. All the other colors differed not only from day to day but also from hour to hour and from season to season.

And the trees! All the trees. The individual trees, especially the English walnut at the foot of the driveway, almost at the little culvert bridge by the dirt road. Faith loved to look up through its leaves to the stars late at night. It was like looking at diamonds glinting through filigree lace. Breathtakingly gorgeous!

The two towering pines and all the huge maples on the front lawn that enhanced the house in its setting—these were the things that mattered to Faith, part of the eternity of God. Not the hurly-burly bustle for daily bread but rather the constancy, the glorious involution and evolution of the Universe, these things filled her consciousness. These things thrilled her. She was part of them. She heard all this world speak to her, fill her with joy and gladness.

What harmony permeated the very world around her. Harmony! Lovely word. Science erred in its cold concept. The world had not come forth from chaos. Whirling energy, yes. Not chaos. Constant creativity filled with intelligence. This is God at the heart of the constant creativity. Limitless God. Only good coming forth from Him. Even the horrible war . . . more good came from it than destruction. Medical science advanced. And little by little man was universally getting to know other races, other nations, other religions—yearning and learning to love them, and thus understand them. Why even here, in the country, up the road a bit, an American lad had brought home a Japanese wife, and everyone within reasonable radius was learning she was beautiful even though her "eyes were differently made." And all the neighbors took the beautiful little girl-children to their hearts. So the ripples were spreading out from the pebble dropped in this little pond.

Surely in the heart of this fabulous Energy are peace and harmony. Love, Wisdom, and Understanding. These are the Law of God. These qualities make the world go around! Not the little personal loves and plans, for often they have selfish little motives; they are merely subplots which—often in spite of themselves—are lifted up and transcend the finite. Only the good lives forever, all else fades as a nightmare fades into oblivion with awakened consciousness.

In a sense such was her life: The turbulent childhood and teens. As John came into her life the storms began to diminish. Once Faith found the full peace within herself, dissolved her old-time resentment, her whole world benefited. She smiled slightly, remembering Pierre's namecalling. "God intoxicated." No, not intoxicated with senses dulled and inept. Rather she was divinely enthused, responding at long last to His love.

Doug came beside her, pointed out the sprouting corn.

Faith came to his world. "Can you see it, Honey, tall and green and sending forth its good crop?"

"I can taste it," Doug countered and Faith hugged him close. "Metaphysically you're ahead of me, sonshine."

Sometimes Faith wondered if her planting of truthseeds into the minds of the little men were sprouting. She wished she knew, but one can't go digging around the little seedlings and still expect them to thrive. She could only hope, continue to plant—and of course live the life! Then one day Faith's silent question about truthseed planting was answered. Rob dashed in breathlessly from his homeward walk, large-eyed, speaking in a trumpeting voice, "Ma, a kid at school says when you die you go to hell and sizzle if you're bad." He paused to catch his breath. With a rush he finished, "I told him God loves everyone—and never, never hurts. *Not ever!* I told him you said God even loves crooks and yearns 'til they come back to Him."

He wondered why Faith hugged him so ardently, why she seemed near tears.

So the days moved along, serenely, each day filled with clean living. Faith lived in a white tower, a monastic kind of family life, each day brimful with prayer and meditation and study

106

as well as the chores to be done for John, the children, and the stock. The hours of routine duties were her hours of building the new consciousness when she held His words in her mind, savoured them in her heart, digested them in her soul and intellect, cementing them with the steadfastness of her desire—and listened to Aura's promptings and teachings.

The last Sunday of May Lulu arrived, silently wondered how anyone so large with child could drag around. Ardently Lulu wanted to caution Faith against overtaxing her strength, but her lips remained sealed. She could not penetrate the invisible tower walls around the younger woman. She watched Faith's busyness in the garden from the kitchen window until she could not be silent any longer. When John passed through en route to the barn chores, she pulled him to the window. "John, look at her! I know she does too much. It's all right to be active but there is a limit. That baby'll be all squeezed together."

John patted his mother's shoulder, "Don't fuss, Lulu. The good Lord has endowed her with remarkable common sense and great strength."

In the garden Faith surveyed the growth about her feet unmindful of the kitchen discussion. A few small beets awaited her plucking in the hotbed. A joyous gleam lighted her eyes as she gently pulled tiny beets from the soil. She blessed the divine inspiration that impelled her to plant for early enjoyment. Tops would be delicious in a tossed green salad, and the baby beets would be most sweet and tender. Plodding into the kitchen she offered them to Lulu almost as a peace offering, and continued upstairs to shower.

Faith's personal agenda before her sabbatical, the delightful way she referred to her confinement, was consummated. They would not require Mary Banners' helpfulness, for Lulu was there. Everything was now in readiness for the baby. The garden planted and growing. A large part of the barn gold cleaned out of the barn. Rob no longer required total escort to the school bus, hadn't for several weeks. Now, only the baby had to come and her days of sabbatical be finished, and the city boys arrive . . . and . . . and. . . .

She wished the baby would come. Right now! She was tired. But surely the Lord had helped beautifully ever since that prayer against the fence early in May, furnishing all the extra pep she required. But she was weary of waddling rather than walking. Exhausted with the extra weight. Fifty pounds of it! She wondered why. She had watched her diet. Blithely she continued gaining. Was it some silly personal law she had set up for herself during pregnancy? Or—could it be twins? That would save another pregnancy! If they hit the jackpot with this pregnancy. . . .

She didn't enjoy being pregnant. Of course, she liked the end-result. She appreciated the miracles occurring within her body to nourish, protect, and grow this bit of divine life. Surely she was co-creating with God! The other two had been early, Rob a couple weeks, Doug six weeks. This baby even ruined her private theory about keeping active to expedite the days of gestation.

It would be good to stand up straight, behold her knees again and her feet. She hadn't seen her feet from a standing position for many weeks. It would be wonderful to bounce out of bed mornings instead of laboriously pushing herself up and out, fists hard in the mattress.

She was packed for the hospital. Besides five pairs of pajamas and a housecoat, her valise contained books rather than the usual femininities. A volume on Buddhism, Sugrue's *Stranger in the Earth,* Fillmore's *Twelve Powers of Man,* and a huge volume named *Bibles of the World.* Wedged in a corner of the valise were a toothbrush and a tube of paste.

June, with its gentleness of breezes and lazy warmth. June with its deeper green hues, freshness and exotic perfumes tantalizing the countryside. June, the month of romance and weddings—and new babies. And the days were accomplished for the fulfillment of the new baby.

John awoke before Faith the first day of June. He lay quietly beside her, lovingly considerate of her sleepiness. He watched her eyelids flicker in the full morning light as she slowly journeyed into the world. One eye half opened. Reclosed. John teased his index finger under her chin, down her neck to the dimple at the base of the throat. "What's the procedure for the day, Love of my life? Do I take you to the hospital or do I shove off for Newark?"

Faith emitted a long, trembly sigh. A slight pucker rested momently on her forehead and she pursed her lips together, opened both eyes.

"Well?" smilingly.

"I have to call Doc. He will want me to go."

108

"Do you have pains?"

"No."

John threw off the cover. "Then I may as well go to Newark." Standing at the closet he selected his attire for the day. Sensing Faith's thoughts he turned quickly. She lay still, meeting his gaze.

Slowly and with deliberation. "No. I have to go today."

"Why?" banteringly.

Faith pushed herself over in a roll, prepared to get up. What she had to say she wished to appear casual. Busying herself with dressing she spoke offhandedly. "Because my history shows Doug was jaundiced at birth . . . because we want Quota—unless this is twins and there has been enough activity for four legs! . . . because my blood is RH negative and yours RH positive . . . because what they call antibodies build up terrifically if one carries over the normal period . . . so he will check the baby's position and induce labor."

John crossed the room in swift strides, lifted her face upward. "What is all this about, Honey?" His voice was grave and there was a haunted expression in his eyes. Dad Sanford's words shot through his memory, "watch her . . . she isn't like most girls. She doesn't cry, goes off by herself like the animals in her pain or to die." It had not occurred to him anything could be amiss. She had been well and happy, seemingly unworried. He had done much watching and worrying, heavy with great concern through long months while Faith recuperated from a miscarriage. Then he had watched carefully, wondering how long the deep emotional pit would hold her, hoping her mind would not slip during the depressed months. That was before Faith discovered the "Unity stuff." She was a new girl since then! Gently, "Why do you carry these burdens by yourself?"

As she met his look he knew this wasn't the Faith of long ago. There was no fear or worry in her eyes. No beaten down expression. No lines of self-pity around her sensitive mouth. Emphatically she moved her head from side to side. "No burdens, Hon. When they told me, I just turned the whole thing over to the Lord. If He makes all life, He surely wants it perfect. Whenever a silly little fear arose in me I just told myself that. Then that affirmation precluded my talking about adverse possibilities, dear."

Her heart deplored the gulf in their spiritual understanding.

109

She knew he didn't comprehend how talking about a situation empowered it. She must try to increase his comprehension, not by thrusting these ideas on him. No, much as she loved him she would not force his acceptance of this philosophy. For herself, she could see and understand the theory that talking about negatives—or bad luck—keeps the negatives perpetuated. This to her was the esoteric meaning of "false gods." Not always the golden calf. Sometimes intellectualism, or germs, or science, just as easily as an overstuffed bank account. How could she explain the principle of removing one's vision from the appearance, fastening it rather in faith upon the desirability! How could she condense the principles she was studying, sincerely trying to work with?

In the silence of her heart her prayer-thought went upward like incense in the temple. "God, he's so wonderful and You have brought us together for this life. I don't want to thrust my beliefs on him, but I do want to bring us both closer to You. Help me explain this Unity stuff, this practical and wonderful self-psychology. Help me show him these principles—these laws of spirit and mind."

Aloud she said slowly, "I can't explain all the ramifications—but I understand the principle. So I must work with it, keep my faith in it by using the faith I have. One can't pray for one thing—perfect life for our baby—and then spend time contemplating or talking about the opposite, wondering if God has heard or might be a little deaf. It's like a delicate scale: one hour's worth of prayers on one side—and it wouldn't be fair to put twenty-three hours' worth of worry and fear on the other."

John remained silent. At his closet he substituted his business garb for the at-farm things. Faith's eyes were filled with unspilled mistiness. She wished to avoid hurting John. Surely, too, she wished to not appear holier-than-he. His back was toward her now. Was there an example she could use to clarify the whole thing? Was there?

"Job said 'that which I fear cometh upon me.' Do you see, John? This is self-psychology. Spiritual psychology. We've always thought of psychology as rules to handle other people and really Jesus' teaching was 'he that ruleth his spirit is greater than he who taketh a city'."

John continued dressing, silently, deliberately.

"Forgive me if I erred in not telling you. I thought you might

110

worry—and that it might decrease the potency of my prayer. I *know* the baby will be perfect." Almost fiercely, "And it won't have a blood problem either. I know Quota will be perfect. Yes, Doug wasn't—but I didn't know these things then. I didn't understand God as Life, perfect Life. Not death. *Life!*

"When Doug was born I believed 'God gives and God takes.' Now I realize this is a limiting concept. People think of God as they are themselves, maybe. I'm beginning to think no one dies until he relinquishes the desire to live. God gives us free will even that far. And if people are His self-expression, He wants us alive and perfect. He can't express through a corpse. Death is a negative, the opiate of life. Perhaps death is merely a digestion period between incarnations. Jesus underscored eternal-life-in-a-perfect-body by resurrecting three people before His own Easter. Perfect life, not merely long days. Not old age with dentures and a wheelchair. Fillmore quotes Dr. Alexis Carrol as saying 'man could live forever except for a brain and a nervous system.'

"Do you see the immensity of that! The nervous system is merely the telephone setup from the brain. When we individually learn to use our brain perfectly—thinking constructively—no fears, no worries, no greeds, no hates, no lusts, no criticisms— we will live forever in perfect bodies. It merely takes self-discipline over every thought." Softly. "Merely! It's the most stupendous task I have ever undertaken."

John was still silent. He did not understand completely but he was receptive to Faith's explanation, and surely her sincerity. He realized she caught sight of a great ideal. He had never witnessed such depth of sincerity and yearning in her voice and manner before.

Faith remained before her dresser, brown eyes intense with an inner glow. This was more than philosophy to her. This was the whole message of Christianity! Yet we seem to get lost in the idea of Good Friday rather than Easter, she thought to herself. But even as she reached her right hand God-ward, her left hand would extend toward all those who come after in her little world —especially John and the children.

John climbed into his trousers.

Faith could think of no parable or story to make a verbal italic to her remarks. She wondered if she had talked too much. How

111

could she prattle about mind being the beginning of everything, that all life moves from within outward? It sounds so abstract. How could she modernize "whatsoever ye believe and ask for, believe ye receive it and it shall be done unto you?" Or Paul's vast psychology—that "whatsoever" stuff of his—"Whatsoever things are lovely, whatsoever things are true, whatsoever things are of good report . . . think on these things." Why if that isn't psychology, what is? Don't the experts say whatever you fill your thoughts with comes into your life, so doesn't that mean health or illness, good or trouble, and so on?

She went over to John, put her arms around him. "We didn't understand this when Doug came. But we do now. So we must work with it."

He kissed her, reassuringly patted her, left for chores. Standing at the window Faith watched him walk the hilliness to the barn. Aura comforted her. John would mull it over awhile. The baby would prove all emphatically.

Slowly Faith dressed for the hospital, best underwear instead of the farm quality. Meditatively she wondered if she would ever have the courage to tell John she now believed she had caused that miscarriage some five-plus years ago. Not by straining or stretching. Simply by worrying something would happen. Now she recalled a weed seed planted in her subconsciousness by a fortune teller when she was very young. On a lark she and several girls sought out a gypsy, who suggested she would marry and have only one child. Having spent lonely years after her mother's and brother's death, she tangled with that idea. By meeting it with force and fighting it, she firmed down the soil of her subconscious mind, then when the second pregnancy appeared she had forgotten the gypsy's suggestion—but the worry and fears blossomed. Had she known metaphysics! Had she denied the suggestion and affirmed the opposite—like she was doing regarding this new little life in her care. . . .

But she must not do as Lot's wife. God had forgiven her because she had not known these laws of mind and heart. Now that she did, she was responsible to keep the high watch in her heart and over her thoughts or it would be as "the worse thing befalling."

Yes, she admitted to herself. It's a mental discipline. And

"disciple" and "discipline" are from the same root word. One has to achieve mental self-discipline to attain Christhood. At-one-ment with God. This is the whole object of being!

Faith made the telephone call to the doctor, then matter-of-factly announced to Lulu he would induce labor. She made no additional comment to Lulu's well intentioned warning such steps don't always work. Faith merely smiled at Lulu, hoping it was not a patronizing grimace. Understanding and will were the guards against every incoming or outgoing thought to be judged. It was as though she were living in a castle of old with a moat around it. She had to learn to lower the drawbridge of acceptance only after the thought or idea passed the sentry's inspection.

Aura gave Faith a warm feeling the inducing would work. Simply because she believed it would. Aura said gently, "There's another reason too. You get your heart's wish. How often have you complained, laughingly, to Mary Banners or Lucille Landemere or anyone else, you wished you knew when the baby would come so that you could plan? Those were your words. Remember? The subconscious has no sense of humor. It carries out all the directives. The heart's desires. Now you do know precisely when the baby will come. Today."

They drove to the doctor's office in congenial silence. The examination over, they headed to the hospital, Faith already a little lonesome for the two at home. They would have wonderful care with Lulu. She knew that, but she also knew both boys would miss her. They had stayed so close to her these last few days.

In the admission office she managed to be casual, kissing John and whispering, "Bye. We'll be two soon." Then she was whisked off, leaving John to furnish details for hospital records and while away the time amid incessant thoughts.

In the labor room Faith was efficiently bedecked with the bizarre hospital gown, shot with an injection of pituitrin, supplied with the customary offensive castor oil cocktail, and left to meander the spotlessly clean and impersonal corridors. Each half hour another injection with the laughter-filled warning to "perform—or else." The "or else" included stories of the many times the injections are not effective. All six injections, the last a few minutes after seven that evening, accompanied by the dire threat there could be no more. This was the maximum. Far down the corridor a few minutes later Faith had the first intimation of performance. She quickened her pace toward the labor room. That first pain was extremely intense. The experienced hand on her abdomen led the little nurse to press a large watch in her hand with the admonition to clock her pains.

"You'd better call my doctor," warned Faith.

"You've just started. We'll watch you. Don't be afraid."

Faith was alone. Only the large watch to tick out the time. How could she convey to the nurses she was working spiritually on this delivery? This wouldn't be as a normal delivery—not even a normal one spiked with pituitrin? This would not be like the usual case where a woman merely depends on nature and science.

A routine peak around the doorway ten minutes later brought the nurse swiftly across the room. Mute, distorted agony on Faith's countenance. Two more nurses appeared instantly.

The little one, leaning over Faith, asked, "How fast are they?"

In the middle of another onslaught Faith could only roll her head in speechless agony. With the subsiding of that pain she gasped, "I can't clock them . . . they are erratic."

Another pain followed, seconds after.

The rolling table was beside the bed now, two nurses prodding her by words and actions to move over, knowing how quickly cooperative strength ebbs at this point. Faith raised her hand, silently pleading for recovery time.

Ruthlessly, "You can't wait. Move over now! Come on!"

In the delivery room, they worked in synchronized coordination. The pretty brown-eyed one with the southern accent fastened Faith's arms, elevated her legs, booted and strapped them.

Precisely at seven thirty-five the new boy child exploded into the world, lustily protesting. Doris, the little nurse, sang out "It's a boy!" efficiently clamped his umbilical, wrapped him amid his loud protests. Upsidedown to Faith's perspective he was placed on a separate table.

Two shining tears slipped from Faith's closed eyes. Almost imperceptibly her lips moved in silent prayer while the trio of nurses held a gossip session at the foot of the delivery table. "Look," Doris whispered, "she's praying."

Their conversation ceased. Perhaps they joined the congregation of Faith's happy thanksgiving in the cathedral of her soul.

Faith's eyes flew open. Grinningly, "Well, we made it, didn't we?"

114

A burst of laughter. The southerner drawled, "Ah'm sorry we couldn't give yuh anesthetic, Honey. We aren't allowed unless there's a doctor in attendance." Lamely, "We couldn't locate him."

"Thas'll all right," Faith unwittingly drawled her response.

Another burst of laughter.

"May I see him please?"

Doris moved instantly, deftly cuddling him. "Did you want a girl?"

"Not really. We wanted whatever we got—really . . . He's kinda squeezed together, isn't he? Looks like an Indian rubber eraser my grandmother gave me when I was very little. My! I forgot how tiny they are."

"He's a big baby!" protested all three.

Doc stood enframed in the doorway, his glance ascertaining all the details. He proceeded to scrub up, don his whites while the nurses worked in silent skill. "We'll have to give you some ether while we repair the damages," he informed Faith.

One of the nurses prepared his equipment, another adjusted the nosepiece to Faith, one tied Doc's whites. It seemed to Faith airplane motors roared in her ears and the room revolved. Through it she heard him lambast the girls. "She had no right to be torn that way! This could have been prevented with you on your toes! I told you the very minute she started labor you were to call me. You will never make good nurses until you can obey orders."

Faith tried to free her hands from the brackets. She must tell Doc the girls were not inefficient. She couldn't tell him God and that pit stuff removed all normalcy. He'd think her crazy. But she could exonerate the girls.

From a million light years away a southern drawl wafted to her, "There . . . honey . . . you . . . breathe . . ."

The next instant she was being moved into a bed, trying powerlessly to cover her femininity, faintly heard the girls laugh a little, one of them relieved her anxiety with "don't worry; you're covered." Doc's voice penetrated, bidding her lie quietly, not move. Faith had an inclination to laugh except it required more energy than she could muster. Even her eyes wouldn't open, the lids were so heavy.

Sometime after that she was aware of John's presence. With stupendous effort she opened her eyes once. He was beside the

115

bed surrounded by a peasoup fog. His voice came from Africa maybe, or further. Valiantly she tried to speak, tell him it was another boy. A perfect boy. No jaundice!

It took such effort.

It ebbed to her that John was fussing with her arm, fastening a wristwatch. He was whispering thankfulness of her welfare, of the perfect baby. His kisses were dewdrops.

The fog shut off everything.

Even John's voice could not penetrate.

Summer

June's warm days and pleasant nights blended into composite sunrises and sunsets. Confined upstairs, Faith surveyed her world. The lush garden, strawberries as large as a first thumbjoint; growing spinach, beets and corn; emerald green parsley. Each succulent vegetable within easy accessibility of the kitchen. At night low stars over dancing fireflies and the air smelling fresh and clean. June was positively intoxicating. Faith announced to John and Lulu she felt as a little girl, ready to burst with happiness! Everything was so perfect! The new baby! All the farm fulfillments, little joys and big joys filled her with ecstasy.

Little joys—like the morning Doug came in from play, tiptoeing upstairs, Lulu's voice following him, "Don't go waking up your mother now. Let her rest. She'll get precious little when I leave!"

Feigning sleep Faith watched Doug through her eyelashes, saw him reach into the bassinet, hold Don's tiny foot affectionately as he whispered, "Hi, you dear little Stinky. Hurry up and grow so you can play with me." Momentarily he moved over to Faith, then tiptoed away as softly as he appeared leaving Faith deweyed and radiant.

A big joy of that June was the sale of the first cockerels. John pronounced them nothing exceptional as though questioning Faith's precepts. The chicken dealer, Finestein, confirmed John's opinion. Twenty-five cents per pound of weight was all he offered, precisely the open market price.

Faith's heart took a little dive. All that water lugging. The weeks of dragging her heavy body up the hillside every two hours to check on the chicks. The quantity of their feed. Their water. Their temperature, for too cold and they would bunch together, smothering one another. Too hot and they would be dopey, eating insufficiently, not actively running around and growing.

A quarter per pound!

Only a few cents profit on each cockerel above the feed costs. No recompense for her labor.

Nor for John's labors! John set up the battery. John readied

117

the hennery. He moved them, "promoted" them when they were six weeks old, able to be without heat. Catching them, bulking ten to fifteen in a carton, ponderous trips to the larger quarters. John's work continued a whole Saturday. He had come in to lunch so full of perspiration. Dog tired! Yet he had returned to the chore that afternoon while Faith did the less arduous job, scrubbed the battery, readying it for the new group to arrive the following Saturday.

Well . . . regardless . . . they would be faithful to the covenant —even though to tithe erased all profits. This was their promise to Him. This they must fulfill—generously. As generously as God had led them and given them this farm.

Forty-five cockerels in the first batch. Finestein counted $36.60 into her hand after weighing them, toting up the amount. He proffered his figures to her. She waved them aside with a smile, "I trust you," simply.

"Sometimes people make errors," he grinned.

She let the comment fade. But Finestein persisted, expecting her to check his figures. "You're doing the Lord's work your way and you're honest. So are we. We're spiritually attracted to each other."

Finestein's eyes narrowed. Sharply he scanned her face. Almost imperceptibly a smile edged across his beard-studded countenance. A note of almost-wonder crept into his tones as he weighed, "You say that to me, a Jew, and you a Christian."

Faith shrugged her shoulders, shoved her hands into pockets in a definite manner. "Only one God though." She met his gaze fully. Idly she pondered his reaction if she were to pronounce him filled with a Christ Self—whether he be Jew, Moslem, Buddhist or even atheist. It's time for a removal of all the old fences and isms, she reasoned, and we have merely used different names—and now the psychologist comes along and adds a new one, Higher Self.

As Finestein moved to his truck Faith's voice followed him, "Interested in our other broilers next month?" His back to her, he nodded an answer. The crates in the rear of his truck joggled with the motion. For a fleeting moment Faith visualized the whole rear of that large truck filled with their broilers.

Down in her kitchen Faith held "the Lord's pot" in one hand, the money in the other. Silently she thanked Him as she rounded the tithe to four dollars.

Four dollars! Truly this was as the "widow's mite." Of their living!

"Of their living!"

The first tithe check went out in the noon mail.

So it was, a big joy in the sense of covenant fulfillment even though profit seemed disappointing.

Late in June Faith and the little men trekked to the city to accept the gift of Kim, a handsome cinnamon and white Gordon Setter. Brought from Massachusetts to Irvington, Kim was tied to the mammoth poplar tree in the Sanford yard to await Faith's arrival. Apprehensively Mrs. Sanford followed Faith into the yard explaining. "Polly gave him a sedative, dear. It may be wearing off and he may be ugly. Do be careful."

Speaking in low tones and extending yummies Faith approached. Kim wolfed the goodies. Faith giggled to the children, "Look, his ends disagree. His front is full of noise and his rear waving delight."

At the farm Lulu watched from the kitchen doorway, her manner full of distrust and forebodings. Faith tied Kim to the big appletree up the hilliness from the kitchen. There Kim could rest in the shade, sleep off the remains of the sedative. Only a few hours later, however, early evening, both John and Pete approached the appletree to view the new dog. In an instant there was bedlam, Peter cussing, John scolding, and Lulu screaming from the kitchen. The slam of the kitchen door behind Lulu was the crescendo.

Upstairs Faith strode to Doug's north window overlooking the scene. It was impossible to project her voice over the commotion. She wanted to shake everyone of those people in the act. Individually and collectively! Kim wasn't vicious! He was confused. All these different people. All the miles from Massachusetts to almost-Pennsylvania in one day! And people's fears got in the way, messed up things. Faith approached the group near the appletree. Teeth bared and a menacing noise rolling upward from his throat, Kim stood against the tree. Faith's hand extended to comfort him.

"Don't you go near him!" John commanded. "He's vicious

119

and mean. I'm surprised Polly would send him where there are children. We'll have him destroyed." Having delivered his ultimatum John limped toward the house, the large rip in his trousers flapping with each angered stride.

Lulu and Pete followed, a running flow of negation between them. "It might be good to have a watchdog on the farm." "Might be a good thing too with Annandale so near." "If John's skin is broken we'd better get him to a doctor for a shot."

Scowling at their comments Faith eased to Kim. All these silly fears and worries! How confined! How in bondage, people are to their fears! But she must not contend with them. One must dissolve errors, gently erase them, Gandhi's passive resistance. To meet the negatives with anger or annoyance only multiplied and intensified the whole situation. Gentling to Kim in body movements and tones, "You're no more mean than I, are you, Honey? You just thought 'here's someone else to take me away and I like it here.' Poor baby. All the way from Massachusetts to here in one day—and you don't even know geography. All these people. Polly, Nana, me, the kids, now John and Pete and Lulu. No wonder you're confused."

Her outstretched hand aimed for his ears. Tall and tense, tail moving uncertainly, large mouth parted in a mixture of bared teeth and a canine smile, Kim's throatiness ceased. Faith's fingers contacted his fur.

"Faith!" John's shout from Doug's window started her. "Get away!"

Meekly she backed away, for John was in no mood for reasoning or cajoling. Her soft explanation reached only Kim, "I'll see you later, Baby. They'll get busy and forget us. We'll go for a walk and get acquainted so you know we love you and you belong here."

The episode upset her. She wanted to get alone and think it out, feel the dirt road beneath her feet away from all the family, even inarticulate Don. Surely principles are truth! For all time she had substantiated the principle of faith and love herself through baby Don, that growing bit of pink and white baby. If she had acquiesced to the doctor's suggestions of Rh factor problems, had worried and fussed about the blood matter each time the thought occurred on the screen of her mind. . . .

But she hadn't! Instead when a pesky fear thought appeared

she had affirmed God's perfect life and love for the little one, reminded herself that God is good and produces only good, that He delights in perfect bodies through which to express and work. And that had manifested! Manifested in spite of the fact that the previous baby, Doug, had been so badly jaundiced at birth.

This "Unity stuff" teaches there is *only* good, that if one keeps beholding the good, "turning the other cheek"—"keeping the eye single"—only the good manifests. Sometimes it means "leaving father and mother for My sake," she acknowledged. Not physically, like going to a far country, although in today's world it might. More importantly, mentally and spiritually leaving them. Forsaking the old environ*mental* habits. Going into a new thought country. Scrapping the inherited or acquired attitudes of the family climate.

Sometimes this leaves one alone. Solitary on life's journey with vast mental self-discipline. A challenge to be met.

Alone.

But never lonely.

She was intoxicated with this spiritual life, sometimes finding it a distinct test of interests to leave the spiritual mountaintop, descend to the practicalities of living. It was so wondrously clean and invigorating in the immaculate atmosphere of pure love and pure thought, walking in close communion with God and Aura.

There is a rhythm in all of life, she reminded herself. Jesus practiced it. He communed alone, sometimes walked alone, apart from His disciples. But He always returned to the world to do the Father's work. It isn't enough to pray. One must also work. One must be strong to withstand the mortal world—be "in it but not of it"—stronger to lift it up, rise above one's emotions and thoughts.

Life moves from within outward. From idea or thought to accomplishment just as good healing commences at the heart of a sore, building new tissue and cells from the basic fount of the body. First, the bleeding to cleanse the wound, then coagulation to form an outer protection. Once the protective covering, immediately the healing commences deep within, far from human sight.

Surely there is a parallel here. First one catches sight of the potential of Christhood and there is true repentance. Then one's baptism within his very heart. When his newness appears, he steps forth into the magnificent challenge of self-discipline. Christ power is not to bulldoze others. One must use Christ power on oneself!

And that's a full-time assignment, she acknowledged.

I must remain impervious to the attitudes of others. Tend the garden of my own mind and soul.

Aloneness.

Occasionally she felt aeons apart even from John. Odd. They were so alike in many ways. Since the early days of their marriage, they seemed to think through one another. It was that now she had begun to weigh every idea appearing on the threshold of her mind, separating the goats from the sheep. This led to aloneness. Sometimes when friends visited she felt a planet apart from them, only the similarity of womanhood or yesteryear memories a common social oasis. It seemed she even spoke through the idiom of a new language, with interpretations and shades of meaning known only to herself.

Once too, she and Lulu seemed to dwell in the same mansion. While there was outer harmony, Faith realized that within herself she was judging everything the older woman said, felt as though she had to stand guard against Lulu's constant stream of speech, mitigating the negative seeds Lulu scattered in the young minds about her—Lulu's seed ideas of the virulent belief in germs and divinely ordained punishments, accidents or whathaveyou.

That matter about whether or not to increase Don's formula upon their return from the hospital, for example. With the doctor out of town and the hospital formula barely carrying him two hours, Faith suggested a little cereal. Loudly and at some length, Lulu predicted convulsions and other dire consequences. Faith met that negation head-on, succinctly, "He ate well prenatally and apparently requires it now."

But Lulu's screamed warnings to the boys, "Keep climbing trees and you'll break your neck," "Come in out of the rain or you'll get pneumonia." On and on it went. Those things Faith did not collide with in the outer sense, but felt she must mitigate them in the young minds lest the weed seeds get rooted.

Originally Faith rejected Fillmore's idea that man himself creates germs by his thoughts or through his negative emotions of hate, greed, lust, fears, and so forth. Yet Fillmore's words haunted her. Needled her. Hounded her for months. Until one day she took out the idea, tabled it in the laboratory of her conscious mind, dissected it, evaluated the findings. Summing it up she now accepted it as wholeheartedly as she had previously scorned it, climaxing her self-sell with, "It's time people stop buckpassing, blaming misfortune—even disease—on God or the government. Surely it is the logic of the universe that if everything God makes is very good, then nothing destructive comes from Him."

Now, alone with herself, she faced all of the situation, realizing she must live the truths within her own consciousness. No quarrels with Lulu. Not even inner conflicts with only Faith's mind the battlefield, for in God's plan of things Lulu and everyone were growing and evolving at their proper speed. Each individual spiritual growth pattern. Some of us learn negatively, and some learn positively. Each of us is in a state of becoming—reaching toward our potential Christhood.

Besides—these truths that Faith now embraced might not be ultimate truth. Newer, more comprehensive revelations would continue to come to her from within her own Christself. Meanwhile, she must remain steadfast. She must constantly behold the good and the positive. Then more good would continue to flow to everyone, radiating to each individual. She must continue to realize God as the only Power, the only Presence! Hold to that awareness constantly, and silently. And within her heart and mind she must extend free will to others—even as He grants it to all!

As for Faith, she was finished with the John-the-Baptist kind of consciousness, the eating of locusts and wild honey. No more devastating worries and bitter sweets for her! So, Faith triumphed in her inner battle while the others busied about the house.

Later, Faith and Rob walking Kim, she unleashed the dog a short way from the house. Running in great circles he bounded back for reassuring pats. Rob and Kim frolicked for a half hour or so before Faith suggested they return to the apple tree. She left to procure a pan of fresh water. Returning, the water slopping gently against the sides of the pan, Faith paused. Rob and Kim were romping around and around the tree in a charming boy-dog dance, the massive white and cinnamon head plopping on Rob's shoulder with each of their combined movements. Kim vicious? Why, he was just a great big baby of gentleness. He might even develop a lap dog complex.

June finished its days.

July ushered humid heat and Lulu's return to her personal nursing schedule, promising to "come give Faith a hand between cases." Good Lulu! Faith felt constricting remorse for her inner censure of Lulu's speech or worry attitudes. Lulu gave so much of herself! Surely Faith was picayune to sit in judgment of Lulu's babble of talk.

July . . . and the farmers haying in the first east field. Faith climbed the hillside with coffee and ice cream to two astonished, overheated men in the fields. (She thought Jim seemed less suspicious.)

July . . . and John commenced painting the house exterior on his weekends, working diligently so that he would finish before the city boys' arrival.

July . . . and the second batch of cockerels due for market.

While the Wells waved farewell to the last carful one Saturday evening Finestein reappeared. Faith groaned. Such a day! The kitchen sink stacked with dishes. Read-aloud time to the little men. Don was settled for the night, but all the other loose ends!

"Hi!" Finestein enthused. "I marked my calendar. Your cockerels should be ready. Thought I'd amble over after sundown and collect 'em for ya. Cuts your feeding costs, you know. Builds profits faster. Say!" He leaned from his truck, pushed his hat back. "Those others were just fine. Every one of my customers told me 'bout 'em. I'll be glad to take your broilers any time. *Any* time!" Readjusting his floppy hat Finestein urged his truck through the open gate John held.

"Coming up later?" John called to her.

By the time Faith reached the hennery Finestein had caught most of the stock. The tally sheet lay beside the scale. "These go much heavier than the others," Finestein greeted. "Look!" He invited her inspection, expertly crossing the wings of two cockerels before scaling them. "What did you do!" It was a demand, not a question.

John's expression was one of utter incredulity.

Faith's face glowed while Finestein's enthusiasm crescendoed to effervescence.

She was deaf to Finestein's windiness. Her heart was shouting praises. This was dramatic proof of the dynamic workability of God's silent laws. "Give and it shall be given unto you, good measure, pressed down, shaken together, running over!"

The sheer magic of tithing!

Not magic in the sense of conjuring. Magic in the sense of demonstrating invisible principles right into visibility! This *had* to be God's work, for she and John knew nothing different to do. Same water. Same brand of feed. This was a demonstration in the face of odds: hotter weather when the cocks stood around, beaks parted, wings aspread, appetites dulled by July heat and humidity. Well, if she wanted the good Lord to sell John on this principle of tithing, He surely proved Himself.

Thirty-five cockerels in all this time. Ten less than the first batch. Each twosome weighing heavily. "Can't give you more per pound," Finestein explained, "but they weigh so heavily your returns are substantially greater." Lips moving Finestein totaled the figures on his tally sheet. "Forty-five dollars and ten cents," he beamed. "If my customers were satisfied before, they'll be more than happy now. Who's the family treasurer?" John signified Faith, and Finestein counted the cash into her palm.

Repocketing his wallet Finestein scrutinized Faith from narrowed eyes, "I'm in the chicken business twenty years, ma'am. Ain't never seen anything like this. What did you do?" It was a quiet, expectant demand.

How explain it? Should she throw at him all her digested understanding of the little metaphysical books? The divine work of love, the power of blessing, of working with God. The principle that everything responds to praise and blessings in all the kingdoms. The law of personal expectancy. Or even the Wells' covenant with God!

In all fairness and courtesy Finestein didn't require that. She was not withholding divine law explanations because of religious differences. Indeed, if he were an Orthodox Jew he might well be a tither too. All Finestein wanted was a quickie—not a book review nor a sermon on Being, nor her personal interpretation of Jesus' parable of the talents.

"It's the magic of tithing," gently. True magic, she thought to herself, more than ten dollars increased profit yet ten cockerels less.

A responsive glint appeared in Finestein's eyes. He made no

answer, however. Stooping for the last crate he swung it into his truck, bolted the rear panel in one rhythmic movement. Pausing momentarily, "Call me anytime. I like doing business with you." And the truck rolled down the hilliness.

Thoughtfully Faith ambled down the hillside by herself while John remained to close the gate. The magic of tithing! Man can never live in lack when he works with God, she reflected. The magic of tithing!

"Give and it shall be given unto you . . ."

"Bring ye the whole tithe into the storehouse now . . ."

The last was Aura's whisper, but Faith was not yet always able to distinguish her divine promptings from her mortal thinkings. She was busy rejoicing and praising God, too busy talking to listen.

July . . . and Jed. Jed Shepherd.

Kim's persistent "people bark"—quite different from his "peer bark" at other animals—alerted Faith one Sunday morning to visitors. John was easing the ladder against the house, preparing to resume his weekend chore of painting the exterior. Kim was not objecting to John's movements for the misunderstanding between them long since evaporated like early dews in strong sunlight. A white pickup truck and its occupant at the foot of the driveway was the target of Kim's noise.

Having just shoved a cake into the oven Faith strode to the den window in time to see Kim romp up to a tall, lithe bearded chap who approached John, hand outstretched. A luminosity seemed to billow around the stranger, like a walking halo, Faith thought. John must have noticed too, for she saw him look above the English walnut tree briefly even as he warmly responded to the handclasp. Surely the sky was normal. There was an effulgence about him, something vaguely familiar too. Was it that he resembled someone they knew? Who? She searched the files of her memory. No, no one.

"I'm Jed Shepherd. My place is over toward Hampton. You can see the Water Gap from my porch—if you know just where to look. Heard you moved in, and although tardy I came to say welcome to the community."

"Thank you, Mr. Shepherd."

"Call me 'Jed.' Everyone does." Nodding toward the razed

126

tin garage, "I see you've made quite a few changes. Going to fill that in?"

John dug in various pockets for a match, holding the freshly filled pipe between his teeth. "That's going to be kiddie corner, although my wife contemplates a flower garden eventually. We have much to do, but we love it here and visualize it completed."

Jed's spontaneous grin displayed even white teeth, their whiteness emphasized by the deep tan of his countenance. The twinkle in his blue eyes spilled over, as though annointing his whole face. "Good!" heartily as his chin lifted a trifle so that the reddish beard appeared to be pointing upward. "That's practically what the Lord meant when He told Abraham he could have all the land he saw. That which one can imagine or believe is part of God's plan for you. 'Except they have the vision the people perish.' Only hitch is that the vision always has to complement one's talents." There was warmth in his heartiness. "I see you started on sheep. They look fine."

Thus the inception of a deep friendship. John found himself telling Jed that in spite of only four of a kind shortly there would be several hundred. John painted a picture of the barn renovation, the prospective loafing shed, the wagon house rehabilitation and all the other ideas on his agenda, finishing with the testimonial, "You see we are expecting wonderful things to happen."

Abruptly Jed faced John. Peering into the latter's face, his rich voice measured, "You've taken God into business. That's a powerful and wonderful thing to do."

Spotting Faith at the compost pile, John called her over. Slowly she approached. The introductions finished, any shyness Faith customarily experienced evaporated in Jed's friendly presence. Jed bantered, "The country grapevine is quite an institution. Probably most of the countryside knows as much about you as you do. No reports about the color of your laundry—just that you have three boys and are moving the hills on your place."

They laughed with him. Jed moved to his truck, and reaching into the rear he pulled a tan feedbag toward him, carefully carried it, placed it at John's feet. "I took the liberty of bringing a gift to your sons. Hope they like it."

At a call from John the boys came running and laughing from

127

the meadow. At sight of Jed they stopped abruptly, silently surveyed him, unresponsive to his easy greeting. Prodded by John a mumbled "hi" in unison. "Mr. Shepherd brought you something. Care to open the feedbag?" Their attention directed to it they were startled by peculiar and rhythmic undulations. Doug returned to staring at Jed's bewhiskered face. Rob suspiciously watched the bag movements.

To divert Doug's too enwrapped attention John offered, "Your mother and I are consumed with curiosity." Rob stooped and began working at the knot. Doug's attention remained riveted. Many minutes elapsed, then out popped two white rolypoly piglets, snorting, grunting, cavorting, squinting in the full light of day.

Jed laughed pleasantly at the surprised facial expressions around him. "They're going to be wonderful conversationalists. Just listen to them."

Immediately both boys were on the ground with the piglets. Over their heads Faith explained, "We were going to get a couple of pigs."

"Say, this is something," John enthused. "Can't we remunerate you, Jed?"

Smilingly Jed shook his head, patted John's shoulder briefly. "No, my friend." He dug hands deep into his pockets, rocked on his toes and heels a moment, enjoying the scene of the snorting, running piglets with two little men in avid pursuit. Once the piglets stopped abruptly, sniffed the boys' shoes, tested the digestibility of the metal tip of the shoelace. Squeals of protest from the startled youngsters. Simultaneously all adults laughed at the antics of children and animals.

"They are brother and sister of the same litter. If you wish to breed once, okay. Otherwise slaughter when they weigh about a hundred sixty," suggested Jed. Then he cautioned about sturdy fencing, right down into the ground and furnished suggestions about feeding. "Tell me more about your sheep husbandry. Born on a farm? I heard you came from the city."

Amused at the accuracy of the country grapevine, John knocked his pipe ashes against a fence post. Then he briefed the new friend on their progress since the Farm Miniature of Chatham days, finishing with, "Once out here we got sheep as live lawnmowers to keep this back stuff down. Then—fell in love with

128

them. When Claude was born we got sidetracked. Now we contemplate sheep as the first crop, chickens as the second."

Jed nodded seriously, only the hint of a glimmer in his eyes, an effervescent bubble in the tone of his rich voice. "All the result of an 'a-tion'. I always say it takes three 'a-tions' for success. Inspiration. Aspiration. And perspiration." His deep toned words flowed, inner joy permeating them, ringing through them with clarity and warmth, encompassing them. "John, you have limitless vision. God bless you! You are truly using your imagination divinely."

Faith silently regarded Jed. He sounded precisely like the little Unity textbooks. "May I ask a personal question?"

Jed's manner invited the question. Faith had the feeling he knew what she would ask. "Are you affiliated with any particular movement—or something?" Her voice trailed off as his smile broadened. She felt she was being stuffy, that she was one of many people endeavoring to categorize him.

"No," just that one single syllable, gloriously mellow, suspended itself. "Whatever is Truth, wherever found, in any religion, is acceptable to me. I believe all religions, esoterically, each in the clothing of its individual vocabulary, teach the same truths—that man is eternal; that he is three-fold in nature. It seems to me the only error through the ages has been the theological teaching that Jesus is the *only* Son of God when the Master Himself plainly taught 'ye are all Sons of the Most High' and 'that which I do ye shall do and greater works.'

"The truth is that man is one part of the holy trinity and the trinity itself is also indivisible unity."

Jed's tones were gracious and kind, a simple and charming humility permeating them, reflecting his whole mien. "No, Faith, I belong to no specific movement. There is essentially only one Teacher for each of us. The inner Guide, whether we call it 'Higher Self' like the psychologists or 'Christ' in the religious term. Perhaps in the beginning of each individual's unfoldment we require outer teachers. Ultimately, each of us must make his own at-one-ment with the Father—whatever name we use for Him."

Although Jed's speech was in a conversational tone, softly spoken, Faith heard his phrases ring throughout the countryside.

She heard them spread up and down Spruce Run, magnify themselves, bounce from the hills. This was of the innate joyousness of the man, and the effulgence she saw billowing about him as he walked from his white truck. Jed's very presence had a godliness about it. One felt good, clean, wholesome, uplifted in his company.

"I've about finished my . . .'homework,' shall I say?" Jed grinned. "Soon I shall go forth. I don't know where. Or when. But at the right moment the Father will instruct me. Perhaps somewhere in this country. Perhaps in another. It makes little difference." His smile flashed. "I'll shave my whiskers," laugh lines in his face, laughter bubbling in his voice. "In Biblical days when an individual grew to another spiritual consciousness he either changed his name or moved to another country. . . . I'll just change my face—and probably move." Now he openly laughed, his manner invited theirs.

Perched on the power lines a mourning dove sang its haunting refrain. The romping boys and the piglets made noise. Otherwise there was silence, not an embarrassed silence, rather one of empathy and oneness.

As the men resumed talking, Faith's attention wandered to Jed's hands. Large capable beautiful hands. Not typical farmer hands. No scars of manual labor. Rather massive hands, a trifle large for Jed's over-all structure perhaps, yet magnificently sensitive and strong. The men were talking of crops when Faith tuned in again, Jed was speaking.

"A practical farmer without concept of God's limitlessness would advise you to have as many crops as possible, a hedge against failure or a poor year in one of them. Diversification. In our mortal vision we err in limiting the Limitless One. He never shortchanges anywhere in order to bestow more to another. In God's world there is good abundance, 'enough and to spare, pressed down and running over!'

"Man seems to forget the invisible principle of the universe: Work with what you have, be thankful for it, praise it, bless it—and it multiplies. Use it freely. Our good must never be hoarded Like the daily manna in the time of Moses, one's good should be used. I do not say don't save your money. I do say save it for an opportunity—whatever surplus funds you have. Let the surplus funds work for you, and let its work be a blessing. But—

130

the Chinese say something like 'that which you give away you have forever' and that is a truth. It goes out to multiply.

"I feel strongly about these laws, Friends. I am eager for the dawning of a new day, the new age when all people everywhere will be co-workers with God and no one anywhere will be hungry, sick, out of work, or out of harmony with himself or his neighbors.

"I want to see the day when everyone nourishes a global consciousness rather than a global charity. Not charity! That's bondage to want and lack. At this moment I don't know the outer solution, frankly. But I believe international financiers can work out international monetary exchanges so that our huge surpluses are not stored to rot but will be used for the betterment of all man. I know this requires education too. I know many prefer rice to potatoes, that some peoples will eat no meat and drink no milk. And it is not right for us to smugly laugh at these ideas. Perhaps they are further along His road than we. Could it not be that the East can teach us some spirituality—and we could teach them practical science matters? But we must learn tact and humility and that the yardstick of materiality is not alpha-omega . . ."

Jed paused briefly, his head slightly tilted, his expression most earnest. "I don't like the word 'sin' . . . but I do believe it is a spiritual sin for a nation to pay farmers not to grow crops, to let surpluses rot in storage bins, and the other sins we perpetuate while many in the world starve to death. There is a silent law of usefulness, the law I referred to about opportunity funds. Use or lose. Or call it the law of appreciation . . .

"Wendell Willkie was ahead of his time when he coined the phrase 'one world'. It must come to pass. Not with guns and cold wars and hot hates. First the inner awareness of peace and understanding must be born in individual hearts. As that quality grows strong and full of grace it will penetrate the whole universe."

Jed's expressed ideal drew no comment. He expected none. Jed had sown a seed-thought deliberately, for intuitively he knew the soil to be receptive. His hand extended to John's shoulder. "You will be divinely guided to the right third crop, my friend. With God in your business you have the greatest Efficiency Expert. The Infallible Infinite. Even if you start with the proverbial shoelace you will not fail. You will succeed—gloriously."

And Jed was gone. His little white truck bumping merrily over the dirt road toward Hampton. Arm in arm under the walnut tree at the foot of the driveway John and Faith watched to the turn of the road while the boys and the piglets still cavorted untiringly.

So it was Jed came into their lives, a casual and friendly beginning, destined to make its tremendous impact.

During the days to follow thoughts of Jed and fragments of his conversation returned to Faith. With all her heart she believed his prediction of divine success. Hadn't the good Lord brought them a lovely investment? To say nothing of bringing them to this particular farm and all the stipulations they desired. It seemed a divine development they should move into Jed's neighborhood and friendship. Even the white truck set Jed apart! What farmer had a white truck! John, too, mentioned it seemed foreordained that Jed's and their paths should cross at this precise time of their lives.

Jed's happiness was infectious, permeating the atmosphere. He became a frequent visitor, sharing an hour or two of an evening, bringing a humorous experience to them, offering it with his special variety of joyous laughter or the silent mirth reflected in his blue eyes and the minute laugh lines in his face. Now and then Jed's inferential teaching was so homey they almost missed the application, for unfailingly he brought a spiritual offering.

They grew to love this strange man, this combination of Christlike mystic and farmer, responding to the very joy resident in his individuality. There was no inane constant grin on his countenance, but rather a pleasantness of expression, emanating from the deep inner well of love for all life. There was a completeness about Jed, a harmonious weaving of poise, humility and a dynamic dominion. Faith believed Jed could probably control the weather, so great was his air of authority without a taint of arrogance. Jed's visits inspired the Wellses. His ideas and words became part of their household.

In a most objective way Jed fascinated Faith. Everything about the man intrigued her, lingered in her memory. She tried to fathom him, his words, all that he represented. She could not. He was a perfectly complete person, a most integrated individual.

When Jed visited evenings, letting the men talk back and forth,

Faith studied Jed's hands. Masterly hands, exquisitely strong and sure but with a tender quality apparent in his gestures or the way he touched the stock or tousled the heads of the little men. Tanned by the sun, strong from habits of work and usefulness, they made few unnecessary movements. Usually as he talked they rested before him, fingertips to fingertips as though perhaps relaxed in prayer. If she could paint, Faith thought, she would select such hands to represent God's hands. Her thought momently shocked her, seeming almost sacrilegious.

Jed's eyes were the other magnet that invited her attention. When he laughed or his face crinkled in the manner of his silent mirth, gold flecks danced in their blueness. There was a far-seeing quality about them also. One had the feeling Jed sustained X-ray vision although there was no impersonal coldness in his expression. Rather, there was a wondrous compassion in his habitual mien as well as the eyes of one who looks to the mountains.

Yes, compassion was a word befitting Jed. Compassion and peace. Whatever he saw in the world not to his liking he neither criticized or condemned. In his own, sometimes unconventional way, he set about extending help, Faith was positive of that idea —but they would never hear about his helpfulness from him, surely!

Late July brought a humid period, even nightfall in the country brought no appreciable relief of temperature. Ardently Faith yearned for a complete set of screens. Yet screens throughout the house would be only part of a solution. Most of the windows did not remain open except by a prop. Half screens were an excellent prop but with the outsize windows of the big old house a perfect fit with this improvisation was not achieved. The real job required equipping each window with sashcords and a storm/screen combination.

There were many things to be accomplished, each of them urgent on Faith's agenda:

Cement the cellar.

Discard the old electric stove, convert to an Anderson gas range.

A new refrigerator, for surely the six cubic foot job would be overtaxed when the city boys came.

More stock for the farm. Lots more! Although they had purchased ten more sheep, each of the boys buying a bred ewe of the ten, many more were needed to put the farm on a self-paying basis!

And the thousands of nails to be added to the outbuildings. New doors there. Stonework to be repointed.

And Itchy! That monstrosity misbehaved more as each day passed.

So many things to do. And never anything left from the monthly income.

When such thoughts rolled over Faith in waves, she abruptly shook them off, affirmed all the more vehemently their divine prosperity and its manifestations. Nothing was impossible to God! she shouted in her heart. Aura, the Friend within, comforted her with whisperings and Faith kept those sayings close, pondering them, gathering sustenance.

The vacillation of early spiritual growth is great. Sometimes Faith lived more from the old intellectual plane than her newer spiritual. It is easier to witness appearances, for it is the inbred training of the earth—easier to see the worn out, dilapidated buildings, look to investment reapings—than it is to abide in the Invisible Presence. Logic dictated screens would have to wait the actual evidence of greater prosperity no matter how they panted for a breeze on humid July nights. She tried to see the positive viewpoint, encouraged herself by their blessings—they did not have to hang out a tenement fire escape in a hot, stifling city. They could open more windows, prop them with a stick when their supply of half screens was exhausted. No mosquitoes serenaded either, although admittedly there was a tremendous assortment and population of other bugs that buzzed, rasped, flitted, and nocturned. Extinguishing the lights helped.

Not quite six weeks old, Don still required the nightly bottle and Faith followed her routine during the humid spell. Downstairs to put the bottle in the warmer, light the lamp in the living room, arrange the small Unity textbook beside the green leather chair. Back upstairs for the babe, change his pants. By then, the bottle was just right. Ensconced with the baby in her left armcrook, the bottle in her right hand, the small book held just-so by her left hand, thumb ready to turn the page, she studied.

Spiritually and mentally Faith ate the very ideas, for since the impact of Fox's *Sermon on the Mount* everything in the universe was explainable. To her, now, everything was the result of Cause and Effect, God's deeply profound, silent laws. Everything was an aspect of the same law of order and harmony that moved the stars and the planets, kept them from collisions, impelled man toward higher evolution. These truths were so valid, so logical, it seemed she had always known them.

Greedily Don worked on his sustenance. Outside the night noises serenaded. Faith only vaguely conscious of time. She was minutely aware of Don's movements, and completely aware of Aura's ideas; those glowed in her heart and mind as though in luminous print.

Something swooped into the living room, plumping against the fieldstone fireplace for a split moment, then whirring the length of the room in a peculiar undulating flight. Faith's mouth went dry. She could not scream.

A bat! Of course they don't tangle in long hair. Or—do they? That's a silly old superstition. There is nothing to be afraid of. She had affirmed that for months. Nothing to be afraid of. God is the only presence and power. Surely she wasn't afraid of a tiny, blind little bat. Recall how she mentally accused John and his folks of being afraid of Kim? Well, this little bat wouldn't floor her!

She half rose from the chair to put Don down. Conquer the bat. No precise plan occurred to her. The bat swooped low over her head, zoomed up from the table lamp beside her. Dropping the bottle and book she clutched Don tightly. Replopped in the chair, congealed while the creature continued its flight. Tortuous long moments after the bat gracefully paused with outstretched wings on the fireplace. Instantly she was up, through the den, at the foot of the stairs.

"John! . . . JOHN! . . . J O H N !"

Completely nude, shaking sleepiness from himself, John appeared at the top of the stairs. "What's the matter?"

Terror now abated in John's presence, "There's a bat down here," sheepishly. The bat in the other room, she was composed.

Down in the living room, Faith's nude knight grabbed a farm journal from the reading table, approached the resting bat. The little thing did not wait for his onslaught. Instead it swooped merrily around the room in its rhythmic flight. Once it swooped into the den and back again into the lighted room. John lunged.

135

Whammed. Darted after it, missing by mere fractions. Once, with well rolled up magazine, John connected as it rested between the fieldstones of the fireplace. It flew away gracefully, unbruised. Perspiration glistened on John's body, ran down in rivulets. He stalked from the room, returning shortly from the kitchen with the broom.

In the doorway between the living room and the den Faith was suddenly overcome with giggles. This huge, handsome, naked chap wanging away so forcefully and ineffectually at one little mite of a bat. Rivers of sweat gleaming on his body whenever he crossed the pathway of light from the solitary lamp struck her as hilarious. Patting Don's back to encourage the burps, she pressed her face into his clothing to stifle any sound lest her hero walk off in high dudgeon. Her hand motion was also to convince the baby the balance of his meal was coming.

Then the little thing clung desperately to the fieldstone, his tiny chest heaving. Noticing it Faith felt great remorse. Poor little thing. Just because she was momentarily frightened. It wouldn't have harmed Don or herself. Probably wouldn't have tangled in her long hair either. Now her mouth was too wet. She couldn't swallow sufficiently, nor quickly enough.

John delivered a magnificent wham at the heaving bat, killing it instantly. It fell at his feet. Leaning over the fireplace apron, John ran a finger across his forehead. The stream of perspiration poured off to the stones below. "Good night," matter-of-factly. He returned upstairs to continue his slumber, leaving Faith alone with the hungry but unprotesting babe, her studies—and the dead carcass.

At bedtime the next night John asked casually, "What are you doing about the window tonight?"

"It's open," getting into bed.

"They see in the dark. Original radar, you know."

"There's nothing here to invite them. I'll close it when I get up to bottle Don."

No further rejoinder. John's even breathing an indication of immediate union with the masters in sleep. Faith rolled over on her stomach and relaxed. She would surely be happy when this humidity was finished. Everything else about New Jersey she liked. What purpose had humidity anyway? Didn't everything in God's world have some purpose? Well, she couldn't figure out the purpose of humidity, but she could be thankful for the one window with the built-in screen, and she knew divine prosperity would produce screens throughout . . .

Pleasantly weary, she fell asleep. Hours slipped by. Only the various sleeping sounds of five people within the house blended with the nightsounds. Far off in the hills a late freight, pulled by a Diesel, strained up the mountains, and the mountains cradled the song.

"There's a bat in here," whispered Aura.

Faith awoke instantly.

No mere bat would render a sissy of her! Hadn't she been raised by Tarzan Dad Sanford! All her life he taught her self-sufficiency and independence and courage! Perhaps they could perceive in the dark, she couldn't. She snapped on the dresser light. On the radiator by the screened window lay an old copy of the *Ladies' Home Journal*. Faith grasped it firmly, rolling it slightly for increased whopping power. With set determination she approached where it clung high on the wall beside the dresser, temporarily immobile.

No bat would render her eighteenth century-ish. Until the preceding night she had never awakened John. Not for children's needs. Nor for herself. This bat she would take on. She was resolute. With steady tread and high courage she approached. Perhaps she had weakened last night about killing a harmless thing, but these creatures belonged outside if they wanted liberty. Not in her home. She didn't invade their home. Arm raised she was poised for action. One firm whack would end its life and her problem. Blissfully John slept on, unmindful of the slaughter about to be perpetrated. Her vision was on the inert victim.

A whirr of wings. Yet, there was the bat before her eyes.

The mate had swooped in!

Involuntarily a scream tore from her throat. Another scream wrenched itself free. And another.

Bolt upright in bed John stared momently at the crouched figure behind the corner chair, wide-spread fingers spanning the top of her head. Swinging his body from the bed, he kept up a running stream of encouragement, "All right, Honey. Just you stay there. I'm experienced at this stuff now. Two tonight, eh? Just stay there, my sweet. I'll get them both. Let's not make a habit of this though, eh?" In passing, he picked up the dropped magazine, discarded it for something heavier, his weightier bedroom slipper.

From her corner, wide-eyed, Faith watched every move. No smidgen of laughter in her throat or her heart. Nor compassion. She was silent, strained white beneath the summer tan.

Taking careful aim John let the slipper ride against the bat clinging to the wall, all the might and beauty of masculine follow-through apparent. "Pitching baseball for the high school team did this. Don't ever scream like that again. It may not be apparent, but I lost a whole year of life expectancy. This will stain the wall."

One lifeless form lay on the floor.

The lone mate swooped in rhythmic glides about the room. For a moment it rested atop John's chiffonier before reflight. Accident or instinct, it flew out the open window.

Picking up the still form John dropped it outside, closed the window, dusted his hands together in a gesture of having finished the business at hand. "Let's stay hot nights, my love."

He approached Faith tenderly. This capable woman who took on farming and its chores. Brave enough to move into a new way of living, remote from old friends and the city. Gently he helped her to her feet, steadied her to the bed where she sank into its welcoming softness. Very slowly the depleted, used-up feeling left her. "All right now?"

Almost imperceptibly her head moved in a nod.

"Lie down," his suggestion rather than a command.

Hardly audible, "Might as well stay up for the bottle business." With great apparent effort, "Was it having biology makes you so brave?"

John patted her shoulder understandingly. "Want a drink of water?"

She shook her head.

"Want me to do the bottle stint?"

Again her negative reply. Her backbone felt like jelly, but pectin was slowly manifesting.

"Well, mind if I get some sleep?"

Upon hearing her weak response, John walked around the foot of the bed, lay down to sleep.

City newspapers screamed about the heat, the drought, the ruin to farmers' crops. In the places where farmers congregate they stood in clusters, alternating between sky scanning and head shaking. Some country folk were already filling milk cans with water from nearby brooks or rivers as household and barn springs or wells went dry. However, the Wellses suffered no drying of springs. Their only program at that point was to finish the exterior painting, ready themselves for John's vacation and the arrival of the city boys.

How the house drank the paint! The two-storied annex portion on the west side sporting four huge windows, two smaller ones and one door, consumed ten gallons of primer alone. John used a spray machine, moving its gun from left to right as far as his reach permitted. By the time he attained the extreme right the far left portion was completely dry. The thirsty pores drank it all. John demonstrated to Faith just how dry, rubbing the palm of his hand across a clapboard immediately after spraying, showing his hand completely free of paint.

All in all the job went smoothly. Many weekends, but smoothly. The entire house, now fortified by its paint, caught the sunlight, its whiteness scintillating among the lovely lawn tree greens. The second coat applied even more easily, for John knew the peculiarities of the spray machine by then. Also, he had overcome his fear of height—he too praying his way through a challenge. Ascending or descending the ladder John affirmed God's loving protection. Standing atop and working with the spray equipment, he affirmed it. He did not recognize the precise moment the specific fear dissolved, but long before the job was finished he was free from that fear burden forever.

So it was that the Wells' farm became a proving ground of their souls and character and the Unity teachings, individually—and as a family.

The house painting finished, John made a platform for the shutters, spreading them on a drying trellis, spraying with a re-resplendent green. With deep satisfaction over a job well done, he drew forth his pipe, filled it, took some well-spaced puffs as they stood arm-in-arm, admiring the glistening house. "The shutters will be dry enough to hang tomorrow before we go for the youngsters."

Holding Faith close he kissed her.

In the late afternoon sunshine Rob and Doug romped about the house with each other and Kim. Kim, circling the boys, kept up a running yapping delight. Tramp joined the happy melee also, but a little more conservatively in view of his advanced age. On the side porch Don lay in a last minute nap before dinner, unmindful of the hilarity.

"I hunger," murmured John, his lips on Faith's.

"It's doing," meaning the dinner. She met his kiss perfunctorily.

"How's the freezer ice cream situation?" His kiss more pressing. No response from Faith, she coy and playful.

"Need some."

"Give," demandingly.

She pecked.

"No. Hollywood style."

A tiny smile played at the corners of her lips. Teasingly she permitted her ardor to warm only slightly.

"The real thing!" He held her in his arms, covering her up-turned laughing face with warm affection. Between his kisses her mirth burst forth. "Now I am refreshed," returning her to an upright position, laughing together.

Dinner over and Don's evening needs met Faith removed a five-pound container of cheddar cheese from the freezer, and they all sallied forth to the Glen for the evening paper and a supply of ice cream for the freezer. The paint being tacky dry—as John put it—they left the house doors ajar.

"Do you fellows remember tomorrow the city boys arrive?" Faith asked.

"A-huh," they dueted.

"Where are they going to sleep?" practically from Rob.

"Daddy's going to move the daybed upstairs. It comes apart, you know, into twin beds. They can sleep in Don's room and we'll move his crib into the hall until they go home. He won't mind a bit," Faith smiled. Rob eyed her contemplatively. Doug seemed to take it all in stride, no questions.

John took the long way home, riding through the countryside briefly in the cooling evening air. Approaching the house in an hour or so, he slowed the car, admiring his handiwork. "Looks like a million, huh, Baby!"

A groan from Faith. Horror filled her face. "The screen door is wide open. I left the dishes! Every fly in the county will be visiting the kitchen!"

True. The kitchen walls and ceiling were ecstatic with polka dots. The air was filled with the exultant song of thousands of

140

wings. Stacked, soiled dinner dishes were alive with whirring noises. "I hate these things! I positively loathe them!" Venom in her tones. Armed with a flyswatter she attacked the gigantic project.

John did not laugh, although it struck him the job was like transferring the Atlantic Ocean to the Pacific by the teaspoonful while on a crosscountry run. Suddenly they were both distracted by a loud thumping noise in the playroom. They stood absolutely still a moment. Each silently questioned the other. Noiselessly John tiptoed to the door between the dining room and playroom. Turning the knob cautiously, he eased the door open, abruptly thrust it wide. He had expected a huge rat, weasel or other marauder. "You *soandso!*" John bolted into the room. With one graceful leap Kim went through the screen doorway, a gaping Kim-size hole in his wake. Behind him on the playroom floor lay wrappings and meager leavings of the five-pound tub of cheddar cheese.

From the open doorway Faith was saying mildly, "I hope we get him filled up soon. My favorite cheese, too."

"Look at this room! Just look at it! And it took a whole Saturday to get it tidy."

Faith returned to the flies. John's voice followed her. "Just close up the kitchen. We have some spray left, Hon." As Faith closed the door John talked between his teeth, "Bats! Flies! A wolfish dog! Damn! Damn! Damn!"

In the light of early grey dawn sleepy birds tuned up, commencing a slow twitter, gradually accelerating to full rhapsody of the day's harmony just as the eastern light spread over the world. Over all the earth a fine mist fell. Greedily the dusty foliage reached for the wetness, and the dry ground lay receptive. It would take hours of continuing wetness to appease the vegetation, really penetrate. This was August 9th, the first rain since early June.

This was Thursday, *the* Thursday the city boys would arrive.

All the Wellses scampered through chores. Little men did theirs. Faith sudsed the baby, bottled him after cereal, whizzed through breakfast dishes, assembled chocolate pudding, set the dining table for noon while John chored the stock and rehung the shutters despite drizzle. At last, all in readiness, it was time to dress and leave for the twenty-mile trip to Flemington Junction.

The little men were silent the whole trip. Occasionally Faith interrupted their thoughts with suggestions about putting the visitors at ease. Her words were greeted with attentive silence, but no comments.

Many extra cars were at the station, parked in a straight line down the centerway between commuter cars. Groups of chatting people gathered, awaited the train. A gentleman with a close-cropped haircut and a Boston accent seemed to chairman the project, visiting from group to group. Several times he glanced at John and Faith but did not approach.

Faith nudged John to notice a red-haired family. Five red-haired girls and a set of fiery-haired parents. The girls ranged from two to twelve in age. There was no perceptible variance in the shade of red hair. Passing the family Faith overheard the mother answer a stranger, "Yes, we've been doing this a number of years. It's most rewarding. We only wish we could squeeze in more than two guests." The mother's hand fondled the youngest girl's curls. "We always ask for redheads, so if we go anywhere they look as though they belong to us, you know."

The Wellses exchanged glances. Faith hugged Don a little more closely. They continued to the train platform, and the noise of an approaching Diesel came from the east, concealed by the grey mistiness. A muted whistle, the signal for the release of pent-up enthusiasms from the youngsters on the platform. Such jumping, skipping, running, shouting! Both Wells lads were startled. The idea of entertaining complete strangers began to expand in their imaginations. The long train slowed to a stop. Through rivulets of moisture on the windowpanes those on the platform saw hundreds of small faces pressed against the glass. Eight full cars. Fresh Aires in assorted sizes, colors, and temperaments.

Boys and girls began to file out from the two middle cars. The youngest appeared about five. The oldest twelve. Faces wore mixed emotions. Some stood quietly, large solemn eyes roving the scene. Others jumped off, ran in gleeful circles, uttering peculiar sounds of unrepressed delight. Some few older ones attempted an immature poise. Some were docile, neither frightened of the new adventure nor delightedly expectant. Ten exuberantly whooping ones circled the hosts, yelling, "Yowie! Yowie!" After several com-

142

plete circles they were outshouted by the owner of the Boston accent.

"Please! Please!" extending his arms, palms downward, to quell the racket. Peace sustained, he stretched on tiptoe, overlooking the entire group. His voice carried to the perimeter. "Let's get this straightened out, see who goes to whom." He motioned the hosts to one side, grouped the Fresh Aires on the other. Each group awaited the apportionment.

Behind the groups, face determinedly set, the conductor started up the stairs, leaned far out to give a signal. This trip was noisier than usual; he was not enjoying it. From the corner of his eye the Bostonian saw the conductor's movement. "You can't move this train until I have everyone accounted for!" It was a command. And somehow in New Jersey the peculiarity of the Bostonian "a" gave impact.

Arms akimbo the conductor half-mocked, "Oh, can't I? Well, we can't stay here all day. We've got a schedule to keep." The last of his mockery disintegrated into a whine.

"I can't care what you've got. You can't move until I say so!" With a gesture of effortful patience, "If you wait just a moment and everyone is quiet. . . ."

While the count began, the conductor maintained a glare at the back of that closely cropped Bostonian head.

"Fifty," pronounced the Bostonian, head up from the list. He moved among the children. "Fifty-two! That's what I got last time." He scrutinized his sheet of names. "Will someone help me count?"

A large matronly woman stepped forward, counted off the children into tens, moved them over like so many pennies at a bank teller's window. Shyly, hopefully, patiently, the children awaited the counting. Some few worried. Would two be returned? Without a vacation? Faces lengthened, eyes grew wistful. Even though the unknown lay ahead, hopes were high. Promised a vacation in the country, they wanted it with all their young hearts, even at sacrifice of leaving familiarities of family, city, and known modes of living. One little Negro girl, braided pigtails jutting at angles, buried her face in a larger girl's skirt, softly sobbed. The two red-haired guests stood hand-in-hand.

"Fifty-two," the consensus of both matron and Bostonian.

143

John approached the chairman. "Is our name on your sheet?" His low baritone carried to Faith and the boys.

"Who are you?" The Bostonian's tone cool, almost insolent.

"John Wells. We are scheduled to receive John and Robert Warwenski of Brooklyn," proffering the Tribune's notification.

His back to the train he waved the conductor forward. "Now why in the world would they neglect to notify me!"

A toot-toot and the train moved, pulling slowly into the mistiness of the west. Little faces from within peered through bespeckled windows at the disappearing station.

"We wrote direct to the Trib," John outshouted the train noise. As he spoke he reached into the group, gently pulled forward two boys of the exuberant classification. One, tall and skinny, wearing horn-rimmed glasses, clutched a crumpled brown paper bag. The other, a trifle shorter and equally skinny, oversize ears protruding, monitored a big, battered brown valise that bumped his legs with each step. "I believe these are our boys."

The Bostonian verified the orange colored tag each boy wore, matched it with John's card. "Yes, they are yours. Thank you for stepping forward," in a mollified voice.

The effervescence of the two little Polish-Americans rebubbled. It was capable of frothing right over the brim, and the nodding of the Bostonian head toward John was the awaited signal. With startling whoops two synchronized human dynamos chugged forward, gaining momentum with each vocal chugging, battered valise bumping between the smaller one's stick-like legs. From the older boy in the rear emitted a blasting shrill whistle simulating a locomotive. The train episode was finished.

Abruptly they catapulted themselves into the mien of real live Indians—from Brooklyn.

Many in the host group looked with sympathy on Faith and John as they led the four children to the car. How could she manage those noisy visitors with a new baby and her own two-some! Momentarily Faith closed her eyes, shook her head as though freeing herself of an apparition.

While the Wells group continued to the Studebaker, the Bostonian parcelled out the children to the hosts, matching orange-tagged names to his list. Little groups, each with a city child or two, broke away from the large group. Some of the smaller groups felt their way into friendship. Others renewed friendships from former years. The red-haired family strolled off with two golden-redhaired girls.

John ushered the four boys into the rear seat while he and Faith settled in front, she with Don on her lap. The city boys immediately began a running torrent of conversation as the car eased to the highway.

"We've never been away from home before," began Robert, the older.

"We crossed five East Rivers," offered Johnny of the outsize ears.

"We seen cows and sheeps and pigs and cats and—everything!" Robert again, large brown eyes wide with wonder.

A moment's pause, then, "Our grandfather, my mother's father, died," Johnny's contribution.

"That's too bad," condoled Faith. "But I'm glad your mother let you come."

"He died Friday," matter-of-factly from Robert. "Not last Friday. Back when snow was." He spoke quickly, the rush of the city in his voice and mannerisms. Faces forward, John and Faith swallowed their smiles.

"Look at that behind horse!" Robert's ejaculation. (Faith is still analyzing that comment.)

Again the little one brought up the affairs of grandpa, "Yeah, he drank too much."

"Now whoever heard of anyone dying from drinking too much water," teased John. Faith shot him a glance plainly saying perhaps-his-mother-used-this-as-an-example. John understood and withheld further comment.

"Oh, he didn't drink too much water!" contributed Robert with proper emphasis.

"No," expanded the younger lad. "Hardly ever. Not even soda pop. Just whiskey and beer. Mostly whiskey."

"I love cows. I ride 'em," interrupted Robert.

"Sorry, fellas. We don't have cows. Just a few chickens too young to lay eggs, some sheep, and a couple pigs. Robbie and Doug each bought a bred ewe. Until Daddy fixes the outbuildings they are going to keep their sheep with ours. If their sheep have a boy lamb, we will buy it for the freezer. If a girl, it's an increase in their flock."

Silence. But not long.

145

"I like gooses," offered the little one. "I swim underwater and stab 'em with my knife."

Faith's eyes popped. What were they getting into! Then she smiled straight ahead. This was empty bragging. As the Pennsylvania Dutch put it, "this is for so not for real."

Each time John slowed the car for a crossing or merging traffic two lads synchronized, "Do we live here?" Each time a negative answer from John or Faith. It must have seemed an endless journey from the railroad station.

"What would you like for lunch?" from Faith during a lull in their chatter.

"We et," they dueted.

"Oh? We haven't yet. Do you think you could eat again?"

"Naw," together.

"Perhaps by the time we get home and you're settled in your room you will be able to. Country air keeps one hungry most of the time." Deliberately Faith planted the suggestion.

At length, the Wells' driveway.

"Do we live here! Whew-ee!"

The boys poured out of the car. Rob and Doug were detailed to introduce the city boys to their room. All were requested to change to play clothes, get ready for lunch—and those assignments were completed long before Faith had waffle batter prepared. They all whooped outdoors, including John. When Faith rang the big bell four noisy hooplas approached from the wagon house, John following slower of pace, a grin stretched across his jovial face.

Johnny was first into the kitchen. A look into the batter. "Blintzes?"

"No," a questioning tone in Faith's voice. "What are blintzes?"

"You make with pot cheese and potatoes and water."

"No eggs? How much of each?"

"Yes," vaguely. "I think eggs. I don't know. . . ."

She would try her cottage cheese pancake recipe. The boys would tell her soon enough if it were the same thing. "All up and wash your hands. Towels are on the rack behind the sink. A different color for each of you. Rob, please show them which color belongs to each of them."

The noise and commotion out of the kitchen Faith checked the waffle iron. John stood behind her as she dipped up the batter. He rubbed her neck caressingly. "Anything I can do?"

146

"No, Hon."

Four boys trooping noisily downstairs. John slipped into the dining room, tactfully designating places for each boy. "You, Robert, will probably pal up with Rob because of your ages. You sit beside each other on this side, Robert next to mother, Rob next to me. You, Johnny, sit next to Doug and beside me." Going to the head of the table, John readied Faith's chair as she came into the room bearing a tray of plates with waffles and milk glasses to set around.

A short grace offered and the syrup passed. Two city boys dove so abruptly into their food that even the country children were startled. John and Faith exchanged glances, swallowed a large lump of emotion apiece, then seemingly ignored the speed of food consumption. Conversation was spasmodic until particular hollownesses were alleviated.

"Do you have a nickname?" Faith asked of Robert. "Your name being the same as Rob's there might be some confusion."

"Yeah. 'Cheesecake.'" An extra size piece of waffle was held calculatingly on his fork a moment. The estimate proved slightly in error, for a protruding edge had to be tucked in with his forefinger.

"'Cheesecake'? Where do you get that name? Because you like it so much?" from John.

"No. Last name sounds like 'cheesecake.'"

Faith's right eyebrow shot upward in question. Inaudibly John's and Faith's lips moved through a "Warwenski-Cheesecake" routine. They shrugged. Perhaps with Polish tonal sounds it did.

Turning to the younger boy John asked, "Do you have a nickname? You and I might get confused, you know."

"Johnny," tentatively. "Mother calls me Jashu," giving the name a 'Y' sound.

"Jashu," repeated Faith quietly, only her eyes smiling. "Sounds like a sneeze." Large solemn brown eyes regarded her. Eyes too large for the thin face surrounding them, too solemn for a six-year-old. Serious, hungry eyes.

John picked up the conversational ball, infectiously laughing, "Sure. 'Kerchoo-Jashu.'" Magically John's warm personality, vibrant in his voice and manner, saved the day. Suddenly it was hilariously funny, and everyone laughed heartily, especially Jashu. Social ice was smashed.

As the social weather inside improved so the climate weather changed, the mists and drizzle of the day vanishing. Radiant, full sunlight spread over the wet countryside, dappling down through the front lawn trees. It became a lovely mellow August day, the humid heat relieved at least temporarily.

As the laughter subsided, Jashu queried, "What shall we call you?"

"Our fellows call us 'dad' and 'mom.' You can too if you like," offered John.

Zing! Cheesecake bolted from the table and out the kitchen door before Faith realized he left. "Where are you going?" she called to the emptiness beyond the banged screen door.

"Out," floated back.

Quickly at the door lest he get beyond the reach of her voice, "Wouldn't you like dessert?"

"Dessoit!"

They heard the thrill in his voice. He was reseated at the table before the door closed. Blinkingly Faith observed him an instant. Surely this youngster moved with the speed of a New York taxi! With almost exaggerated calmness she removed the soiled dishes, set out individual chocolate puddings before each plate.

"I hate chocolate pudding!" from Jashu.

Both Wells boys scrutinized their mother. This was direct assault on a family rule. John and Faith glanced at each other. Deliberately Faith busied herself, stacking dishes, bringing in coffee, all the while reflecting on the most tactful but firm way to handle the matter. She must be fair to Rob and Doug yet not press the visitors' adjustment too assiduously. Yet if there were no selfish pressure on her part it would be good for the city boys to learn "to do as the Romans while in Rome." Always there is the middle of the road policy, she thought, only sometimes the middle white line seems too faint.

"More milk!" demanded Cheesecake. No courtesy in his voice at all. His very tone an insulting command.

Consternation was in Faith's reply, "Oh, Cheececake, I'm so sorry. I can't give you more now. This is a between-delivery day for our milk comes only every other day. I ordered extra milk, of course, but I only allowed an extra quart for each of you. We shall have abundance tomorrow." Cheesecake's dark brown eyes measured her.

"I hate chocolate pudding!" Jashu reminded.

A perceptible twinkle in John's eyes. His silent laughter plainly said "one-two-three-testing" just like the telephone man after his new installation. Then John came to the rescue, tactfulness and authority in his manner. "Jashu, in this house we get only good food. It is simple in its preparation but it is good and nourishing. It will bless your body. God gives it to us and we are thankful for it. Unless there is a distinct argument between a specific food and you, you are to eat it. No comments. Food rebuilds your body, keeps its engine going by your food intake just like a car uses gasoline and water and oil. I think you'll find it tasty—and you'll be a member of the Scoopers' Club."

Jashu's too large eyes met John's. He was fascinated by the idea of his body being like a car. He pondered the matter after the fashion of a six-year-old. Disdainfully he lifted the spoon, held his breath, got the first mouthful in successfully. Then like the sunlight after the drizzle, his face brightened with surprise, "Why, it's good. I do like it."

The Wells boys had suspended food operations during the trial period. They now returned to their enjoyment and nourishment. As the clouds blew out of sight Faith wondered if John's suggestion about an argument between a specific food and their bellies would backfire. Well, she reflected, family principles were maintained with love and wisdom and understanding—at least for the present. At any rate the Wells boys were not undersold and neither were the city boys tread upon. There would not be two standards.

Just before everyone finished Faith spoke, "Before you all go out to play I'd like to make a speech about the do's and the don'ts." The city boys were very solemn. "Oh, it isn't that bad," smiling quickly. "There are only a few things and it is better you know them immediately. We require it of our lads and while you are here you are our lads too. Your folks loaned you to us for a short vacation." Their spoons rested on their plates.

"You may be excused from the table. Come over to the window so I can show you one of the don'ts," Faith led the way to the dining room window. They gathered around her. "See that pipe sticking up in the lawn?" Eager heads nodded. "That's the vent pipe for the septic tank. It is very important. We never throw sticks or stones down it for we would have trouble in the bathroom and the sinks. That's rule number one.

"Two: Always close the screen doors because flies on a farm are a nuisance.

"Three: We play cooperatively and share toys all around. Everyone." She glanced meaningly at each young man.

"Four: If you don't feel well, tell us immediately.

"Five: Don't leave the farm unless we know where you are going or unless one of us is with you. This is most important, for if you were to go somewhere we wouldn't know where to look for you. You are our complete responsibility.

"Six: When the bell out back rings, come. I shan't ring it unless it is necessary. It means meals or something important. It is to be obeyed implicitly."

Faith paused. All four boys stood expectantly. "Okay? Got all that?" Meditative nods. "All right. Out in the sunshine to play." Her right hand gently urged the last of the foursome outward. Single file through the kitchen they went. One comforting slam of the door. Rule number two was being followed meticulously.

"More coffee?" Faith moved toward the kitchen, assuming John would agree. Noisy yellings from the outside, and the sound of Doug's tractor going full tilt to the accompaniment of lusty shouts. Seemingly from nowhere Kim appeared, big, graceful, effortless bounds overtaking the tractor and driver, Cheesecake. A bloodcurdling scream!

John recovered first. Faith remained frozen, coffee spilling over her cup. The noise of the slammed door was the signal for Kim's barking, his whole frame reflexing after each deep throated protest. Each bark elicited succeeding staccato yells from Cheesecake.

"Kim! Stop that! Cheesecake! Hush!" John's deep voice boomed over both their noises.

With great joy Kim placed forepaws on John's shoulders. Quietly, "Down, Kim." Two front feet hit the earth, the plumey white tail waving like an allegro-set metronome. Scream echoes ceased. John's right hand rested on Kim's head, his left on Cheesecake's. Calmly, "Cheesecake, this is Kim. He is the boys' dog and he is harmless. Although he is large, he is still only a puppy and he is playful. He knew you were on Doug's tractor and he wanted to race you. See, Cheesecake, he is laughing with you."

Gradually faint color ebbed into the pallor in the lad's face. Cautiously he eyed the big dog standing over him, large teeth bared. The boy's expression indicated he thought the dog's smile wore a degree of taste anticipation. John continued, slowly and deliberately, "Now, he wouldn't hurt you. Jash, you come over too. Jash, this is Kim. Kim, this is Jashu." John made a production of the introductions. Cheesecake was still motionless.

"We have another dog," John continued. "He is a little black cocker spaniel. His name is Tramp, and he is your friend too." John whistled for Tramp who appeared at the annex portion of the house, peeking around the corner. John talked gently a little longer until the terror vanished from the young face. "Now you lads go back to play. You have no reasons to be afraid here. Nothing will harm you." John patted Kim's head, his gesture toward the dog encouraging the children's resumption of play. Hesitantly they began.

By now the sky was startlingly clear, strong sunlight playing on the world of Red Mill. An azure sky with huge billowy cloud puffs waiting in the limitlessness called the heavens. The fields and roads were splotchy with sunlight and shade. One could smell the freshness, the sweet cleanness of the newly saturated earth. One could feel the difference on his skin. Vegetation again sparkled, looked alive, dustless, and fresh.

When they finished their second cup of coffee, John suggested a walk around the farm boundaries to forestall juvenile wanderlust. They started up the dirt road toward the far east field. (Faith loved to call it that; it gave her the feeling of far-sweeping horizons). Along the way John pointed out interesting things to the four boys trudging along the hedgerows.

On the return trip they cut through the fields. The hay was making second growth. Four boys raced and romped, interrupting the ambitious bees, the white flowery embroidery of Queen Anne's lace swaying in their wake. Big, free-striding Kim bounded ahead, encircling easily every now and then, talking in joyous barks while the short-legged Tramp eagerly followed rabbit scents, emitting staccato yips of interesting comment as he ran. All the way to the horizon lush summer growth extended, resplendent against the now clear, fresh-washed colors of the summer sky. Except for the darker hue of the trees it seemed a day in June, so clear and fresh the world.

The joyousness of the children emphasized the freedom and beauty of the country. They raced. They jumped. They tumbled.

They tagged. They leapfrogged over blossoming weeds, knocking the powdery whiteness into the air. They followed the leader up the incline of the field, achieved the top with abandoned laughter. One after the other they rolled down. Abruptly, in reverent hush, they crouched over an anthill. Kim trotted to them, plopped his largeness atop the object of their curiosity. Sternly he was reproved for his bad manners. Unmiffed he bounded away, leaving them to marvel at the minute world before them.

John and Faith trailed along the edge of the field in the background, Faith still hugging Don. "They'll sleep tonight," John laughed as congregating emotions lumped in his throat and his eyes held the mistiness a man hides from all but his wife. "Honey, you've sold me . . . this is an annual institution with us . . . from now on."

After dinner and family fun, Faith cheerily prodded the children toward bed. Washing the city boys she strongly repressed the urge to shudder at their skinniness. Their extremities were mere bones covered with skin. Jashu, two years older than Doug, easily fit into his handmedowns. Cheesecake, two years Rob's senior and a whole head taller, weighed the same. Hopefully Faith questioned them, "Are your dad and mother slender?"

"Nope. They're fat," succinctly from Cheesecake.

"Are they as tall as dad and I?"

"Naw."

Four little men herded into beds, four separate prayers to be supervised. "Want me to hear your prayers?" to the visitors.

"Sure. Where's your cross?" Cheesecake knelt on the bed facing the headboard.

"We don't have one. You pretend one is there. If you close your eyes, it's easier to pretend."

Cheesecake and Jashu rattled off their prayers in Polish. Momentarily Faith was surprised. It had not occurred to her they would know another language. Then, she remembered they weren't saying them to her.

Polish-American kisses were cloyingly sweet. After extinguishing the light and a cheerful, "See you in the morning, sleep well," Faith left to join John. Abreast of Rob's room he whispered, "What were they saying?"

"Prayers," matter-of-factly.

"I couldn't hear them."

"Sure you could. You mean you couldn't understand them."

"Hmmm."

"They were speaking in Polish." From the doorway in the diminishing skylight streaming through his window she saw his freckled nose wrinkle. "They're smart. They know more than one language and God understands all languages—as well as the un-worded feelings in one's heart, Honey." Robbie scrunched down in the bed. Faith leaned over, kissed him again before continuing on downstairs.

In the morning, thinking they might be a bit homesick, Faith asked heartily of the visitors, "Did you sleep well last night?"

"Naw! Your crickets don't sound like our trolley cars!" Jashu's instant rejoinder.

Relatively no conversation during breakfast. The entire meal was composed of rapid movements from plates to mouths. Peaches from Jed, a ready-to-eat cereal, eggs and bacon, coffee cake and milk.

The weather pattern was as the preceding day—mist and drizzle and greyness. To keep everyone busy, John suggested they build a large doghouse for Kim and Tramp. So, outside the kitchen door, lusty sounds of wood gathering, sawing, hammering, shouting and laughing. In a couple hours the project was complete, even the roof. Four boys were delegated to fetch straw from the barn. With great fanfare, dogs were corralled, introduced to the doghouse while four boys—quite unsynchronized—yelled, "See! Your new house."

Then, immediately with noisy hoopla, they succeeded in chasing the dogs away. In the twinkling of an eye the doghouse was transformed to a fort. Except for luncheon, the fort provided hours of enjoyment and at bedtime it again became a doghouse.

Later that afternoon, it cleared as had the day before, a beautiful, warm, delightful summer fragrance and a glistening world appeared. Faith settled herself with Don under the now green flowering cherry tree. As she gave Don his orange juice concealed by the lush foliage she overheard one of the city lads. Peeping through the drooping greenery she saw Cheesecake, arm lovingly around Kim's neck as they walked side by side. "Kim, you scared me silly yesterday," Cheesecake was saying. "But, you know, last night when I got to bed I lay there and figured out your angle. I bet I scared you silly too. I'm sorry, Kim." They

153

stopped walking. Faith saw two lanky arms encompass the mastiff's neck and a dark head plop on Kim's white one. All she could see of Kim was his long tongue dangle and his eyes protrude with the ardor of Cheesecake's hug. "I love you, Kim! You are my friend. I like it here very much. They are my friends. But you, Kim, I LOVE YOU!"

Kim panted in blissful understanding. Walking close together, the boy and dog continued their friendly stroll around to the west of the house, up the hilly pasture, out of Faith's hearing and sight.

By and large it was an easy adjustment for everyone. The visitors tested the discipline, mostly table discipline. It was not done in the sense of what-can-I-get-away-with as much as do-the-rules-hold. There was one scene at the bathroom door, Faith combing her long brown hair when Cheesecake appeared in the doorway, extended filthy socks toward her and with insolent tones commanded, "Here. Wash these. I ain't got more."

For a fleeting moment Faith failed to appreciate his youthful embarrassment. Even ordinarily he spoke in italics. The way he demanded more milk, for instance. She told herself their kindness and courtesy would win. This time though, stung by his manner, invisible icicles encircled her words, "I beg your pardon?"

Mollified and in a surprisingly mature way understanding, he corrected both his attitude and grammar, "Will you wash these for me, ma?"

" 'Please,' " hintingly.

"Please."

"I'll be glad to. You have asked so nicely. Would you like to put them in the hamper?"

Cruddy, they thudded in. He took off for play.

And there was a series of tomato episodes. Tomato wedges behind the china closet, under a radiator, behind a bookcase. Neither Rob or Doug did that. Only Jashu fussed at the table about tomato eating. Faith or John reexplained about the family food rule. Faith talked informally about vitamins and nutrition values, about the wonders of Jersey tomatoes fresh from the garden. She used many approaches.

Tomato wedges still hardened in odd places. Faith wondered how to proceed. She loathed food waste, prided herself that nothing at the farm was ever wasted. What they didn't eat or the chickens failed to appreciate, the compost pile accepted, utilized, converted to humus. This behavior of Jashu's deliberately violated family rules. It was sneaky. She felt she had been reasonable. Even kind. This was now a matter of principle. Well, she would let her inner Lord guide her.

The opportunity presented itself at a family picnic at Voorhees Park. She just happened to see a speck of red under the long picnic table. She knew it to be a chunk of tomato and the time seemed propitious. Aura prompted kindly and wisely. "My goodness," Faith said. "Someone dropped a piece of tomato." From the angle she knew it to be thrown, not dropped.

Instantly, loudly, Jashu spoke up, "Not me, ma! I didn't do it!"

The other children protested mildly. John looked across at her, and she made no outer answer. Within her heart she held to the idea that Jashu's higher self would manifest. Her countenance bore no trace of emotion; it was as bland as she could achieve.

Several minutes elapsed. Minutes not weighted with anger. Merely silent time. Jashu whispered, "I did it, ma. I'm sorry." Chin down on his chest.

Faith's brown eyes regarded him. "I'm glad you're honest, Honey. What do you think we should do about it? What would your mother do?"

Instantly his head bobbed up, dark expressive eyes widened, "She'd whale the tar outta me."

"Oh, I can't whale you. You aren't my little boy. Besides it doesn't solve our problem."

Jashu sat respectfully, thoughtfully eyeing her, awaiting the verdict.

Silently Aura suggested, "You've tried every approach but the spiritual. Why not put it on the spiritual plane?"

"Do you know the story about Jesus feeding the multitudes?"

Only a few weeks earlier something Jed said clarified her understanding of that story, underscored her own thinking. Wasting food was like destroying a crop or being paid not a raise a crop. Spiritually dishonest Jed said. Faith had their complete attention. Everyone at the table. Even John wondered what she would say.

"Remember?" She smiled at them. She loved to tell stories, and the warm interest of the little ones and John quickened her desire to teach truth principles.

She painted the scene of two thousand years ago, of the multitudes seated on the hillside in groups. Friends and neighbors together. They had listened to the Master's teaching, so interested time had slipped by. Now the teaching was finished and everyone was hungry. It was almost night. They were a long way from home. Knowing their needs, Jesus determined to feed them, asked His disciples' assistance. Andrew told Him about the little boy with the five loaves and the two fish.

Andrew doubted how that little could be distributed among four or five thousand people, but Jesus received the loaves and the fishes. He gave thanks to God for the substance. Then He blessed it before commanding it to be passed to everyone. With His blessing He split the atoms* of the bread and the fish, and there was an abundance of bread and fish for everyone.

"Such abundance that when all the people were finished the disciples were instructed to gather up the crumbs 'so that nothing would be wasted.'" Faith paused dramatically. Every eye observed her. Breath seemed abated until the end of her story, especially the city boys' attention was caught. Rob and Doug lived with her story-telling tendencies. The little city visitors were deeply stirred by Faith's simplicity and quiet humility. "You know," she continued quietly, almost as though thinking aloud, "I believe we have all missed the crux of the story through our jubilation and wonder of the mere multiplication. We have missed the spiritual teaching—that we are not to be frugal. Neither are we to be wasteful. Rather we are to accept all good, give thanks for it, bless it—and *use it completely!*

"Did you remember that twelve basketfuls of crumbs were collected!"

Little men's heads slowly moved from side to side. Tentatively, meditatively, Jashu solemnly resumed eating, snipping tiny bites from his food as though busily digesting Faith's version of the old story. The other boys resumed eating too. At the foot of the long picnic table, atop it, Don lay kicking merrily in his lined washbasket.

Tree-filtered sunlight played upon the scene, scintillating light patches, simmering reflections moved slightly in the gentle breeze.

---

* Charles Fillmore's scientific explanation—in 1898 he arrived at that conclusion.

Down the slope of the pine-needled hillside the little lake lay in full sunlight. "Jashu, suppose you pick up your piece of tomato, take it to the lake, wash it, and bring it back here to eat."

Jashu carried out Faith's suggestion. It was the last instance of his food disposals while at the farm.

Faith and John constantly enjoyed the city boys, sometimes laughing together over their way of putting things, occasionally poignantly aware of their deep requirements. Such a time occurred one morning during the week following the picnic. Faith was at her desk writing their mother when Jashu sought her. On the top of the desk lay a book. "Whazat?"

"The *Bhagavad-Gita*. Can you say that?"

The word rolled off his tongue without effort. Faith silently marvelled at his linguistic ability. Conversationally he continued, "Yeah, poor grandfather, he had only one liver." He placed himself in the rocker, gave a few backward-forward movements. Suddenly, "Hey! Whazat?"

"That's another fireplace," explained Faith. "It is blocked off because they utilized its flue for the oil burner. We can't use this fireplace until we put in a two-way flue."

"You mean you're your own janitor!" He was aghast. He paused only long enough to receive Faith's confirmation of his deduction. With a whoop he ran full tilt through the hall, the dining room, the kitchen. Yelling from the doorway as soon as he reached sunlight, his words projecting before him as well as wafting behind him, "Hey, Cheese! They're their own janitors!"

Choring finished, John came indoors to find Faith engulfed in a mixture of mirth and marvel. Between gulps of laughter, " 'Poor grandfather had only one liver' . . . 'You mean you're your own janitor!' "

Their laughter subsiding John said, "You know Doug's ewe . . . what does he call her, Dorothy? Well, she seems aloof to me. I wonder if we should get the vet?"

Faith put up her writing equipment. She would finish the letter to Mrs. Warwenski later. The last click of the washer in the kitchen signalled the end of its task. "I don't think so. I believe she is ready to lamb."

"Dan said the boys' ewes weren't due until September or October. This is only August."

Rising, Faith nodded, "A-huh. I think she'll have twins—and she won't wait until September or October."

"You don't know any more about it than I do," John's instant rejoinder.

She tossed her head the merest bit. "I won't tell you how I know. But I know she'll have twins—and it will be this week."

"I'll bet you've had one of your prophetic dreams again," John's voice followed her.

She tweeked John's round cheek and left the den.

A case of milk, twelve quarts, every other day to be somehow wedged into the six cubic foot refrigerator along with all the other foodstuffs. Blessedly Don was on formula made from canned, evaporated milk. Four noisy boys and a baby filling the household and the farm with their fun and their demands. Four big boys constantly banging in and out. City lads eager to glory in their new constant delights. "Mom! Mom! See the frog I've got!" . . . "Dad! Are you taking us swimming today? . . . Dad! See this! Whatzit? Alligator? . . . OOOh, a sal-a-mander. Whatzat?" "Dad! Come see this with me."

Thrilled boys. Eager, observant. Voices almost coloratura in excitement. Boys whose little bodies rounded out as their knowledge increased. All the surrounding world new and fresh to them, vibrant, crawling or winging with interest and intrigue.

Mostly it was John who spent time with the lads during his vacation. He took them on walks about the farm, worked with them, showed them the wonders to be found under rocks, amid grasses. He played ball with them, invented games on the lawn, swam with them, frolicked with the aid of an inner tube in the not too deep waters of sparkling Spruce Run. John read to them, whittled small boats for sailing down the brook during the swim programs. John wrestled gently with them. He was their pal. He was at their incessant call except during chores. Somtimes they trooped along, inspecting the salt for the sheep, getting in his way while he filled the feed troughs for the thriving chickens, marvelling with him at the almost perceptible growth of the pigs. When Faith asked John to pick tomatoes or another vegetable, four boys assisted. Tramping up and down the rows, inspecting each tomato, interrupting John's concentration with constant demands, "This one ready yet, Dad?"

Yet with great sensitivity John sometimes disappeared from the foursome. Perhaps this was his greatest genius with the boys. He could play without intruding. He could fade out. By magic he could reappear when boredom or exhaustion of long undernourished bodies threatened.

Rather than clanging the dinner bell one night, Faith meandered to the garden, the site of joyous commotion. From a lawn chair John matched the boys in noise as four little men lustily engaged in obstacle tag. Infectious laughter resounded from the hills. Hilarity dominated the countryside. Faith eased on the chairarm, and John slid his arm around her waist. "How long has this been going on?"

"Couple hours. Since we returned from swimming. Not the same game. They won't play unless there's a stake."

"Meaning what?"

"A prize. No sport for the sake of the sport." They laughed together. "Swimming is going fine. Cheesecake's tube sprang a leak today. If that happened last week he would have been hysterical. Today it was just funny. . . . When's dinner ready? I'm starved!"

"You sound like the kids. It's ready now. I came out to call you all."

"Okay, fellows." John's voice projected to them, topped their noise. "Inside and wash up. Dinner's ready."

Cheesecake first in the house, first up the stairs. The house reverberated with the gusto of four boys. Arm-in-arm John and Faith followed leisurely. "I enjoy my swim every day. I'm going to miss it—and them—and you—when vacation's over." They paused in their stroll. Cupping her thin face tenderly in his hands he kissed her.

"You have a few more days," when her lips were free.

Cheesecake yelling from the doorway. "Hey! I'm through washin'." Their lovemaking interrupted, they laughed good naturedly. Faith's hand found John's as they parted from the embrace.

"Our life is less our own each year," John protested. "Gets worse too. As they get older they stay up later."

"The city boys don't seem so surprised now when they catch us kissing," softly put in Faith.

"No, guess they don't see much affection at home," John's answer low so that it would not reach their ears. They were at the door now, Cheesecake holding it open for them.

"What's for eats? Smells good. My belly hoits I'm so empty. What's dessoit?"

The next morning Faith awoke with a start. Rob and Cheesecake stood motionless at the bedside. They had neither touched her nor spoken. She had sensed someone's presence. As her eyes flew open Rob leaned over and whispered, "There's a baby in the pasture. Two of 'em."

Faith shook John awake. Not at all gently. "Wake up. Wake up. We got twins."

Groggily, John started forth, vainly shaking the sleepiness from himself, fumbling on the dresser for his glasses. "Huh? Huh?" It had been a reflex action. Even his voice was befogged. Now by sheer will power he stood staring at Faith.

Perceiving his thoughts she explained, "Out in the pasture."

"Ooooooh," and he was horizontal on the bed before the last note of his exclamation faded.

"Shoo with you," to the boys. "I want to get dressed. Come on, John. Let's see the twins," proddingly.

A protest from the bed. "Me dreaming of making Quota and you announce twins! Don't do that again. Twins, like they're a dime a dozen." He raised to his elbow, watched her. "First it's bats. Now twins. Either double my life insurance or yours."

All but baby Don trooped out of the pasture, Faith carrying a bottle of iodine. Skillfully John caught the new white lambs, Faith dabbed the iodine on the umbilicals, John elasticized their tails and returned them to their mother. Admiringly they watched the wet, wobbly lambs try gamboling about their mother's legs. Reassuringly Dorothy licked them as they frisked.

"Well, Doug, your ewe has given you the start on a flock. They're both girls. Congratulations." John patted Doug's shoulder as he might a co-worker announcing his new paternity. "And your mother's right about the delivery date and the quantity," looking at Faith who managed a degree of smugness.

To many that summer stretched endlessly with excessively hot days and torrid nights but to John it was wondrous relaxation on his farm full of children and stock beginnings, of dreams. To Faith it was almost a blur of time, so swiftly did the days begin and end. All waking hours were crammed with small fulfillments. Food to buy, meals to prepare, dishes, laundry—endless laundry. Lines and lines of it every hot day to be hung, taken down, folded or ironed, put away. Mending at night. Cleaning. Don and his growing demands.

But it was not a treadmill period. Faith remained steadfast to her quiet time with the Lord. Her time tithing. Each morning after the boys streamed outside, while John chored and Don cat-napped before his bathtime, she maintained this sacred time. Her constant sabbath. Only once did she omit it, and so many things went amiss she returned quickly to her armchair sabbath. God first in thoughts and in life's affairs. God first in the little matters as well as the big ones.

Before the visitor's second week Faith witnessed how the physi-cal tithe program with these little lads prospered. Their little bodies filled out. The day of the family picnic in Voorhees Park she glimpsed the project as a spiritual one. There were many ideas she and her Johnny Truthseed could plant in young minds and hearts!

She smiled slightly, remembering the first time Cheesecake asked to say grace, then rattled off, "Dear God, bless all the poor people. Amen." Immediately he proceeded to stoke his anatomical furnace while she and John exchanged glances. In the light of Unity's and Jed's teachings such a prayer held masses in bondage to poverty.

"God loves everyone, Cheesecake," she had said softly. "Some-times the rich need His blessings more than the poor—although for a different reason."

Yes, Faith could visualize this work as being a spiritual tithe as well as a physical tithe. It required loving understanding and gentleness. No holier-than-anyone tendencies. And no jimmying of doorways of hearts. Rather with simplicity and sincerity, an al-most reverent respect for the right of the other fellow to believe his way. Jashu's offer flashed into her memory, his suggestion to duck a turnstile to save a fare inferring it to be his family prac-tise. On what far-reaching winds could this project of theirs soar!

Right now, of course, there was tremendous reward in seeing their young bodies fill out as the result of good nutrition, ample rest, relaxation in a happy homelife. Both boys were less jittery. A measure of poise and peace appeared in their very speech, rosi-ness in their cheeks, a sparkle in their formerly lusterless eyes.

These were treasurable moments with the first Fresh Aires. So much happiness through their filling the big old farmhouse with their lustiness and the Wells' hearts with their needs, the implied ones rather than the spoken ones. The second Sunday of their stay was fabulous, tremendous for everyone.

As the car needed repairs John could manage, they held Sunday School in the "backyard" under the apple tree near the laundry lines. Four boys, two dogs, and two kittens—given to the Wellses by a friend whose female cat was too sexy—John and Faith of course and Don kicking contentedly in his washbasket bed. Rob wanted the "noisy hymns." John taught the lesson and led the singing. Faith verbalized the story time. And all the surrounding countryside vied for boyish attentions, projecting its beauty, verily shouting, "Our beauty and fragrances are part of divine manifestations too."

After supper Jed came, the familiar white truck appeared just as Jashu shouted, "Moider! Look at this woik in the doit!"

At the side door Faith stood shuddering and laughing, "English as she is spoke. Only the purest English is used on this farm. Long ago a friend of mine left her Pennsylvania farm to become a teacher in the New Jersey schools. She vowed she would never stoop to the sloppy manner of Jersey speaking. I did not understand then. Now I do. My ears are offended by pure Brooklynese," holding her ears. "Forgive me. That's pretty catty, isn't it? But there are moments these past couple of weeks when it is a bit too much."

Jed grinned. His manner and smile offered understanding with no admixture of commitment. "Thought you would bring the boys to see my pigs."

"We have pigs here. Some of your very stock," matter-of-factly from John.

"I have many breeds. Children like to see differences. By the way, I brought you some more peaches. They are truly lovely this year. Indeed! Every year!"

It was Jed's way of praising the Lord, giving thanks for all his gifts from God. His face glowed and his eyes danced with glee as he set the blushing, fragrant fruit at Faith's feet. "I would have brought more but I know your canning time isn't abundant right now."

"They're gorgeous. Thank you very much," Faith acknowledged, silently wondering how a bachelor could be so judicious of her canning time.

The four boys came racing down the hillside at that moment, the city boys in the lead. They stopped instantly at sight of Jed. Rob and Doug came forward happily. Jash trumpeted a whisper, "Who's he?"

162

"Mr. Whiskers," Doug answered, adding a hearty "hi" to Jed.

Faith almost visibly winced but Jed turned, affably greeted the boys with an easy manner. He didn't wait for an introduction. "Hi. What is your name?" he asked of Cheesecake who was nearest, holding the bony hand in his firm, gentle grasp.

"Cheesecake. My name's really Robert but all my real friends call me Cheesecake." A moment's analysis. "You can too."

"Thank you," Jed acknowledged the ready friendship. Turning to Jash his manner invited self-introduction.

"I am Jashu. That's Polish for John. You spell it with a 'J' but it sounds like a 'Y'."

"I see." Jed appeared to be digesting that iota of information. Faith loved his manner with the children, and she watched him in utter fascination. He was so charmingly simple without condensation. Faith's eyes glowed, watching Jed.

"I hope Mr. Wells brings you over to my farm. You should see all my rows and rows of heavily laden peach trees. When you stand on my hillside surveying them—and you can smell them for miles too—they are like seasonal Christmas trees, only they have peaches instead of tinsel and lights. It is a glorious sight." Jed put an arm around each little city shoulder, hinting the boys toward Faith's garden. He need not have employed physical means for the boys were magnetized by this friendly stranger with the resonant voice, the shiningly incandescent face. Jed paused at Faith's garden. His head bobbed up and down. "Good. Very good. Who's the farmer?"

"Faith," John acknowledged immediately. "She plants it, weeds it, talks to it, waters it occasionally and loves it. Sometimes she even picks the vegetables." A twinkling glint in John's eyes.

"No drought here," Jed was saying. "Mrs. Stashi's and yours and mine seem to be the only gardens hereabouts that aren't crying for water. Most of our neighbors complain about lack of rain. Many have dry wells and are using Spruce Run by the milkcanful. Your fields look good too. You must be blessing them."

Jed required no answer. Faith and John made none. Jed's hands were now deep in his pockets, and he was completely aware of the intense interest from the boys. He knew the adults understood he was sowing spiritual seeds, that such seeds must be sown at propitious moments even as cornseeds and limas are

163

not planted in wet soil but only when the ground is well warmed, receptive to those seeds yet well before the calendar runs out and growing time too short.

So now Jed smiled broadly and especially included the boys in his miniature lecture. "Yes, the enthusiasm—the love—you give your garden by your thoughts, speach, and action does an immeasurable part toward a big yield. Everything responds to love. Universal love is the whole law, and by 'law' I mean the deep cosmic laws, not the kind man sets up to correct social conditions.

"You know, many years ago I knew a lovely old colored lady. She was big of stature, had a great deal of padding on that stature too. I loved her and she loved me. She and her husband were caterers, preparing, cooking, and serving delectable foods to large gatherings of people. Sometimes when the catering business was slow, she sewed for our family. That's how I got to know her.

"She had another talent. A great talent with plants and flowers. All her neighbors enjoyed the colors of her garden, for with the first breath of spring until the killing frost of autumn her yard was a gorgeous riot of color and fragrances. When fall came, she moved all that was portable of the garden indoors. It continued to bloom behind her windows. I remember a poinsettia of hers. The blooms measured eighteen inches across and every passing florist propositioned her for it." Jed stretched his hands, measuring off eighteen inches. The boys were "with him" the way a theater audience breathlessly drinks in each word and gesture of the hero.

Jed continued, "Once she said to me, her black eyes flashing with lights and laugher, her voice hearty and expansive and so musical, 'You know, I talks to my flowers and they talks back to me by bloomin'. When I comes downstairs in the mornin' I says 'good mornin', you beauties.' I remember she paused a moment, let me digest that and then she said, 'I thinks all people when they dies gets to be flowers. Good folks gets to be roses and violets and pansies. And the bad ones gets to be stinkweeds!' I can still hear the way she spit out the last word."

"That isn't true," blurted Jashu.

Jed laughed pleasantly. "No, son, perhaps not. But isn't it a gentle thought?" Jashu nodded seriously, relieved the hell-purgatory-heaven idea was not banished for him. "You see, she was saying that everything has a soul and is part of God. She was

164

saying more than that. She was telling me the story of the fig tree in modern version."

For an instant Faith saw herself talking to Lulu beside the fireplace the first week of their arrival. She noticed the children looked puzzled. Jed removed his hands from his pockets, strolled to the stone retaining wall at the foot of the hillside pasture just behind the house. The children gathered around him, Doug leaning against him and Jash wiggling in so that Jed's arm encircled the little shoulders.

"You remember the story of the fig tree, don't you?" he began. He did not embarrass them by waiting for an answer. It was merely his easy introduction to an interpretation, a way of alerting them to the source. "Remember the Bible tells the story of Jesus and the disciples going down the road, the Master reaching for a fig. But there was no fruit. The scripture says it was not the season for fruit, although another version of the story implies the tree was barren and could not produce fruit. Jesus condemned the tree. 'Cursed it,' the Bible says. Spoke disparagingly to it. When they passed the same tree the next morning it had withered and died."

Jed paused, letting his words penetrate. "Did you know that's the only example we have of a destructive act of our Lord? It wasn't completely destructive if the tree was barren or that fruit out of season. . . . I believe," and his voice was very quiet, sharing his personal opinion with the little group, "He did it purposely . . . to underscore all His other acts. Through that example He emphasized one can work either destructively or constructively. For evil or for good! He wanted to show His followers dramatically. He said 'every tree must bear fruit or it is cast into the fire.'"

Jed's tones became more expansive, "I believe He was showing His followers each of us, then and now—one can use the power of thought . . . and speech . . . and act . . . to destroy by criticism or condemnation . . . or to bless by prayer and praise."

Jed strung out his words, releasing them deliberately, individually, into the air, pausing between them as though to tamp down good soil over the seed, patiently await the work of God's light and rains. He resumed the thread of his explanation, gently as though not to intrude too harshly into their reflections. "Do you see? The disciples might have missed the point had He not

165

given them this negative example of principle at work." His slow smile wreathed about his words, "And my lovely colored lady was telling me in her way that she blessed her plants, loves them, encourages them to respond to her love. And they do."

Several minutes elapsed before anyone interrupted the stillness. Then Rob shyly asked, "Is that true?"

Deliberately, slowly, Jed nodded. "Yes, Rob. More truth than most people realize. Scripture says 'we have power of life and death in the tongue.' Jesus said His words were 'spirit and life and would never die.' We now find that whatever one condemns dies and whatever one blesses thrives. This is a law that applies to everything—your body and all its members, your money, your relationships with people. It applies in the vegetable and animal kingdom. They say that a pearl responds with a special lustre to those who genuinely love it for itself.

"And all people have this power. This blessing power. All the time. It is a constantly active cosmic law. Like gravity. But it isn't so apparent as gravity.

"You see, all around us is what Jesus called 'the kingdom.' Science calls it 'ether' or 'atmosphere.' Metaphysicians call it 'substance.' It is like the soil of this garden," gesturing to it. "Except that it is invisible. The thoughts we think and the words we speak are the seeds planted in our substance gardens. They grow, each seed according to its kind, each harvest according to its own timetable. Joy—and love-seeds produce bountiful crops! Criticism and hate seeds are deep-rooted prolific weeds that keep the world harvesting strife and discord.

"Your thoughts are the most important seeds of all, for they are the very beginning. They are the cause. Whatever you see was once a thought, an idea. Light bulbs, toys, even improved garden seeds, *everything*. Whatever you perceive with your senses . . . sight, smell, touch, and so forth, is an effect. This is how 'man is made in the image of God and after His likeness' for man has creative powers too. Man is co-creator with God.

"Always remember your thoughts are your treasure and in your mind you are complete monarch of that treasure. Only you have the complete power—the blessing attitude or the cursing attitude— no one can do this for you." Jed tousled the head of the nearest lad, Doug. "Big stuff, little man. isn't it? Good seeds for your garden."

166

Jed glanced at John and Faith, opened his lips to speak when the group was startled by a peculiar whinny from the truck. "Why, I forgot Garry." He laughed outright at the puzzled expression on Faith's countenance. Half apologetically, "I should have requested permission but I couldn't resist. I saw him, and he just invited himself to your place through me. Come on, boys."

The boys required no second invitation. They raced Jed to the truck, stood peering inside before he reached the tailgate. Jed gently set a young brown goat before the boys, handed the leash to Robbie.

The goat was small and friendly. All four youngsters tried to hug him simultaneously. He shied but there was no other protest. "I named him for you. 'Garry' for 'garrulous'." The twinkle in Jed's eyes sparked the amusement in Faith and John. Unsnapping the leash he added, "He'll stay with us."

Then the fun began. Four boys romping after Garry, and he skillfully remaining just beyond their reach, his whinnies acknowledging their gleeful shouts. The three adults laughed at the antics until the fading light reminded Faith of little men's bedtime. She asked the men to help the children bed down Garry for the night while she went in to peel off the bedspreads, and place pajamas in readiness. When the boys noisily trooped in, exchanging ideas on how they would play with Garry the next day, Faith was ready to assist in their washups and hear their prayers.

Afterward she slipped outside with the men in the big lawn chairs. The evening dark deepened and the stars appeared. Early katydids began their song about ten, and the men moved to the living room while Faith prepared coffee and a tray of assorted cheeses.

"This is one of our favorite snacks," put in John as Faith offered the tray to him.

"Did you know I have hired help?" Noting their surprise Jed continued around mouthfuls of provolone and crackers. "Are you going to be busy after the city boys leave, Faith?"

"I expect to have lots more time. Less laundry. Fewer beds. Fewer dishes. School starts shortly for Rob too." Her tone held a question.

"I'll bring Hilda to see you. She's learning English rapidly. She speaks five languages already. Hilda does my housekeeping while Otto helps with chores. He's a doctor. They're from the Iron

167

Curtain and have been bunted about quite a bit. He's a bit older than Hilda and the toll on him has been a little heavier. But he's finding himself. The farm and country quietness are a big assist to his soul—and the rest will follow."

Faith felt this program was related to Jed's plans, that he was anticipating his divine assignment. No one interrupted the silence. There was merely the irregular noise of cracker crunching, the occasionally scraping of a coffee cup on a saucer. During the lull in conversation Faith fell to studying Jed, his hands that fascinated her. Innately clean and artistic. Firm and positive she would categorize those hands. Looking at his face she would classify Jed as a mystic, she thought, but being mindful of his hands one would designate a practical category. Aware of that peculiar radiance, that full-length walking halo he wore, one just couldn't determine the right pigeon-hole. It seems ridiculous, she told herself, and surely not subject to analysis. It wasn't that he was handsome, feature-by-feature. But there was surely a certain indefinable quality that he radiated, that permeated the very atmosphere of Jed's presence. It was really as though a high powered electric bulb somewhere deep in the recesses of his being, invisible to human eye, extended an incandescence about his whole body.

Correspondingly Faith sensed a vast sensitivity about the man in a universal sense, a conscious understanding or awareness of others' and their needs, and Jed's empathic ability to fill such need or mitigate it. Without listening to his words Faith was aware of the man's booming voice, a musical resonant series of tones that compelled attention or its quality that was muted and vibrant, confidential, as when he told the fig tree story to the children. His voice is like the sea, she thought. Sometimes like the breakers pounding the shore, sometimes soft and hushing when they merely lap at the beach. Somehow all of these aspects of Jed's is not completely Jed, for one also has to credit the philosophy he is living.

"Would you?" Jed was directing his question to Faith.

Startled from her thoughts Faith covered her embarrassment by picking up the coffee pot, refilling Jed's cup murmuring an empty apology.

Smiling at her he repeated, "I was asking if you will help teach Hilda some English."

"I don't know how good I'd be. I don't know any other language."

"You don't need to. You'll find her an apt pupil. I take her shopping and sit in the car while she goes forth. I tell her what to ask for. She must be doing well, for she always returns with the right things." He laughed a little. "Sound tough, don't I? But she claims she 'vants to learn American queekest way—she vants to be America.' And the fastest way to a goal is to practise with whatever equipment we have."

John interrupted with the episode of Jashu and his rattling off *Bhagavad-Gita*. "He has real linguistic abilities. They both say their prayers in Polish."

"Really? Children's natural aptitudes fascinate me. A while ago I concluded most of us are God-inspired during childhood, say at puberty, as to the individual purpose in life. Like Jesus at the Temple at twelve, knowing 'He must be up and about the Father's business.' And until we obey that inner prompting we never truly express individual divinity." He turned to John. "What did you want to be at twelve? Farmer?"

"I really don't remember, Jed. During High School days I wanted to be an architect. There was a depression on and it wasn't feasible."

"You, Faith?"

"At twelve?" Wistfully, "I remember writing a book at eleven. Saved the manuscript a long time. It never sounded as good as those I read."

"Why not write now?" encouragingly from Jed.

Faith just smiled at the preposterous idea.

Jed broke the few minutes silence. His voice no longer boomed. It held the soft lappings of the quiet tide, the constancy and rhythm, the clarity. "For myself at twelve, I would have said missionary. I wanted to travel and faroff lands beckoned romantically . . . Perhaps 'metaphysician' best describes my ambition now.

"I used to pore over the Bible." He smiled a bit at himself. "I thought it very peculiar and badly translated. I mused about the lack of punctuation and other poor translation qualities. The skipping around of tenses—'Father, I thank Thee that Thou heardest me and I know that Thou hearest me always.' I wondered why such valued books weren't translated by better qualified scholars!"

Jed leaned back in his chair, stretched his legs full length. In the lamplight his eyes were full of mirth at the memory of an audacious and reflective, puzzled very young man. "Also, I began to be intrigued with numbers. Forty days Jesus was in the wilderness after His baptism. Forty days of rain during the flood. Forty years the Israelites wandered. Moses was forty when he fled from Egypt, tended sheep forty years. Lent is forty days. Pentecost forty days."

Reflections poured from Jed, sometimes intermittently, sometimes with a rush as though the memories came too fast to be measured by words. "And 'wilderness.' Did it mean only wild country? Why did John the Baptist come out of the wilderness as a 'voice'? I could understand his diet of honey—but not locusts. And Jesus was 'The Word.' But didn't a voice make more noise? Yet John had no mighty works to his credit, was given to condemnation—and lost his head . . . It took me many years to appreciate the mysticism of the Gospel of John." Jed grinned broadly at himself standing in judgment of scholarly translators via young lad questions.

"For months I puzzled where the comma belonged in 'I AM that I am' or 'Before Abraham was I AM.' And many times those of whom I asked questions thought me either sacrilegious or insane, one even told me 'people go daft with too much thinking on such matters.'"

A long slow sigh slipped out, and Jed smiled dreamily, triumphantly, "Then one day I saw that 'I AM' is the constant, eternal name of God!

"It came as a revelation although it was years before I comprehended the Creator as limitless energy and love and wisdom, plus all the other attributes of Being. Or even that evolution is a constant and continual law, still at work! Through 'I AM' God is continually individualizing Himself in each of us."

Jed's vibrant voice stirred the very room, the qualities of light and joy permeating each syllable.

"I know all that I am is the result of my inner search. I believe everything I ever thought or experienced led me to today—although at times I seemed to live on a spiritual plateau, a kind of digestion period."

Abruptly Jed was profoundly serious. Deep understanding and compassion glowed from the blueness of his eyes, the flecks

170

of gold subdued. Leaning forward, "I said that 'I AM' purposefully. . . . All through the ages scholars and priests have believed there is a lost word or a lost pronunciation, a magical way of intoning the name of God to produce miracles. Some think it a special name but untranslatable. Some think it contained in 'Jahveh' which we understand to be the Allness of God, the Father-Mother Principle. Some think it to be 'JHVH' from the Hebrew. We can't pronounce it in English and 'Jahveh' is believed inaccurate." Jed hushed, "I believe the lost words are 'I AM'. Not lost! Horribly misused. Downgraded!" His voice dropped to a whining mimicry. "Listen to the average conversation: 'I'm sick— or broke—or lonely.' Whatever the moment's lack."

He sat back in his chair, swung his right leg over the other knee. "Yes, most of us keep working imperfectly with this perfect power man calls God. We set limits of time, space, conditions. In His name—the glorious I AM—we claim and perpetuate the very errors from which we really wish freedom!

"We keep our minds filled with fear instead of faith, and then we behold fear manifest as illness, depressions, wars, death. Don't you *see!*" His tone pleaded for their perception, his hand outstretched as though to give them this gift of enlightenment.

"This substance in which we live is plastic to our thoughts, our words, our acts. When we incorporate I AM we have hold of a live wire. For the mass of mankind the effect of his words does not follow immediately because he has not spiritualized himself sufficiently, so he does not perceive the connection between his thoughts-words-deeds. Jesus, the Master, so perfect and so self-disciplined, produced instantaneous results by His touch, His words, His thought."

The Wellses sat quietly receptive, and Jed, encouraged, began again. "Read the Gospels anew, my friends. Note that whenever Jesus prefixed a statement with I AM it was tremendous in scope. 'I AM the resurrection and the life.' 'I AM the true bread out of heaven.' 'I AM the vine, ye are the branches.' In all these affirmations He was saying that through the Christ part of man one attains this kind of fulfillment . . .

"I said earlier that so far Jesus is the only one to so discipline His speech it reflected only divine and good fulfillments. He didn't condemn the Pharisees but rather their attitudes . . . He didn't 'hate the sinner but only the sin itself' as we are fond

171

of putting it . . . We keep wondering why we don't have absolute power. Even a cursory analysis of the steady stream of our words would reveal how much havoc we would create until we go through the fire of that self-discipline of every thought, achieve a positive divine love attitude. Even Peter, once pointing an accusing finger at a husband-wife expedited their death!

"Ah, my friends, it is not by outer laws and their enforcement this world moves to perfection or peace. It is by the spiritualization and enlightenment within each individual. The lighting of all lamps among all peoples. Divine be-ing. Divine do-ing. Perfect fulfillment is from within—outward! For as the Master put it, 'He who controlleth himself is greater than he who taketh a city.' But—the world is always impressed by the conquering hero rather than the simple one who wears homespun or a cotton sheet, collects no titles or medals."

Jed's fire of eloquence subsided. Neither John nor Faith spoke. Faith sensed Jed's whole talk was deliberate and planned. Not that it lacked sincerity, rather every word had a clarion ring of sincerity. But he seemed particularly to reach to them. In a subtle, controlled way he employed every art. She could not analyze her intuitive feeling. Something was quite indefinable about the whole visit.

"Yes, my friends, the deep wisdom and love of God are not learned from books or teachers. They come through enlightenment, pure flashes of comprehension from one's indwelling Christ self.

"Remember the Lazarus story?" He didn't wait for their answer. An eagerness to share his interpretation filled his voice with enthusiasm. "Used to wonder as a boy why my compassionate Jesus did not go immediately on hearing of Lazarus' death. In all other instances He did! The little girl of twelve. The widow's son. But with the death of Lazarus He paused two days before starting the journey and the journey took another two days. The number four again!" His chuckle invited their enjoyment.

"When I understood the Lazarus resurrection it didn't come as one piece of puzzle after another, but rather as full comprehension. Lazarus was Jesus' friend. He loved Lazarus. Wept at Lazarus' tomb. Nowhere else in scripture does Jesus demonstrate negative emotion. Great love, compassion, joy but no weeping.

172

Sometimes a steadfastness that almost seems cold and aloof. Perhaps 'controlled' is a better word. Like when He reproved the disciples huddled in fear in their boat during the storm. Evidence one must control one's personal emotions before one can command the elements or circumstances—even life and death!"

Jed paused briefly, letting his words stretch their imaginations. His speaking was clear. Each word separate like a crystal in the sunlight of their understanding. "Jesus had to pause before facing Lazarus' tomb until he achieved a balance between His Son-of-God part and His Son-of-Man part, the divine and the human. His dual Self. Then only could He stand and without a quiver in His voice but rather 'in a loud voice' command friend Lazarus to come forth! . . .'Be ye perfect even as your Father in heaven is perfect'. . .'Heaven is within you'. . .'Ye are all Sons of the living God'. . .'What I do ye shall do also—and greater works . . .'"

Jed searched their faces with keen penetration. "Have your hearts been gladdened by the newspaper accounts of the modern miracles? On operating tables surgeons massage human hearts to new activity—and the patient returns to life.

"I sometimes wonder the thoughts of the surgeons. . . . The day is now when all doctors and nurses everywhere know themselves to be divine channels of healing . . . when they recognize pills, serums, transfusions, etc. as mere channels for healing.

"And psychosomatic medicine is blazing a trail, taking up where the church left off some three hundred years after the Master. This new science will one day say with modern metaphysicians 'until you remove the mental correspondence—or the soul problem—no healing is permanent.' Then there will be no headcolds, no cancer, no illnesses and death and sorrow shall have passed away.

"I honestly believe a new age is dawning. A new world. I believe thousands of people are now ready to accept their divine sonship and its responsibilities, understanding the power of thought and word, growing in self-discipline, able and eager to use this potent power for good—selflessly. Cooperating with Divine Love and Wisdom. This is truly glorifying the Father and working to the honor of man. Now is the time for world unity.

"World harmony—understanding and cooperation among all peoples — scientists, doctors, clergy, sociologists, nutritionists, teachers, statesmen, *everyone*. Everyone to harmonize and work

173

in unity with one another, collectively inspire and uplift. Here and there individuals have been doing it through the ages. Now is the time for groups as well as individuals to chord with His universal symphony for the harmonious, wondrous blessings for all His children."

Jed's deeply resonant voice was still. Quietly, reverently, he had given the distillation of many years. He had spoken beyond the scope of dictionary definitions and that which intellect alone can perceive. He had given generously the fruits of divine realizations, deep understandings that come to one working and walking in constant God consciousness.

John pointed his unlit pipe at Jed, enthused, "Why don't you go forth and teach?"

A slow smile spread over Jed's face. Meticulously he fitted his fingertips together, observed them carefully before answering. "Yes." Reflective a moment, he continued, "Yes, I will take these interpretations as one might call them, to all people. I want folks everywhere to know how beautiful, how free, life is for the privilege of working with the whole law—Love. This taking on of the Christ yoke. Want to do it so intensely I know it is God's divine assignment for me . . . and my time is soon."

He smiled easily, glanced at Faith who experienced that quick rush of feeling, confirming her intuitive knowings. "And some day Faith will write her books. Perhaps her message will be that man is a spiritual being, co-creator with the Infinite, that God is the center of the universe within each individual as well as the universe of the atoms, planets, and stars."

The melody of Jed's words lingered the way instrumental music lingers, vibrantly, clearly. The dimples above Jed's beard deepened as his smile flashed and a note of humor warmed his tones, "You'll see me one day—clean shaven and joyous. You'll know it is my silent farewell, that I've been commanded to go, and a destination given me."

Jed arose, moved to the screen door. A large luna moth climbed upward, winged downward, climbed again, its gorgeous colors set off by rings of black visible from the underside. "It carries the marking of Infinity with countless prisms of colors in each circle."

They laughed slightly together. Jed pulled himself slender in

174

a long stretch at the doorway, partly stifling a yawn. "Well, morning with its chores comes quickly."

John too stifled a yawn. "Nice of you to drop over, Jed. We could talk all night, eh?"

The men shook hands. Faith remained in the background, irked by the degeneracy of an illuminating evening into yawns and comments about chores. From the mountaintop of ideas we crash to earth, she thought.

"I'll do a quickie so that all these bugs don't invade you." Jed stepped outside, cupped his hands around his face on the screening, "How'd I do?"

"Not a one," laughed John.

"Thanks for the peaches," Faith called to be retreating figure.

"And Garry," John added.

They stood in the doorway until Jed rolled to the road. A few birds in the lawntrees chirped dreamily when the headlights and the truck motor disturbed them. The noise of the little truck was swallowed by the night.

Yawning profoundly and noisily between the sheets John mumbled a weary goodnight. Faith undressed slowly. Staring into the dark she pondered Jed's ideas, her whole being stimulated and alive. In bare feet she padded into the hall. Don was covered. She touched him lightly, her right hand following the curved beauty of the baby form caressingly.

"Substance," Jed named it, this in which we live and move and have our being. Plastic to our every thought and word and deed, he claimed. She patted Don's buttocks and smiled faintly in the dark. In the analysis of Jed's teachings even Don was accounted for. She laughed softly, delightedly, recalling the picture of herself running to the doctor every spring—just like the birds and the bees—seeking professional permission for another baby. Don was bound to be! Unknowingly she had worked with what Jed named divine laws, the law of hope.

But now she *knew!* Now she could work consciously with His laws—just so long as she kept her purpose pure and high, selfless!

She slipped into bed beside John, lying awake a long time reflecting on the facets of Jed's words, his teachings to the children at the garden, to John and herself later in the living room.

"Substance" is like the garden soil . . . ours the choice to sow good seed in this Eden . . . ours the choice to weed out mortality's error seeds of hate, criticism, fear, discord . . .

"It's a never-ending job," she thought, recalling the constant struggle against weeds in the vegetable and flower garden. She rolled on her stomach. "Thank you, Father—and bless Jed for the truths You revealed through him this day!"

Monday brought the return of the long schedule. Up at five-thirty for Don's early bottle while John chored; breakfast for John and herself, John driving the long distance to Newark. Breakfast for the four boys, her meditation and study time, the baby's bath, and then the continuity of laundry, beds, luncheon, dessert-making for dinner, choring the stock by mid-day. A long day, dovetailing all the requirements of the home and farm, this day alone with five children—well, a rugged day.

The boys missed John. He had been their constant companion, fading from their horizon tactfully now and then, miraculously knowing when to return. This first day without John was smattered with bickerings and squabbles, shoutings and yellings. In the beginning its din did not penetrate Faith's ivory tower. Now and then a whisper permeated, but to those whispers Faith replied that most children's squabbles are best settled by themselves. But the din tended to grow with the day's heat. Their arguments became like the dripping faucet—irritating, annoying, constant. Faith found it a struggle to remain atop her holy mountain.

By eleven the quarreling reached huge proportions. Faith halted. She removed the pudding from the heat, stepped out the kitchen door. It slammed mildly behind her as she paused on the stone step, hands in the slit pockets of her pastel plaid summer dress. Strolling to the foursome under the first apple tree, she silently asked the Lord's guidance in handling the matter. "It's just that quarreling can become a habit, Lord."

To the children she said, "What seems to be the trouble?"

Four versions were simultaneously offered.

She waved the youngsters silent with a gesture. "Doug, you're the youngest. Tell me your story."

"I want to play with the road scraper and nobody will let me."

She nodded to Jashu. "I want to play with it too and nobody will let me. "

She indicated Rob with her eyes. "It's my road scraper and I want it."

"Cheese?"

"I had it first and I want it."

Quietly, hopefully, four little men waited. She did not answer immediately. Her heart affirmed understanding, love and wisdom in guiding these small matters. She glanced from face to face, noting shallow lines of anger already receding. Flittingly she thought of the plasticity of youngsters, yet we should not impose adult will, she thought. It should be a drawing forth process of love and wisdom, guidance and a readiness to assist the divine design of each young life.

Slowly she dropped to the grass, spread out her dress. The boys settled around her. Her every movement was slow, calculated, dramatic. Within her heart she waited for divine prompting; in the outer sense she was stalling until she received it. She flashed a smile around the little circle, began to speak in a friendly philosophical tone.

"You know," she began, "I have a theory. It might not be right, but I believe many of the world's troubles come from our social attitudes and habits. It seems easier to yell and push and shove and grab than to. . . ." She paused momently, wondering how to put metaphysics on a juvenile level. In a flash she remembered Cheesecake's conversation with Kim.

". . . to get someone else's angle. We forget that 'hatred ceases not with hatred.' Folks have done it this false way in families and in nations since Cain slew Abel. But now the world is at the dawn of a new era. Now we must remember everyone is part of God and God loves us all. When we play and work in harmony with other people, we live in harmony with Him. When we don't stay in harmony with Him, we cut off our good. *He doesn't* cut it off. *We* do it by breaking His law of love. That clogs the good streaming from Him to us, clogs it with discords.

"Har-mo-ny." She let the word stretch out, let it trickle syllable by syllable. "Harmony. Do you know what it means?"

Four earnest-eyed boys watched her lips, her face, her gestures, solemnly wagged their heads. "Say it," she encouraged.

Together they repeated the word and Faith smiled inwardly, reflecting that perhaps she seemed a frustrated teacher using the children to satisfy any professional longings of the past.

"Harmony," she took up the word herself, looking away to the hills with the late morning sunlight dappling them, patches of tree and cloud shadow. The settled, dusty color of late summer lay on the horizon. Despite the slight breeze there was the overhanging quietness of the day's heat, the lull when temperature reaches its peak and the birds rest from their songful delight and their perpetual food searchings.

"Harmony means peace. It means universal love at work. In music it is a delightful blend of sounds. It means God's love that is impersonal, limitless, and forever. This love of His sends rain into the fields of those who love Him, those who don't accept Him and those who ignore Him.

"Harmony means the growing fields, all the lovely blend of colors in the world about us—trees, flowers, shrubs, ferns in the dells, the sky. Some people call this nature and they say nature is cruel, warring upon itself—birds eat bugs, bugs eat plants, plants absorb food from the earth and the air, animals graze on the plants—and we eat the animals.

"Harmony. I see all this as God's divine design, as the Mother aspect of God, that our every need is supplied, and everything has a purpose in life. I see it as harmony because nothing in the universe is wasted. Everything God makes has a purpose and that purpose is very good. Plants don't deplete the earth; they come to maturity and if no one harvests them they rest until the changing of the seasons. During the resting period they enrich the ground from which they sprang by decomposing. When this happens for eons it is transmuted to coal or humus—or even diamonds. Although it has changed its purpose, it is still good."

She was still a while. She knew some of the ideas were well over the four-year old and perhaps the eight-year old thinking, too, but the children had caught her mood and through it were receptive to something from her dreamy philosophy at work.

"Harmony is also the rhythmic movement of planets and stars. No collisions in space. 'The morning stars sing together' and glorify the Creator. Harmony is order and beauty all about you.

"And harmony is within you too. When each of us carries no grudges or gripes against a friend or neighbor, or creed or race, his whole body is full of light, happiness, joy. This is health and wholeness.

"Harmony is easy—it takes real soul unfoldment to be a blessed

178

peacemaker, for it doesn't mean being willowy and bending with the breeze, the 'yes-man.' It means demonstrating the courage to live one convictions while maintaining tolerance of the other fellow's convictions. It requires discipline over your thoughts and your words. One is constantly thinking—it's always a busy street up there," pointing to her forehead.

"Harmony is thinking and working in tune with everyone, all God's children. It is chording with oneself. It is courageous and generous and selfless. Jesus was always in perfect harmony with God. Harmony is God working through people. Harmony is all people working together toward the greatest goal—universal good and peace for everyone.

"Har-mo-ny. The music of the Universe . . . God."

The children sat motionless around her, fascinated with her intonations of the word, thrilled with its music. She wondered if she had hypnotized them. She wondered too if she were too abstract for them. "Did you notice the other day how the kittens and dogs ate from the same dish? Then one of the pigs was loose, strolled along and joined them?" Yes, they remembered. Four boys nodded their heads. Faith continued, "When everyone lives in self-harmony and understanding, that kind of thing will happen everywhere in the world. The Bible tells us the day will come 'when the lion and the fawn shall lie down together' and no one will be unhappy. Everyone will know his purpose in life and will do it . . . Now we are at the dawn of that new day . . . Let there be peace in the world beginning with me."

Jashu's lips moved slowly, forming the word 'harmony.' He was tasting it. Faith watched him. "Don't you love the very feel of the word, Jash?" Jashu noded vigorously and Faith rose to leave, return to the pudding. "See if you all can play in harmony, sharing the toys among you." It was a gently worded suggestion, perhaps not necessary after the lengthy talk. Faith swung down the hillside amid the song of the ciciada on the slight breeze wafting through the trees, her thoughts returning to the mystical mountain.

Clanging the big bell at noon she had forgotten the morning's episode. At its signal four exuberant boys came on the run. Cheesecake's lanky legs brought him in first. "We done it, Mom! We done it!" shouting as he approached.

As he breezed through to wash up, Faith asked blankly, "Did what, Cheese?"

His rush propelled him into the dining room, around the corner and up the stairs. "Played in harmony!" His voice crescendoed back to her, "No stinky fights!"

For an hour after lunch Faith read of Tom Sawyer's doings, enjoyed the wide-eyed entranced audience as Cheesecake and Jashu were transported to the Midwest of long ago. Rob and Doug, more accustomed to the family read-alouds, noiselessly maneuvered tiny boats and cars through imaginary canals and roadways.

At two o'clock Faith resumed the needs of baby Don, then it was time for the laundry stint, take it down, fold it, put it away; check the stock and begin preparations for the boys' evening meal.

Summer was almost over, Faith reflected. Still hot and the hint of autumn in the air rather than the temperature. One more week of August, then school for Rob. A nice long winter in which to hibernate. Hibernate! The very idea intrigued her. Summer had been fun, but it surely was busy, with no vacant moments.

It would be extremly quiet when the city boys left. She would miss them. She had not always realized how noisy they were. Contemplating their return to the crowded household from which they came and their inadequate meals, she felt remorseful. Could three-plus weeks in the country achieve any lasting good, she wondered?

In a way John's and her gift backfired. They meant well by giving a vacation to a couple of city urchins. But these fellows had given so much to the Wellses! Their appreciation and unreserved, uninhibited joy! Who is it says 'what you give away you have forever'? Yes, that is truth. One can't give without receiving a greater inflow of good.

Jesus' divine admonition of 'give and it shall be given unto you.' Simple as that. Just *give*. Anything! Everything! Launch your ships. Keep launching them. They'll return to the docks. The only concern should be to keep sending them out, fully loaded with love-wisdom. The world is wrong in its teaching to save for a rainy day. The divine teaching is to put God and the things of God first, then all else falls into right proportion.

Well, she, Faith Sanford Wells, was wondrously thankful for this farm and the glorious opportunity to work with this divine law, the chance to know God more intimately—to make up for the "lost years," the years she was materialistic . . . in fact, she was now a bit like Jed, letting God do things through her.

Truly that was it . . . letting God do the chores through her. Everyone who had trekked out since spring remarked she looked different somehow. Where once she was a mortal Atlas with the weight of the world across her shoulders, intellectually battling the family problems, stewing about the affairs of the world, now she too wore the Christ yoke, letting God work through her. Life was revolutionized! Meekly she realized she had not personally helped the Hottentots—or whoever—but then fussing about them as formerly had not helped either. At least, now, she was helpful to her immediate world, and the perimeter of her sphere of influence was extending.

Not everyone wanted the same gift. A sadness appeared in her eyes as she thought of her friends' reactions. When she tried to tell of the magic of tithing, its results with the cockrels; when she tried to tell about the Power that helped upend the one-hundred pound chicken feedbags into metal bins while John was on the road and she was great with child. . . . the incredulous, disbelieving expression on their faces! They thought her crazy. She wasn't bragging about tithing. She was marvelling about God's mysterious ways, and in her discovery she wanted to share this . . . this security! . . . with those she loved. And they didn't want it.

And once the custom farmer, commenting about the lushness of their crops and the color of their wheat compared to his, prodded her testimonial, "We bless our crops, pray over them." He had gasped, "Why you don't even go to church!" Then he had gunned up his tractor and taken off as though it were the greatest piece of heresy!

What she tried to do was to give of this foolproof formula.

Well. . . .

Probably the saddest episode in the whole Bible, Faith thought, is the scene of Jesus on the cliff overlooking Jerusalem, aching because He had so much to give—and they didn't want it. A little like a salesman who has a miracle for an inexpensive price that he wants to sell to everyone, and so few wish to buy.

Aura interrupted, suggested Faith check on the pigs. Hefting the bulging basket Faith lugged it into the dining room, continued on through the house to the side door by the driveway.

181

Yes, they were out. John had improvised and improvised on their fencing. They were most adept at lifting it, obtaining freedom.

Still in a philosophic mood, Faith returned to the kitchen for her broom. Her gentle persuader. The broom bristles on their buttocks urged them without hurting them. In light of experience with pigs, she now thoroughly understood the old fashioned term "pig-headed." In fact, handling the various stock she comprehended much. Certainly "separate the sheep from the goats" is a most graphic phrase now that Garry was with them. As to the pigs, they were highly intelligent. She knew they remembered precisely their exit. When she chased them, they deliberately swooped past it, gave her a real run, antagonized and infuriated her.

She grinned a little to herself en route through the house for that broom, remembering their first week on the farm. One of those little rolypolies, weighing at most twenty-five pounds, outnosed a full-grown sheep, at least a hundred-fifty. Piggie backed the ewe right into the barn, stole her food, then waddled to the spring grunting triumphantly all the way!

At the kitchen closet Faith paused. No broom. Probably John or one of the boys borrowed it. Well, John was in the office in Newark and the boys sounded as though they were in the hayfield. Usually she was annoyed when something was not replaced. This time she strolled to the side door, out to the pigs again. Their heads remained down, but she knew they were aware of her presence. Beside Winky, the boar, she spoke in a conversational tone, "I haven't got my gentle persuader this time, so I shall appeal to the divinity within reach of you. . . . You must have some, for you are alive and God is life."

Winky tried to rub against her, grunting the while. He was big now. His friendly gesture could send her sprawling. Faith patted his rump as she sidestepped the gesture. "Go on now, divine piglets. Into the barn with you."

Nancy moved toward the barn first. Winky followed. Ambling to the spot of fencing under which they scrunched, Nancy lifted it efficiently, flattened herself under it, waddled right into the barn. Winky followed.

Mouth agape Faith remained at the lilacs. She was there when the boys hollered their way down the hillside to her presence. In wonderment she briefed them on the episode, ending with, "If you've ever seen how many times I've raced after the blooming things, getting so angry and steamed up. . . . Maybe that's it," wonderment in her voice. "I wasn't mad . . . and I called forth divinity, didn't I?" She talked more to herself than to the boys, analysis aloud in mental transit. "That's it! First control yourself, and then you have dominion over animals and conditions."

Reflectively Faith walked into the house, mentally reviewing the many times she chased the pigs. The time she ran after Nancy, up and down the hilliness of the pasture while Nancy danced in and out among the sheep. She saw herself finally catching hold of that silly curly tail, holding on with all her strength, Nancy squealing and pulling valiantly to both retain her tail and elude her captor, all while Faith sat on the hillside gasping for breath, her long legs extended before her. Or the many times she dashed up the road to recorral those thriving pigs. All this before she discovered the art of the broom and its persuasive powers. Now, in her patience she discovered this greater power, the appeal to indwelling divinity in all degrees and levels of the universe.

As John stepped out of the car that evening four boys raced as one. In a swoop of excited talk, the whole day's activities were telescoped into one singing chorus while they bounced and jiggled on bare toes in the dirt floor of the wagon house. "We played in harmony! We played in harmony!" was their theme song.

"Did you now?" chuckled John. "That's fine." He patted their pates or put his hand on bare browned shoulders, listening to their enthusiasms. Then good naturedly he sent them forth with a friendly, "Did you save me any dinner?"

Noisy assurances floated to him as the foursome zoomed away at their play, and smiling to himself John approached the house. "How'd it go?" as he kissed Faith.

"Rugged for a while—but fun," laughingly uptilting her face. "What's the 'harmony' bit?"

While dishing up their dinner she briefed him and they enjoyed a hearty laugh. They bowed their heads for grace, then enjoyed a leisurely dinner together. The pig story, however, she saved. Part of her was still too awed at the spiritual discovery of the truth that 'he who controlleth himself is greater than he who taketh a city.' Although she shared it with the children, it was a verbal reflex, a thinking aloud process. Now she was before the altar and worshipping.

183

All of Faith's activities that week revolved around the return of the city boys to their home that Thursday. Seeing the sparkle in their eyes, aware of their healthier endurance and bounce were almost tangible rewards of the Wells' expenditure of time and energy.

Wednesday was a day to top all days! John suggested he remain in the city overnight so that Faith and the children could have the car to meet their train Thursday morning from the Gladstone station. That meant Wednesday morning they had to take John to Gladstone. Then eighteen-plus miles back again. Then: the laundry, shoe shining; an extra batch of Don's formula so that Mary Banners could care for him the following day. On and on the day's activities went, for she wished to send the boys home with everything clean and ironed.

Mary appeared at the front door Wednesday night at bath time. Faith called down, "Ever hear of the Ford assembly line? Well, we've got the bath assembly line. Come on up. I'll wash. You dry."

Hardly any conversation throughout the baths. They took the boys in chronological order, youngest first, oldest last. Four-year-old Doug's instant comment, "Hey, her dries yuh real good. Me not sticky."

Mary giggled her appreciation, "That's my nursing training showing up, Doug."

The boys abed, Faith and Mary enjoyed coffee together while Faith briefed Mary on Don's needs for the following day. "If Don grunts while sleeping and tries to twist, he wants to be rolled over. When you do it, he'll heave a sigh and pretend he achieved it all by himself."

Mary's eyes danced with glee.

"The banana for his supper may seem pretty large to you for an eleven-week-old baby, but he'll use all of it plus a full bottle. When you see what he eats you'll be glad to return him." Giggling with Mary, "Every night our prayer is 'Thank You, God, for the farm.'"

Mary's enjoyment spilled over into full laughter.

Then Mary was off, up the road with Don's formula and his Thursday's clothes, and Faith was left with four basketfuls of laundry to be folded, their suitcase to be packed, and her personal needs before closing her eyes on that full day.

184

Up before the whole east was light, caring for Don, choring the stock, awakening the boys and getting a hearty breakfast of fruit, scrambled eggs and ham, toast with jam and plenty of milk. A last glance around at the four faces before take-off time. Only two faces required egg wipings.

Stoically they watched. No answering smiles. No empathic enthusiasms. Wish we could keep them forever, she thought, picking up the padded washbasket full of Don. Wonder what's wrong with them? They're so quiet. Perhaps it's the early hour. Guess they were stinted an hour's sleep.

They single filed behind her to the black Studebaker, each one toting a package. Sliding Don in the car Faith suppressed a giggle. Coming toward her they looked like a humanized version of ducks following the leader. Settling into the seat and adjusting her skirt, running her right hand expertly around the nape of her neck, her gesture as well as her schedule triggered something in her memory, Lulu's telling someone Faith was "like an old maid school teacher." Lulu's words were graphic, Faith acknowledged to herself, for she was plain. But today, today she was glamorized. John would be pleased, would beam his warm approval when they met him that evening after the city boys were home and just Rob, Doug and she would be awaiting John at the Newark station. She smoothed her black faille skirt, poked in her white dainty nylon blouse—a little on the frilly side for her. Glancing in the little mirror even the lipstick was applied already. Her feet were trimly shod in high heeled pumps, no comfortable running shoes today.

Mary waited by her garage to accept the washbasketful of Don, and they were off, Faith headed toward Woodglen, the Dippsydoodle Road, on to Califon and Gladstone.

Silence in the backseat.

"Cheese and Jash, this used to be an old waterway. The roadbed dips are former rapids. When it dried up they made a road but they didn't level it off. It may have been a waterway for a grist mill. There are many in the area. Rob and Doug called this the 'Dippsydoodle Road.'"

Receptive silence, then a spurt from Cheesecake, "Lemme see if I got that straight. This used to be waterfalls and the water went away and they made it a road?"

"That's right."

185

A snort of an answer.

Miles of silence, up and down the Califon mountains.

"Hay! I'm deaf!" a scared shout from Cheesecake.

"Just swallow," Faith's calm suggestion.

"Ain't got nuttin' to swallow."

"Swallow the wetness in your mouth."

A pause. "It woiks!" in shrill surprise.

Faith smiled slightly to herself. In this last bit of togetherness she didn't object to the pure Brooklynese.

No further conversation. From time to time she glanced at the boys in the rearview mirror. They looked all right. Not really even sleepy. But this was surely strange behavior. They had chatted constantly on the farm. Sometimes she was more weary of the constancy of their talk than of the physical demands on her in the way of food preparation and laundry. Sometimes she had found herself hushing them with, "For goodness sake, I can't think you're so noisy."

In the train she settled comfortably. The boys paired themselves off, the younger two sitting across the aisle, the older two directly in front of her. This was her day. She would not even contemplate the unmade beds nor the sinkful of breakfast dishes. After all the city boys wouldn't need their beds that night and she had done a quickie on Rob's and Doug's.

She could relax, for she had forgotten nothing. Their toothbrushes were packed. Each little city man had something special from the farm—a couple jars of homemade peach jam and a large bag of freshly picked garden beets they had loved so thoroughly. The conversation from the elderly couple drifted her way; they were betting between themselves as to which were her children. Naively she wondered how they guessed all four were not hers.

A lengthy stop at Basking Ridge. Faith arose from her reverie to glance out the window. Across the field a conductor ran toward a little cottage several thousand feet from the tracks. It looked like a couple cartons of eggs were under one arm and his other hand reinforced the position of the precious cargo. Apparently it was a personal express delivery. Faith enjoyed the touch of hickiness. No one else seemed to notice.

In New York they taxied to the Tribune office amid the blare of city traffic. The country boys eyed everything. The Warwenski boys stared stonily ahead. Faith looked sharply at them again. What in the world bothered them! They had not missed that much sleep. As she watched, Cheesecake emitted a huge sigh, and in a strained tight monotone said, "Wouldn't you like to come visit us now?"

Why, bless his heart. This was from his own wonderful self for no mail had come to him from home suggesting this touch. "Thank you, Cheese. We would like to—but not today, Honey. May we have a 'sunshine check'?"

He questioned with his eyes.

"Well, it isn't raining so we can't have a 'raincheck'." She smiled. "We'll take a sunshine check."

Not even a glimmer in his eloquent eyes.

The smell of printing ink permeated the whole Trib building. Miss Allen tried conversation with the boys. Only polite monosyllables at best or silent headshakings. Tactfully she turned toward her desk, "We'll have to find someone to take them home."

"I'll do that," a deep voice boomed behind Faith.

"Who are you?" coolly from Miss Allen.

"Their father," with a nod toward the Warwenski boys.

Faith glanced at the boys for verification. What ailed them? Why didn't they fling themselves upon him with happy shouts. They greeted John that way every night.

As though pulled by puppet strings of filiation Cheesecake and Jashu moved stiffly to his side. No exuberance. No joy. They were solemn. The formerly verbose Jashu drew in a long breath, expelling it slowly with weak words, "Pop, we caught frogs . . . butterflies . . . saw bees and sheeps . . . and chickens . . . and pigs . . . and Mr. Whiskers . . . and. . . ." He had made a tremendous effort. He stopped abruptly, returned to the bench against the wall, sat in silence. Cheesecake joined him, having made no comment at all.

Faith looked from one boy to the other. She felt keen sympathy for Mr. Warwenski. Seeking to cover their lack of affection, she smilingly extended her hand. "They were up pretty early this morning, you know, and we've had a long trip. Probably they're quite weary."

Mr. Warwenski shook her proffered hand, then silently urged the boys into the hallway and stepped out after them. One hand

187

on the doorknob he paused and smiled at Faith, "I guess I ought to thank you for all you did. I'm sure they had a fine vacation."

"That's all right," answered Faith. "Thank you for loaning them to us. I hope you'll loan them against next year."

He nodded appreciation of her invitation. The door closed after them.

My, it was quiet on the farm the day after. Catching up on the laundry was as prodigious as the day before the trip. Six loads spun around in the Maytag. Faith had to wait for some of the laundry to dry before she could hang up the last of it. Even at that she had some sheets at right angles instead of parallel.

Rob and Doug seemed to settle down to their former routine of play, and during her busyness Faith reflected on the many tender episodes with the city boys. That gem of a conversation between Cheesecake and Kim while she orange-juiced Don under the tree. Little tooth-gaping Jashu and his holding to the story of grandpa and his one liver. And, perhaps best of all was the played-in-harmony-no-stinky fights. She laughed to herself.

Somehow the project had grown far beyond their hopes. In the spring it seemed mostly a good stewardship matter with the overtones of physical tithing, and some play material importation for their boys. It had grown into personal fun. John had truly enjoyed them. They had done a world of good for John too, mitigating the city pressures.

She loved them. Cheesecake and Jashu. It had not been totally work for her. The boys were truly a love project. Some lines of memorized poetry welled up within herself. "He who gives himself feeds three: himself, his hungering neighbor, and Me." She idly wondered who wrote those lines. Wasn't it a true idea?

The welling up of those lines from subconsciousness was good, for it led to another memory. A time when she and John doubledated back in the early years of their marriage. Jo and Tom. It was only a movie date and then they all went off for hot pastrami and coffee to the Jewish section of town. Jo and Tom were both teachers, a bit older than Faith and John. Now, many years later, she couldn't remember what triggered the seriousness of their conversation that night over the Jewish sandwiches, but she could hear Jo ask, "What do you kids really want to do in life?" John had remained silent and Faith had answered, rather wistfully, "I'd love to work with kids. Other people's. Not just our

188

own." She recalled John's enthusiasm and remembered Jo's follow-through with "How?" Their dreams were nebulous. . . .

"This is it!" Aura whispered.

Faith paused. Suddenly every fiber of her being was alive! Radiantly. Ecstatically. This *is* it! she shouted. The very world must have acclaimed the truth. This is the beloved third crop Jed predicted would come through the Lord's guidance.

John would label this a natural. John with his years of working with Boy Scouts. And was there a child anywhere who didn't love John? John was like Lulu, a regular Pied Piper with children! For herself she loved children. She didn't care if she knew their parents or what background they came from, nor what skin color they happened to be wearing.

They wouldn't have a camp. That's too regimented. A large family. A farm summer home. Not an institution. A family. A farm family. Where city children, rich ones and those not so materially favored, could learn the wonders of country living, animals, rural harmony.

A smile crept to her lips. Would that word "harmony" ever reduce itself to mere dictionary definition? Forevermore it would be colored with overtones of "we done it, ma; we done it. No stinky fights!"

That was the crux of it, of course. This could be their contribution toward peace in the world. Building up the ability among many types of children to live and play in harmony. Each little bit would help. If she and John mixed it up internationally and interracially—had little Chinese, little Negroes, little Catholics, little Jews, little Protestants— why there's no telling where interfaith and international harmonies could travel!

The day whizzed. While her hands were busy with practicalities, her mind was busy with dreams and plans of a newer and bigger project. Late in the evening, with all the children in bed, she made up the next day's formula and eagerly awaited John's homecoming. She must remember to hold her ideas in check, give him a chance to talk about his day. Surely once she "had the floor" she would really hog it.

She stepped out the kitchen door, away from its light, looking up at the infinity of stars. All the milky way appeared in its glory. Only the droning song of the katydids stirred the quietness. The grass under foot was dew-drenched. In the garden

189

immediately off the kitchen, where a ray of light caught it, a spangled spider web, diamond drops of dew glistening on its strands, gave her delight. Truly God had led them to fulfillment! How could she ever thank Him enough!

She reflected too on Mary Banners' comment one day. Enthusiastically Mary ejaculated, "Faith, I believe you've been sent to Red Mill especially to help me."

She rejected Mary's remark that day, secretly thought it a trifle sacrilegious. Now she looked at it anew, sweepingly could understand the role an individual plays in God's realm—that each of us is a sphere of influence on others in each one's world. And each should be our brother's keeper in this sense, this sense of spiritual-mental helpfulness.

Yes, truly both she and John were increasingly aware of a growing divine purpose. She was most conscious of spiritual unfoldment. Not that she had arrived. One never has. One must remain meek and humble, teachable by Spirit. But in her heart she knew both she and John were new people, born anew since the Chatham days of their lives.

She returned to the kitchen to put the kettle on. John ought to be about at Woodglen now. She selected one of her prettiest plates too, this was an occasion. The plate with the red and yellow tulips, the bone china plate Auntie brought from Canada. As she reached for the cups and saucers the little black Studebaker crunched on the driveway.

Walking out to meet John her heart pounded with excitement. She must hold this enthusiasm in check, not usurp the whole evening. They met under the lilacs and stars, kissed warmly and together strolled to the kitchen doorway. John was weary. It had been unbearably hot in the city, August's last fling. One of the little stenos in the office fainted from the heat. He finished, routinely asked, "Anything special in your day, dear?"

She picked up the coffeepot, cups and saucers and threaded her way through the dining room darkness to the living room. Casually, "Had a wonderful idea. Can hardly wait to tell you. I've been so busy with it I don't recall what I gave the youngsters or myself for dinner. I must have fed them, for they're all sleeping."

John laughed, "If you don't remember what you ate either it must be quite an idea."

Settled in the big green leather chairs opposite the fern-filled fireplace Faith picked up the thread from the past, the double-date with Jo and Tom. She omitted Aura's suggestion; that would be a little too much mysticism for John. "This is our beloved third crop, John! Children handicapped by city living. Children who might not know the riches of farm living or country life. Not a camp. Not just a farm. Rather a farm family. A big farm family. We can fill their bodies with good food, their senses with the joys of rural living and appreciation of animals and crops. A way of life. . . . And," dreamily, "perhaps by taking all kinds, strata of society and backgrounds, we can plant many seeds for world peace and tolerance. We can always have Fresh Aires as our tithe arrangement between the Lord and us, always ten percent of our paying guests.

"We can plant truthseeds in their hearts and minds, Honey. So they learn to walk and work with God—like Jed and us. Let's specialize in teenagers when Rob and Doug get there. Around a campfire at night is a magical time to sow rich God seeds!"

In the beginning her words poured forth with a rush. Her eyes were a hallowed glow in a radiant face. "I don't know a name yet, but that will come in time. We'll ask the Lord for the right name."

John paced the floor in his excitement. "I like it, Faith! Especially when I can be here all the time. When we get this farm into a going business—sheep and chickens."

"It might be a slow start," Faith acknowledged. "I don't know how we go about beginning. Do you suppose we could handle up to fifty youngsters without losing the personal touch?"

"Fifty?" John echoed, pausing in his strides. "Fifty? Sounds a bit steep, but it would depend on their ages. Let's begin with ten and see how that goes. We can begin with youngsters our lads' ages and work up to the teenagers."

John was at the north window. He was thinking of the winter night when he invited Pierre to look up at the apple orchard with him. Faith joined him and he brought her to himself gently. "There's always a breeze up here. Excellent for kites, you know. I suppose some city boys have never had a chance with a kite.

"Faith, we can fix up the wagon house for a dormitory. And that field," pointing to the west one, "can be converted into pasture when we're at the peak on sheep. It can be a playfield for

191

ballgames during some of the summer without injury to the pasture."

It was John's turn to romp with plans.

"We can fix up the cellar under the playroom to be a laundry for a battery of automatic washers. That would be an additional facility the families could count on. And a way of giving full measure."

They moved away from the window. "When do you think we can start?" John continued.

"What's the matter with next summer?"

"I thought we were planning Quota for then?"

She laughed, "I never saw having a baby retard my progress any, did you?"

"No," John joined her laughter. "It doesn't seem to."

Imaginatively John bulldozed a lake back in the hollow beyond the north field, up on Christmas Tree Hill where acres were given to the growth of loblolly pines. Atop that hill would be an excellent site for a log cabin when they were at peak performance on this project!

Eventually ideas and conversation petered out, their full days required the balance of sleep. Rambling off toward bed Faith reiterated her concern about the city boys' quietness all the long miles to New York. "They didn't act as though they were afraid of their dad. But they were so clammed up. They seemed under some kind of strain. I can't believe it was merely the hour's sleep they missed."

"I wouldn't worry about it. I doubt if they wanted to go home, for one thing. I think at heart every child enjoys the freedom country living affords."

" 'Warwenski—Cheesecake',", Faith intoned. "I still can't hear how they are supposed to sound alike."

John laughed shortly. "Me neither."

Monday's mail brought a bread-and-butter from Mrs. Warwenski:

"Dear Mrs. Wells,

"Thank you so much for the wonderful vacation you gave our sons. They have done nothing but talk of the farm and Dad and Mom Wells since they got back. Except when they talk of your boys, your baby, the sheep or Garry. You must be wonderful people to give them such a good time.

192

"They were so quiet when they first got home. After the second day of it I finally asked Robert are you sick? Do you need a doctor? What's the matter with you? Do you know what he said? It's so noisy here I can't think!

"Thank you again, and God bless you both. How I hesitated to send them and how wonderfully it turned out. God bless you all.

Sincerely,

Rosemary Warwenski"

Faith put the letter down and laughed until the tears streamed down her cheeks. "So noisy I can't think!" My very words. I wonder how much of their speech shows Brooklyn and how much Red Mill. Now they miss the crickets and not the trolley cars.

Dear little fellows. God bless them, and bring them back next year.

She sat in radiant happiness, holding the letter in her hand a long time, reflecting on the city visitors who so unknowingly directed them to one of the greatest projects of their lives, the beloved third crop.

"Dear Father," she whispered, "it is true 'he who gives himself feeds three, himself, his hungering neighbor and Me.'

"We received so much more than we gave—although smugly I thought we were giving an awful lot.

"Thank you, God, for the good gifts we continually receive, and bless the good gifts we are privileged to give."

Autumn

Almost imperceptibly autumn came. Careful observance expected it before the first hoar frost. Spiders intruded, determinedly spun webs in the house. Crickets appeared indoors, not only on the hearth but anywhere they could winter-up. Theirs the lone voice within for the nocturnal chorus outside quieted completely.

Days commenced and ended with spanking crispness and clean fragrances. The air was exhilarating. With the first hard frost, killing summer flowers and the produce garden, autumn splashed reds among the evergreens of the hills. As nightly frosts became the pattern, the hills' colors deepened, orange shades, yellows, even red-purples touching the designs. Exotic splattered carpet effects covered the Wells' lawn as the heat and busyness of the summer vanished. Week by week the design underfoot faded to leached browns, rustling musically as young lads ran through the fallen leaves or raked them into piles for jumping purposes.

Seasons were fulfilled. Hens laid eggs, noisily bragging of their accomplishment. After many weeks of cold nights, corn would be harvested, the cold temperatures evaporating the moisture, hardening the kernels. "Very good harvest considerin'," commented the farmers.

Considering the drought, they meant. "Very good," Faith reiterated. "Indeed very good! God pays handsomely for this sharing of His wealth, this taking Him into active partnership!

"The world is wrong. One doesn't attain wealth by saving and scrimping. By giving and giving—in wisdom and love. By giving as He guides. Not charity of baskets at Thanksgiving or Christmas or outgrown clothes. That also, of course, but rather the kind of giving that inspires people to lift themselves. Incentive giving. Gifts that are enwrapped, permeated, with universal love and divine wisdom shall never hold one in bondage. The law of truth is 'give and it shall be given unto you, good measure, pressed down, shaken together.' But the 'give' comes before the 'given unto'."

So she thought and the musical theme "very good" revolved in her mind. With it a recurrent idea wove itself into the fabric of

194

her thinking like a small babe squallingly insistent. Like the tiny babe. But more like the blending of harmonies, the way a musician takes two melodies, interblending them. Slowly in Faith's consciousness one melodic theme predominated as the other lessened, established itself as harmonic background, foregoing personal identity.

The theme crescendoed in Faith's mind and heart one day as she maneuvered the wheelbarrow from the barn to the garden. Spilling the "barn gold" onto the garden, she was suddenly aware that the thought was thinking itself through her. She had not chosen the thought. She had not looked about with cold intellectual detachment for an affirmation to use in building the new consciousness like the quotations she tacked above the kitchen sink or sometimes wore on a slip of paper under her watchband. These words were running through her whole being as harmony weaves through the order of the spheres. These were welling up within her, gathering momentum and radiance with each passing day. Supplying new meanings. These were divine whispers as when Aura communicated.

"Bring ye the whole tithe into the storehouse and prove Me now, herewith . . . if I will not open you the windows of heaven and pour you out a blessing that there shall not be room enough to receive it. . . . And I will rebuke the devourer for your sakes and he shall not destroy the fruits of your ground. Neither shall your vine cast its fruit before the time in the field. . . . And all nations shall call you happy for ye shall be a delightsome land. . . ."

She did not know the origin of these words. But atingle with zealous understanding, she let the words sing themselves through her again and again as though standing under a perfectly tempered shower. As she let them wash over her, various phrases accentuated her understanding, "Bring ye the *whole* tithe . . . Prove Me *now* . . . *herewith* . . . *Prove* Me . . . Prove *Me* . . . *herewith* . . . *herewith* . . ." with that which you have right now. . . .

WHY NOT?

According to appearances they were behind in accounts payable, and Itchy's big drinks would increase with the colder season. The manila folder of bills would fatten before the investment harvest. But the date for that was almost ready, she reminded herself. Faith's heart knew all would work out in accordance with God's plan, and "God's plan is always good!" she affirmed steadily.

In Faith's mind, however, there was a lag that debated and reasoned, looked fearfully at the appearances, weighed them. The kerosene as fuel instead of oil, more expensive, less heat retention, recommended by the oil company technicians to overcome Itchy's sluggishness.

Glorious October was near. Surely, somehow they could struggle through until the end of the month, the investment harvest time. Then they could pay off the bank note taken to obtain fluid capital, and with the interest really reconvert the farm. Tithing on all income would demonstrate active faith. "Faith without works is dead," she quoted.

The first reconversion would be more stock, she planned. Wouldn't it be wonderful if they could add a hundred sheep immediately! Or even fifty? Or twenty-five?

A new stove in the kitchen! She loathed her antiquity. Well, not "loathed" for nothing good comes from the emotion of hate, not even when directed to an inanimate object. But surely she didn't enjoy using it, the old antiquity!

A cemented cellar. No more dank smelliness after two or three days of continuous rain.

And screens/storm windows—remembering last winter's icy blasts through cracks as well as the bat episode of the humid summer nights. True, John had filled in all visible cracks, and the exterior paint job eliminated the porous quality of the old clapboards. Modern windows would finalize the whole package, preclude any more of those drafts that swayed the curtains winter nights. They were a necessity, not mere nicety.

She smiled dreamily—and the beloved third crop. The summer farm home for city children. That would take much capital. Beds, sheets, summer blankets. More play equipment. Perhaps a couple of horses. Reconditioning the wagon house.

Too, John required a tractor as well as an extension on the barn, sheep loafing shelter, he called it. A larger hennery. After all, they purchased the farm to go into the chicken business and seemed to be sidetracking into sheep and children!

A hothouse for Faith.

And . . . and . . . and . . .

More stock!

Here was something positive. Why not—acting metaphysically —since one's faith should be supported by one's acts—write Mr. Dan, asking prices and a possible delivery date for late October? That would give her all the facts, ready for the right moment when their investment harvest check arrived in the mail.

Yes, now they would tithe on everything, even John's salary commencing that very payday. In spite of appearances amid accounts payable, they would tithe. This was Faith's divine order. The words wouldn't have sung themselves through her if this were not Aura's guidance. Nothing, absolutely nothing, must stand in the way of her execution of divine guidance.

John? John would say, "Honey, we could go bankrupt tithing."

Intuitively she felt John was not ready to tithe on all income. John would claim it unfair to their creditors, compelling them to wait longer for funds already overdue. John was appreciative of the magic of tithing. He too witnessed its very witchery with hens and the corn harvest so abundant despite the drought. Plus the wellsprings that were abundant throughout the summer. Only the Stashis, Jed, and themselves—the only families in a wide radius—to have household water through the long, hot, dry summer. All others fetched water from Spruce Run daily for household and stock needs.

In a practical sense tithing paid. Not that one tithed to achieve success and prosperity, she hastened to add to herself. Tithing was their covenant, that's different!

Faith's divine guidance had to be obeyed. John need not know. During the war years, when John worked eighteen hours daily, he gave Faith all his salary—as well as all the responsibilities. He never withdrew that authority. Faith was family exchequer, hers the financial juggle each payday between income and outgo.

At the right time her Lord would direct her to tell John—or He would tell John Himself. Here she was limiting Spirit, forgetting God works through everyone, not just Faith Sanford Wells.

Never in their married life had she been underhanded with John—except about the Fresh Aires, she admitted, and she was rather highhanded about that. She smiled. This trying to live one's religious ideals to the highest understanding is upsetting. One learns to junk much. Putting God first means even before a husband, children, or parents. But it is always a blessing to all.

197

To be honest with God does not abrogate the law of honesty with people.

The initial tithe day was fabulous! Even the weather was unusually clear and sparkling for the middle of September. Faith felt the warm, powerful influx of spiritual substance as she set down the week's groceries on the kitchen table before stowing them away in cabinets, refrigerator or freezer. Right at that very moment, the full tithe check was somewhere on a train, rushing along with other mail to the advancement of God's work as He suggested. This was intangible, practical, and a deed executed in love. This is a 'second coming of Christ,' the individual awakening in the heart-mind of the soul self.

Now were the Wellses substantially part of His program, knowing God fully as prosperity as well as Life and Health, Harmony and Peace. Prosperity that is constant, abundant. God as co-creator for every moment, not merely in the beginning or as Something to worship on Sundays. God as All-in-All, pouring His ideas into the mind of man, bestowing understanding and the ability to work with His ideas. Surely this warm, comfortable feeling that engulfed her was the faith substance of the storehouse. She was heady with joy. Her whole being felt permeated, drenched with faith and strength, divine love and wisdom—the foursquare of the universe. Surely this was the firm foundation, the house builded on shiftless rocks. Surely this is the only pathway to spiritualized wealth—Christ consciousness of wealth—even though this would be as 'the widow's mite,' truly of their living, vitally needed.

Tremendous waves of happiness washed over her. Now He was truly their Senior Partner. On the payroll, so to speak. Nothing could go wrong. This was like insurance. Better than insurance! Insurance is negative, fence straddling, paying for something one hopes won't happen.

Taking God into business is a *guarantee!* Real security.

At the zenith of Christ consciousness a metaphysician knows how to dissolve old errors, the tares in the wheat field growing in the subconsciousness so that only the good crops produce. During unfoldment, before one attains this understanding and power, there is a time the tares grow with the wheat. They can be cleaned out only by burning at harvest time. It is a matter of spiritual chemistry as well as soul growth.

Some of the Wells' tares manifested as termites' work one morning during the autumn before the investment harvest. The termites did their work in the dark silence many years before Faith went through the kitchen flooring, her ankle gripped by jagged wood. John ran to her aid, freed her carefully from the imprisonment of the splintering spurs. Improvising he placed half the ping pong table over the hole.

Another substantial bill for floor repairs; the underpinnings required replacement and this was beyond John's improvisations.

Bathroom plumbing revolted too before September finished its time, necessitating the septic tank man. Under a kind of grace, he came immediately and the Wells were hardly inconvenienced. In his wake, another huge bill for the septic tank cleaning as well as the dry well he recommended be dug across the road. And no liquid funds with which to pay the bill. Just the blessedness of knowing the investment harvest was closer with each day's passing.

One glorious day as September slid into October Mr. Dan appeared at the side door in response to Faith's inquiry. The day was exhilaratingly alive and fresh. Colorful leaves danced zestfully on the trees, and the constantly shifting splashes of color in the hills delighted the eye of anyone who paused long enough to watch. The very countryside seemed to be singing holy alleluias.

Mr. Dan, hat in hand in the doorway, was the epitome of kindness and tact. He cleared his throat a little self-consciously, "I got your letter, Mrs. Wells, and thought I'd stop by while in the vicinity." Faith refrained from smiling, knowing he came down from the Allamuchy section and could hardly be just in the vicinity. "You know, sometimes folks get started with sheep and they get them from us by the truckload, then along comes a little hard luck and they want to get rid of the whole kaboodle." His eyes besought her acceptance of his guidance. "They don't always get their money out . . . Maybe if I see your sheep I can make some suggestions, save your going through that."

Faith loved him. Why, bless his wonderfulness. He really is like the Biblical shepherds! Not only does he care about the sheep no longer his—as in the spring when he refused to bring them until assured there was a shed for them—but also now mindful of the customers' problems.

199

"They're up in the first east field," she smiled. "Want to come see them?"

Together they crunched up the driveway, stepped through the gate, headed for the field. Part of her mind listened to Mr. Dan's further conversation, part wondered how she could get the sheep down. At that hour they were well back in the eleven acres. It seemed needless for Mr. Dan and herself to walk the distance. The sheep could cover the hilly terrain much more capably. She wondered how Mr. Dan called his sheep, only he was manager of a large farm corporation, probably had lots of farm labor. She recalled the time the Banners and they went to one of the sheep farms in Lebanon. That farmer had stepped to the fence and called 'here, sheep.' He felt very foolish about it. His sheep didn't come either. Must have been either his hired man chored them or that he normally used another kind of call.

Her sheep would come to a lusty baa-a-a. Helene's head would go up first, then Helene would trot toward Faith's voice, and all the others would follow. No matter where they were they came to her. Beautiful Helene, the leader of the whole group. She would feel a little ridiculous baaing for them. But that was the call they knew and obeyed. At the top of the incline, where the barn pasture meets the first east field, beads of perspiration stood on Mr. Dan's forehead. Those drops convinced Faith she must call the sheep, even if she were to feel foolish. Well along in his seventies, Mr. Dan stood moping his brow, his white hair ruffled by the breeze.

Faith made a pretty picture standing tall and slender on the hillside, her colorful dress billowing a bit behind her, wisps of brown hair moving about her face. She wasn't beautiful in the glamorous sense. Rather it was her healthiness, her vitality, an inner harmony permeating her being and radiating from her very pores to establish her prettiness. It was something in the sparkle of her eyes and the glow of her rosy wholesomeness.

Removing her hands from her pockets, cupping them around her mouth, she gave forth a lusty, deep-toned baa-a-a-a. From the tail of her eye she saw his startled expression and she suppressed the desire to giggle. Standing on tiptoe she could barely see Helene rise from where they all rested in the shade at the far hedgerow. She called again, her baa-ing note carrying on the breeze. Helene answered. Mr. Dan turned slightly, smiled an aside.

Slowly the other sheep arose. Faith encouraged them by one more call. Several voices answered. They started toward her voice, following Helene, gained momentum, rolling toward Mr. Dan and herself with a beautiful graceful rhythm. As they neared, Mr. Dan involuntarily gasped and Faith looked askance. Quickly he commented, "They look fine!"

The sheep stopped before Faith, milling about her. Helene and Bertha each nosed a hand. Mr. Dan pushed his hat back dramatically, openly stared. "They look fine. Just fine!" It was several minutes before he resumed. A few of the sheep moved to the grasses, nibbling, lifting their heads to munch while they surveyed Faith and the visitor.

"Tell me what you do to them," he thoughtfully invited. "They look better than my stock—and I've been in the sheep business all my life, forty years of sheep." He turned now, faced her. He had already noted the sheep were grazing on timothy—not much clover in it either. Apparently this was their hay field, and sheep don't usually do well on timothy. The Wellses were breaking many of the cardinal rules—yet these sheep appeared better than his.

If Faith ever required a sign, something tangible as the outpicturing of their tithe, this tribute from Mr. Dan was it. First Finestein about the cockerels. Then the custom farmers. Now Mr. Dan. Surely she was well guided to tithe on all income. In each instance they knew less than these local authorities about chickens, lands, and sheep—yet the magic occurred in the dark of the nights and in the light of the days. They witnessed no spectacular occurrence. Nothing measurable by any senses. Yet here at hand the effect of the magic, the manifestation of God's increase, appeared.

Mr. Dan pressed for an answer. Gently Faith acknowledged, "It is the Lord's work, Mr. Dan. We don't know anything special to do. We've had no husbandry experience with sheep, not even schooling."

Mr. Dan was silent. Faith wished he would ask specifically what she meant by 'Lord's work.' He didn't. Whatever her phrase conveyed to him she would never know the degree of his comprehension.

He moved to leave the field, and Faith gave Helene's ear an affectionate tug before accompanying him through the gate and down the hillside. It was such a scintillatingly clear day. That azure sky, the very breeze clear and brisk, alive. Faith felt so good, so clean, so joyous. Like a little child, that free, abandoned happiness. It was so good to be alive and healthy, to have all the Father's protection, guidance and supply, to witness His loving care, His part of the covenant.

At sixteen she thought she had to study hard, learn a great deal, push and drive herself. Now, at double that age, she merely relaxed and let God use her as a channel. True, prayer does not preclude work—God does it through us and we have to do our part, but that former stage was the old Atlas consciousness. Now, she whispered within her heart, if she were very humble and filled with a great amount of divine love-wisdom, remained clean and pure in her thoughts as well as all areas of her life, He could use her in His world.

Faith's hands found their way into her pockets again. The song in her soul was apparent in the rhythm of her stride. Mr. Dan was saying, "I see no reason you folks shouldn't invest in more stock. What you have is surely doing fine! How many were you contemplating?—And you said something about the last of October. Why not take them now? Then you have a chance to get well acquainted before they begin to lamb."

Faith was receptive to his suggestion, but in all honesty he should know they couldn't pay immediately, not for another month. Surely this too was acting in understanding faith. She didn't like to tell him about the investment harvest. That was John's and her affair. But it was good to pronounce the word of expectancy, aware of the power of the spoken word, its ability to bring things into manifestation.

Distinctly she said, "Frankly, Mr. Dan, we can't pay for perhaps a month. We are expecting . . ." She paused several moments. What was the best creative word to use? One that would conceal the investment matter from Mr. Dan yet be honest and be the most metaphysically powerful word? Her thoughts raced with the speed of light.

"Windfall," she chose. "We are expecting a windfall around the end of October, and can't pay you until then."

She heard an etheric clap. She glanced up. The sky was matchless in serenity. Odd. It had not sounded like mine blasting in Pennsylvania. Surely it wasn't thunder. The air was still exhilaratingly clear. Not a sign of a storm. Distinctly she heard a clap.

It was not her imagination. It was like recorded instructions . . . like where the Bible says 'some thought it thundered, some heard a voice say . . .'

A momentary wildness within. Was she alone too much!

"Suppose I bring them down the latter part of this week," Mr. Dan was saying. "You can pay me when it is convenient . . . You said something about Merinos in your letter. Know anything about them? They handle a little differently from the Hampshires you have. Why not take only a dozen Merinos and find out how you like them? I don't like to sell a breed unless the buyer likes it . . ."

Details completed, Mr. Dan left.

There was no recurrence of self-doubt. Rather the little song of joy rose and fell . . . Thank You, Father . . . Thank You, Father . . . Thank You, Father . . .

At dinner John remarked casually, "How long have we been tithing on my salary too?"

Faith glanced up quickly.

"Since the middle of September."

More tares in the wheatfield.

The cellar waterpump misbehaved beyond John's mechanical fix-it genius. The plumber advised its action indicated leaks in the underground line somewhere from the springhouse to the house. "A modern pump would perform more efficiently. Also, it's too near hard-frost time to lay new piping."

Amid all the items of septic tank, dry well, waterpump, termites—and the one glorious item of more stock—Itchy rumbled temperamentally and noisily. Exasperated one Saturday morning John blurted, "Gosh. We just about get caught up and something else goes bloop!"

Faith walked away. Up to the high place in the hayfield. 'Caught up!' Between the new stock now on their farm and unpaid for, and all the items of bad luck and Itchy's tremendous fuel bills now increasing in galloping proportions . . . "fuel bills higher than the monthly mortgage payments, and heaven knows that's high enough!"

'Caught up!'

The investment harvest would have to be plethora itself!

Only God's miracles could help!

203

Surely, surely she had been divinely guided to tithe on everything. The full tithe. Surely it was a divine instruction she was impelled to obey! Aura never led her astray . . . all the times Aura prompted her to check on the stock or whatever. Surely she was not prompted to this step from mere mortal selfish motives. In the honesty of her soul she loved the sheep. In a sense they meant more to her than their own children, for in the words of Gibran "the children were loaned from God" but the sheep were theirs. The sheep were her personal tutors, teaching simply and profoundly the esoteric meanings of scripture. From their very first night on the farm they gave lessons in depth.

Yes. In all inner honesty she had acted in high faith and in the light of her spiritual understanding.

Then . . . why didn't things seem to be working,

Was it her impatience? Was she subtly trying to force God to a bargain she cunningly connived?

High in the hayfield, looking to the mountain ridge of Kipp and beyond, Faith pondered what action to take. She could not talk it out with John. Right now John was still riding her apron strings of prayer faith. If her faith wobbled at the sight of mountainous bills . . . if her faith did not fully abide in spite of all the studies and her conscious rebuildings through meditation and prayer . . . if her faith wavered despite those beautiful, clear prompts from within . . .

She had to maintain faith for two!

Alone on the hillside, Faith had a vision of Jesus coming to her as she sat at the desk in the den, sitting beside her, gently asking for the folder of unpaid bills. She handed it to Him. He promptly tore it to shreds. "But we must pay them!" she protested aloud. The vision faded. His smile lingered but briefly.

Weeks slipped by before Faith understood the symbols of the vision, knew them to be indicative of the mental state she must achieve—and there abide—not run in and out of the rain. Weeks before she knew her protest to be tares in the subconsciousness, that if she gave complete attention and power only to God, the good, rather than looking at the negatives, entertaining debt fears, the demonstration would rush into view.

These were weeks of inner conflict between the mortal part of Faith and the Aura part. Not constantly, of course, but now and then like perky little cold germs. Sometimes she contended within

204

herself. Sometimes, through prayer, she gently removed the tares and diligently planted the good seeds of abiding faith and high expectations, ideas of God as All-Supply—people, bonds or investments merely channels of that supply.

There were moments of torture when she tried to balance between her active faith and her all too abiding fears. When the dogs barked or a car crunched on the driveway, part of her trembled lest it be a creditor. Realizing how quickly fear produces its offspring, she was fright compounded. Where in the spring she was strong in the Lord, able to use Principle in overcoming all fears about the unborn Don and the RH factor, debt was as the unmoveable mountain to her. Mere thought of the swelling folder of bills produced an exceedingly dry mouth and rigidity of her whole frame.

The only saving grace was the imminence of October, the investment harvest that would save them. In a subtle manner the investment harvest was becoming a false god.

Persistently Faith worked with herself. Aura teaching firmly, constantly, wondrously. The fear thoughts must be dissolved. It must be done the only perfect way, the Christ way, the way of denial, repudiation, truth. The inner cleansing of the subconscious garden, weeding out the old fears, worries and anxieties, attaining dominion and mastery over her every thought and feeling. Gently but firmly she must tell the old junk of her subconsciousness to go, washing it away as one bathes an open wound or as one pulls up a weed too near a precious seedling.

Then—going the next step, the important part for no garden remains clear of growth if the soil is good. Unless good seed is planted, more weed seeds blow in with every breeze, drop from every passing bird, or brush off the coat of every domestic animal. Unless the healing manifests itself from within outward, Faith realized, it is an imperfect healing. The scab is merely the protective covering but the deep wondrous healing takes place underneath.

So it must be in her consciousness and subconsciousness.

Truth seeds must be planted firmly, confidently, trustingly. And in praise and thanksgiving the good seeds would increase. Her prayers, her cathedral time in the living room, were the watering and cultivating of the new garden.

Truth seeds. The truth that God is continuous supply. Supply for every need. A constant blessing, for God never has to subtract from one to give more abundantly to another. Supply. Always on time, always in divine amounts, a blessing to all.

These seedlings must be nurtured in the silence of her heart, must come to be mental reflexes.

So it was that Faith sang affirmations to her own ditties or to the popular tunes of the day. Sometimes she danced to them with the broom or the vacuum, part of herself laughing at the pleasant foolishness. While her hands were busy with the physical chores of bedmaking, meal preparations, pitching hay to the beloved sheep, feeding the chickens or collecting the eggs, breadmaking, caring for the children, her mind-heart was free to work in the spiritualization of the Wells' affairs. Her soul was free to partake of the Master's words, appropriate them as spiritual food. Digest them. Relish all their substance and essence. Daily Faith deliberately built the new consciousness. When John came home nights she was able to meet him, serene and smiling.

Day by day her inner garden became a place of greater beauty and joy, of stauncher faith, strength, and courage.

There was much outer good too that came to them that autumn. Good that appeared more than health for all the family and the growing baby, for 'Quota' was definitely scheduled. More than the fine condition of all the stock. More than bargains in the grocery store. Good that slipped in as a little friendly pup.

He was Faith's good luck omen, arriving as he did out of the blue. The boys named him Pal. Faith fed him. The children loved him. Black and white, a huge black patch on one eye and a much too long tail, he was mostly 'pure dog' with a heavy strain of fox terrier. He was patient with the boys, permitting Don to poke a chubby finger in his eye and Doug to experimentally thrust an inquiring arm down his throat while he juggled his tongue and teeth to keep the young arm safe.

Pal's one erroneous delight was to chase the sheep. Barking and laughing, running behind them, they fled terrorized in a packed herd. Pal enjoyed it immensely. Faith reproved him. Gaily he wagged his tail, explaining, "But it's such fun and they're pretty stupid to behave like that."

Caught again in the act Faith corralled him, depriving him of liberty as one would a mischievous child. "You must not do it,

Pal. They are pregnant and it isn't fun to run or be so scared when one is pregnant."

Pal had a Houdini complex, freeing himself from every halter or contraption Faith concocted. Shortly he rushed the sheep again with complete hilarity. It seemed impossible to teach the sheep a sense of humor. The only recourse was to train the dog.

And the dog defied training.

Pal broke collars guaranteed unbreakable. Pal slipped out of a knot or chewed it. In desperation Faith called the Humane Society in Washington and gave Pal away, explaining to the boys he would not be destroyed but that a good city home away from farm stock would be found for him. The little truck with its one high screened window came while Rob was at school.

Early the following evening a commotion at the kitchen door brought Faith on the run to investigate. Tail wagging, canine grin, his manner plainly said, "I really prefer it here with you."

Opening the door wide Faith laughed, "Pal, we love you. But you must not chase the sheep!"

John was furious. "Were they in the sheep business or the dog business! And what kind of dog business with all male dogs?"

When the children were in bed for the night Faith pleaded. "Honey, all my life I wanted to bring home every stray dog and cat nobody loved. My dad always made a scene. I never could keep them. I was so wretched. Possibly down inside I felt as lonely and forlorn as those strays. . . . Everythin' needs love, Darlin', and these things are all part of God. Can't we keep the little thing? He loves us—and he's so good with the children. They love him."

John weakened.

"Okay. But he stays tied up. I will brook no sheep chasing!"

That was the line of demarcation.

Pal was confined except when the boys strolled him. But keeping Pal tied up remained the problem. His Houdini complex was miraculous. One day, in desperation, Faith wound the chain twice around his neck, rehitching it in the wagon house. It was not too tight. She verified that. Verbally she defied Pal to chew through it or slip through it! In triumph she flounced down to the house.

Almost at twilight that evening Rob rushed howling down the

207

hillside. Hysterically he screamed into the kitchen. "Now you've done it! Pal's gonna die or have to drink blood. And where are we gonna get all the blood!" His voice ended in a desolate wail and he flung his body at Faith.

She hugged him until he quieted. She was angry with herself for sharing a gory farm journal story with the boys. Fascinating pictures of a mammoth western wolf spurred their interest. She read them of the marauding wolf that feasted on ranch cattle through a hundred-fifty mile circuit. It was trap-smart and its devastation continued for several years. Finally a most cleverly concealed trap succeeded but the wolf had torn himself free. In a few weeks the killings increased. Apparently he was only able to drink fresh blood instead of returning to a carcass; the havoc worsened.

Gradually Rob quieted and amid upsurging inner sobs he told of Pal. Hand-in-hand they went to the wagon house. No noisy, happy upleapings at their approach. Pal lay almost inert, pain filling his brown eyes, only whimpers issuing from his mouth. Faith winced, bit her lip. She too could have howled at sight of Pal, for the chain was doubly embedded in his neck. The raw flesh lay open like a sprung trap door revealing the bones of his neck. "Pal, forgive me," she whispered.

She dared not jiggle the chain lest in trying to free him she torture him and damage the bones. The freeing maneuver would require most tender handling. Thank God John was coming home that night! Thank God John usually was expected home when something of magnitude occurred. Perhaps if she held Pal and spoke soothingly to him John could cut it off.

She touched Pal's head tenderly. "Don't move one speck, Pal! We'll make it better—please God." In the gathering twilight she entered the kitchen, prepared Pal a fluid supper of freshly beaten raw eggs and milk, Rob looking on in big-eyed wonder.

After John's and her dinner she carefully broached the subject of Pal. She knew how John hated the sight of blood—to say nothing of his annoyance over Pal's residence. She hoped John's compassion would eclipse both points. She held to a continuous flow of silent prayer while John gently handled the dog. The operation of removing the chain complete, Pal lay motionless on the kitchen floor.

"Now what do you propose to do?" asked John quietly. "He's more dead than alive."

She was silent some moments. Then with firm conviction, her chin lifting spunkily, "He'll get well. God is healing him now."

"What are you going to put on it? The bone is visible. You can't leave it like that."

She was again beating together a couple of fresh eggs, pouring some milk with them. Quietly, "We'll put nothing on it. If we bandage it, he'll scratch. We shall bless it and him, and let God heal it perfectly."

John grimaced impatiently, walked from the kitchen. There were moments her metaphysical studies left her a little daft, he thought. Faith knew his thoughts. Alone in the kitchen with Pal she presented the liquid. "You've got a divine spark in you, Pal. Man calls it Spirit or God. Right here and now you are already being healed . . . regardless of appearances. You are practically proving God, Pal. You *have* to demonstrate perfect healing!"

It was a command.

A new light in the brown canine eyes. A faint response in the tail. Tentatively Pal flicked his tongue toward the fluid. Faith stood by, eyes tightly shut to the appearances of that loose flap of fur and raw flesh. Silently she blessed him, affirmed divine healing, tried to visualize the neck and fur intact. Pal scrunched down again and rested.

In the living room, each of them in a big green leather chair opposite the fireplace, Faith pretended to read. Instead she kept up a running stream of thanksgiving for Pal's perfect healing.

Every day that week Robbie was dispatched to feed the dog. Faith could definitely hold to the mental picture of Pal's perfect healing if she did not witness the appearance. At the end of the week Rob bounced into the kitchen and announced brightly, "Ma, Pal's flap is shut up and new fur is growing in the crack."

Moist-eyed she patted Robbie's head before turning to hide her emotion. God had not failed! Not that *He* ever did! He had used Faith's belief and the power of her decree in spite of John's dire predictions about the dirty chain in an open wound. Later that evening she saw the awe in John's face and the significant light in Jed's eyes when he was shown Pal's miraculous healing.

Pal's healing, the whole episode, was a signpost to Faith. She had more growing to do, more becoming aware of the universe. The Pal incident was as though she stood atop a mountain, able to sight a destination ahead. While coming down the mystical mountainside to the regular duties of living, the goal became less visible.

In the beginning of Faith's awareness of the studies, she did most of the talking to God. Talking of her personal desires and the corporate family ones. As the months slipped by, she grew more receptive to His desires. She gradually learned how to hush the outer world, hear Him—and obey. This was a gradual accomplishment, a slowly maturing ability, a habit of mind and soul she had to sensitively build. Daily she tried to practice the relinquishment of the personality so that individuality, the inner Christ consciousness, could expand. Aura had leaped forth the night of the Landemeres' visit. Since that evening Aura had grown.

But there was much universality, discipline, and patience to be interfused. During the growth process Faith thought often of the apostle Peter. When he tried to walk the waters to Christ he was sustained only so long as he kept his vision on Christ and the outstretched hand. But he sank when he beheld the wetness of the sea, the height and strength of the waves, measured the wind in his garments. At those times, it seemed there were two distinct women travelling through life as Faith Sanford Wells —the old Faith being pulled into the swampiness of race consciousness and mass human thought, old mental habits. And the new Faith, perfectly protected, enwrapped by the aura of Christ, persistently, determinedly striding forward and upward. There were moments she had to outshout her mortal thinking, affirm again and again, belief and trust in God, even convince her old self. As the months slid by, her faith changed from, 'O Lord, I believe, help Thou mine unbelief' to the quiet, serene, complete and conscious knowing God face to face, attuning herself and hearing His voice within her heart.

The former Faith Wells made decisions first, weighed pros and cons, balanced them in her mind. The new Faith remembered to consult God first, abide by His desires for her. Sometimes it was easy to remember to consult the Senior Partner first. Occasionally she forgot. When the way seemed blocked she remembered the covenant. God first. Always. In all things. Small as well as big. Know Him well through the small bits of life, then one knows Him perfectly when the bigger things require His wisdom-love. Daily reconsecration and rededication. Paul's 'I die daily' admission. Die to the old consciousness and resurrect each morning to the new.

Of vegetation Jesus had said, 'Except a grain of wheat fall in the ground and die it cannot bear fruit.' Faith pondered His words in her heart, was nourished by their substance. His word is the seed, she thought, falling into the surface of the ground, the consciousness of man. As it reaches downward into the soil, rooting out and gathering unto itself the elements of nourishment from the soil, so in the subconsciousness of man, the talents and abilities one has within himself, the understanding, and the capacity to use that understanding. Even as the rootlets reach downward, the seed sprouts upward too, reaching to light, superconsciousness, inspiration.

Faith had ample opportunity for her ponderings. John's boss dubbed him 'the roving ambassador of good will.' Faith liked her nickname of Johnny Truthseed better. There were many occasions when the Lord worked inspirationally, intuitively, through John.

Often alone on the farm during the week Faith had the full brunt of farm management. Her truth lessons, her angels of light, came to her aid. In a sense she was much alone and staunch in spiritual courage. In a universal sense, she was never alone.

Daily there were living moments Faith treasured apart from her studies, gems from the children she shared with John when he called or on his return weekends. Like the time Doug burst into the kitchen with, "Ma, you should hear the hens praise the Lord!" meaning their enthusiastic cackles after egg laying.

Or the bedtime conversation Rob began one night with his earnest, "Ma, where were those cows going that we saw the other day? You know, down by the railroad overpass where the farmer was getting them into his truck. Were they going to be meat?"

"Not necessarily," Faith answered, hanging up his clothes. "Perhaps the farmer was taking them to another farmer for servicing."

Doug became part of the conversation at this point, staring at his mother in wide-eyed wonder. Rob frowned slightly, followed with, "What's 'servicing' mean?"

Faith sat on the edge of his bed. "Perhaps the cows want to have a baby—or the farmer wants them to."

211

"Why?" a duet from both boys.

"When a cow has a calf, her milk supply increases tremendously and that makes more income for the farmer."

"O-ooo-h!" understandingly, little voices blending. "Where were they going?"

"Perhaps to the bull. Maybe the farmer wants those cows bred to a particular bull. It's sometimes easier to move cows than bulls. Sometimes a certain bull has a reputation for 'making' female cows. 'Heifers' one calls them. Heifers increase the farmer's herd because they grow up and produce milk—and more calves. Little bulls are not worth much unless they are highly pedigreed and can be retained for sire purposes. Otherwise they are sold young as veal. Sometimes farmers have an animal doctor come, a veterinarian he is called. He brings along equipment to impregnate the cow. That is called artificial insemination."

A long pause. Each boy digested all that while frozen in his undressing procedures. Then slowly from Rob, "How does that happen?"

"What?" asked Faith, "Pregnancy in a cow?"

Both little heads bobbed up and down, eyes large and solemn.

"The bull and the cow have a love affair—or if artificial insemination is used, the vet injects a sperm—I guess you call it that. The sperm goes through the cow to the proper organ where it merges with the cow's seed called an ova. The cow nourishes the life within her just as I did each of you and Don. It grows within her and when it is complete and ready, it is born. Sometimes a vet or the farmer help deliver it just like a human baby has assistance from a doctor. In a cow the baby is called a calf, you know."

"Why doesn't she just lay an egg? Wouldn't that be easier?" from Doug.

"Because a cow is a mammal. She can suckle or nurse her offspring. The ova I mentioned before could be called a seed or an egg. Most four-footed animals are mammals and have their young who look just like themselves but smaller. Miniatures." Faith smiled reassuringly. "Birds or chickens are not mammals. They lay eggs but in their egg, if it is fertilized by the male bird, is the potential little bird. Sometimes—like the whale and the platypus, you find a mammal that isn't four-footed." Faith drew in a long breath, hoped she had covered everything. Mentally she thanked John for teaching her Nature's interests many years ago. But she also wished that once in a while their profound questions would be directed to John instead of herself. She beamed on Robbie though, for all but the last question came from him. Robbie was breaking his shell of quietness.

Doug surveyed her with narrowed eyes of concentration. "Now say all that again," he demanded.

Faith repeated it, then gently with her hand on his shoulder urged him toward his room. "Do you say a bull 'lays' or 'delivers' milk?"

In spite of herself Faith laughed slightly, "Neither, Doug. In the first place a bull is a boy cow and can't give milk. Only the female of the species can furnish milk. She neither lays it nor delivers it. She is milked by the farmer, either by hand or machinery. The milkman delivers it."

"Oh," profoundly from both of them, Doug heading across the hall to his room.

"Come now, both of you, the prayer of faith," she said, tucking Doug in. Standing in the hall between the two bedrooms her mellow voice joined two low-pitched little boys' voices in Unity's prayer:

> God is my help in every need;
> God does my every hunger feed;
> God walks beside me, guides my way
> Through every moment of the day.
>
> I now am wise, I now am true,
> Patient, kind and loving too.
> All things I am, can do, and be
> Through Christ, the Truth that is in me.
>
> God is my health, I can't be sick;
> God is my strength, unfailing, quick;
> God is my all, I know no fear,
> Since God and Love and Truth are here.*

Kissing each sleepy little man, extinguishing the lights, and with a soft 'night, see you in the morning' Faith went downstairs to her metaphysical studies.

---

*Unity's Prayer of Faith by Hannah More Kohaus. Permission to quote granted.

Yes, although Itchy misbehaved and the water line clogged or the pump seemed temperamental, or any other magnitudinous mess, it was all worth the struggle for the privilege of learning to walk more intimately with God and the benefit of bringing up the children on a farm. When Faith watched the boys romping in the sunlight of the fields or took pleasure over their healthy appetites at the table, everything was worth the investment of love, talents, money—and sheer physical brawn. Perhaps the biggest advantage—although it did sound matriarchal, was the opportunity to guide their minds and hearts. Here in the country they could teach the truthway to the youngsters. They could weed out negative influences of literature, radio, movies. Here the family had to demonstrate innate abilities and resourcefulness not only with broken equipment or stock needs but also in the art of self-amusements. At the risk of sounding Pollyanna-ish, she told herself with a smile, even Itchy's temperamentalities occurred when her Johnny Truthseed was home to express his fix-it-genius!

So there was slow but steady growth in Faith's awareness as she persisted in mental self-discipline while her soul stretched toward compassionate cosmic consciousness. She was coming out of mortality's dream of 'my family, my friends, my neighbors, my country' and growing to the universal ideal of one world.

Faith found new uses for the power of her spoken word after the Pal incident. One day the milkman limped through his deliveries. Faith spoke the word for his healing, and he seemed to walk more uprightly. The limp was gone. She spoke the healing word instantly for Rob's teacher when he reported a drastic illness—and the teacher returned to school that very week. And neighbors—other than Jed and the Banners—began to drop by just to pass the time. Invariably the conversation took on deeper tones than the usual casual pleasantries.

In the silence of her heart Faith claimed God's guidance and the channeling of inspiration, upliftment, healings. To each she gave richly of this practical, workable self-psychology, this blend of love-wisdom, co-creativeness with God. To each she gave as much of this teaching as she felt guided to impart. Her speech became clothed with homey little phrases . . . "Did you ever notice communication with God is like a two-way radio? . . . No prayer goes unanswered. Every answer manifests itself at the divine time for God works *through*, us, not merely for us, and when

214

our consciousness is receptive the prayer answer appears. . . . One can pray about anything. Not just virtues. Also the desires of the heart, one's social life, or even one's financial needs. . . ."

It was a supreme joy to see friends leave seemingly refreshed, full of energy and joy, renewed in mind and spirit.

About mid-October another jigsaw piece of Faith's divine design appeared. Mary Banners came one afternoon, deeply depressed and discouraged. Faith let her talk out her woes. When she finished Faith suggested two things: That Mary sing, and sing, and sing. That Mary sing as she do her housewifely chores, sing to accelerate the very atoms of her being. Sing for self-therapy.

"It's funny, you know," Faith explained, "but with our words or our songs we can change our attitude. It is self-psychology that by dwelling on a cheerful thing we can uplift ourselves . . . or the reverse. In our minds we are complete master. We can think of something—or we can refuse to entertain that subject and substitute another subject."

Faith had Mary's undivided attention. She did not add 'this I discovered and practice' but Mary sensed this was Faith's personal recipe she shared.

Faith's second suggestion was that Mary return to her profession. In a week or so Mary Banners became the R.N.-in-charge at the Magnolia Nursing Home. Here she became a link in Faith's greater fulfillment.

That happened almost incidentally. One morning as Mary bathed Jane Allis, an elderly patient, she noticed some Unity literature on the bedside table. Making conversation with the little old lady, Mary said she had a friend interested in Unity. A few weeks afterward when Jane Allis took a bad turn she pestered Mary to "send her Unity friend."

Going off duty Mary stopped to see Faith. Her manner was apologetic. Choosing her words with care she explained, "I never mentioned your name nor committed you in any way. But she's very bad, Faith, and keeps asking for 'my Unity Friend.' I know you are terribly busy with the children, but somehow I feel you could do her a lot of good—if you could manage to visit her."

The plea in Mary's eyes plus the echo of Mary's words some months earlier propelled Faith to promise a visit. The day that Mary straggled to Faith in her need and then was refreshed by

Faith's friendship and guidance, she enthused on leaving, "Faith, I believe you were *sent* to me. Sent to this vicinity just to help me." Now these words revolved in Faith's memory although Mary did not reuse them.

So it was that the expression in Mary's eyes interwove with the echo of her words and Faith's expanding spiritual horizon. All these qualities blended to impel Faith to commit herself. John was sitter Saturday while Faith visited Jane Allis. There were many thoughts sifting through her heart as she drove to the nursing home. Ideas of what she might chat about. Thoughts strong enough to be prayers that she say the right thing, be an instrument of enlightenment as well as joy and cheer. Thoughts that were humble and invisibly prostrated themselves before Almightiness, and the growing idea that she, Faith Wells, had a larger divine assignment than marriage to her Johnny Truthseed and motherhood of four. Thoughts that somehow this Jane Allis was a link in the chain of Faith's greater purposefulness.

Mrs. Allis was in a large comfortable chair looking out on sunlit fields when Faith arrived. She turned to the doorway when Faith was shown in by a nurse. Several moments passed before Faith could make Mrs. Allis understand who she was and why she had come. Unfamiliar with the mental flights of the very old, Faith began to doubt that this woman was a link in her divine assignment. Suddenly Mrs. Allis' face lighted with joy and she exclaimed, "Why, you're that nurse's little Unity friend, *my* Unity friend!"

Faith stayed an hour. Mrs. Allis asked many questions. Most of them were about Faith's farm and the family. It was a very gradual progression to questions concerned with Unity teachings and the manner in which Faith 'came to truth.' When Faith arose to leave, Mrs. Allis asked her to pray for her. Her tone was so expectant Faith could not refuse, although part of her felt this woman was putting her on the same basis as a visiting clergyman. Faith had never prayed with anyone before. But she could not refuse this expectant, smiling little old lady. Mrs. Allis desired the cleansing, authoritative prayers of a metaphysician. Apparently she believed Faith was such.

Faith didn't feel she had grown to that status. Not yet. But, she acknowledged to herself, her silent declarations for the milkman, Rob's teacher, Pal . . . all those 'worked.' Why even the frost had not affected the pumpkins and tomatoes the night she decreed protection for the unharvested garden things. Surely all these things were too numerous to be mere coincidence. And weren't the prayers of those least in the kingdom just as worthy, powerful, as those of the saints! In good conscience she could not refuse this little old lady looking upward so happily, so expectantly.

So Faith sat down beside Mrs. Allis. The little old lady reached her hand over to Faith's, inclined her ear toward Faith's soft speech. When Faith left the nursing home she felt glowingly strong and clean, immeasurably good, at peace with the world.

There were subsequent visits with Mrs. Allis. Usually upon Mary's prompting, sometimes a telephone call from the Magnolia Nursing Home. Unfailingly, after each visit Mrs. Allis improved. All the nursing staff noticed it, commented among themselves. Mary did not carry their gossip back to Faith.

One time when Faith visited Mrs. Allis seemed confused and meandering, and their conversation peculiar. Afterward, in the silence of her heart Faith talked with God about it, haltingly, wonderingly. How should she pray? What words should she use? What should she decree?

"God . . . Jane Allis is very old. Only You know her needs and can fill them. . . . I give her and her needs unto You, so that they are filled now. . . .Once I believed You 'took' people in death. I don't believe that any more. You are Life Itself, and thus require all people through whom to express. A corpse isn't suitable. . . . I give You Jane Allis. If there is no further work for her in this incarnation, and You and she know it is time for her to leave, let her going be easy . . . very easy."

Faith reflected on her prayer all the way home. A prayer to truly stack up against Christian principles has to be an instrument of good. If death is the last enemy to be overcome. . . . But she hadn't prayed for the death of Jane Allis. She had put the whole matter between God and Jane. No one has the right to stand between God and another soul. Faith no longer believed God 'takes a person through death.' Now she believed one dies only when he relinquishes the desire to live and to learn or do . . . or just *be*. (Glory! How she misunderstood Hamlet's suicide speech in school days!) Yes, she could let the prayer rest. She had not betrayed her inner Lord.

The next morning Mary telephoned.

"Faith, . . . Jane Allis died this morning. . . . Faith, I've seen death many times . . . but this was the easiest going I ever witnessed. . . ."

Amazing!

Precisely Faith's words. "Easy . . . very easy."

Our words come home to roost like chickens, she reflected.

October's page fluttered to the wastebasket.

November dawned grey, bleak, full of greys and blacks on the horizon.

November! The investment harvest should arrive any day!

November!

Now they could clean up all the old accounts. The septic tank. Dry well. Termite bill. New stock. Itchy's big drinks. All the accumulated odds and ends. A new kitchen floor. The children's winter clothing needs.

The first week of November poked along. No big fat check in the mail, either from Jerry or the investment people. Faith gave it a mental deadline. If nothing came by Friday, she would write Jerry.

Aura suggested, "Suppose there is something sour about the investment?" Aura guided Faith, gently and firmly, but Faith hit out at the suggestion and a horde of pessimistic thought-people came to do her battle. The multitude swarmed about her. With all the human courage at her command Faith struggled with them, struggled through a slowly losing battle.

It was a full day misspent in Faith's battle against herself, engaged in a thought-to-thought encounter like knights of old parrying with swords and staves and spears. One thought persistently slammed at her until Aura's whispers were lost. The battleground was her mind, although invisible nonetheless bloody.

Faith demonstrated extra patience with the children, a strained patience loaded with tensity. By bedtime she was fatigued beyond measure, emotionally weary from the day's lacerating self-battle. Even the metaphysical books could not reach her while the angry thought-people milled about stormily. Discordant noisy brasses and metallic clanks came to her as the music of the spheres that night, and the dissonance fortissimoed in her heart.

In the darkness and the aloneness of the large house when the children were abed Faith's hopes almost died. Aura kept whispering, "You are not alone. God and Christ are with you forever.

No matter how it seems. Faith! You have work to do here! You know where one door closes a larger one opens!"

Faith did not hear Aura's assignment of special work to be accomplished. Even as the majestic words sounded her heart babbled, "O, God, where are You?"

There was no quietness within. Discords ceased but Faith stood upon a sandbar. She could not return to the old way of praying, supplication to God. Now she knew God as Principle and Law, and that man has co-creative powers with Him—and therefore disciplining responsibilities. She was too distressed to know how to pray and thoroughly frightened she might pray amiss. She could find no quietness within to rest upon a denial-affirmation, to hold a thought until the quietness and power of that holding could produce the manifestation.

Hours later, when it seemed the Goliath-like thoughts were at least held at bay, an aggressive peppy youngster bounded into her mind, "Suppose the investment fails entirely?" he teased.

Faith met that idea instantly. Impossible! We prayed the investment into manifestation. Breathlessly she met this impostor, put him to rout. In her own way she shot David's first stone at the giant of fear as well as at this malicious fellow. Why, the investment could be likened to the multiplication of the loaves and the fishes. She had brought the matter before Christ-consciousness, given thanks for it, blessed it. To question the success of that investment was like saying 'Is there God?'

A long trembly sigh escaped her lips.

So much of their capital, their fluid funds, was ploughed under in the soil rehabilitation program in the north field. Like the Communists it went underground. A wan smile flickered across her face. Somehow it wasn't too funny. Also, it was very late. The new day would bring its physical demands.

She felt her way up the stairs to bed. Exhausted mentally and emotionally she tossed in sleep, dreaming frequently that oversize people pursued her, screaming the while, waving bills as they ran. Elongated bathrooms with twenty to forty toilets all spilled over simultaneously and a bludgeon-faced master demanded she tidy up the mess instantly. From each dream she awoke drenched in perspiration.

In yet another dream she stood alone at a mountain pass, armed only with a club; steadily, relentlessly, through the narrow mountain pass marched personified billboards, gigantic red figures of debt, a speechless terror. No matter how hard she swung her weapon they bounded up, continuing to come at her.

Wide-eyed and beaten, eyes smarting from unused tears and too little real sleep, her back wracked by excruciating pain, she lay inert as the east changed to pearl greyness. When the dawn became a rosiness Faith at last fell into a refreshing sleep. All those junk dreams arose from subconsciousness, God and Aura unable to reach through the noise of the thought-people. Now, exhausted and the milling thought-people vanquished, Faith could see and hear His message of compassion and infinite love. The white-robed Jesus stood at the foot of her bed, arms outstretched, a smile of joy lighting His beautiful countenance, His rich voice ringing invitingly, 'Come unto me . . . I AM the way to the truth and the life . . . ye shall know the truth and the truth shall set you free.'

Faith walked to Him, surrendered her affairs, slept deeply, refreshingly.

On awakening, she could once more trust—and wait.

It was a glorious day for November. A living day full of sunshine, and all the world sang. Not actually, for birds were south and crickets were hibernating. But the vision had been vivid. It comforted. It sustained her. Yesterday's worries and fears, last night's nightmares were vanquished. Today was a new beginning! Resolutely Faith went about the early morning chores, getting Rob off to school, Doug and Don cared for, the chickens fed, the sheep and Garry out to pasture, and hay pitched down to them, the pigs tended.

If nothing came by Saturday she would write Jerry.

Nothing came.

If nothing came by Monday—so many offices are closed on Saturdays—she would write Jerry.

Nothing came.

She might as well wait one more day, just in case the mail took an extra day because of the rural delivery, and one more day wouldn't matter.

Nothing by Tuesday.

She wrote Jerry, briefly, almost casually.

By Thursday an answer from Jerry which eager fingers tore at:

220

"Dear Faith and John,

"It was good to hear from you. As they say in China 'no see long time' or however they put it.

"I hope you folks aren't inconvenienced. You must have mis-understood. The agreement on that investment was that the fiscal year ends the last of October but they give themselves a grace period in which to get the bookkeeping in order. Checks should go out late in December. Frankly, I don't know how much your returns will be on $3000, but I suggest you consider it in the nature of a long-term investment. It has taken the business longer to get rolling than antici-pated. Regardless—it is a good investment. I just wish to warn you that the 'investment harvest' (the term is yours) may not reap for several years.

"Don't you get down to the city? Why not drop in on Tish and me. Delighted to have you any time you can make it, you know. . . ."

Faith reread the letter several times.

'Several years!'

She was incredulous. She murmured the phrase many times to herself. They had counted so heavily on the investment. It was to be the channel of supply. Not only the septic tank and dry well and the stock. . . . She rehashed all the items. It was to be the channel by which they could procure their bonds from the bank, the bonds used as collateral for the note, get back to cou-pon clipping. Even commence the farm home for children project!

Faith huddled in one of the big green leather chairs in the living room while her soul walked the floor restlessly. They just couldn't continue at the rate they were going and remain finan-cially solvent! She winced at the thought of adding up the unpaid bills. A hundred dollars here, five hundred there, another five on the termites' damage. The kitchen floor improvised with half the pingpong table. The accumulated fuel oil bills and technically it wasn't winter yet.

Oh, it's probably a good adage, this bit about not counting the chicks before the hatching. But this was a prayed-about-thing. Prayer is always answered. They'd prayed this farm into their lives . . . received all the items their hearts desired. God isn't

221

mocked! Not just because the Bible says so. Because it is Truth it is in the Bible. Truth personified. Truth manifested.

Then, what . . .?

Why . . .?

Was she trying too hard, selfishly putting her personal desires ahead of God's? Even though Unity teaches ardent desires are the very inner voice of God.

Was this the reason for that dreadful day when she battled all the Goliath people, and then nightmared with them too? Was it Aura trying to tell her? And her comprehension lagged drearily?

By now she thought she understood Aura's voice as separate and distinct from the mortal part of herself. On the day she covenanted to full tithing—John's salary as well as the farm projects— she thought she could always recognize the difference between Aura's guidance and the mortal personal self. It didn't seem she did.

A slow sigh escaped.

'All the way.' One must go all the way.

She searched her remembrances. Had she covenanted only on impulse? Was there a hidden fear that propelled her to do this as a kind of insurance or guarantee? Had she been travelling along in intellectual pride or self-will? Was she subtly trying to trick God into increasing their supply . . . and not honest enough with Him or herself to admit it?

Doug called from outside. Faith did not hear him. She was facing facts. Not including the mortgage they were now in the red several thousand dollars. Mechanically she toyed with her wedding ring, staring at it with unseeing eyes. Gradually the gesture alerted her, awakened something. Gladioli for joy, lilies for purity, bells for their union. John designed it. She smiled slightly, thinking of him as the earnest boy showing her the design. John who moved heaven and earth to please her. John who fulfilled all her hopes. All their hopes. John, still her ideal even after twelve years of marriage! There was still nothing about him she wished to change. He was so wonderful!

Everything they had truly wanted had come to them. Four children, for 'Quota' was now being designed within her body. The farm. Even the conditions they wanted with the farm . . . 'an old place to fix up.' . . .

"Please, God, not so much fixing!"

Strange. Now that she knew the status there was quietness within her, a kind of serenity. Idly she wondered if those awful dreams the other night were the Lord's way of showing her the many weed seeds yet to be plucked from her old garden? And that last one, Jesus at the foot of her bed, encouraging her, convincing her the only lasting way is to do the upweeding spiritually, that to do it only from the mental level is 'the thief and the robber.'

A long, noisy sigh.

Well, they weren't bankrupt! She stared into the barrenness of the dark fireplace, elbows on knees, face cupped in her hands. They would have to sell the bonds, pay off everything. They could sell the other Chatham lot; the folks who bought the house had made an offer some months ago. John thought present day traffic merited a higher offer, but perhaps he too would see the matter differently now. Perhaps he could get his little red Jeep to commute over the Califon mountains if any funds remained.

And, if worse came to worse, she had her mother's engagement ring. When she sold her grandmother's diamond ring to get the freezer, she was offered quite a substantial sum for her mother's large, perfect stone. That amount would cancel some more bills.

Also, she could convert her life insurance policy to cash. She had already bequested her eyes to the Eye Bank and her body to a New York hospital. When she finished using her body, it would still benefit the world.

So, with hardness of heart and practicality of reason, she planned the full tithing would have to stop until they were in the clear. It wasn't just to the creditors, forcing them to wait. Every cent belonged to them as fast as it poured in. She could well imagine raised eyebrows on the part of friends if she were to tell them about tithing. She could imagine their smirking expressions too. Up on the hillside that clear day in September Mr. Dan thought her harmless but a little peculiar. They'd still tithe on the farm products though. That was the original covenant. That had to be honored.

Somehow she could get through without discouragement weighing too heavily. In fact, it was good to have the suspense finished, to know the precise facts. No sense in waiting for the weekend to talk over matters with John. Tomorrow, via the telephone, she would put the machinery in motion for the sale of the bonds and she would contact the Chatham people about the lot. She knew John would agree that it was all right and most proper. They would miss the bond coupon clippings. During the years of their inheritance from her grandmother they had enjoyed the rich blessing. They planned an ocean cruise when the bonds matured. That would be gone now. Perhaps, she thought wistfully, they had both forgotten the Source of those bonds! Gram was merely a channel. The Source God, of course. The bonds came during a materialistic period of their lives, a kind of taking all their good for granted, without acknowledgment to the Source.

She slept unusually well that night. No terrorizing dreams. No drenching sweats. Toward morning there was one dream. A strange dream, wherein she was taken by The Presence to a high place. It was exceedingly dark within. Gradually, as her eyes became accustomed to the darkness, she realized it was a large building. There were people, men and women, within this place. The occupants worked furiously but unsuccessfully. As she watched they seemed to complete nothing. Always fulfillment and its joy was absent. At her elbow, The Presence drew her attention to the bars at the windows and to the height of the building above a moat. She looked closely at the faces of the people again. She had not understood the room to be a prison. These were not the faces of criminals.

As the early light streaked the east she awoke, lying quietly, letting the details of the dream filter through her understanding. The moat. The bars. The exceptional darkness of the huge room. Atmosphere of unsatisfaction—rather than dissatisfaction.

Odd, too, how her Lord conveys His message. Usually her dreams came from Superconsciousness. The dreams she sustained which were prophetic or where she was aware of The Presence were always full of light, brilliant light. Sometimes these visions in the night were in technicolor, occasionally full of fragrances like a mystical flower garden that could reach her senses. Always when she dreamed from subconsciousness—like that horrible night . . . they were darkened like this one. But she was vividly aware of The Presence at her elbow. No, she didn't see Him. But she knew He was there, invisible Guide and Friend.

In a flash she understood.

Those were the faces of people confined by materialism, living in the darkness of mammon's gods, denied spiritual fulfillment by their very attitudes. Those people were slaves, imprisoned by the dark conceptions of their consciousness from which there is no escape—at least not until they invite Christ, let Him be formed within.

Faith shut her eyes tightly. The impact of the dream hit her silently, forcefully.

Rolling over on her stomach, hiding her face in the sheet, "Okay, Father. I'll tithe on everything—no matter what. I don't want bondage—not for me, not for John, not for anyone. . . . I'll keep trusting and walking with You. Forgive me, please."

So it was a pruning time. Bonds sold. Chatham lot sold. Faith's insurance converted. Life insurance on John suspended. Children's policies liquidated. Faith did not mind the suspension of life insurance. There was no inner subtle quaking. With all her being she knew their lives and health to be divinely protected and guided. Now if only she could achieve—acquire—the deep conviction of God as Supply!

Those persistent, virulent little fears still bounced in her consciousness every time Itchy's motor sounded peculiar or Itchy took a longer period than usual to kick over or when a car crunched on the driveway, setting the dogs to barking lustily. Then it was Faith contended with thought intruders, aware that fears manifest in outer circumstances when given lodgings in the mind, knowing one must not contend with the fears but rather dissolve them through substitution. Some of the fears were like alfalfa roots, extending twelve feet and deeper into the subsoil. Constancy of faithful denials—repudiations—and firmness of affirmations loosened the root holdings. Day by day and week by week, Faith walked more courageously in stronger trust and confidence.

As all this was accomplished on the silent planes of the soul, Faith was gradually more aware of the greater purpose of her life, the purpose beyond that of wife and mother. Aura's whisper of "There is work for you to do here" became stronger with the passing of the days.

The Saturday before Thanksgiving John and Faith awoke to the slamming of rain upon the windows. "This is quite a blow," John commented leaping from the bed to survey the world outside.

Coming from the east the rain poured down the panes in such torrents the world outside was invisible. Between gusts of wind blowing sheets of water, they could see Spruce Run leaping and frothing above the rocky hedgerow, dark brown and turbulent under the dirty foam. Then the noisy wind again, everying bowing before it.

John went out to do the choring while Faith cared for the children. She was serene and the children absorbed courage from her attitude. Breakfast was consumed normally, Don taken care of. It was only when John did not return within the customary time Faith felt alarm. Rob and Doug busy on the living room floor with their games, she slipped quietly upstairs, hoping she could see the barn and pasture from Doug's north window. What she beheld astounded her! Five of the huge apple trees lay uprooted, giant tendrils reaching nakedly into the rain, their hulks resting on soggy saturated earth.

Wondrous, the vast limitless sense of calm within herself. Not too long ago a sight such as that would have frightened her. Part of her was surprised at her inner quietness. It was as though part of her could stand apart, dispassionately and objectively look at the other part of herself. Regardless of the havoc she witnessed in the pasture, a great inner reservoir of calmness and quietude permeated her whole being, reached out into the very atmosphere of the house.

As she watched the rain streak earthward, the remaining orchard trees doubling over before the wind, a gigantic section of the barn roof lifted off. Intact, it blew four hundred feet. Then the sustaining current of wind let it crash. The crash propelled her into action and she flew down the stairs, donned raingear in the kitchen at the closet. The boys came into the kitchen, asking for John. With sustained serenity she replied, "I'm going out to see. You both stay here so that you are warm and dry."

Out in the wind, her head bent into it, each step a struggle to cover the distance between the house and the pasture gate, progress was extremely slow. Once the wind stopped abruptly. The relief from its pressure almost toppled her to the ground. When she reached the crest of the first incline, John came into view from the barn, five fingers of one hand spread across his head to hold his hat. With a slight warning the wind signified its return and John shouted, "Go back! Go back!"

They reached each other, arm-in-arm turned to the house. The going was easier when they breasted the wagonhouse, protected from the east. From that building, they held to the fencing, pulling themselves along, each step an achievement. High in the orchard pasture a great whoosh. Another tall tree plopped to the wet earth. No resounding thud. The saturated ground passively received the large tree, yielded with the impact.

In the kitchen, removing their soaked clothing, John commented, "I don't remember a storm like this in my whole life. This must be a hurricane."

"Are the stock all right where the roof isn't?"

"Yes. They can get over to one side. It's blowing so hard though that the hay will get wet—doesn't keep it in good quality."

One of them noticed the electric clock stopped. "It'll be days before they get the power on. This storm covers a wide area. They'll have miles of lines and poles to replace," John predicted.

She made no comment to his dire predictions. She did not relish the coming days. Powerless dark nights and days that projected them back to the historic Revolutionary era, compelled them to cook at the fireplace. Lug all the water—for cooking, drinking, baby's laundry, toilet flushing, dishwashing. Only fireplace heat—no grumbling Itchy. Heat the dishwater on the fireplace. At least drinking water wouldn't require boiling!

Well, she'd been through it before. Back in Chatham, during the winter of '48, the ice storm followed by the blizzard—or was it the other way around. Five days without power. But no baby then. Little tykes, to be sure, but no infant. Nor a farm and stock to be cared for. Also, that fabulous Anderson gas stove! What they cooked on the Anderson sustained their bodies, even a measure of their souls, during the unusually cold days and nights in a heatless house. And city water flowed through taps and toilet tanks, not requiring a water pump in the house for civilized decency!

Still this measure of calm within herself! Remarkable.

She moved quietly, steadily, preparing to cook the noonday meal on the fireplace. With a teasing grin and a twinkle in her eyes she chided John, "Had I suspected long ago that you took me hiking and taught me the joys of outdoor cookery as a preparation for marriage, I might not have let you catch me."

Little to do but hover over the fireplace cookery.

For his part John wondered if he would be able to discover a supply of dry wood when the small accumulation disappeared into the hungry maw of the fireplace. About midafternoon John moved surreptitiously toward the cellar doorway. Sometimes after "too much weather" the cellar became wet. No need to alarm Faith until he checked. Little light from the small high windows down there. It was like looking into the black hold of a ship. Quietly he closed the door behind him, lit a match. At the instant he determined the cellar to be full of floating cartons and half submerged boots, a tremendous jolt shocked the entire house. The sound came from Don's room. He heard Faith dash upstairs. Slowly he withdrew from the cellar, mounted the steps too.

Faith was leaning against the doorframe, her vision fastened on the huge elm resting against the baby's window. The pane, infinitely splintered but miraculously intact, was still in the frame. Reaching for his hand she murmured, "Truly we are divinely protected this day."

John's eloquent expression of askance went unnoticed. He was inventorying the uprooted apple trees, the gaping barn roof, the cellar full of water and floating objects. Now this huge tree leaning against the house itself.

Knowing his thoughts Faith added, "But none of us has been touched! The stock are safe!"

Simultaneously they heard a new sound. Cascading water. Faith's first reaction was that it was a burst pipe. Without electricity, no pipe could burst. No time for wide-eyed contemplation. This was an avalanche of water.

The boys yelled from the living room where they stood entranced at the east window watching an impromptu river foment and churn from high in the apple orchard. The force bolted down the hilliness, divided itself around the base of the wagonhouse, crashing, foaming and pounding down the driveway to the road where it merged with the miniature brooks in each ditchway. It carried everything with itself, large stones, sticks and branches, a battered cat.

"Was that Susy?" worried Doug.

"I don't know, son. We'll have to wait and find out." John patted Doug's shoulder in a comforting gesture.

About four o'clock the wind ceased, abruptly. Soon after that the rain stopped. The sky lightened.

"How's the cellar?" from Faith.

John didn't answer immediately. Her calm, like the eye of the

228

hurricane itself, impelled his admiration. "Not good," slowly. "I've been wondering how I can rig up the lawnmower motor to bail it out. The water's above Itchy's motor level."

Moving toward the cellar doorway, "Suppose I start bailing with a couple buckets while you rig up." She fastened the cellar door open so that she would be able to hear the children. Everything not stationary floated. As she let herself to the cellar floor the water topped her boots, slopped inside as she moved.

Atop the stairs John watched. "I honestly don't know whether to help you the slow way or expend my energies improvising."

Faith made no comment. Her genius lay in physical stamina and courage and rearing children and tithing and working with the Lord. John's lay in improvising and rigging. She bent to the work at hand, a bucket on each side. Easy to fill two buckets. Just let them down anywhere. The muddy water gurgled inside. More difficult to tote two buckets, swishing and slopping through water to the cellar doorway, ducking the overhead odd-level pipes, making the gigantic step to the outside, walking twenty feet to the driveway, emptying the buckets so their contents joined the flash pasture river coursing through the driveway to the road. This required brawn, persistence, and endurance for hours. To stand on a cellar-doorway step and heave it might not work. Better to do it the slow, methodical way lest it seep back into the cellar. The long way, toting from cellar all the way to the driveway. . . .

"I can do all things through the Christ in me," Faith silently reiterated, moving in rhythmic procession from cellar to driveway. Pools lay atop the grass already. Letting the buckets down, swishing through the dirty water. It would be time to get supper started soon. Slow supper. Via the fireplace. Don would be yelling shortly. At five months he would be unaware of family inconveniences.

"I can do all things through the Christ in me."

Would the waterline never lower!

"Through the Christ in me I can do all things . . . Through the Christ in me . . . The joy of the Lord is my strength . . . I am strengthened, renewed, sustained by Spirit. . . ."

Back and forth. No lowering of the waterline. Surely two hours had elapsed. Two full buckets each trip. Four gallons. Why was there no lessening of the water level? Countless quantities of four gallons ought to demonstrate something visible to her handle-dug

229

hands, weary back. That last gigantic step of twenty-six inches from the cellar doorway to the lawn seemed four feet. Now, each time, she set down the buckets, climbed to the lawn, reached down for the buckets, proceeded the twenty foot to the driveway to dump the contents.

The arduous demands on her physical being triggered a memory. A short time before Don's birth, John was away on a trip and she needed to dump two one-hundred- pound feed bags into the metal bin, the chicken feed. She had been SO great with child and the chore was so gargantuan. As she struggled she had remembered to call on the Lord's help. Wondrously, like magic, the bag seemed to lift itself.

With self-renewal, "Through the Christ in me I can do all things. . . . The Lord is helping me right now, right here and now. . . . When I was a child, standing at the window at night looking to the heavens and thinking God is out there . . . blessed is it to know He is within me yet all about me too! Blessed the day I discovered Emmet Fox and Unity! Blessed the day I comprehended the omnipresence of God, how He is everywhere evenly present. . . . If John would only get that lawnmower rigged up!"

John came splashing through the cellar, toting his rigging. "Trouble is the water's seeping in faster than you can bail it out, Honey. I was standing outside a minute and I could hear it gurgling in by the foundation."

Faith stood upright, rubbing the back of her muddied hand across her forehead. She could think of no spritely answer. A grumble would help neither of them. Silently rebending to the task, "Through the Christ in me I can do all things."

The improvised lawnmower-sump pump worked while they had a sketchy supper, got Don fed and off to bed for the night, set water to heat on the fireplace for the supper dishes. For several more hours in the cellar, both of them worked with the improvised pump. If they could only get that water level below Itchy's motor before it did permanent damage—if it hadn't already!

Darkness settled. The noisy driveway river stopped as abruptly as it began. They took courage from that.

The Banners dropped in. Mary had to get to the nursing home. However, all roads out from Red Mill were blocked by fallen trees and downed high tension wires. Telephones were out as well as power lines. They did not stay long. When they left they marvelled between themselves over the degree of calm in the Wells' home.

With the aid of flashlights John and the boys located dry wood, stacked it on the side porch. While they busied with that, Faith did the day's diapers, stretching them to dry before the living room fireplace, trying to ignore the desecration of that beautiful room.

All the children were in bed and they sat silent in the large room, only candles and kerosene lamps providing light by which to read. "Always makes me appreciate Lincoln's education," she offered. Reflecting a moment, "On the other hand, it's kind—leaving this . . . this mess . . . in shadows."

John smiled acknowledgment. He was far more concerned with the condition of Itchy's motor and enjoyed the sound of the improvised sump pump, evenly and monotonously reducing the cellar water. "By the way, I have corncobs soaking in kerosene at the cellarway."

"What for?"

"Quick start in the morning," motioning toward the fireplace. "Seems uncannily still outside after the roar all day. And no farmers dashing through to a grange affair by night."

During long spaces of quietness between them each was busy with his own thoughts, John thankful he was home during this day of devastation, able to share Faith's burdens; Faith in communion with her Lord. Occasionally John arose, stirred the fire a bit, added another log or turned over a half charred one.

Steps in the driveway. No vehicle had come by since the Banners left. They looked in askance at each other. A knock at the sidedoor followed by a hearty, "Hi!"

"Jed! How'd you get through? The Banners were here awhile ago, said this part of the world is space-bound."

Jed stepped into the large, cluttered room, set down an old fashioned kerosene lamp, moved to the fire to warm his hands. "Getting crisp out. How did you folks fare?"

A deliberately casual question. Faith let John answer. Intuitively she felt Jed already knew the extent of their damages. John told the story of their day, finishing with a question about Jed's damages. Jed shook his head. No damages. Pointing to the lamp, he said, "Thought you might not be prepared for blackouts.

At least if you use that along with your own you can save your candles." With a slight bow to Faith, "I realize you prefer dining by candle."

Faith made a peculiar throaty noise.

"How'd you get through, Jed?" John persisted. "Hike over the fields after the first downed tree across the road?" He did not see that Jed's boots were free of mud.

Jed's wordless answer was a gentle smile.

Busy lighting the new lamp and moving the same match to his pipe John seemed unaware his questions went unanswered. "We can get plenty of kerosene, you know. Itchy drinks it now. We have at least 500 gallons right below us," his voice full of laughter.

Jed turned to Faith, "How about packing up and moving in with us until power is restored? We have enough bunk space. There's ample food whereas you can't open your freezer until power returns. Also we have central heating—old shovel method, you know," he grinned.

John accepted immediately. "Yes, why don't you and the children go? With stone-filled walls this house won't be comfortable in a day or so. Now the walls are still giving of their retained heat. Once the stones get cold and frosty it will be unpleasant. I can manage here, chore the stock, do whatever is necessary until the emergency is over."

Faith's large brown eyes regarded John seriously, wistfully. "No. But thank you," directing her appreciation to Jed. "We'll stay together. The children are strong and we all have ample sweaters. I believe it is more important for them to stay together as a family, important psychologically."

"It could be a party for you, dear," John persuaded. "Hilda's there and you always enjoy her."

Faith shook her head. There was firmness in her manner rather than stubbornness.

"It is a kind offer, Jed," thoughtfully. "Jed . . . what brings about storms? Not scientifically. I know those answers. What is the metaphysical cause?"

Jed's blue eyes regarded Faith's thoughtfulness, searching her earnest face, scanning John's also. "I believe *we* cause storms . . . affect . . . influence . . . create the elements."

"Humph!" from John.

232

"How?" quietly from Faith.

"God has given man dominion over everything—even the elements. But first man—to have that mastery—must control himself. We build conditions by our mental climate, even of the elements. Shall I say it in the language of science? Britain's Sir James Jeans says, 'It may well be that the power of our minds affects the universe around us.' In the poetic language of spirituality, I would clarify by adding that those who dwell in love, universal love—that which Jesus called 'The Kingdom'—have only love and harmony surrounding them. The hate campaigns engendered by nations during wars become the Frankensteins of post-wars. 'Love is the whole law?!" quoted Jed.

His words came ringingly clear. Eyes filled with compassion and understanding he searched the faces of the couple before him. Quickly he continued, "Are you careful to use the highest language at your command at all times? 'Man is held accountable for his lightest word.' The ether in which we live is the garden soil for our words, although the process is invisible. This ether substance is malleable, plastic to our thoughts and words. We create by our words even as God. Remember? 'God *said*' the whole universe into manifestation.

"Orientals refer to Akashic records. The Old Testament implies the same meaning in the phrase 'The Book of God's Remembrances' or 'The Recording Angel'. This ether substance in which we live—Paul called it 'in God I live and move and have my being' —is not only moldable by our thoughts-words but also retains impressions like a master photographic plate. Listen to the average small talk and you will comprehend why there is chaos in the universe and confusion. Stack that against the divided households, people who say one thing and mean another . . ."

Jed smiled gently, remembering the scene last summer in their garden when he deliberately planted these same ideas in the minds of four little men, Faith and John standing in the background. Jed thought they understood. Actually he had used the children to get his thoughts through to the adults. Surely, Faith understood! How long would it take the world to reach spiritual mountain tops when such as these did not perceive!

Jed looked beyond John to Faith in the dimly lit room. Perhaps that was only intellectual perception she experienced last summer in the garden. Now she would experience spiritual-mental

233

understanding. "We live in substance," he added softly. "We can drift willynilly in it—or use it purposefully, deliberately, creatively. We can use it merely by speaking to it—like the genii of Aladdin's lamp. It is an aspect of God. It is Holy Spirit in action. Some of us use only part of it—like praying for guidance or bread or friends or a new job—well, that's bread, isn't it?" he laughed. Becoming serious again, "This is the esoteric meaning of Jesus' temptation by Satan. The mortal part of Him understood this, knew it can be the 'thief and the robber of the sheepfold,' perverted to selfish ends. His temptation is the inner struggle between the Son-of-God and the Son-of-Man. Scripture clothes it with the form of 'Satan' because early Christians did not understand abstracts as easily as this generation; they needed a form to depict an idea."

His voice seemed unusually deep and rich. Neither John nor Faith made any comment, and Jed softly quoted.

" 'Death and life are in the power of the tongue.'

" 'Man does not live by bread alone but by every word that proceedeth out of the mouth of God.'

" 'Be still and know that I AM God.'

" 'The words that I have spoken are spirit and life and they shall never die.'

" 'And I, if I be lifted up, will draw all men unto Myself.'

" 'I said ye are gods and all of you Sons of the Most High.'

" 'That which I do ye shall do and greater works.'

" 'I AM that I am.' "

His voice trailed off, its resonance lingering in the room, filling it with bell-like tones.

In a new way John comprehended Jed's quotations. As a child he too understood the simple profundity of spiritual teachings from the ages. Right thinking and right living. Now he also understood these principles as spiritual self-psychology. Now the curtain was parted and the passageway flooded with light.

They sat in silence, thoughtful a long time, unmindful of one another.

Sometime during the deep quietness Jed slipped out into the cold night. Only the light from Jed's kerosene lamp bore testimony to his visit.

Cold, sparkling morning revealed the devastated countryside. Tiny icicles pointed from dropped power lines. All the world was washed clean, and light was scintillating from myriads of gem facets, shining from upended trees, encrustations on rocks, and icy patches in the holes of the dirt road.

Neighbors rallied to one another's assistance, forgetting former petty annoyances, and offered themselves or their belongings. Invitations came to the Wellses from the Banners and the Farnsworths to either move in or come for the cooking. But the Wellses remained at home, meeting each day with its involvements as it came along, hopeful each hour would bring the sound of repair gangs.

Rumors collected, travelled abroad with each winterish hour. "The power was on in the Glen." "The power was not on in the Glen but on in Woodglen." "The crews were at Bunnvale . . . or Changewater." "The road gang had removed all fallen trees. Now the utility crews could get through." "Destruction was so bad they had imported utility men from Ohio." "Hampton had power. The Glen would have it tonight." With each rumor the line of truth wobbled.

For John there was much to do, changes for the stock now herded into the lower portion of the barn. Salvage the hay as much as possible. He fenced in the pigs in the lower level while Garry and the sheep shared the remainder of the lower barn. Unaware of inconvenience the hens merrily laid eggs, cackling continuously, until full egg cartons towered in the playroom, awaiting John's return to the office for his regular egg customers.

So the family stayed together, working steadily. Little men were kept busy within their strength limitations, mostly helping tote and stack wood on the side porch. Despite John's cutting up the fallen trees and their toting, the house grew increasingly chilly. Stones between the walls grew cold, gave off a penetrating chill. The living room fireplace fought valiantly to maintain some liveability. Faith stopped consulting the den thermometer when it reached 36°.

Time did not drag. Each day was so full of physical activity Faith wondered how people of the preceding century, into which they were catapulted by the hurricane, managed to enjoy life. How did they ever manage to read, make babies, fill the needs of the soul as well as the physical requirements of life! Merely physical requirements consumed all of each day! And how could the women be beautiful, she wailed to herself, looking at

235

her fire blackened hands. "I've never been glamorous. Even Lulu says I look more like an old-maid school teacher than a former secretary, but gosh!"

It snowed the third morning and the boys took to their sleds. The Banners insisted they all come to dinner that night, Mary having taken a turkey from her freezer lest it spoil. Mary had gas for cooking. How Faith yearned for that Anderson gas stove! It was wonderful to have a full dinner, not an all-in-one-pot affair. A dinner with side trimmings, even a salad and cranberry sauce. It was less formidable returning to the big, cold house.

Road department trucks got to Red Mill on the fourth day. Power and telephone trucks could get through now. Morale zoomed upward throughout the countryside. That night they all had dinner with Jed, Hilda, and Otto. The party was festive, not only with good food but also the comforting awareness the century-retrogressive nightmare was ending.

On the fifth day utility crews appeared. Women rallied to give coffee to these martyrs of long working hours whose strained, unshaven faces furnished ample testimony of their diligence. Farm men appeared spottily to watch, technically unable to help, many of them equally devastated by the requirement of milking huge herds by hand in an age geared to power. Often they finished the chore of milking only to recommence, then spilled the fruits of their labor on the snow. Roads remained impassable for several days and no one had extra milk tanks or methods to safeguard the precious fluid.

At three minutes after seven in the evening of the fifth day the power returned.

A whole day was needed to get the house cleaned, the bathinette back to the kitchen, blackened pots shining again, laundry blowing in the windiness and freshness of the backyard. Several hours for John to get temperamental Itchy happily resuming her peculiar mechanical song.

On the seventh day John returned to his Newark office with the backlog of eggs. That day's mail brought a letter from the Landemeres, inviting themselves for a short stay before wintering in Florida. They would arrive Saturday.

They came in time for lunch, enthusiastically calling from the car. Lucille was almost breathless in her manner, kissing Faith, patting the boys' heads, reverently hushed before the sleeping

Don bundled outdoors against the bleak November sunshine. Pierre was unusually quiet in contrast to Lucille's verbosity. Pierre's youthful fires seemed banked. There was an air of detachment about him, a kind of withdrawal although he hurried to see the stock, compare everything with his memory. But the lively quality was absent, missing even in his gait and the blueness of his eyes which seldom twinkled. When Lucille bubbled, "Faith, what have you done to yourself! You are positively pretty. You even look younger somehow, but I can't place my finger on what it is about you."

The old Pierre could never refrain from some facetious quip. The new Pierre merely gazed absently at Faith as though to make his own appraisal, await her answer.

The men and the two boys toured the outbuildings while Faith assembled a luncheon of chow mein and hot rolls, quickly set the table, keeping an ear tuned to Lucille's report of their trip the preceding summer.

Pierre's attention kept returning to the gaping hole in the barn roof and the uprooted tree trunks. Startled at seeing the flock and the busy hens, he wryly commented, "Your stock all look fine in spite of know-not."

John laughed merrily, "Where we lack knowledge God supplies us with wisdom." Privately he was thankful he and the boys had sawed up most of the apple tree mess, removed the tree limb leaning on the baby's room, and replaced the glass pane. He was mindful of Pierre's frequent glances at the gaping barn roof.

Appetites whetted by the late November cold, Faith's bell clanging brought them on the run. Interesting aromas from the kitchen assailed them, tantalized their enthusiasm for luncheon. Seated at the dining table, steam spiralling from each plate, there was only polite conversation after grace until hunger was somewhat appeased.

"Got another Anderson range?" Pierre queried of Faith.

Smiling easily, "Not yet. All in the Lord's time."

"You two sound God-intoxicated!" Pierre's tone nettled.

John glanced quickly at Faith, well remembering when such a retort could well prompt some temper. Furthermore, the Anderson range was her Achilles' heel. To himself John thought Pierre was probably right. They did sound queer. Even the children spoke familiarly of the Lord as though He were part of every moment of their lives—as indeed He is! But folks just don't talk that way, I suppose, he reasoned. Why, Doug was nightly thanking the Lord for the pony he wanted. Pierre should know that! Sometimes during a meal one of the little fellows would pipe up with, 'Isn't the Lord good to give us this delicious food!' Whenever one of them did John usually added, 'And to inspire Mother to cook it so well.' Yes, in a profound sense each member of the little family was deeply aware of the Creator. Naturally the awareness permeated the very atmosphere of their home, affected their way of thinking and speaking. John thought of Jed's words, 'words are the clothing of thoughts and everything manifests itself in thought.' Only Jed spelled it with a capital 'T,' or referred to it as Divine Mind. Well, for John's part the family's constant awareness of God was fine! The Wells' difficulties all began when they were smug and self-sufficient, thought they could get along without Him.

Now watching Faith closely, John saw a soft smile begin in her eyes, witnessed a new expression encompass her face as she looked up at Pierre. John was positive she was praying for him, blessing him. He knew it was not a you-poor-misguided-dope expression; nowadays her prayer would be a tender, compassionate plea, perhaps a poetical bit of mysticism like 'Divinity in me beholds Divinity in thee' kind of thing she was fond of discussing with him.

She did look different. Prettier. Lucille was right. Beyond the new prettiness Faith usually experienced during pregnancy when her thinnish face rounded out. This new prettiness was lasting, born of prayers and songs. She seemed younger but with no sacrifice to the charm of impending middle age, the love-maturity and richness that completely eclipse youth's superficial gaiety and shallow beauties.

"Everyone will think you queer if you keep on!" Pierre added didactically. He too watched Faith intently, knowing this whole Lord-stuff began with her, since the woman sets the tone in a home. A slight pucker appeared between his brows. He too noted the indescribable difference in this woman, could not account for it.

Faith did not answer immediately. A whole parade of thoughts marched before her memory. Her covenant with God last spring, the full kernels of corn despite drought, His work with the second

238

batch of cockerels regardless of extreme heat and weather disadvantages, His work with the sheep, so that even the experts felt impelled to seek formulae from the Wellses! She thought too of the seeming slowness of the investment harvest, the need to liquidate the personal insurances. She reflected too on her mother's engagement ring—that it hadn't brought the huge sum, for the diamond market was different from several years ago. Now diamonds were in good supply. She'd had to sell the sunburst pin too, and she'd loved that, prayed for a miracle which would let her retain that pin. But the miracle had not come. After a bit, somehow it didn't matter so much. Not really. Now with the bonds sold and the Chatham property and all the debts cleared away—again—John could get the little red second-hand Jeep to ease his commuting problem over the Califon mountains. It would help clear away the uprooted tree stumps too. It was a practical move not a luxury, or a gadget to impress the mythical Joneses.

Everything was so much easier with the Lord's help, she admitted to herself. Somehow former standards . . . well standards just aren't the same. New, higher standards are formed and all old junk fades away. Literally everything is easier. Easier down within oneself. She simply couldn't have lived through some of this—this junk, this bad karma, these seemings—if it hadn't been for God's guidance. Sometimes His visions—sure, sometimes she had wondered if she were completely sane! Some of those dreams she had, especially the prophetic ones. Why didn't other people have prophetic dreams? Why just she? Well, John had had a couple. But nobody else they knew ever said, 'I had a beautiful dream and it all came true.' Even Mary Banners never said that, and Mary was a most spiritual person. Eventually, of course, she had taken comfort from the fact that Biblical people of old seemed to be guided through their dreams too. It was rough going within herself for a while until she remembered that facet. Then, in her logical approach to the phenomenon, she reasoned perhaps she was too troubled for God to get through to her in any other way. When she was able to silence the mortal part of herself, God communicated directly. In fact, He often did— through Aura.

Yes, this is a cleansing period, Faith told herself. Some might call it a sacrificial period or a testing. 'Sacrificial burning!' That

239

was it! Not rams, or calves or doves or goats like in the old Biblical days. Rather old errors of belief, old limitations, old attitudes. Maybe that was the very symbolism of the Bible—calling the error attitude by these animal names to depict specific kinds of mental errors, habits or attitudes. She could comprehend that since being on the farm. There were many times when her attitudes were more goat-like than sheep-like or pig-headed, determined to have her personal way. Where once she had intellectual, dictionary knowledge, she now had the beginnings of wisdom. Yes, surely working with the stock she had learned much of Scripture semantics. Funny, Jed working with pigs! She thought of that oddity often, puzzling too why the old Biblical writers and prophets so despised swine. Was it because they were the scavengers of old, the ancient garbage disposal system? Might it be the old superstition that one absorbs the spirit of the food one eats? Eating symbolizes a state of consciousness, and because pigs were not discriminating they represented beings too low in the spiritual scale to serve as food.

Ah, sheep! How she loved the sheep. Sheep were so obedient, completely obedient to their shepherd. But only after they knew his voice, had confidence in him. They were not stupid. Merely meek. That isn't being stupid nor lacking in courage! She thought of herself as being meek—well, sometimes. Like when she received the divine instruction to tithe on everything. Surely it took courage in the face of seemings. Yes, sir, she'd go to bat on that idea! Sheep. Meekness. Complete trusting obedience. Goats might be like the agnostics who claim they are self-made. She'd claimed that too many years, thought one 'got somewhere' only by dint of his own efforts. But sheep accept divine leadings. Sheep seem to know a divine arrangement, a partnership kind of thing. No wonder they called Him 'the Lamb of God!'

Pierre was expecting an answer. She met his gaze steadily. Quietly, with a wispy smile, "Perhaps I do seem God-intoxicated, Pierre. He has more than held my seams together. My first day here with the children after John left for his business trip was enough to tax mortal me. It's true Lulu was here, but all the decisions and responsibilities were on my shoulders. Also . . . we've had many miracles. One I could cite is with the little Donald who was supposed to be jaundiced because of my RH-negative blood factor and because he's technically the fourth pregnancy and because Doug was badly jaundiced."

Faith's words came slowly, filled with patience. Between them she saw the mental pictures of herself busily choring with children and stock during John's many absences from home, nights alone with the metaphysical books, a kind of sublimation as well as a divinely impelling urge to know and understand, work with all of God's laws. She could easily see the division between her spiritual self that she called Aura and her mortal self named Faith Sanford Wells. None knew of the conflicts within as she did. John might suspect, he knew her so well. But no other person can know all the little thoughts and feelings and naunces of spiritual evolution.

"In a measure we all walk alone, Pierre. Just as no one else can eat or breathe for me, so no one else can meet my challenges. In the big sense, however, we are never Alone! With all the honesty at my command I acknowledge that when I learned to put Him first, I became different. Our lives are different. If old friends think us queer, well then . . ." She made a freeing gesture with her hands. "Perhaps, though, they will see His demonstrations through us—and get on His bandwagon. People are fond of quoting this thing 'no man is an island.' It's a great truth. We can't put it in a test tube but perhaps there is an invisible empathy so strong that even our thoughts affect a passer-by, although I hastily add there must be a receptivity too."

There was such disarming charm in the simplicity of her testimonial that Pierre turned his attention to his silverware, fidgeted with it. But he did not interrupt her.

"These haven't been easy months. It is a new life. John and I bit off a big chunk. We knew that before we moved in. After we were here, this first spring, we learned the soil needed rehabilitation as well as the house and the outbuildings. There've been moments I thought the job stupendous! That's when my working religion carried me . . . Beneath all our experience is the abiding conviction we were divinely guided here, and it will come out all right."

Her voice dropped so low Pierre could hardly hear her.

"Perhaps not the way I might outline," she continued. "Maybe that has been my error—like Garry in the barn and Saul of old

241

—telling God how to run my part of the universe . . . I hope I've cleared that out of my consciousness forever . . . It takes a lot of true humility to pray 'not my will but Thine be done'—and mean it!" She smiled slightly. "Unity teaches God's will is always good. To put it slangily, that He wants the bestest for the mostest. We go through a stage where knowing that He sends only good makes it easier to pray 'let Thy will be done in me.'"

She was silent briefly, thinking again of her mother's sunburst pin. That was her hardest challenge, to hope for a miracle that would enable her to retain that pin, and to finally relinquish it, give it up mentally as well as actually.

"I believe God is preparing us for a bigger divine assignment. Whatever we have experienced in the past few months has produced an inner transmutation necessary to fit His assignment. All my life—even as a youngster—I've had glimpses of a glorious goal. Now it's more than a glimpse."

"Bringing up three children in this day and age is task enough!" Pierre shot back. Might just as well get her off those clouds of glory.

"Four," she corrected, eyes glowing mischievously, a tender glance toward John.

Lucille had remained quiet, a shade of tensity in her manner. "I expect you had a houseful of company this summer," she offered, hoping to steer the conversation to more mundane areas.

John's eyes laughed. He knew Lucille's aim, and he also knew this could lead right into Faith's dissertation about her divine assignment.

"Yes." Faith did not launch into the favorite short stories of Cheesecake and Jashu episodes.

"We had city kids and we're going to have lots of 'em," enthused Doug. "One's name is Jashu and the other's Robert but we called him 'Cheesecake.' They came from. . . . Where was it, Mommy?"

"Brooklyn," Faith supplied.

Their glances met in silent laughter.

"We teached them to play in harmony and once Kim scared the dickens out of Cheesecake but Daddy introduced them and then it was all right." Doug continued his voluntary information while Rob sensitively glanced from one parent to the other.

242

"What's all this about?" invited Lucille. "I thought you were dyed-in-the-wool Jerseyites. I didn't think you knew any New Yorkers."

"It's a long story," John answered. "How about the coffee, Faith?"

Faith arose, assembled Danish pastries and coffee, arranged cups and saucers, cream and sugar on a tray, silently praying as she worked. God bless them. We seem to have drifted eons apart from the Landemeres, Father. Pierre and all he represents from the old Chatham days are a world apart. Help me, Father. Help me remember everyone is a spiritual being, each unfolding at his own rate of speed toward fuller Christhood.

She checked the stove. All the knobs were turned off. Pierre would label her more than queer if he knew she prayed over the stove and the food. Her smile widened, a small giggle escaped. The small giggle romped about, put a new zest in her brown eyes. Serving the dessert and pouring the coffee, Lucille reminded, "Well, who's going to tell us about the city children? There's such an atmosphere of mystery about it all."

Faith opened her lips to say, "We stepped into a new way to serve the Lord this summer" because that was the way she thought nowadays. Aura remonstrated. No sense in thrusting one's convictions. Keep blessing instead. Let John talk. John used a business man's vocabulary, wouldn't offend, wouldn't sound holier-than-they.

So it was that John launched into the story of their beloved third crop, their dreams for the future. His enthusiasm carried him to the plans for Christmas Tree Hill, the pond at its foot. When the boys slid down from their chairs, murmuring a plea for dismissal, John fetched his sketches of the wagon house reconversion.

"Well!" in unison.

Then Pierre brought up the matter of capital in a blunt but well-intentioned manner.

"We're trying the local banks first. If none of them can see it our way—since our original plans regarding an investment didn't jell as quickly as we hoped, we'll go to Uncle Sam. He has many arrangements for farmers. Naturally I haven't forgotten my farm plans!"

"All under-privileged children? No sponsor?"

"We'll always have a few under-privileged, the rest will be paying guests. There needs to be a healing of the have-nots as well as the haves."

"Healing!" ejaculated Pierre. Blinkingly he surveyed John.

"Yes," affirmed John, his voice ringing with abiding conviction. "A healing of the twentieth century error—materialism. We want to plant truthseeds that putting God first, absolutely first in every department of one's living, is a matter of spiritual law. This is a spiritual affair, not the letter of the law that merely carries one to a place of worship on his sabbath.

"I was raised in a hellfire-brimstone kind of religion—that heaven is upward, that one must be good, that the rich are probably unscrupulous, that only the poor are good. Those are error-teachings, for truth-searchlight reveals that people are individuals, whether rich or poor, of whatever nationality, religion, or race.

"My point is that many were raised on false spiritual diets. I have read, for instance, the Rockefellers were raised to be tithers, taught the stewardship of their wealth, that it brings responsibilities. In any age we have the Rockefeller attitude toward wealth—and—unfortunately—we also have the Jelke attitude. Among the poor some think they have the right to be lazy and get what they can from the haves.

"It's a big challenge. My main point is that life can be quite a struggle without sufficient supply but man should know God is supply, that He works through us, not just for us. Pierre, since teaching myself this idea I have so many ideas with which to work in business I can hardly keep up with them. Daily I see new, larger doors open to me. Even in the business world, the market place, I witness His miracles."

Silence from the Landemeres.

Aware of the new mood Faith began to speak, choosing her words with great care. "I suppose the have-nots need to grow to an awareness of fulfilling a divine purpose. They need to learn to use their imaginations constructively, their intelligence to work with God, to give of themselves. In one of Fillmore's books he attributes famines in the Orient and depressions in the Occident to man's fears of lack. Group fears. Man worries, thus visualizing, talking and thinking, lack by his fears. So lack manifests itself. In the Orient what we call a humble manner of speaking is false

244

spirituality—'this lowly crop,' 'this poor son.' Fillmore quotes 'whatever Adam called a thing that it became unto him.' I suppose we have thought this meant the naming of cats, dogs, elephants, snakes, and so forth. But Fillmore means the deep thing of attitude and quality."

Incredulity and amusement combined on both Landemere faces.

"I didn't accept that in the beginning either," admitted Faith, rhythmically moving the salt shaker in a circle while she spoke. She was seeing herself descending the hillside with Mr. Dan on the glorious autumn day and employing the word 'windfall'. Surely she hadn't meant the devastation of the barn roof and all the apple trees. Who is it says 'the subconscious mind has no sense of humor'! And that quotation of Jed's a week or so ago, that British scientist he mentioned, 'it may well be that the power of our thought affects the universe around us.' Probably those scripture writers of long ago tried to convey more than their period of civilization could comprehend.

Aloud she continued, "I see much more than I understood a while ago. I see the occult law of the power of the spoken word. I see what can be termed self-psychology. Most of us think of psychology as the power to motivate others to our own aims. Its biggest power lies in its use on ourselves."

Still they made no comment. Faith talked, almost in self-defense. "I can testify we have worked with some of these principles. John will corroborate my statements, I'm sure. I can't say I saw the working of miracles but I surely saw the results. Couldn't it well be the miracles occurred through our right thinking. Is this a Buddhist precept because he taught the principle of 'right thinking'? Isn't that same precept indicated in 'as a man thinketh in his heart so is he'?

"All I know is that these new-old interpretations of His teachings work and prove themselves! We have denied—in the sense of repudiated—the seeming appearance and affirmed the reality—that God is always good and sends forth only good. We have blessed the hens, the sheep, and all the stock. The hens lay eggs bountifully, and even Mr. Dan declared our sheep have no worms.

"This way of Spirit works beyond one's highest flight of imagination. Malthus judged by his senses, put a limit on the Infinite, said the earth cannot support more than so many people.

245

Would a just and loving Creator witness the starvation of multitudes of His children? Isn't it rather that He gives us intelligence to work with chemistry, raise vegetables in tanks, rebuild soils . . ."

Softly Lucille raised the age-old argument, "Dear, people have been praying for centuries. Prayer isn't a new idea. Ever since the recording of religious history people have asked God to remove all wars. We still have them. They have asked God for bread. We still have famines, whether we call them that or depressions or the cycle theory."

"Yes," Faith smiled spontaneously. "We have prayed amiss. We have asked disbelieving. The wars are man-made, not Divine surely. Perhaps we have forgotten the enemy is His too. But even from wars comes forth good. Medicine made tremendous advances during the last horrible international mess. God is well able to establish Himself regardless of what low level man sinks to. Unfortunately in our good intent we have been a bit crude too. So filled with our enthusiasms and our know-how we have gone into some less developed countries and have said, in effect, 'You're pretty stupid to do things that old way. Here, let's do it this way.' We have given them money and our bad manners—and have robbed them of their self-respect. We must learn to help them help themselves. This world has no more ivory towers or desert isles. We're going to have to live by the law of love—even if we call it by another name or refer to God with varying tonal effects. Each of us must so fill his own consciousness with divine love and peace it will overflow to all the world . . . this we want to help achieve through our farm summer home program."

Absolute stillness in the room, silence and a mystical light encompassing those at the table.

After a while Lucille said softly, "God bless you both—and your noble purpose."

Pierre was his old self. In a jocular manner, "Faith Wells! When you lived in Chatham and we came to your home for dinner I was most dissatisfied with my wife's cooking thereafter. She does as well as she does because I taught her all that she knows. But tell me," he leaned toward Faith confidentially, "what do you do to make such light yeast rolls?"

Faith's eyes were brimful of laughter. "Pray over them."

An explosion of spontaneous laughter greeted her admission. In each heart arose a faint suspicion she spoke truth.

On the Thursday before Christmas Lulu came to the farm with John, bringing her usual assortment of surprises and gifts in her commodious purse. Bustling in with her perennial good humor and natural verbosity, the children fell upon her, eager to see her as well as the delightful surprises.

Christmas was Sunday that year. Sunday! And Faith hadn't done one smidgen of Christmas shopping. Fortunately it could be done in one day. Faith would go to Newark Friday with John, accomplish it all while he worked a half-day, attended the office Christmas party the other half.

So Friday was Faith's day. A day to really enjoy. No stock to care for, John would do that before they left Red Mill. This a day to restore her perspective, even a dinner date with her beloved Johnny Truthseed at night.

On arising Friday morning Faith felt queer. Her feet lagged and the day she had looked forward to seemed gloomy. John noticed her attitude, the degree of perplexity on her face, the familiar gesture of rubbing her forehead when troubled. She felt as though something were missing, as though part of herself were off on a vacation or hibernating.

"Something?" asked John, concern in his voice.

After a long interlude Faith looked at him. He came to her, enfolded her in his arms. "What is it, Honey? Don't you feel well?"

Faintly, "I seem to have misplaced my Aura—and I can't find it."

He dropped his arms, walked impatiently to his dresser, selected a pair of socks. "Anyone listening to you would think you're screwy, and me too for sympathizing!"

Perhaps it did sound silly. But she had such a premonition. The absence of light. A dark cloud sat upon her, weighed down her spirit. She felt she should not go to Newark, remembering the children of Israel moved forward only by the pillar of light and not at all under the dark cloud. But this was the last opportunity. How could she explain no Christmas to the children?

She glanced from one face to another at the breakfast table.

The big fellows. The baby. Lulu. John. Everyone looked hale and hearty. There were no misgivings about any of them.

How stupid to feel as though Aura could leave her. This Christ consciousness couldn't leave her! Was it Jonah or Job who moaned to God something about when I go to hell You are there also. She laughed silently, but returned attention to the cloud. The vague premonition seemed to be formless but dark, foreboding. She would jot down the doctor's telephone number for Lulu, and the oil burner repairman, leave them by the telephone. Then she would invoke divine grace and protection on the farm and all within it.

It was a cold, raw day. Felt like snow. Faith snuggled in the seat, the car heater blasting away at her feet. They were comfortable, she and John. It was merely the world outside the car that looked bleak and stark. In a measure she usually had this struggle with herself on a 'day off.' It was the usual struggle between her selves, the part that decreed all mothers should have a time to themselves and the self that enjoyed hibernating on the farm, disliked the impersonal attitude prevalent in the city, plus its foul smells.

Abruptly she jammed on the mental brakes. Non-resistance. Love for everything. All the way. Divine Love, not the selfish, possessive personal variety. Today she would even love the city. Today she would bless all passersby, refuse to see strain, stress, unhappiness in their faces. She would 'keep her eye single' and behold spiritual perfection everywhere. In the measure she could maintain it within herself she could contribute to the universe. Today she would look beyond appearances, look deeply into the heart of Truth itself. This day she would bless and bless and bless.

She glanced at John busy with traffic. They spoke intermittently during the long trip. For about fifteen minutes she read aloud something from a Unity tract in her purse. Each relapsed into quietness.

Regardless of her high resolves a haunting persistency, a nagging awareness of the cloud claimed her attention. Doggedly Faith used affirmations, blessed the cloud, spiritually reached out to it, questioning it. No hint or comfort came from Aura. Gradually the cloud grew larger and it darkened as time elapsed. Again, faithfully, she decreed divine protection for John, the children, Lulu. There was no comfort returning to her, no intuitive

248

feeling her prayers accomplished their purpose or even rose higher than the car ceiling.

The trip to Newark was longer than usual because of holiday traffic. An hour and a half after leaving Red Mill they parted in Newark, John to the office and Faith to seek out a coffee shop and refresh herself until Hahne's would open its doors to the shoppers.

In Hahne's vestibule she awaited the store's opening. Each time the outer doors opened the Salvation Army Christmas music from the corner drifted in, fading to a tinkle as the door shut behind the newest arrival. She whiled away the half hour in prayer for each newcomer, her glance moving from face to face. Occasionally someone met her gaze, flashed a quick smile as though an outer response to her prayer vigil.

Her shopping began with the children's gifts. Waiting for service at each counter she decreed divine guidance in selecting the right gift, blessed the sales personnel, blessed each purchase. Attired simply in her grey herringbone tweed coat and blue accessories Faith was the personification of radiance, peace and composure. Inwardly the cloud increasingly worsened. She stabbed at it periodically, using words of truth, affirmations designed to dissolve the cloud, effect light. Sometimes she paused, awaiting inner guidance as to the specific thought to hold.

No guidance.

The cloud steadily blackened.

It began to overshadow her. It could overwhelm her, so gigantic became its proportions.

But the shopping demanded. There had to be Christmas for the children, for the few adults—Peter, Lulu, her folks, her favorite aunt, and of course John!

The dispelling of the clould could be consummated only by getting away from the Christmas shoppers, becoming utterly quiet. One's ships come over a quiet sea. She must get still, remain still long enough to scatter the cloud. Her metaphysical stabs and jabs were ineffectual. Occasionally while waiting for service at a counter she thought there was a lessening of its intensity. But each time she left the prayer vigil for the material matters, there was a renewal of her fears rather than her peace.

Rapidly she checked off the Christmas list. Only the men of the family, the hobbyless men. It was this way every year. Men shouldn't receive shirts and ties. Gifts should be heart's desires not practicalities.

It was almost two o'clock and suddenly she realized she was extremely hungry. Perhaps while having a sandwich a divine idea would come along regarding the two dads, and so lunch would be more than an infilling of her physical needs.

A few minutes before three all the shopping was consummated. She waited in line while the girl tied together all her vast assortment of boxes and bags.

The cloud was enormous.

There was no peace from it.

Black as a tropical storm. Sullen. Faith felt as though she were in the very midst of it, borne aloft amid frightening winds of sound and velocity.

Purchases all neatly and strongly held together she crossed Broad Street, entered the quietness of Trinity Cathedral at precisely three o'clock. Here was the haven of quietness. She was alone in the Cathedral's silence. Light from the candles on the altar flickered interesting patterns on the stained glass window above. Faith did not pray in words, or even in thoughts. Rather there was an emotional reaching Godward after some moments of quieting her misgivings and her fears, hushing the cloud-like premonitions, disspelling the darkness and the clamor of the world.

Finally, calm within and the feeling of mastery increasing, Faith asked aloud, "God, is it the children?"

Instantly a bell-like word rang, "No."

The single note lingered in the cathedral vastness. Never had she experienced the Voice from the atmosphere. Always it came from within as intuition, silent conversation. She was too intent to reflect on this strangeness.

"What is it, Father?"

No further answer. Neither from within herself nor from about her.

Only the cloud still lingering. Seemingly unshakeable. Heavy. Dark. Ominous.

She sat motionless a long time, forehead resting on her hand against the pew in front of her, affirming divine protection, divine power, reminding herself 'nothing is impossible to God.' Nothing! Reaching out to Divine Love.

Of course! Someone said there's nothing enough Divine Love can't do!

She would call on that aspect of God.

Deliberately, quietly, with a growing serenity, she imaged the golden circle of Divine Love around the beautiful old farmhouse and all its occupants. The golden circle intensified. She could see it so perfectly. She maintained this mental picture, bathed the farm—in the gold light of love. Minutes slipped by, although she was unaware of time.

Gradually great peace enveloped her. The peace that surpasses understanding. Such a wondrous calm enwrapped her in the mantle of quietness and light. No definite words came. No communication from her Lord. Rather the blazing conviction that whatever had been amiss was taken care of.

Peculiar. She was neither aware of the cloud's being dispersed nor of Aura's return. Just this unalterable conviction the matter was remedied. Not repaired. Rather 'taken care of.'

For some inexplicable reason, perhaps merely her appointment to meet John at four-thirty, she glanced at her watch. It was exactly three-thirty.

She remained in the cathedral for a half hour, praising and thanking God for His work and protection, His all-encompassing Love, thanking Him for being with her through the day as she made her purchases, thanking Him for 'all the good they had that day and all the good they were going to have.'

Her relief from the cloud was immeasurable. Truly she had known God face-to-face that day!

About four o'clock she gathered up her purse and bundles, buttoned her great coat. Her heart and mind were still busy thanking God. A little tangent thought recalled itself to her and she smiled slightly, an episode with Rob. How wondrously and completely their lives were enveloped with children. What a wealth they teach us in our efforts to teach them, she thought.

A small episode it was. Rob wanted something very much, had tucked it into his prayers at night. Then one afternoon he apparently thought it would be helpful to campaign a bit whereas she and John never removed the prayer requests to their own hands. "Will I get it, Ma?" he had asked while Faith was busy preparing the dinner.

Matter-of-factly she had answered, "Yes, if you faint not."

"What's it to faint?" he had asked and she made the routine answer.

"Lose consciousness."

Of course it required more answer than that to a seven-year-old, but Spirit taught her through herself in one brief instant. "Like a great sleep while one is unaware of one's surroundings," she had finished to Rob.

In the Cathedral, knowing God face-to-face, she truly comprehended what it is to 'faint not.'

It was already a winter evening outside. A wet snow had begun. Traffic swished in the wetness. Lights shimmered, elongating reflections on the streets. Everywhere the sounds of Christmas, Salvation Army Santa Clauses on street corners and the sound of their bells or recorded music. The bustle of Christmas. The joyous spirit radiating from every face, overcoming tiredness and heavy bundles. The man-made Christmas tree in Military Park shone into the heavens, jostling crowds surged below it.

Faith's large bundles bumped into her legs the four long blocks to Raymond Boulevard. She was to meet John by Kresge's, on the Boulevard side. The snow and the enormous traffic muddled the whole traffic problem. John was late, unusual for him. It was five o'clock before she heard the familiar horn beep. The bundles and herself in the car she leaned for her kiss, "Have a good party?"

"Yes, everyone did."

His answer was short as he negotiated the traffic. Police whistles. Cars swishing. People, thousands of them, trudging the sidewalks, spilling over into the gutters.

People. People. People.

Some faces beautiful with inner radiance, caught and retained from the spirit of long ago. Other faces, more earthy, yet even they caught some of the reflection of that spirit too.

"I didn't ask this morning," John interrupted her thoughts, "where would you like to have dinner?"

Quietly, "Did you call home?"

"No. I usually do when Lulu is there alone. I didn't today."

"I think we should call before we make personal plans."

John parked at the first available spot, sought a public telephone. Faith watched the people go by. Blessed the people. Thought of her own vast blessings, this fabulous day. Thought of herself as being a channel of their blessings, an open hand for the infilling of all the multitudes of good desires. His people, wherever they are, whatever they are or can become.

John slid beside her. Putting his arm on the seatback he toyed with the lobe of her ear. Gently, "I imagine you will want to go right home. . . . The oil burner, our Itchy," he forced a little laugh, "blew up. Lulu thought she smelled something peculiar about three o'clock. Suddenly realized Itchy had been running since we arose this morning. She pushed the thermostat but the controls didn't work. That frightened her. She called the oil burner people. Whitey was out. She remembered the name of Banners. Thank God! And called Parry. He came down about three-thirty and pulled the house switch."

John stopped. He'd put it simply, omitting the terrific consequences.

"So, they are without power. Can't cook . . . and so forth."

He removed his arm from Faith, started the car, maneuvered from the parking space into the stream of traffic, headed for South Broad Street and the ramp to highway twenty-two.

"Has Whitey been there yet?"

"No."

John gave all his attention to the traffic. It was thick and slow, everyone impatient and in a hurry. Wet pavements. The driving became increasingly hazardous.

Wondering how Lulu was managing with three hungry children, one only six months old, Faith closed her eyes, re-entered her inner cathedral. Interwoven in her declarations for Whitey's speedy arrival at the farmhouse was the awareness of the time coincidence John had mentioned!

Three o'clock she felt that stupendous cloud!

Three-thirty when she knew the danger had been 'taken care of.'

She mouthed her lip. "God bless God! . . . I'm so thankful for Your wondrous love that protected all in spite of Itchy's temperamentality!"

Silently her thanksgivings flowed. She reached a sabbath of consciousness, rested in the awareness He would inspire Lulu despite the distress of no lights, no water, no electric stove.

Driving worsened. By Plainfield the slush was frozen into ruts. Cars jolted along, in, or over the ruts. As they climbed to the hills beyond Plainfield, pavements became sheer ice mirroring the

253

traffic lights. That which was wet snow in Newark was raining ice west of Plainfield. Cars moved cautiously. Seldom did anyone increase his speed, the resultant spin sufficient to remind all witnesses of such foolhardiness.

From Somerville on cars crept half on the highway, half on the shoulder. On the steeper inclines three or four cars, abandoned on the roadside, caused oncoming cars to gingerly leave the safety of half gravel, edge beyond the stranded ones, cautiously return to the shoulder. An exceptionally bad accident near Whitehouse, The ambulance was already at the scene. Scattered glass and twisted steel strewn over the highway, a ghastly sight in the shining wetness of the icy night.

She glanced at John's white, strained face, returned to her prayer vigil. John always called these vigils of hers "watering the flowers." She smiled slightly, appreciating his light, poetical turn of phrase.

Atop the Glen Road just before the little country church, they saw car lights winding up the mountain. They waited at the side of the road. Whitey's truck passed them, headed to the Glen. Poor guy, he had seven miles over the very road they had travelled. The dirt road down the mountainside was safer, stones and gravel giving them a purchase on the ice.

Almost four hours after leaving Newark they turned into their driveway. Empty-handed they picked their way to the house. Whitey had established power. The lights were on.

Don was in bed. The older twosome seemed calm, unfrightened. Lulu was in the kitchen finishing her supper. She was tense but outwardly masking it. "Did you walk through the den?" she shot at them.

"No." John's voice was exceptionally quiet. Faith looked at him in the glare of the kitchen light. He was colorless, little purple veins projecting under his eyes.

"Don't. Floor's too hot."

In word bunches the story came forth as the details returned to Lulu's memory and her mouthfuls permitted. "That Whitey's something! If I don't blow up, he'll scare me to death! . . . Stands there before your furnace and says 'Jesus Christ! How the hell did you hold together! Geez, lady, when they go like this you either blow up or burn up! Look, lady, look at the crack you got here! If it's an inch it's eighteen. Look, here this fissure. . . . Then

I asked him what was in that tank a couple feet from the burner. I almost had a stroke when he told me kerosene like it's water. . . . John, of all the damn dumb things! I usually try to mind my own business, but that's about the. . . ."

Aware the children had come into the room her fount of censure stopped. Lulu wiped her mouth forcefully, moved her bulk out of the kitchenette and took her plates to the sink.

"We had to use kerosene, Mom," Faith quietly defended John. "The oil people recommended it because Itchy wouldn't take the regular fuel oil and use it properly."

"Oh," mollified. "Well, your burner's dead now. Whitey said to call him up when you get in if you want to arrange about an installation. Said they can't do anything for you until Tuesday because Christmas is Sunday. All the supply houses are closed tomorrow, Sunday being Christmas they won't open until Tuesday. You'd better call."

Neither John nor Faith moved.

"Did you have your dinner?" kindly.

"No," they dueted.

"I'm not hungry," Faith added.

John leaned against the kitchen sink as Faith walked to the living room, principally to be alone. She felt as though an avalanche had buried her. Here, practically on the eve of getting everything settled financially . . . now the burner! O, God!

There was no strength left in her to rise to the occasion. No talk. No petitions. No communication, not even with Him.

Just, O God!

"You gotta eat for that baby," Lulu's voice following her, high pitched and penetrating. Good Lulu. Always dependable. Always wonderful. Always thoughtful. But if she just wouldn't talk so much. Just give Faith some time to regain some inner peace.

As John entered the living room the Banners arrived at the side door, Parry and Mary, anxious for their welfare. Had the burner chap been there? He, Parry, had never been so scared in his life! Had John seen Itchy yet? "When I went down those stairs I thought I was walking right into hell, John. There sat your burner, violently red, ready to explode any minute. I came back up for an instant. To gather courage, I guess," Parry laughed a bit. "Then I went down and pulled all the switches. I didn't know which one took care of the burner, you know."

255

The men went down together, their talk rumbling to the girls. Mary and Faith stood alone. Outwardly Faith was calm, inwardly she was depleted. Mary made an admission, "This was quite a test of Parry's courage, Faith. He was in a house a few years ago when the oil burner blew up. That's why we heat with coal. He won't have one in his home."

"I'm glad divine love in him is stronger than his fear," simply.

The men returned, Parry commenting to Mary. "Their burner is still red, dear, and it's almost six hours ago." Turning to John, "Why didn't your controls work?"

"Insulation had burned off. They couldn't."

"Is your den floor cool now? I couldn't walk on it this afternoon. I never saw anything like this in my life!"

Both men stooped to touch the den floor. It was still warm.

Faith knew the miracle. Only by Grace, divine love in action, had they been saved. Divine Love had kept the roof intact. Kept the fissure from disintegrating, puncturing the large tank of kerosene. Divine Love! She was deeply aware of Divine Love. Divine Love had worked through Parry. . . . Mentally she retoured the issues of time elements again. At three o'clock . . . at three-thirty. . . . She should be shouting praises to God! Her heart dictated that.

But her heart was split, for her mind thought of another bill. A gigantic one, and no apparent supply to pay it. There was nothing left. No more insurance to sell. No Chatham lot. No diamond engagement ring, nor even a spare hundred dollars from the relinquishment. No cherished sunburst pin. The thought of the end-of-the-year investment harvest failed to lift her spirits.

Somehow she couldn't—just couldn't—rise above these appearances.

The Banners left. Hearing the door close behind him, Lulu chirped from the kitchen, "I made you two a couple chicken sandwiches. How's that? You can make your own coffee. I never made it to suit you. Mail's on the dining room table."

Mail!

For a half instant Faith's spirit almost rallied. Quickly she and John sorted it. Mostly Christmas cards. One or two business letters. A long yellow envelope, an unknown return address. Faith tore it quickly, sensing its contents would be uncomfortable. A form letter with a check direct from the investment people rather than through Jerry. Briefly she noted "that despite the small interest at present the business is building; they could confidently expect greater returns next year. . . ."

The check was nine dollars and forty cents.

Silently they looked at each other.

After a few moments Faith managed to whisper hustily, "All right with you if we endorse the whole thing to the Lord? Only He can save us."

Wordlessly John nodded.

They endorsed it together, stuck it in an envelope, John sealing it firmly.

With great effort Faith said, "I just can't believe it. I had such faith in it . . . in Jerry as the channel . . . the whole thing came to us through prayer . . . and I'm sure we didn't ask amiss."

There was nothing more to think—or say.

With great effort they took up the balance of the mail. A few more Christmas cards. At the bottom of the pile a plain white envelope in Lucille Landemere's heavy-handed penmanship, its firm up-and-downness revealing her European education in its similarity to German script. As John opened the envelope Faith said, "Pierre's dead."

Skimming rapidly John confirmed, "Pierre . . . cancer . . . on Wednesday."

Faith absorbed the words, turned away to the kitchen, mechanically filled the kettle, placed it on the stove. The experiences of the day engulfed her. She stood before an inner altar in humility, the timing of the miracle, the coincidence of desperate awareness of that cloud at three o'clock and at three-thirty. . . .

Why had nothing come to her from the Landemeres?

If God could hold their home together and keep its people safe, surely He could heal Pierre. In the Cathedral she felt so intimate with God, and in that high consciousness she knew she could be a channel for healing. God did the healing—even for cancer. All she had to do was maintain the high watch. God could have healed Pierre just as easily as He kept the house intact!

Welling up within herself came an answer. Pierre had relinquished the desire to live. God doesn't 'call us' or 'take us.' God is Life and He requires Life through whom to express Himself. And death is not 'a sleep and a forgetting' but probably a spiritual-mental digestion period of the soul's lessons. As mortals we have the freedom of choice, personal will. We have the ability to live as long as we have a purpose in living or a willingness to learn. When that attitude vanishes we forfeit life. That which man calls death is merely a rest and a soul digestion period between incarnations. Life is a weaving of two threads—karma or fate and free will. The Orient believes fate or karma is irrevocable but as Fox gloriously puts it, 'Christ is Lord of karma. He is the overcomer of past debts' and Christianity is an active religion, not a passive one.

From Aura these thoughts came.

Now Faith's intellect and reason stood reviewing, analyzing them. Jesus' quotation came to her, 'I have the power to take my life up to lay it down.'

Couldn't that mean reincarnation as well as the crucifixion-resurrection?

While the divine part of her sang praises to the Creator the mortal portion wobbled and wallowed with worries of Itchy's demise and the agony of another bill.

And neither portion of her was in ascendancy.

Faith wanted to be alone. She wanted to walk off to a mountain top, regain her inner poise. Think it through. Think it through? No, probably worry and fuss it through.

She felt so used up inside. Absolutely depleted.

"God, forgive me. There have been so many things. I know instead of worrying about the payment of another thousand dollars I should be shouting Your praises. I know the principle I discovered today in the Cathedral should be topmost in my heart. . . . O dear God, Quota and I are suddenly overwhelmingly hungry and SO weary."

The kettle sang. It snapped Faith's attention from the cosmic to the personal, reminded her afresh of the $9.40 check. Almost automatically she patted the stove with her right hand as one placates a fretful child and a long, slow sigh escaped her lips, peculiarly out of harmony with the now furiously boiling water.

"Well, Stove," she whispered. "I've secretly hated you! Wanted to junk you ever since we came. In the beginning you responded by burning my meats and making my cakes less than exotic—sometimes. In desperation I began to bless you. In all honesty, my blessings were prompted because I hoped we could replace you at harvest time, so I was doing the letter of the law and not the spirit. . . . It looks as though we're going to have to live together, you and I, perhaps a long time. I'll have to praise and appreciate you a great deal."

She poured the water into the top of the drip pot.

Nine-forty, she reminded herself. Nine-forty!

Her disappointment was boundless. Her eyes were moist when John entered. Enfolding her in his arms he kissed her. "Pierre's better off, Honey. He was a very different man from the Pierre of old." He rested his cheek against her hair.

She glanced up, sniffed a couple times, appropriated his handkerchief. "I'm not weepy because of Pierre. And it isn't Itchy or the nine-forty check," she fibbed. "*We* are suddenly cold and violently hungry."

She wouldn't admit, either to John or herself, that the financial recovery seemed so distant or so precipitous.

They slipped into the nook seats, John offering the grace. They ate in silence to the music of the coffee pot's steady drip-drip. On the other side of the house's U-design, the boys played at Lulu's feet while she read the paper John brought from the city.

Faith had yet to mention the Cathedral experience to John. It was an emotional and spiritual demonstration she could not quite enclothe in words. It might sound a bit smug. That coincidence of time. Yet—it certainly was an omen of the Good God's divine protection! And if He could hold together a badly fissured furnace —well, He just could right their finances and bring about Itchy's replacement under grace!

As the food and warmth permeated her being, the financial road appeared less bleak and barren. "With God there is nothing impossible," she reminded herself.

She tried to tell John—not about her Cathedral experience—but rather about God as Divine Love. Her words came forth meditatively, sometimes in phrase groups like clusters of similar flowers in a florist's spring mixture. Much of her new understanding was in the realm where pure knowing does not consist of reason's logic but where God's revelations to the individual pour forth in mystical realizations of the soul.

"Honey, I can now understand Divine Love more fully. I know Divine Love held the roof on this house . . . kept Itchy from disintegrating—four miles from the nearest inadequate fire company. Now I can better understand Divine Love as a political defense,

259

know it can dissolve Communism like we talked when Pierre and Lucille were here. Why, Divine Love can even create chinks in an iron curtain and then widen the chinks so that light, love and wisdom can pour through. Jesus taught 'those who live by the sword perish by the sword' and only the Quakers and Gandhi seem to be practisers of Love as a perfect panacea. . . ."

Her thoughts rambled. She didn't seem to be teaching John about Divine Love and its miracle regarding Itchy at all. Somehow now that she was warm and comfortable again the world seemed more important than just their little struggle with Itchy or bills. Her ideas about the universe tumbled forth, sometimes in profusion, sometimes paced apart as she sought meticulously for a shade of meaning. Her thoughts were the effect of much inner seeking and measuring through many alone days since she found Unity. Shades of Jed's influences too. John was listening. In a sense John accepted more from her than from Jed, she knew.

Earnestly she continued, an intensity in her eyes.

"You know, I believe if everyone in the world who considers himself religious would go apart daily for fifteen minutes and let God fill him with love toward everyone—everywhere—there would be perfection in body temples and among the nations! There would be no diseases. No famines. No fears. No greeds. No hates. No wars or even national incidents. No disasters. There would be just immeasurable love toward God and all men. Real harmony."

Her eyes shone, her face radiated. Wistfully and softly she added, "Old stuff, isn't it? He said it simply and profoundly. So simply we reject it and hold it to be an after-death condition, forgetting 'heaven is within you.' Or we hold it to be oriental poetry instead of the universal law of mind and emotions. 'Love is the whole law,' He said. And 'I come not to condemn but to fulfill the law.' You know, one can't even criticize the government or friends with impunity. . . ."

"We can too," hotly from John. "This is still a free country!"

Faith shook her head. Softly but with authority, "Not spiritually. Criticism only invites more criticism. Condemnation intensifies itself and begins a vicious cycle. The only way is Love. Universal Love that sees everyone as God's child, the living Christ within each of us regardless of skin color or the name we use for God. No criticism. Only Love. It's Jed's lesson of the fig tree. Remember what Jed said about it?"

She smiled faintly, more to herself than to John, for her heart silently reminded her, you must not even say 'Lulu, you talk too much. You must just bless and behold the Christ in all—even when you want to wrap the mantle of silence about you and flee to your mystical mountaintop.'

Hilda telephoned excitedly Christmas morning. In her accented English she said, "He gone! Last night, at dinner, he come with shave face. This morning, when we get up, a note on the kitchen table. All it say—vait, I read. . . . 'I go now. This place is entirely yours to work with to the glory of Gott and the honor of man. Attached is executed deed. Vat that mean?"

"He has signed over the entire farm to you and Otto," Faith explained. "It is all yours, no strings attached." Somehow Faith managed to chat further with Hilda, congratulate her, explain Jed apparently felt farm produce provided sufficient capital for their needs.

John and Faith could hardly think of anything else that Christmas Day. Not knowing Jed, Lulu wondered what all the fuss was about, and with no Itchy to provide warmth over the long weekend she felt it was good someone could work up steam. There was an absence of the normal kind in that big house. And they were so filled with their thoughts about Jed and whatever he meant they didn't seem to recognize practical needs. Oh, Faith didn't neglect the children nor John the stock, but they seemed to live in a kind of dreamworld Lulu wasn't part of.

How typical of Jed to just turn over that fabulous farm to a couple of people he trusted to love his stock and whom he felt deserved a good start! So John and Faith marvelled to each other after the shock of the news.

Apparently he had taken his little white truck. Faith smiled to herself, reflecting on that. The very fact it was white put it apart from ordinary farm equipment. Jed had ordered it white deliberately, no doubt.

For themselves Faith felt as though Christmas had a blight. No Jed nearby. They would each miss him! John would miss Jed's casual visits, their pipe talks together, Jed's personal brand of jolliness. Faith would feel as though her personal preceptor had vanished. Often Jed, intuitively perhaps, had supplemented Aura's early teachings.

Through the days to come Faith would wonder where Jed was, what he had been divinely guided to do—and where. She could have asked Jed about that little virulent whisper, 'you have work to do here,' could have received his guidance. Gradually it occurred to her, Jed's departure was divinely arranged for their good too. Now they were forced to plumb their depths, make their own at-one-ment with God.

So they had to be up and about their business, their business of prayer and work, study and growth. They recast the mortgage to take care of Itchy's replacement. They had their little red Jeep for John to commute over the Califon mountains. They sent out their tithes.

Winter, a period of industry and preparation for spring, patience of fulfillment, steadiness of purpose. Winter, longer than the usual three months in the temperate zone, but not a time of frozen vastness. Rather a time of fortitude and high courage, endurance.

A time to study and apply the lessons.

Send out the tithes and grow in courageous faith.

A time to grow—imperceptibly but determinedly, expanding a root system already sturdy in the soil of ideals and dreams.

Winter, a time to prune.

Winter, a spiritual plateau period. There had been autumn, a time when the old wealth had to go as leaves fall to prepare for the new spring. Now winter, a time for absorption, a preparation for new growth. In the steadiness and faithfulness to responsibilities and chores, each of the Wellses grew. John graduated from the consciousness of constant yearning to be full-time farmer to the willingness to work along patiently during the intermediate period with good humor and grace. Gradually Faith passed from the consciousness of wishing she could sleep until the day of a financial demonstration sizable enough to take care of the Farm Summer Home and all John's desires to farm full-time.

So she ran, by letter or by car, to banks and government agencies, altruistic millionaires, a rich relative. Everywhere the door to their dream was not only closed but bolted. Yet Faith continued to dream, dreamed she chased raggy urchins down the byways of twilight city strets, waving on two men standing atop a city wall, "Come on!" she shouted. "Help me get them. When it's dark we'll never find them!" Her shout so full-throated she awoke.

Because so many of her dreams were prophetic she continued to search for the two men of her dream.

Yet—if the Farm Summer Home were the divine assignment—why didn't she receive instant guidance?

Meanwhile her body prepared for the new baby, and Margery Joy was born, a lovely brown-eyed lass. The lovely blessedness of the new baby, their little Quota!

Sometimes, choring the chickens and watching their busyness during the day, a whisper stole to Faith. "John has too much personality to hide it here among stock. He's needed out in the world." She rationalized it away. The Farm Summer Home is sufficiently "out in the world."

And they pursued their search for funds.

Again the need to seek, for once more mortgage payments fell behind so that the full tithe could go forth. Faith juggled John's salary and all income. The sheep were building up in quantity; the purchase of hay and grains increased. The "girls," which is how they referred to the hens, paid their own way with the eggs that John sold in the office, but profits were small, very small. True, they weren't as far in the red as the preceding year when all the second-hand equipment 'they' installed broke at inconvenient times and required expensive replacements. But they were forever juggling all the income! No budgets seemed to stretch.

No direct news from Jed through the many weeks.

Direct communion from Aura, the increasingly incessant whisper, "You have work to do here. . . . I will restore unto you the years that the locusts have eaten. . . ."

So they prayed and worked, worked and prayed. In the outer sense they continued to appeal to government agencies or any channels they felt guided to contact. Sometimes government agencies were sympathetic and almost helpful, but there was always a provision they couldn't meet—like John had to be a full-time farmer to merit the government assistance. To Faith's explanation they needed his city income to make payments until they could be on their feet, they were so sorry. . . . Finally one agency could loan them a fabulous sum for the buildings! Four men came, walked the whole farm, toured all the buildings. Yes, they could be helpful. They could loan a sizable sum for the buildings. "But," pointed out Faith, "just buildings don't lay eggs or produce lamb or wool. Some has to be applied to increased stock too."

They, also, were so sorry.

So it continued, the search for the two men on the city walls at twilight.

Then one day when Mari was a few months old and Don little

264

more than a year, the mortgager's field man came to the side door. Shifting from one foot to the other in the den, he said what needed to be said, "I can see you are doing a wonderful job, Mrs. Wells. Your stock looks well cared for, not hungry or neglected. The people who had this place before you thought of it as a subsistence farm but I can see you have replaced nails and boards, the barn roof.

"But you're four months behind in your mortgage payments. Frankly I've never known my company to wait this long. They're fast with foreclosures. I can't say how much longer they will wait. If you've bitten off too big a chunk, sell out and go back to the city."

He meant kindly. He was doing his job. Faith appreciated that. She stood looking out the den window, up the hillside in front of the barn, a stubborn tilt to her chin. How could she tell this handsome representative her husband loved this place? Or that she had an inner authority to remain here, perform a divine assignment—even though the way to that assignment didn't seem to open. She didn't believe they were to remain here forever—but for right now this was their divine location. That she knew! Also, the tithe would stay their hand.

"We can't sell out," simply.

The fire in her eyes would have surprised him, but her back was to him. "Why not? Lots of people do. You need lots of capital nowadays to get into farming. I'm selling out myself, find it a bit too much to carry."

He waited for her answer. It was slow.

"My husband thinks he wants to farm—and I believe he should have the opportunity if he wants it."

He couldn't understand if she were to say she had 'found herself' in a spiritual sense on this farm, that they were in partnership with God, that John too should have the opportunity to work in continuous harmony with God on this spiritual mountaintop, away from the noise and bustle of the business world.

"That's a wonderful idea, but he has a family to support. Most of us have to do the things that reimburse adequately. I want to teach school and I am qualified. But school teachers don't make much money."

Faith wanted to debate that. She wanted to say softly but firmly, 'then your ideal will haunt you until you satisfy it; it's the very voice of God in you.' Instead she turned from the window and faced him. "Most of our initial capital is underground, in soil rehabilitation or water pumps or oil burners. It replaced the second hand equipment 'they' installed which all seemed to break almost simultaneously and inconveniently. We have to get this place into the 'going' classification to get our money out. In the meantime we are increasing our equity."

He shifted his weight again. He detested this part of his work. It wasn't so difficult when the mortgage was deliberately mismanaged. He tried again, "Mrs. Wells, I come from a farm background. I know how tremendous it is to get a farm from subsistence level to the going classification unless you have a great deal of money. Why not give up now before you lose everything?"

This time he saw the flash in her eyes. Her answer was low but each word distinct like a jewel suspended in the air, scintillating in the light of day. "The Lord is helping us magnificently."

Her words surprised him, left him bereft of speach, possibly because he could not see their justification. "Well, I sure admire your guts! You've got more than I have," his tone a mixture of wonder and amazement.

Faith remained in the den after he left. What could she do? There was nothing more to sell. There were no channels of unexpected supply. The 'investment harvest' was working apparently in silence and perhaps in darkness too. How could she tell him of their divine guidance and protection, the guarantee of the tithes? Family and stock health were fabulous. Did a lamb get out of the fencing someone stopped and lifted it back. Once a ewe, heavy with lamb and during a snowstorm, fell in the far east field, somehow rolled on her back and couldn't right herself. That time a school bus driver called from the garage. Faith and John were able to find her, massage her legs, get her back to the barn. Surely they were under grace.

The inner little voice was stronger. "You have work to do here."

Perhaps the time was finished for their being in this spot. Someone in John's company at the midwest office had died. John could have that position for the asking. They could sell out here, begin again, anew. They had made errors here. Fed the pigs too long, counted too heavily on crops before harvest time, share-cropped with custom farmers. If they were to sell out, use the wisdom gained on this farm elsewhere. . . . She could learn to live without the beloved hills. Anything, so long as they regained financial solvency!

The time for mental review was finished. She would freshen up the trim in the dining room and as she painted she dreamed. Up and down, rhythmically moved the brush. Imaginatively she "sold the farm at the right time under all right conditions and moved to the right farm under all right conditions." The new place would have no old stuff to break-down inconveniently. Now they knew the bankers' yardstick, "as the outbuildings so goes the land." She enjoyed her game of pretense, the game of using the imagination. It helped keep her vision off the appearances. John had once suggested selling off the stock which she resisted. To her it was like a carpenter selling his tools while intending to remain a carpenter. Besides the sheep were hers. She chored them, helped in deliveries, loved them. They taught her the things she needed to learn. She returned to the vision of selling the Red Mill farm, but when her stream of willful pretenses hushed Aura remonstrated, "You have work to do *here!* You know the power of the imagination. You are to use yours divinely. God's will—not yours—be done!"

Self-defensively she pleaded, "But I'm doing it. I'm using the power of prayer and the spoken word. I'm going to all the money channels that occur to me. My prayers seem to have miraculous success—for others."

Winter, not measurable in ten to fourteen weeks of snow, ice, and freezing rains. Winter that stretched through seasons of recurring greens, dry summers, exotic splashes of countryside color harmonies, and more seasons of sleet, snow, and ice.

Through all the conditions of the cold winter period two projects remained steadfast; the tithes continued to go forth. And there was a steady stream of Fresh Aires each summer. Occasionally two two-somes a season. Sometimes one two-some for several weeks. Each set brought lots of fun, new adjustments, many fond memories on their departure.

The little blonde Greek god, Steve, who on arrival said bluntly, "Your housekeeping's a mess; I'll help you clean up." But got too interested in the assortment of bugs and frogs and the countryside in general.

The little Negro boys from New York's Lower East Side, Bernie and Ronnie. What a joyousness they brought with them! Faith had never seen shy Robbie laugh so much as during their stay. Right from the start they gave more to the Wells family than they received! Garrulous Doug, silent the long trip from the train station. Faith fussed. What would he say when the floodgates opened. It didn't occur to her that he didn't remember seeing a Negro. Finally at the luncheon table Doug asked the younger one, Ronnie, "Do you have tar all over you?"

But Rob and the two colored boys were too busy making the preliminaries of friendship to hear Doug. Faith became overly busy with details until she recovered composure. Wisely she left it all to the children, sure they would handle the educational matter more than adequately. Knowing Doug she also knew he would follow through until his question was satisfied.

Putting them to bed that night, again in chronological order, she slipped, got so far into her sentence it was wiser to finish it than leave it hanging. It occurred while scrubbing Rob whose fair complexion prompted her comment, "I can see where the dirt is on you." She could have bitten her tongue, of course, before she reached the word "dirt".

But it worked out wondrously, for Rob answered, "They told me how they got that way. The big one. [He meant Bernie]. A long time ago they all lived in Africa and the sun is very torrid there, and God gave them black skins so that they could withstand the heat of all that hot."

God bless them! They surely had handled the matter wisely and well. Rob was quoting. None of that manner of speaking was his. He had memorized Bernie's phrasing, and Bernie must have repeated his mother's.

Gradually Faith was to see that Bernie had the soul of a poet, and probably the comprehension too, along with some political motivation. That very first night, hearing their prayers, Bernie campaigned two-ways simultaneously, "Dear God," he began while looking through a slit under one eyelid at Faith, "thank You for everything today and please bring us here next year. Amen." Then he closed both eyes to match, opened them, and grinned charmingly, ready for his good night kiss.

One more episode Faith especially learned from that twosome. Just a little thing, but most profound. Their second full day on the farm, they looked so pooped as they came in to the luncheon call that Faith boomed heartily, "Tired, Bernie?"

His little shoulders straightened, his head went up and he answered, "No, Mom. The me of me is but the I of me never slumbers or sleeps or gets tired."

And if the young Cheesecake and Jashu were unenthused about returning to noisy Brooklyn, the little Negro boys were more so. Little Doug set the matter straight, however, at the breakfast table. Not a word had been said by the city two-some but Doug clarioned to them, "You gotta go, you know, we have to get ready for the next two-some." And they rose to the occasion. Much as they were reluctant to leave, if their going meant joy to another two-some of city boys, they could and would be magnanimous.

So the steady stream through the summers of the winter period. The Chinese lad named Larry, the handsome Irish-American with a face full of freckles and glorious red hair, Italian flavored Tony and Spanish Jimmy, the lad with only one eye and an artist through and through. Tony had specialized in snitching all the green apples en route in the area with the usual consequences attendant to green apples. Faith thought he looked wan but Tony kept his secret for a time. When she finally caught up with it she reproved him, "Tony, why didn't you tell me and I'd have given you some scrapped apple?"

"That's my problem," a moan in his voice.

"No, this is different. Scrapping the apple, like for coleslaw, releases the pectin in it. Then I quickly sugar it and you eat it just as fast as you can before it turns brown. Know what pectin is?"

Tony wagged his head, still looked green.

"Pectin is what makes jelly jell. When that pectin substance gets within you it performs its magic like that," she snapped her fingers. "Usually only one apple works wonders. Come, we'll do it right now. However, if you go to the bathroom again and it isn't normal, tell me and we'll do the second apple. But I think just one will cure you."

So it was, different little things with each.

One season the custom farmers planted several fields of corn for them. This harvest surely would place the Wells' farm records in black ink, get the mortgage really up to date, resurrect the bank

269

account, rehabilitate the family wardrobe, furnish some fluid capital with which to work instead of additional expertise in juggling.

Corn growth that season was phenomenal. Four and five ears on every stalk, each ear filled out completely, ears measuring twelve, fourteen, sixteen inches long. Faith praised the Lord for that crop! Thanked Him for returned solvency! Tons and tons of corn in the crib that time. Tons of corn spilled over in the top of the barn until the co-op could come for it.

But that was a presidential election year. No one wanted to chance a new party's farm policy. The farmer took the brunt of the situation. If he had no modern facilities to store and hold his grains until the moisture level was proper, he sold them at rock bottom prices or held the commodities the best he could.

The bottom fell out of farm markets. Lamb prices tumbled with beef and pork and mutton. Wool brought less than a dollar per pound, hardly enough to pay for their grain feeding. Grain and corn prices sploshed, they went so low.

But purchased feed mixes remained high. The price of tractors and other farm equipment showed no worriment about a new president or a different party. The established farmer could weather this transition period. New farmers were foreclosed rapidly. The Wellses? They prayed—and kept juggling finances.

From late October until a week before another Christmas holiday no one wanted the excess corn. The abundant crop which was to net several thousand dollars waited through the political transitions. At last the new president made a public statement of his stand about farm subsidies. The next day the huge co-op truck arrived. Two men connected the electric conveyor. They worked rapidly for a half hour, the hum of the mammoth machinery reaching the house. Then stopped. Faith idly wondered. In a few minutes one of the men appeared at the side door. The expression on his face was less than happy and he fidgeted.

"All below the top foot is mouldy, ma'am. Not fit for grain. Not fit for feed. Not even fit to scatter on the ground as fertilizer lest the mould affect next year's crop."

Faith was silent and he let himself out the door. She did not understand. The sound of the huge truck leaving the premises italicized his statements. She was stunned, unable to think. She stood in the spot where he left her.

Slowly his words edged into her mind. That huge crop destined to move them into black ink on the farm records had failed. There was no more elasticity in their juggling art. Financially they were at the very bottom of the pit.

"There is work for you to do here," Aura said most distinctly.

"I've been doing it," she retorted aloud and with heat of temper.

"No," welled up within her.

"What more am I to do?"

"Get a job."

The words were clear. Impossible to misunderstand. She was furious, worried, devastated, unreceptive.

"Get a job!" shouting. "I've got four kids to take care of. How can I manage anything more—except the farm summer home. I believe You want us to do that or the ideal would not persist! Why do You haunt my dreams and my awakeness!" She was shouting and pacing. She paused momently, waiting for an answer, some kind of gentle guidance as formerly.

"Get a job," patiently, persistently, the reiteration from within, still gentle. Very definite.

"I'm a homemaker, wife, mother, hired man and farm manager in John's absence. I'm bookkeeper, secretary, nurse, cook, laundress—and a lot of other things I can't think of right now. Besides —what could I do with the children? I can do the farm summer home project around them. No one we know can fulfill our responsibility there as we see it. They are first in priority."

So she reasoned with Him or mercurially fumed. Mostly she told Him "NO!"

The refrain persisted. Gently, firmly, "Get a job."

" 'Get a job!' " she mocked. "I even deliver lambs when necessary or call the vet and then have to help him."

She was loaded with wrath. She did not say gently with Christ 'Nevertheless not as I will but as Thou wilt.'

"I've been doing Your work for me." She stopped a moment in her fast rebuttal. Searched her memory minutely. "In every instance I've spoken the word of healing—or whatever. Jane Allis. Rob's teacher. Even the dog! In fact, Pal started the whole blooming thing! And I've beheld the miracle You did through me."

She paced and she slam-banged through the chores. No pleasantries of conversation with the children. Tense quietness instead

271

and strained gentleness as though a subconscious reasoning were claiming that even if He didn't give her what she wanted she wouldn't take it out on her children.

Very gradually the fury died down, and Faith got the younger two off to bed for the night. Set dinner in the kitchen for the older youngsters, stood in the doorway a moment to announce she would eat later. This was strange behavior for her, and they looked askance at each other across the little table in the kitchen.

Faith repaired to the green chair in the living room, sat in the darkness to think out a procedure. The inner haunting voice had ceased. She heard the boys tiptoe toward the living room, coming down the center hall, and she opened her mouth to admonish them, say please leave me alone. Actually her reflex thought was to fling the words out.

In a flash, as a vignette from long ago, it triggered a memory. One day when she was six or possibly seven she had stayed closer to her mother than Elizabeth's skin, had walked into her mother's bedroom without knocking, been screamed at . . . 'if you don't leave me alone I'll run away and never come back'. She could see herself, the little girl reduced to hysteria. Odd, that emotion. She could not remember crying much as a child. Plenty of stubbornness in her childhood memories. Not tears, rather the fury to lick the world . . . then when mother committed suicide she felt personally rejected. It must have been the aftermath of those words that day. She must have followed her mother so closely because she too sensed something amiss, unable to know or even word a question, just old enough to worry and wonder, cling for security.

So now, thirty years later she could turn to the boys, pull them into the circle of her arms, gently say, "I'm sorry, Fellas. I just have something I must talk over with the Lord right now. I have to listen to Him. You go in and eat, while I listen to the Lord."

It wasn't true at all, for Faith didn't listen to Him. Instead she got up and went to the desk in the den to rebudget figures and plan. But she had been gentle with the children.

Also, she had taken a real look into the past. Perhaps this day she truly forgave her mother, understood her mother's Gethsemane. Perhaps if there were insurance that could be helpful she too might contemplate suicide as a self-sacrifice. She was worthless dead, no insurance left to be helpful to John. Besides she loved John and the children fiercely. She hoped not possessively, but there was a tremendous strength to fulfill her responsibilities toward the wonderful husband and the children she co-begot.

So she got out the books.

Perhaps if they wrote all the creditors, stated the situation, suggested they would reimburse against the backlog at ten dollars a month until the debt was clear. She would do that. It seemed the honest thing to do, instead of continuing to juggle. She rearranged the figures, many times, pared the budget to the bone.

It would work, but it would be years.

Well . . . He had given her strength for bailing out the cellar, and dumping feed bags while pregnant, and running after pigs. . . .

As a tree is pruned so that it will bear more fruit, so the Father prunes with what are sometimes called 'cosmic prods.' A little push. A firmer 'no, my child.'

Peter, John's dad, arrived by taxi from Clinton before the new year was born. Standing at the stone doorstep his bag in his hand, a wounded expression in his eyes, wordlessly he seemed to plead for shelter. It appeared he had come to stay, not only stay but also get into the turkey business, wavingly advising he would take over the power bill each month. Faith wondered with what capital but made no outer rejoinder.

So with another mouth and increased power bills, the pretty new budget was useless. In the bedroom one night Faith said to John, "All right with you if I find a job—something I can do in and around the children?" Her tone was almost insolent, just barely a question.

John's answer was soft, "If that's the way you want it . . . Do you wish me to tell Pete to go?"

She did not respond instantly. Her mind wanted to shout 'yes' in no uncertain tones but her heart held command. All too vividly she could see the wounded expression in Pete's eyes as he stood at the door. She wasn't listening to Aura these days, but Aura often communed through emotional tutelage. At that moment Aura was declaring to Faith she had no right to harbor feelings of resentment, selfishness, or self-righteousness. So she said, "No . . . per-

273

haps the Lord has some spiritual reasons for Pete's being here . . . and I must clean out the resentment of his presumption from my heart."

"What will you do?"

She shrugged. "I've thought much about it. All day in fact. We're too far from town for me to take in laundry. I advertised to do home typing. No answers. I have only weekends—when you can be the sitter—to offer. That eliminates secretarial work. Anyway I don't have a wardrobe."

She looked at him briefly. "The biggest thing is that I can't leave the babes—or the big guys—with Pete or anyone but you. Only you and I can seed their minds and hearts . . . or Jed. Not even your parents or mine. Our goals are so different from either set of our parents. Maybe because I felt bruised in my growing-up-ness I feel so fiercely about this. I can't turn them over to someone else . . .

"So," her voice trickled out, "it's either waitress work or something part-time in one of the local institutions or nursing homes. Cooking or switchboarding. Maybe practical nursing." Her tone was a combination of holiness and resentment. If Pete hadn't come they could have worked it out! It would be a long grind, but they could have done it. All the creditors had called or written, acknowledging her notes, expressed appreciation of their honesty.

Wordlessly Aura reminded her no one is justified in firming down seeds of resentment.

"I'll have to go forth under Divine Guidance, affirming the right job will open to me," she finished to John.

Late the next afternoon Faith parked on the side of the highway, shut off the ignition, let her hands fall from the steering wheel into her lap. Thoughts galloped through her mind, echoes of her words returned. She had dared affirm divine guidance to the right work only the night before, dared it in the face of being angry with her Lord, petulant because she wasn't having her way. Between her resentment at Peter's presumption in coming to live with them and the failure of the corn crop to keep properly, she had not walked and talked with her Lord. She was very lonesome and afraid without Him. She felt naked without His protection. How could she reasonably expect the comfort of His lovingness when it was she who caused its stoppage by her own will?

Despite her personal wilfullness she had walked directly to the right position. Standing in the doorway of the Magnolia Nursing Home, speaking to the nurse in charge, Faith experienced the feeling she was the other half of a reciprocal prayer. Where she had only weekends to work, this position was for a weekend relief nurse. She had no wardrobe. This position's requirements could be met by one white uniform, a pair of white stockings that could dry overnight, and one pair of white shoes. True, at the rate of six dollars a day before taxes, she wouldn't rehabilitate the family finances rapidly. But there was a degree of rightness about it.

In a deep, imponderable way she had the conviction she belonged in the Magnolia Nursing Home and that once there all channels would open. Was it because of Jane Allis she belonged there? Why in the world did God want her there, as a practical nurse? She was thirty-eight. Does one commence a new profession at that age? Furthermore, Unity taught rejection of negatives like old age, death, sickness. She whole-heartedly believed these things manifest only because man expects them, prepares for them—or because of misuse in thoughts and emotions.

Then why in the world did He want her there, amid the negatives of sickness, old age, and death?

Aura offered nothing.

On the worldly plane of experience her only qualifications were in having had four babies. No babies here. The average age was perhaps 75. Well, if her sense of health and harmony could be contagious that would be a mighty contribution!

She rested her head on the steering wheel. There were SO many things since coming to the farm. Adjustments on every plane. Physical. Mental. Emotional. Financial. Well, if God had work for her to do, He surely wouldn't let it be at the expense of the family—yet the family isn't the whole horizon!

If all this financial stress ensued because of her inner demand to tithe, then she would now begin working it off.

Tithe! She hadn't been able to stop!

For that she was a complete coward. She could neither go against Aura's injunction nor the spiritual meaning of that prison-like dream. And, wondrously, in keeping to the steadfastness of the tithe, spiritual strength and courage and faith had grown—even that day she slammed around and told Him off!

275

That thought brought the little scene to her memory of the boys coming to her from the kitchen while she was in the dark, triggering the memory of her mother. Except for this Unity stuff she too might have fled the challenges. Once her attitude toward her own mother was bitter, reacting to the childhood rejection. Now she saw it wasn't personal. Only God and her mother knew that which seemed too mammoth for Elizabeth to meet.

Peculiar. Faith had been required to meet many of the same challenges as her parents. Perhaps this alone is proof one cannot run from a situation. One must prayerfully seek guidance and courage, overcome and transmute the challenge. Well, if acecptance of a situation and the courage to work it out are the keystone, at last she was on the highway!

Her eyes filled with tears. Truly she had never been alone! Every moment God was close to her, she was conscious of Him through Aura. God is so wonderful. She closed her eyes tightly and the tears squeezed out.

"Forgive me please, Father. I've been bitchy, wanting things my way instead of Yours. In spite of me, You've opened the right door. I don't know why You want me in that nursing home, but I do know it must be part of my divine assignment."

A long sigh wavered through her frame. "I'm going to need You a great deal. This is pretty new stuff to me and my mortal knees are knocking already in fright. But like little Bernie said that's just the me part. The I of me is never anything but perfect . . . The I of me, this Aura part, moves forward in divine confidence. . . .

"O God, forgive me. . . .

"At last I am willing to do whatever You want me to do, and I've put my hand back in Yours."

The last Saturday of the old year was Faith's first day as a practical nurse on the 7 to 3 shift. Sally Blair, the pretty R.N., was the nurse in charge and Faith was under her tutelage to learn the tricks of bed baths, half-baths, thermometers, the intricacies of making a bed with the patient resident. Faith could have no better teacher. Sally Blair radiated joy and love to the little old people. As Sally took Faith on the initial rounds, patient after patient looked up into Sally's face and breathed. "Ah, Saturday!"

Keenly feeling the lack of proper training and awkward amid the duties of the three b's—baths, breakfast trays, and bedpans—

Faith sustained courage by humming. Musical comedy tunes or old fashioned songs familiar to these "girls and boys" to which she silently applied her prayer words. Occasionally the hum spilled over, bubbling with cheer. 'Christ is my light and my way, guiding me through this day, blessing through me, healing through me.' No one guessed her words. Some overheard the melodies.

Compassion and patience sprouted in Faith that first day. Compassion, the quality required to gently lift Eliza Brown from her bed, lean her against it as one might a department store dummy, lift the arthritic arms upward into sleeves, zipper the dress; clean the glasses that did little to assist cataract eyes but kept Eliza's morale on a higher level. She went the extra bit, touched the wrinkled cheeks with cologne. Eliza was delighted!

Patience, the virtue essential to meticulously walk Eliza from bedroom to living room with crutches, firmly supporting her from the back. The distance of forty feet required ten tedious minutes. Patience to gently lower Eliza into a comfortable chair so that she could sit staring at nothing, living in her world of yesterdays, isolated by deafness, near-sightedness and intensifying arthritis.

Something silly passed between Eliza and Faith that first day. Some joke or some little spilling hum, for oddly music reached Eliza when speech did not. Eliza Brown laughed. A most rusty noise. Recognizing its rust from disuse, Faith determined to bring love and joy to her new work as well as the contagion of health and harmony.

Eighty-five year old Eliza was not Faith's only patient. In the same large sunny room Clara May and Minnie had a bed. Back in what Faith would call "the boys' department" were Uncle Harry, Pop, and Mr. Kelley. The boys were semi-ambulatory—well, almost. Then Mr. Kelley meandered from bed to living room to dining room. Later there would be a long stretch when he would lie abed and slowly starve, waiting for the exhaustion of a strong heart, battling cancer of the esophagus. Uncle Harry remained in bed for his bath, then got himself in and out, off and on all day, occasionally requiring quick sales talks from the nurses when he decided to go walking in his brief hospital topper during visiting hours. "Pop" was a stroke patient, a heavy one, had to be lugged out of bed, strained back in.

Grammy Bacon, the little eighty-three year old in the very front bedroom, came nigh to being spoiled. Between her sunny disposition and the fact that she was Dr. Bacon's mother, everyone wanted "to do" her.

Faith remained attuned to divine guidance. While listening to Sally's teachings there was an undercurrent of communion between Faith and Aura. This day she knew herself to be a direct channel for Him. Rubbing Eliza's legs after getting her back to bed, Eliza laughed her rusty noise and commented loudly, "Your hands feel like an electric pad, Mrs. Whatdidyousayyournameis?"

"Wells," Faith supplied. Eliza's dead ears didn't catch it.

" 'Smells!' " She laughed and laughed. It seemed to Faith the rust was chipping off with each burst of laughter. "That's the funniest name I've ever heard. Mrs. Smells!" amid a fresh gust of laughter, feebly dabbing at her teary eyes.

Faith joined in the laughter. For some inexplicable reason she already loved this old spinster, felt irresistibly drawn to her. Perhaps it was the struggling shoots of the compassion plant for Eliza's loneliness and isolation deeply moved Faith. In a sense each patient was alone. Alone in a crowd. Compelled to live with strangers, waiting out the days until their hearts stopped. A fresh wave of compassion washed over Faith.

Eliza patted Faith's hand. "I heard you sing before. You sound like Jenny Lind. I heard her once. You are my Jenny Lind. Do you sing professionally?"

The question was so sweet. Faith knew if Eliza's hearing were normal she would not have tagged that last question. She gave a silly answer, anything to bring smiles to that wrinkled face, reduce the rust in the laughter. Leaning over and speaking clearly into Eliza's ear, "No. In my next incarnation I'm going to be an opera star and I'm practising now."

Eliza laughed heartily. "Are you going to be my nurse every day?"

Faith shook her head.

"Why not? I need you."

"I have two little people home who need me and two more who go to school."

"Oh," sadly. "How old?"

"One and a half; two and a half; six and a half; and nine and a half. Halves are very very important now, you know."

Eliza just patted Faith's hand again.

The day was filled with duties. Getting some patients up

and into the living room to look at television or out the great windows at Jack Frost's paintings along the brook or down the long driveway of stark magnolia trees. Making beds. Emptying wastebaskets. Answering bells, sometimes for inconsequential reasons like 'what day is it?' Laundering nighties for the girls. At midday luncheon trays to take around, help feed those patients who couldn't manage.

While making Eliza's bed and Minnie's after getting them into the living room, the hemiplegic patient in the third bed made much noise. Clara May's entire right side and her voice were affected. Faith approached the bed. The guessing began. Did Clara want her head elevated? The feet? Water? Bedpan?

To each of Faith's questions, a fresh outcry of frustration. More guesses on Faith's part. Almost hysteria on the part of Clara May. Faith stood quietly, witnessing Clara's temper. Then she spoke firmly, almost harshly, "Clara, stop your noise this minute!"

Clara did stop. Her eloquent brown eyes glared.

More softly Faith added, "Look, my Honey and I can do mental telepathy. Perhaps you and I can too. Let's try. But you must be quiet and calm or it won't work. Now," authoritatively, "hold the thought of what you want me to do for you. Just think that one sentence over and over. Okay? . . . I'm going to finish Minnie's bed while you do the thinking."

Slight questioning in Clara May's eyes. This surely sounded queer, but something caught from Faith's confidence, impelled her to try. And as Faith resumed Minnie's bed she sent an ardent SOS, "God, don't let me be stupid! Help me know what she needs!" A few more deft pats, heavy handed pats on Minnie's bedspread, more a stall of time than a requirement before she looked across to Clara May. No words or intuition from Aura.

Faith stood a moment at the foot of Clara May's bed. Gently, "You want to be moved to your right side."

Triumphantly Clara's head bobbed up and down, guttural noises of delight. Faith turned her gently. Clara's left hand could move and she caught Faith's to press it in gratitude. Although Faith left the room quietly she wanted to find a crying corner.

The staff ate after the patients' trays were returned to the kitchen. They helped themselves from the big pots on the stove, ate at the table in the office-dining room just off the living room, visible to the stony-faced, silent patients. The staff

279

of Sally, Hazel and Faith ate quickly to be ready for the first bell ringer.

"How do you like your work, Sweetie?" Hazel began pumping early in the meal. Faith recognized the leading question. More questions would follow until Hazel had the full picture of the Wells' family position. Well, as Dad Sanford would phrase it, Faith had nothing to hide, her nose was clean. True they might be horribly in debt but they were honorably working out from under the avalanche.

"Very much," briefly.

"We hardly get paid enough for the lifting and lugging we do," Hazel rejoined, priming the pump. "Goshamighty! I go home nights scared to death, thinking about what's going to happen to me when I get their age. Will I sit around in a chair and wet it like Clara May or be full of poison and snarls like Fisher upstairs or try to see through cataracts like Eliza? Anything awful can happen to you!" Hazel stopped to shove a chunk of pie into her mouth.

Faith made no rejoinder. She too was working for six dollars a day—before taxes. More than that, really! Faith Wells was here for some divine reason she did not understand yet. Some part of her divine assignment! She was like the man building the cathedral, not the man working for bread or the man merely laying bricks!

And how awful! Hazel to go home and stew about the future! If Unity and psychology are right, that we bring into manifestation what we continually think about, then this is what Hazel is expediting into her life! God help you, thought Faith, looking at Hazel with great compassion.

"Ma! Ma!" came from the boys' department.

"You'd better answer that," Hazel volunteered. "When he calls for his mother he means it. The rest of the time he wants you to get in bed with him. He'll be telling you soon how strong you are, and showing you how strong he is, Sweetie."

Faith had time only for a horrified glance at Hazel. Surely Hazel was way out! While in the boys' department, Faith overheard Hazel's whisper to Sally, "She's a deep one!"

If Sally Blair made a comment it was lost to Faith. Again at the table Sally took up the conversation much to Faith's re-

280

lief. She felt she was on a volcano, that whatever she might say in Hazel's presence would be misunderstood or misused.

"I heard my favorite six-year old conversation this week," Sally began. She turned to Faith, "Do you know Andy Mack? He's the son of the musician up in the hills near you. He and my Jonny are bosom buddies and Andy was down for the weekend. While they breakfasted Monday I overheard this gem. (Perhaps I'd better explain that Jonny is rather overwhelmed with three teenage sisters a little preoccupied with boys.)

"Said Jonny to Andy, 'Sex! Sex! That's all you hear around this place.'" Sally further explained, "All the teenagers' favorite name calling is 'Oh, you're sex crazy,' you know. Andy made no comment. Just kept on eating. After a bit, Jonny continued, 'Sex! You'd think there's nothing else to talk about like fishing and trucks and trains and storybooks.' Still no comment from Andy, just kept right on eating. Finally Jonny was suspicious and said, 'Andy, do you know what sex is?' Andy has a foghorn voice and he boomed. 'Sure I know what sax is. My father plays one and makes lovely noises.'"

Faith laughed heartily with Sally. This was safer ground, talk about children and their conversations. She had a couple of family honeys to share too.

But Hazel was waiting at the pump the minute the laughter ceased, "How long have you lived around here, Sweetie?"

"Almost four years." Might as well satisfy Hazel.

"Are you from town? High Bridge?"

Faith could have supplied a one-word answer, but she parried for time, putting in a fresh mouthful, contemplated possible answers. Deliberately she chewed while toying with a monosyllable answer or the comprehensive picture. Hazel waited.

"We bought a farm on a shoelace. Not only the tip but also the string gave out. What money didn't go underground to rehabilitate depleted soil went for replacement equipment when the second-hand stuff the former owners installed died. Inconveniently. Stuff like an oil burner, electric water pump. Gutters and leaders on the house. Septic tank. Barn roof. Quite an endless stream." Faith expelled a long sigh.

"When the money was no more we had to do the work ourselves. One dry well we had dug professionally, the guy had machinery. I helped dig the other one in back of the kitchen. I've bailed out the cellar and delivered lambs. I've painted all the trim in the entire 10-room house and the rooms are large. The living room is 17x32. John did all the walls and the exterior. I've transferred ten years worth of manure from the barn to the garden with the aid of a wheelbarrow, my sweat and my brawn. One summer John spent three weeks' vacation engineering a new water supply to the house when the old one became sieve-y between the spring house up the road, five hundred feet or so, and the cellar. The job required engineering, masonry, carpentry, and plumbing. And I defy anyone to detect it is not a professional job!"

There it was. Hazel had all but the figures. It ought to keep her quiet. Faith hadn't minded the physical work. That was a revelation period in her spiritual growth. Those were the days she learned to walk and talk with God, building with strong affirmations. She learned to let Him work through her hands and her willing feet. She learned to listen to 'the still small voice within' and to differentiate it from the clamorous voices of the world. All she railed against were debts, the breakages of essential equipment that kept thrusting them into the sea's breakers every time they gasped.

"Goshamighty! Digging a dry well! You got children too!" Hazel gasped.

Faith grinned quickly. "We're doing much better now." It was a metaphysical answer, according to truth and not the facts or the appearances. The Pennsylvania Dutch neighbors would word it 'it's for so but not for real.'

"Do they just sit around and wait for the end?" Faith turned to Sally, her head indicating the living room people.

Hazel inserted her crude answer, "What would you expect them to do, Sweetie? Most of 'em have hands that are gnarled with arthritis. All they can hold is a newspaper or fold napkins. With a census of twenty-two we can't keep them folding napkins all day—and their eyes don't hold out for reading."

Faith could make no response. Eliza's bell interrupted further conversation. Lunchtime was over. Barely a half hour. After sitting in the living room two hours most of the little old people were tired, ready to be lifted back to bed.

Sally called after Faith, "Mrs. Wells, all of them but Grammy

282

Bacon and possibly Mrs. Macaulay will want to go to bed. Mrs. Macaulay can stay up if she wishes. If you need help lifting anyone, call me."

"What'll I do with Fisher?" from Hazel. Faith turned to listen, hopeful Sally's answer would be an instrument of teaching to herself.

"What do you mean?"

"She's full of fight. Look how she scratched me this morning," displaying a long gash on her right arm. "I only wanted to comb her hair."

While Sally contemplated an answer Faith interjected, "Just love her, Hazel. That's what most of them need. Lots and lots of love."

"I'll love her all right!" between teeth, eyes flashing.

"Don't you see?" Faith's tone pleaded. "They've been put off by their families. They feel hurt and unwanted. They're alone in a houseful of strangers. Love can cure the world."

"You're a queer one," Hazel shot back, lifting her bulk away from the table and lumbering to the stairs. Later as Faith was quietly busy with Eliza, undressing and readying her for bed, she overheard Hazel's loud, too-sugary tones, "Mrs. Fisher, Sweetie, can I comb your hair now?" Faith smiled to herself. Perhaps just harmony between patients and staff was His reason.

Whatever His reason Faith was now up and about His work, His divine assignment to her.

It was an education of breadth and depth that commenced the first day on-duty in the Magnolia Nursing Home, a gigantic step in learning the spirituality of giving in overflowing measure of loving work.

Eliza reinstalled in bed, ready for a nap. Clara May, overtired, crying to be put back. Clara hardly weighed as much as a sack of chicken feed, managed as easily as little Mari at home. Except for their weight and longer frames they were much like children.

And Minnie. Minnie was an independent spirit who liked to do things without nurse assistance. Minnie was eighty-five, talked of "my boys" with pride and joy. Faith asked politely how many boys. Smiling broadly, Minnie acknowledged five. When Faith expressed admiration, Minnie mentioned "Had two girls also."

But through the weeks Minnie would talk mostly of the boys. It was the boys who could wedge in a visit from time to time. Both

283

of the girls—women really with their mother eighty-five—were the hub of their families. They could not drive and were dependent on their husbands to bring them to see Minnie.

Minnie's babblings gave Faith lessons in psychosomatic medicine from time to time. As Minnie wiggled herself into bed that first day she chatted while Faith elevated the head portion of the bed, poured water for her, "I was doing all right. Wasn't sick or nothin' till I went to live with my youngest girl. Her place is small and there wasn't nothin' I could do. She wouldn't let me anyhow. Couldn't do it good enough, you know. So I just got sick and here I am."

Faith made no rejoinder to Minnie, but surely this stacked up with her philosophy of cause and effect—that we need a purpose in living. When the purpose is subtracted, even though it be a modest purpose, there is no need for continued life. Long life is not only given one because of long living ancestors but also by purposefulness. One must apparently have a goal and keep working toward it. If this is really the law of life, then society is all wrong. By our social security—even by unemployment insurance—we are doing man no favor, showing no real compassion. If these measures were merely assistance steps, if they only helped to bridge a gap—and of course this is what they were meant to be. It's that they are mismanaged.

Only that morning she overheard the nursing home cook explain to Sally she couldn't come to work Sunday, that if she worked too much she forfeited her unemployment insurance. Surely I cannot condemn nor condone this attitude, Faith thought to herself, but certainly Emmet Fox seems to be right; they require pity and prayers rather than criticism. If man's incorrect attitude toward money leads to many illnesses and unfortunate conditions as the hidden cause, if John's words to Pierre that the have's need as much spiritual teaching as the have-nots, then much of what this period of civilization promulgates is very wrong indeed.

Eliza interrupted Faith's concentration, plaintively saying, "I need you more than she does. I need a drink of water please."

Raising the glass to Eliza's lips, she cradled the old frame in her left arm. They're very much like children, she reflected, thinking of Don and Mari and their demands for water and toidy at bedtime, except the little folks at home had "bathroom privileges."

To Eliza's question as Faith removed the glass, "Will you be

284

here tomorrow?" Faith nodded assurance. Eliza settled down, serenity resting on the weathered features.

Hazel and Sally did charts together in the office-dining room. For the first weeks Sally would do Faith's until she knew more about the work. As Faith appeared Sally asked, "Did Clara May have a bowel movement? How was her meal? Would you judge her appetite to be good—fair—poor?"

The next shift came on-duty, sat through the verbal report from Sally Blair. Faith was dismissed. She drove home very slowly. Leaving the long magnolia lined driveway Aura whispered, "Stand ye still, and behold the wonders I will show you."

Down in the city, on hearing of Faith's new career, Auntie commented, "Some day Faith will be a healer."

Faith's conviction about supply channels opening proved correct. Now that she was "up and about the Father's work" doors of supply began to open. John received a salary increase, not huge but neither small. Through the co-op someone came for the mouldy corn. He paid forty dollars. While forty dollars was not several thousand, Faith accepted the whole episode as an indication she was on the highway of the Lord.

In January Faith experienced another prophetic dream. One of those clear, brilliantly etched ones it lived in her mind. She was in the north room of the nursing home, looking out at the landscape all frozen and winterized. Even as she looked, the rollingness of it changed and it leveled before her gaze. A small house took form toward the rear of the field. The foreground became a cropland. The mighty trees behind the little house began to change with seasons. The field was again level, the crop harvested, and the trees toward the rear assumed the magic of autumn. Faith's invisible guide said clearly, "When this comes to pass you may leave."

That's odd, she thought on awakening. That was Jane Allis' room. It's unoccupied. I wonder why I was in that room?

The weeks flew. They were filled with the busyness of being a practical nurse on weekends, fulfilling home responsibilities the other days. John was fabulous. While Faith nursed he filled the mother role—cooking, laundering, working and playing with the children. He even taught the older boys to make their beds. Then he instigated a point system, points to be credited for little duties they performed, to be tallied up and recompensed at the end of each month, a penny per point. Initiative on their part merited a bonus of twenty-five points. The boys scurried around to think up the extras, even little Don toddling out with milk bottles or down from the hennery, an egg in each fat little fist.

Early January produced a shower of lambs in the barn, almost every ewe producing twins. By the end of the lambing season all but four ewes produced twins, one even topped all records with triplets. John and Faith were ebullient, knowing this was the proper answer to their prayer for a flock increase.

In the nursing home Faith volunteered "to do" Cora Macaulay because her boys department required less time. Mr. Kelly was still ambulatory, shaved himself, fed himself. Pop she could shave in the afternoon while the girls napped. Faith liked doing Mrs. Macaulay, her alert mind delighted Faith. So it was to Mrs. Macaulay Faith especially poured her little farm stories, the other patients too for it brought them away from thoughts of pains and pills.

Combing Mrs. Macaulay's hair one Saturday, Faith began her therapy, "It's been raining lambs in our barn. So far all the ewes had twins. We have only a few more to go—deliver, you know."

Mrs. Macaulay clicked her tongue. "I know nothing about sheep. Do they have lambs in twos?"

"No. Twinning is rare among sheep. Just like people."

A contemporary of Faith's would have followed with "how come?" but Mrs. Macaulay said, "To what do you attribute your good fortune?"

Faith resisted the impulse to laugh at the old fashioned wording. "Do you really want to know, Honey?"

"Surely."

"It can be a long story," Faith grinned, a teasing glint in her eyes. "And I love to tell stories. Had lots of practice." Mrs. Macaulay missed the twinkle. "But I'll be brief. . . . We took the Lord into business when the going got tough, and I'm a constant witness to the power of prayer ever since!" She paused, finished one braid before resuming her story.

"We've been praying for 'the right increase to the flock at the right time under all right conditions.' Frankly, I hoped a huge check would arrive. It didn't. Part of me felt a little let down, to be honest. But now I see how wonderfully God does all things. If the big fat check had come, we'd have bought more stock. Then if all these twins arrived we would have attributed it to the new stock—or to putting sheep on new pasture. Scientists and farmers reason such factors that way. But this way—all these twins—and in each instance every set is a boy and girl—one for the market and the other for the flock increase—we are reminded of the spiritual teaching 'It is the Lord who giveth thee riches, and the power to get wealth.'"

Cora Maculay silently blinked. There was no denying Faith's sincerity of words and tone, but surely she spoke queerly. Cora Macaulay had never in all her eighty-nine years heard anyone speak like that. She was fascinated. All she offered was, "My!"

Faith loved her new work. It surely made her feel useful and purposeful in God's world. It gave her homelife a different perspective too, broadened her horizon magnificently. Listening to the patients talk of their lives, hearing their basic attitudes, she correlated her metaphysical studies with the case histories. Too, as the weeks slid by patients began to smile up at her on Saturdays with "Ah, Saturday" like they did to Sally Blair.

Sally was now able to leave Faith on-duty alone downstairs while she helped Hazel upstairs. The little old people waved off the television on weekends, preferring to glimpse Faith on her rounds, listening to the overflow of her songs. When the cleaning girl didn't arrive, Faith interspersed her brush-up duties with clowning, waltzing and singing with the carpet sweeper or the mop. One time Clara May hummed "Springtime in the Rockies" perfectly with Faith. It was the first articulate sounds Clara May offered since her stroke! Another time Eliza Brown turned to a new patient and shouted, "She's practising for her next incarnation. She told me," and laughed heartily. Sally Blair's brown eyes twinkled mischievously when she teased Faith about "the monotonous monotone on the first floor." Occasionally in the living room there was a conglomerate shout of laughter from the little old people, bringing Sally on the rush. They silenced immediately. It was their little party with Faith, and they weren't about to shut off their unprofessional but personal bit of frivolity.

Deep in her heart Faith still pondered God's purpose in placing her amid the negatives in the Magnolia Nursing Home. In February more pieces of the divine jigsaw puzzle fell into place one Sunday afternoon during visiting hours. Faith opened the front door to the visitor for Grammy Bacon, returned to the charts which she was now qualified to do. Sally Blair sat at the desk, completing her report, for it was almost shift-changing time. Before leaving, the visitor stopped off to see Sally. It was impossible for Faith not to overhear their low conversation.

"Who's the new girl?"

"Do you remember the girl Banners used to call for Jane Allis?"

So that was it!

This accounted for some of Sally's odd questions. This explained Sally's attitude toward her from the beginning. Faith could not have pinpointed how Sally's attitude was different. She sensed their stares while she continued charting.

"Funny," the visitor was saying, "Allis always perked up . . . even her death was different from any I ever witnessed—and I've seen plenty!"

Faith didn't dream Banners told anyone. She wondered why she did. Also, what had she said?

Through the weeks Sally had sometimes opened a mental door with a question, then seemed fidgety as Faith began her answer. Sensing some unknown factor Faith was careful to answer just the specific question Sally asked each time. She felt Sally was intrigued but perhaps didn't wish the responsibility conveyed with the knowledge.

Continuing down the charts, part of her mind busy professionally the other part reflected on an episode in the hall between Sally and herself a week ago. Sally had accosted her in the hall that Sunday, tears glistening in her eyes, "Faith, for God's sake do something for Kelly! I can't stand it! I can nurse when there is something I can do, but I can't stand by and watch a man starve to death. You can pray. I order you to go in there and pray!"

She had been startled by Sally's vehemence. She now reflected on her answer to Sally, measured it well in her mind. "There's nothing I can do unless his consciousness can be uplifted," she had replied.

"I don't know what you're talking about," Sally had retorted.

"A miracle is given only when a miracle is expected. 'As you believe so it is done unto you.'"

"I still don't understand. You give me platitudes about 'God is Life.' Last week at the table you said 'Death is a myth' or some such silly thing. My mother-in-law died. My mother died. My puppy died. I have seen death many times. But why this argument? I order you to go in there and try. When you know how to pray you're responsible to use that power. Pray!"

So Faith tiptoed in to Kelly's bedside where he lay. Skinny. A skeleton of a man. He was mostly under sedatives. Above his bed a two foot crucifix. It had come from his mother's casket. Faith had involuntarily shuddered when he told her.

"Eddie. Eddie Kelly," she called to him and his eyes opened in his wasted face. He looked toward her voice. He was conscious. Softly, "Eddie, are you praying?"

His voice was harsh and he answered between gasps. "I can't go on this way."

"Eddie, there's nothing impossible to God. You know that. He told us through Jesus Christ."

"Yes, I know that."

"Are you praying for—and giving thanks for—complete recovery?"

"I can't go on this way," between gasps.

"Eddie, God is Life. Not merely old age. Life! Constant. Perfect. No wheel chairs or incapacities. Not even glasses. Miracles still happen. Eddie," she paused for his full attention. "Eddie," are you asking for the miracle? Jesus said 'whatosever ye shall ask for, believing, shall be given unto you in His name.'"

"I can't go on this way," plaintively.

Coming out of the room she had met Sally's questioning expression. She had said, "His eyes are on the cross instead of Easter, Sally. Prayer answers are in accord with desire and belief and any prayer will expedite what Eddie wants. Death."

Eddie went early the next morning.

When they came on-duty the following weekend neither Sally nor Faith mentioned the episode or its aftermath.

Now Sally was whispering to the visitor, "You know," her tone was frank, a tinge of wonder in it, "she's as good as I am and she hasn't had a speck of training."

Faith smiled within herself. The reason lay in the truth she had come forth in Christ consciousness and whoever doubted His being efficient as well as capable!

Peculiar, this whole matter of being a practical in a nursing home among the aged when all her being cried out to work with youngsters, plant truthseeds in their hearts and minds. Youth would respond to such plantings. Not oldsters. They're tired. It's a lot of work to change one's thinking patterns. Faith could attest to that! She'd had to jettison practically every idea absorbed in her growing up years, teach herself to think through to the divine logic in a statement, scrap it if it did not stack up against Principle.

Unity's teachings are that ardent desires are the very voice of God calling forth that talent. So Faith knew her desire to work with the young must be a divine idea, but for some inexplicable reason it hadn't manifested yet. Also, positively and unquestioningly she knew that right then she belonged in the Magnolia Nursing Home. This too was divine assignment!

As February's last Friday slid into March Faith suffered a restless night. They retired about ten o'clock because Faith had to be up by 5:30, on duty by seven. John lay beside her, his rhythmic breathing accentuating her inability to get to sleep.

Again and again she turned in bed. This was silly. She wasn't worried about anything. Usually when it took her a while to get to sleep she slowly felt her way through the twenty-third psalm, interposing her own modern interpretation between the familiar lines.

> The Lord is my shepherd; I shall not want.
> He maketh me to lie down in green pastures.
> God is my shepherd and He so wondrously provides for me that I am living in constant abundance all about me.
> He leadeth me beside still water.
> He restoreth my soul.
> Just as sheep are afraid of things or water moving too swiftly, He leads me to safe places, and even though sometimes I have slipped—lost my temper or been pig-headed—He forgives me, cancels out the error, keeps loving me, restores my confidence and my courage to go on.
> He guideth me in the paths of righteousness
>   for His name's sake.
> Yea, though I walk through the valley of the
>   shadow of death
> I will fear no evil; for Thou art with me;
> Thy rod and Thy staff, they comfort me.

Even as I have been reluctant to leave the home and the children. He has brought me into right usefulness because He is so wonderful, knows I will help Him, be His channel, co-operative. . . . Even as I have been walking through the valley of debt, I know I am protected. There is nothing to fear for You are with me every step of my way. Your Rod of Power and Your staff to keep my steps from slipping . . . just the knowledge these are nearby is a comfort.

> Thou preparest a table before me in the presence of
> mine enemies:

Even though I err, in spite of character or personality, You patiently still provide for me. My only enemies are within myself.

> Thou hast anointed my head with oil;
> My cup runneth over.

The spirit of dedication I feel You have increased, and now our supply doors open up. No longer do we need to stint on measurements on our table. We have abundance and to spare, good to spare and to share.

> Surely goodness and loving kindness shall
> follow me all the days of my life;
> And I shall dwell in the house of the Lord
> forever.

Even as our abundant good multiplies, we shall no longer forget all our good comes from Thee.

Sleep was not to be wooed.

Even in the worst nights when Faith was tortured by their obligations she was able to pray and drop off to sleep immediately. Turning, restlessly, she felt a growing sense of alarm, like the day Itchy split, she reflected. Tonight it didn't seem personal. But in some odd way she felt she was needed, prayerfully needed. Somewhere. John and all four children lay peacefully sleeping. All the machinery in the house, the burner and the water pump, made proper noises periodically, in accordance with their individual patterns. The new oil burner was a thing of beauty and a joy functionally.

Quietly she slipped out of bed, loped the belt of the blue flannel robe around her figure, stepped into her slippers, felt her way downstairs. The house was cold, the heat having been down several hours. What time was it? Midnight by the Dresden China clock on the mantle.

She lighted the small lamp, slowly paced the living room, not restlessly, rather as though waiting for divine guidance as to whom to pray for. It was a kind of spiritual radar probing into space. No words. No names came to her from within. Aura was silent. On analysis the whole feeling seemed to come to her from outside herself. Psychically. Strong feelings. Undeniable feelings gripped her, held her commandingly.

That big living room was the site of much prayer these last few years. Its atmosphere spiritualized, permeated the very walls and furniture. Slowly, back and forth, Faith walked, communing. It was an emotional reaching upward within her own heaven, the silence of her heart and mind. Minutes passed while she climbed an invisible, mystical mountaintop. Imperceptibly she passed into a stage of silently speaking, praying. Affirming His love and infinite powers. Every name which came to her she covered with prayer. Home with those in Irvington, John's folks and her folks. Back at the old neighborhood in Chatham. Suddenly she stopped walking. Her girls! Her girls and the boys at the nursing home! That was it. Aura did not tell her. She was too preoccupied to wonder why Aura did not communicate.

She settled in the big wing chair, the green leather chairs too cold. Prayerfully entering the Magnolia home's front door she imaginatively visited every room, beginning with Grammy Bacon, Eliza, Minnie, Clara, the boys in the back room. Upstairs to Cora Macaulay. If Divine Love—if working with it in this fashion—held together the badly fissured furnace and kept insulated wires from igniting, Divine Love could reach across a mere seven miles to heal and bless at the Magnolia Nursing Home!

Faith held special love and compassion for her patients. It was easy to pause in loving thought in each room, mercifully hover over each bed, remain in imagination until the very room was bathed in the golden light of love. With little Cora Macaulay, Faith lingered a long time. She filled that room with the vision of Christ, not the Christ of the cross but the healing Christ, alive and among His people.

A sense of peace came as the little clock on the mantle gently bonged. It was one-thirty Saturday morning. Slowly, Faith withdrew from the Home, visualizing the golden light throughout its many rooms, over all its surroundings, thanksgiving in her heart and on her lips.

Now she could sleep.

She was a trifle late, arriving on duty while the report was being given by a lovely titian-haired R.N. Faith had never seen her before and she idly wondered who she was, if the regular night nurse had left. Faith sat on the table.

". . . Fisher—good night. Bloom—restless until 12:30, gave her a nebutal. Smith—soaked this morning but a good night. Rafferty—usual night. Jones—noisy. Macaulay—." She drew her breath, let it out slowly looking up from the report to face Sally and Hazel. She was unaware of Faith's presence.

"We have a new patient in with Macaulay, admitted late yesterday. Alice Starr. Although the screens are up, Macaulay couldn't help but be disturbed. So Macaulay had a fair night, might want to sleep late this morning."

She closed the report book, leaned back in her chair and gave full attention to Sally, her glance occasionally included Hazel. "We had something peculiar happen last night, girls," she paused, seemed to consider her words. "Nothing you can put into a report. Honestly I don't even know where to put it in my mind."

"What?" the duet from Sally and Hazel.

Watching the reporting nurse's face Faith thought her unusually lovely. A spiritual face, Faith thought.

"Well," continued the R.N., "this new patient came in early in the evening." Referring to her chart, "Ten-thirty. Came in wanting to die. I suppose the pain was that bad." Sally and Hazel were all attention. Faith sat bolt upright! Ten-thirty! The beginnings of her psychic disturbance!

"Dr. Steward was here most of the night with her. Mrs. Mason is specialing. Mason called me in. Everyone was there, including the patient's husband and son. By then it was about one o'clock. Dr. Steward had the stethoscope on her, and he said to the family, 'She isn't going to make it. . . . She's going now.' In a little bit, he announced, 'She's gone.' He removed the stethoscope and we all filed out with that hopelessness one feels at such a time. Mason remained to do the necessary. As she rolled down the bed and

293

began, we all came to the living room," her right index finger gestured. "Dr. Steward and the family. We all stood around saying those empty things . . . 'God's will and must be for the best.' Inside me there was revolt! All I could think of was that magnificent woman and all the wonderful things I have heard about her. Do you know her?" to Sally and Hazel. Both shook their heads.

"Well, she has a list of good deeds that would make a Girl Scout green! I've known her years through my aunt and the Eastern Star organization. Well, I just couldn't stand it any longer. It seemed such a waste to me. That lovely woman! I left and came out here to do the morning medications. Dr. Steward was still there with the family when I heard Mason run down these back stairs. I knew by the speed of her step—and then her face—something had happened. 'Come quick' was all she said.

"Up we went."

The R.N. paused, swallowed, and said clearly, "The patient was alive!"

No one commented.

Faith was incredulous! Deeply moved. Relieved no one was mindful of her.

Sally and Hazel looked astonished.

The R.N. was continuing, "She must have been gone—Mason and I calculate—it must have been about seven or ten minutes. It was precisely one-thirty when we saw her . . . her return."

Sally and Hazel were busy with questions. "How could Dr. Steward make such a mistake?"

"He didn't!" The reporting nurse defended him. "Mrs. Starr went through all the usual indications. Mason and I saw them. Furthermore, he had his stethoscope right there. He couldn't have made an error!"

Faith was in a silent turmoil. She wanted to get away, but she feared attracting attention by leaving the room. Definitely she had received psychic vibrations the preceding night. Distinctly she had arrived at the sense of peace—and the time coincided with what the nurse called a resurrection! But Faith didn't know the woman! How could she be a Christ channel of such magnitude! She knew God did the work, but surely she wasn't worthy to be such a tremendous channel!

Yet—how explain what she had been through the preceding night?

How explain the coincidence of time?

"What did you and Mason do?" Sally's practical question.

"Mason came down and got Dr. Steward immediately, told the family to wait a moment."

Sally shook her head in wonderment, finished her cigarette.

"What do you suppose happened?" from Hazel.

The nurse shrugged her shoulder. "All I know is she came in wanting to die. When the pain subsided after the drugs got working she joked and said, 'Guess I'll stay around for a while after all.' Shortly after that she seemed to slip. It wasn't a coma. I don't know. . . . I've heard of patients dying on an operating table and as the surgeon massages their hearts they return. This . . . this resurrection . . . I witnessed. No one touched her."

Where had this little nurse come from? Almost every word of her report seemed especially designed for Faith's receptivity. Even the words 'she came in wanting to die . . . she joked . . . guess I'll stay around for a while.'

The very words concurred with Faith's beliefs that one dies only when he relinquishes his personal desire to live. Not many people talked or thought that way. Faith looked at Sally. Sally was watching the night nurse.

"Is she still under oxygen?"

"Yes. And specials around the clock."

"Imagine the feelings of her family!" Sally added.

The reporting nurse answered only with the eloquence of her eyes.

"What do you suppose happened?" Hazel repeated her question.

"Mason and I talked about it. The only thing she can think of is when she lowered the bed perhaps the law of gravity helped get the drugs where they were needed. . . . But as soon as the heart stops pumping, everything stops. I don't know. I can't explain it. All I know is that it happened. I saw the dying process —and the coming back process, the resurrection."

They lingered over the discussion. There was a note of reverence in their attitude. Finally Sally arose, "We'd better get to our work or the breakfast trays will be ready before we are."

295

Faith was glad to be alone with her first floor duties. She didn't sing. She was deeply humble and full of wonderment, quietly subdued as she moved from patient to patient. Again and again her heart asked the same questions. How could she be a prayer channel for this . . . this resurrection? She didn't even know the woman! Yet if she hadn't been the channel, why the coincidence of time? Why couldn't she sleep until after one-thirty? Why the sense of unrest and disquietude at ten-thirty? Why had her feeling of peace coincided with . . . the return? Where had this strange nurse come from? Was she a link in the whole peculiarity? Every word of her story seemed to be for Faith.

Eliza bubbled, "You're quiet today, my Jenny Lind."

Faith smiled faintly to Eliza's teasing.

"Anything wrong at home?"

Faith shook her head quickly, eyes closed momently.

"Did I say anything to hurt you?"

"Bless you, no!" spontaneously Faith hugged Eliza, kissed her cheek.

She was slow with her work, part of her dreading to go upstairs to do Macaulay. She wished Hazel would volunteer just this once. Silly! What was wrong with her! Why didn't she want to visit last night's scene. Hazel's clarion voice paged her from the second floor. "Mrs. Wells, Sweetie, Mrs. Macaulay's ready for you."

"I'll be there," dead mechanics in Faith's tone.

Well, it had to be accomplished.

At long last Faith stood in the doorway of Macaulay's room, Macaulay's bed hidden behind screens. The first bed was surrounded by a plastic tent, the noise of the oxygen machine reverberating. The special nurse was absent. Bolt upright, the patient was sleeping. Faith approached on tiptoe, eyes riveted on her. The little titian-haired nurse judged well. Strong, capable hands reposed outside the bedcovers. Faith stared at Alice Starr, speechless, her very soul stretching to Infinity in reverence and humility.

The special nurse returned, silently smiled at Faith.

I can't account for it, Faith thought. But, dear God, if I was part of it all, thank You for using me. Help me keep clean to be Your Christ channel always.

Behind the screen Macaulay was muttering to herself as Faith appeared. "She had an awful time last night," Macaulay offered.

"I had a dreadful night! All of them were in and out most all night." Macaulay was complaintive. Faith wanted to reprove her, tell her a miracle occurred in that room. Her lips were sealed. This day she could make no small talk. This day she moved as on an altar, attendant to a perpetual sabbath.

Before going off duty, Macaulay still downstairs with Grammy Bacon, Faith slipped into the room. Now drawn to the scene, her reaction as inexplicable as her morning dread, she stood at Alice Starr's bedside. Faith silently blessed her as wonder and awe flooded her being.

"You will have an unusually high purpose in living now . . . especially if you remember with your conscious mind. . . . And I believe there's going to be an inseverable bond between you and me forevermore. In a strange way, you are closer to me than our children . . . perhaps showing me a potentiality not only for myself but for every one."

The view from the north room gradually changed that spring. Dr. Steward had a bulldozer shove the hilliness around, level the ground. Grain was planted. In the early summer a little house was erected in front of the giant trees. Faith watched. The procession of the seasons and events matched her vision in the January dream. The trees donned their autumnal colors. It was time to leave.

Faith awaited measurements and the issuance of uniforms from the Sanitorium seamstress. As the woman dawdled Faith's gaze wandered about the large, sunlit room, reflected that the assistant resembled Aunt Elsie, noticed the tidiness of the whole area. Returning attention to the seamstress Faith noticed the inner light of the beautiful oval face, dominated by lustrous large brown eyes. Beside the curtained booth where Faith stood a German motto was tacked above the desk. She speculated on its meaning. Knowing the translation would be like categorizing an individual by the books in his library. "What does that mean?" she asked.

Either the woman did not hear or she was concentrating on measurements. Faith repeated her question. Abruptly the woman stepped back, the lustrous eyes seemed to X-ray Faith. Her lips moved silently as uncomfortable seconds flew by. Ponderously, "Are you—do you—know Frances from Hampton?"

"Yes," Faith admitted, wondering what knowing Frances had to do with the German motto and its meaning. "Are you neighbors?"

Ignoring Faith's questions, the seamstress continued, "Are you Faith Wells?"

"Yes." Of course, she was Faith Wells. The very slip she proffered authorizing the issuance of five uniforms and five pinafores verified that. The woman had read it, and reread it before moving to the stacks of uniforms. Her unblinking stare slightly disconcerted Faith. Once more she repeated, "What does the motto say?"

A brief glance at the motto as though it were another compartment of her thinking. "God is love," mechanically. The continuance of her stare.

Faith's brow puckered momentarily. She had the feeling this woman did not wish to translate accurately. She wondered why. Well, the woman had a right to the privacy of her motto. Faith would pry no further.

Mrs. Lance now reached for a uniform. Suspending it from the floor she deftly unbuttoned it. Her next question was deliberately casual. "Are you the Faith Wells who has the backyard prayer-study group and teaches metaphysics?"

Faith admitted to the teachings. Her mind raced with speculation about Frances and this Mrs. Lance, possible conversations between them. She, Faith Wells, was here at the Sanatorium by divine direction. No issuance of orders or handwriting on the wall. No sequential prophetic dreams. The one January dream was sufficient—and complete, for surely the view from the north room changed precisely in accord with her vision in the night. Eliza was dead now. Alice Starr healed, discharged. In fact, it was Alice Starr who propelled the prayer-study group. Faith smiled faintly, remembering Alice's taking her hand between her own one Saturday morning as she said, "Honey, whatever it is you have, I want it!" And Alice was an organizer with know-how. Once out of the nursing home and increasingly strong, she had a little group of interested women assembled, and had called Faith for a weekly date.

Faith didn't believe her work here at Kipp was to be—in the open, so to speak. She was impelled here for several reasons. First, God's, of course. That intuitive feeling she belonged here—

298

for now, at any rate. Also to get those debts liquidated faster. A gross of six dollars per day doesn't accomplish the objective very quickly.

Mrs. Lance stepped back, surveyed the garment's fit on Faith. As from a great distance and weighty with the slow pull of her thoughts, "Frances told me you teach 'Jesus Christ is now here with me, raising me to His consciousness of unfailing faith and I abide with Him.'"

Faith smiled. Truly Frances carried the light. It was a long affirmation. Faith began to speak but Mrs. Lance's words fell in measured cadence.

"So now you are going to work here—and do your spiritual work in what you call 'the silence,' no doubt. Will you do it openly by and by? There is much for you to do here. Much! There are so few who believe enough. All of them hold their TB close to them, afraid to let it go. They are familiar with it rather than with Gott."

Smiling compassion began in Faith's eyes, encompassed her entire face. Softly, "It needs only one to believe, and that radiating faith can produce the divine adjustment. We can never force faith—or the acceptance of these new interpretations, but prayers from the silence of a loving heart accomplish wonders. We must call forth the Christ within each one, letting God do the work while we remain the Christ channel. . . . Sometimes it is better to bless and divinely love from the silence. Other times there are words to say. When we listen to God's guidance, we always know which is right in each instance. Some folks believe the will of God is illness, death, or poverty. If that were so then everyone who tries to heal or prolong life would be guilty of direct violation of God's will. More of us need to realize God as health, harmony, and supply, as well as the Creator to be worshipped. From your light and mine—held high—many more will."

"Amen," softly intoned the seamstress. "Bless you! Bless you!"

Faith walked into the sunshine.

On a Wednesday night Faith began at "The San," working the eleven to seven shift. The first three nights she would be on the third floor with the children. After the breaking-in period she would be delegated to the first floor, attendant-in-charge at the English Pavilion.

Upstairs with the little ones those first few nights she had only to check on them from time to time, recover the squirmers, get the bed-wetters up periodically. At six o'clock in the morning, they were to be awakened for temperatures and pulse-takings, the very young children assisted with morning ablutions. Long ago there were a hundred-plus children in this building; now only ten, for tuberculosis seems to be an old man's disease instead of a children's.

The first floor patients were semi-ambulatory men, preponderantly middle-aged or older. There would be less to do. The supervisory nurse suggested Faith bring her knitting, reading, or mending for the long night hours. Occasionally someone would require an aspirin or rhubarb-soda. Mostly the position required that someone qualified as a practical nurse be in attendance.

Faith approached this new position with many separate thoughts and ideals weaving into a design. Here she would find younger patients, desirous of living, less tired by life, more responsive to spiritual work done in the silence as well as sufficiently virile to tackle the ardous task of remaking mental habits. "For if everything begins in the mind or the emotions—and that's the subconscious mind if I know anything!—then no cure is permanent until the mental correspondent is removed. Man is a whole unit as well as a holy one. Spiritually we are our 'brother's keeper,' yet each must make his own at-one-ment with God."

So Faith reasoned.

Looking out the southern window of the third floor to the heavens this was Faith's upper room. It was easy to commune here, easy to pray for her loved ones, all in her prayer-study group, the patients and those who now telephoned her at home for prayer requests. This was her mystic mountain.

She determined to set aside an hour nightly as meditation time. From one to two o'clock. At five she would watch the dawn, observe the early streaks of light in the east until the colors swept the entire horizon.

Interspersing the meditation period, Faith paraded the corridors, only the starch in her uniform interrupting the stillness of the night watch, the white pinafore glowing in the darkness whenever caught in her flashlight's beam. Sometimes during these dark night vigils, looking down the mountainside toward the air signal at Clinton Point, she reflected on the seamstress' conversation and pondered her rooted conviction she belonged here just as she once

300

belonged at the Magnolia Nursing Home. She had puzzled long about that. Eliza's response to her joy and love were reason enough in the beginning. And then the Alice Starr episode!

But The San was different from the Magnolia Nursing Home. At The San she felt a familiarity as though she had lived there, known every nook and cranny, as though the very mountains were familiar to her. Before moving to this section of the state she'd never heard of The San or Mount Kipp, the familiar local name designating the State Sanatorium. Staring at the star-studded sky she knew precisely how the mountains dipped on the right, the way the five ridges of mountains cut into the heavens directly east on clear days. Morning proved her right.

In retrospect Faith could see the whole divine plan. Wonderful how dreams are fulfilled, much too perfectly to be mere coincidence. Once she acquiesced to God's purpose, obeyed that inner voice to be up and about a job, everything moved along in divine order and harmony, even the beginnings of the Farm Summer Home. And the prayer-study group that began in her backyard. Surely she enjoyed teaching them! All in the group were Alice's generation, twenty or more years Faith's senior, yet they recognized Faith as teacher.

How she had fumed at those closed doors! The little doors of banks, government, philanthropists, or the rich relative. Then Pete came to live and raise turkeys as though to reinforce the bolts on the little doors. All the while God was readying His vast door, the door of divine fulfillment—maturity and the divine assignment. It was as though God said, "I need you both in my world, not isolated among sheep and chickens." Even though the sheep taught them so much!

God's ways are always best, she reflected. Had the Farm Summer Home come through agencies of banks or the government they would be saddled with gigantic debts. Had Mary Banners not talked to Jane Allis . . . had Jane Allis not asked for the Unity friend . . . had the nursing home not requested her to fill in on a swing shift several times, Faith would not have felt she could manage this bigger assignment at the San with its larger opportunity to channel healings and truth teachings—plus its fuller paycheck to expedite their personal freedom from debt.

How wondrously John worked with the children on weekends, drawing them closer to their Dad. Wonderful John! He cooked for them, whether only their own foursome or during the summer when the Fresh Aires were with them. That point system he had invented: five merits for each well made bed, one merit for a milk bottle taken to the milk box, twenty-five when initiative was demonstrated. How beautifully this built for family cooperativeness and good management. Perhaps sometimes children are emotionally hurt when the mother is forced to seek gainful employment. Surely the Wells children were unusually blessed with richer experiences, closer life with Dad, during Faith's career requirements.

And how perfectly God had dovetailed their timing needs, so that either Faith or John could always be on hand!

She smiled dreamily to herself, reflecting on the long lists of divine dovetailings and interrelatedness. Even the fact that Faith had offered to do Cora Macaulay was used to the Lord's good advantages! After Alice Starr's arrival Faith was aware of her eavesdropping when Faith carried family stories to little old Cora on Saturdays and Sundays. Faith stooped—or rose—to deliberately using Macaulay as a sounding board to quicken Alice's receptivity to complete cure. Yes, He brought many miracles and wonders to the Wellses.

Walking the halls at rounds, Faith pondered her current position from another aspect. John had never known how far down they were, but she must not look back to that. She must keep positive with God, keep her vision on deliverance. This position would enable them to reach that goal more quickly. The only sacrifice was her normal sleeping pattern. Since God helped her with so many other details, surely a small thing like a sleeping program would be of no consequence to Him and her.

The only angle that truly bothered her was that there was nothing to do. Not for seven hours. She was not used to goldbricking. Faith knew and taught her prayer-study group that in accordance with spiritual law one must give good value. Here there was nothing to give. Not even beds to make. She was merely a glorified sitter. Yet—if she were to resign, someone else would be hired to meet the state hospital requirements: that a qualified person be on duty all night in the event of an emergency.

Teaching one must give good value she was compelled to obey her precepts. Or—she had not the right to teach it. Yet—she be-

302

longed here. Now at any rate. The conversation with Mrs. Lance, the seamstress, was one bit of proof. Also, that strange intuitive feeling. Looking down the mountainside, watching the stars move from the east across the southern sky through the night, hearing the long, slow freights move up the mountains, feeling and living in the Presence of God through the long night watches. Faith rested in the distinct awareness of divine indispensability. Perhaps no longer with Eliza or Alice. Now in some fabulous way her finite mind could not comprehend yet.

She would give good measure by praying for the patients, silently blessing them, calling forth divinity in each. Anonymously she could send forth Unity literature wherever He directed, make it available in the library. Also, "if thoughts are things" she could truthseed the halls of the building during rounds at night.

And, through all this program, she could study. This would be her sabbatical.

One morning as the supervisor walked in while Faith wrote the night's report, pleasantly asking, "How do you like it here?" Faith's answer was instant, hearty.

"Fine! It smells clean. It's nice. And no one invites me into bed with him!"

The last phrase slipped out. She had not meant to say it. It was the only feature of the nursing home experience she hated, for Hazel's warnings regarding Pop's invitations had substance. Once she had turned furiously on John when he teased about her strength. Some silly thing like opening a pickle jar. She recalled now how her emotion struck the atmosphere. "Don't you ever use that word again—not like that! That's the routine phrase the old boy uses as a build up to a request!"

The weeks sped by. The big dipper more to the south each week as Faith came on at eleven. The soft pastel colors in the morning east commenced sooner. It was established habit now, her only struggle was with sleep. Where the Buddha discovered the deep needs of the body for food and that high consciousness obliterated itself through too rigid a fast, Faith Wells modestly learned the tremendous demands of the body for adequate rest. Coffee and food were laggards in whipping awake her tired body.

She used metaphysics on herself, recalling Jesus spent whole nights in prayer and sleeplessness, that Carver and Edison managed their genius with only four hours daily. Her most difficult night was Friday. As Tuesday and Wednesday composed her weekend, usually she couldn't sleep before duty Thursday. Rest perhaps for two hours, but not sleep. From six Thursday morning until she finished the weekly food shopping Saturday morning after duty, a total of fifty-two hours, she sustained only six hours rest—the two-hour rest before reporting Thursday, a two-hour sleep when the little ones napped Friday, another two-hour sleep after John and she suppered together before reporting. Saturday morning she died! Died to the world around her while John managed the children, ran the day's laundry through the Maytag, kept up with the activities of toddlers Mari and Don, and the little men, Doug and Rob—plus the stock. Saturday evening John and she suppered together, her deep inner powers of being restored.

Social life was scotched, even modest dates with John to the movies. Practically everything now revolved around Faith's necessary sleeping program.

Fabulous though—really!—how well He managed in her! She neither looked worn out nor exhausted. The only hint of inadequate sleep was the purple cast below her eyes Friday morning, darker purple by Saturday. She joked about the program to John, "Someday perhaps I can forego sleep entirely. I always thought it a waste of time."

So, these nights she walked and talked with God, contemplated His universe, His stars. Talked with Him, listened to Him, understood Him more profoundly as Principle and Law as well as indwelling Father of Love and Wisdom. These nights she was a mystic atop her mountain.

Here and there, she became a channel of enlightenment and inspiration to her boys. Combining metaphysics and group psychology with slangy casualness, she awakened the men at six with a syrupy, "Good morning. Time to rise and shine for the day hath come." Or, "Wake up and greet the happy day." She did it deliberately, of course, knew their unflattering thoughts until they accepted this as her personality. They awoke sluggishly, the pattern of TB, and her phrases were designed to establish the day as a good one, a healing joyous day, quicken them spiritually.

Slight responses came during the weeks. Some commenced conversations in the hall when she headed back to the little office to

304

write the night report, conversations about religion, God, or what brand of church she belonged to. Faith knew these inquiries were the sprouts of her corridor truthseeding program.

Once one of them, Bill, reprimanded her for wiping the temp sticks incorrectly, tactfully teaching her about germs. Faith laughed easily, "I don't believe in germs, you see."

"What do you mean?" he demanded.

Faith could give Bill the same silly answer she gave John—like Peter Pan's comments about people not believing in fairies. Or—should she condense five or six years' metaphysical studies in one paragraph? Time was pressing. She had to be home in the driveway by 7:20 so that John could commute.

"It's a long story," she grinned impishly at Bill. Besides, she reasoned, her work was to be in the silence and through the Unity literature. Bill belonged to a fundamentalist church.

When Faith entered Bill's ward the next morning, he resumed, his voice pursuing her from bed to bed as she moved with temp sticks. Insistent as a pneumatic drill, she thought. She admired his persistency. Aura admonished, "You have no right to withhold truth. To ask is to seek. You are here as a channel—teaching as well as praying."

So, humbly she paused at Bill's bed. 'Help me, Lord, to teach,' she prayed silently.

"I don't know what you mean." Bill reiterated. "They see germs under the microscope."

She procrastinated, looking minutely at the temp stick, replacing it in its holder at his bedside, taking and recording his pulse. Bill lay quietly studying her face, waiting.

"Bill, do you believe the Bible?" The staff gossip had it that Bill was there ten years. Only lately, after turning to religion, did he commence to heal. "Not because it is in the Bible is it truth, but rather because it is truth it is in the Bible."

"Yes."

"Do you accept that God made everything?"

"Yes."

"Then just as the sun can only shine because that is the nature of the sun, so everything God makes is only good. If germs are not good, God doesn't make them."

"Where do they come from then?" There was a note of demand in Bill's voice.

Faith's eyes measured Bill a long while before she answered. She took various phrases from her mental files, returned them. None sufficed but one of Fillmore's. Yet that particular idea was an argumentative point with her many weeks. It had hounded her with its logic. Jed later expressed the same thought but by then she finished dissecting it in the laboratory of her mind. Could Bill accept the idea? Benefit from such acceptance? Only that idea persisted. Aura approved.

Slowly, gently, "Man creates germs, Bill, by his error thinking. Selfish thoughts. Fearful ones. Greedy ones. Lustful. Hateful. All the thinking errors."

Bill responded immediately, "I can accept that. Also I know there have been faith cures since the beginning of time." He turned his face from her to conceal his emotions. Faintly he added, "How do you get that much faith?"

She was over the hurdle. She had had no right to judge whom she might teach, whether fundamentalist or liberal. Quietly, "By using the faith you do have. It's a principle that whatever we use grows. Use your biceps and they get strong. Henry Ford said even our money must be used in order to increase.

"Spiritual faculties grow with use too. Use this self-psychology. Silently talk to yourself. Tell yourself you have lots of faith, limitless faith. Tell yourself you are a tower of faith, the faith that moves mountains and that God moves the mountains through you. No longer complain or criticize your lungs or any part of your anatomy. Your body is a holy temple. Bless it. Praise it. Tell your body God is working in it and through it, healing you. Just as you need God, Bill, He requires you to work through and to accomplish His work in this vast world. We are His hands and feet. Each of us. The lesson of the fig tree in scripture is that whatever one criticizes or condemns withers and dies. Whatever is blessed and praised, glorifies God. This is true in the body physical, in nature, in finances. Everywhere!"

Yes, here at The San was where Faith belonged for the present. No longer among the aged and infirm. They were tired of life, only required that their last days be mitigated more pleasantly. Here she could be a channel, either in the silence or by actively teaching wherever He directed.

En route home that morning it occurred to her that sometimes the mental correspondent requires surgery. But it can be spiritual surgery—inspiration, encouragement, enlightenment, and the power of silent blessings.

Not always was Faith's work on a high plane. Very often it was an everyday level of wit and humor, personality category, like the morning she walked into Sandy's ward and he sat bolt upright in bed, a puckish glint in his eyes. As she approached his bed he said, "At home my wife calls me Oatmeal and I call her Jello. Know why?"

Faith shook her head, held the temp stick ready.

"Because she's ready any time and I'm all finished in three minutes."

Faith laughed pleasantly, commenting, "Oh, I like mine cooked slowly in milk."

Proceeding down the corridors to the next ward there was a hilarious outburst of laughter behind her. She froze in her stride, overwhelmingly aware of his meaning.

In a personality sense she accomplished much with Buck too, quipping to his wisecracks each morning. It was so unusual when the patients awoke with all faculties perking! Approaching Buck for his pulse count one time he stretched heartily, his fist extended. "Heavens! Don't do that. My Dad taught me to box and you don't know what my reflex action might be!"

Buck caught the funning ball, "Can you wrestle too?" His eyes laughed full appreciation. Faith could almost hear the wheels of his mind racing. "What hold do you use?"

"Half Nelson," she shot back, thankful that was the end of the verbal sparring; it was the only wrestling term she knew.

Only once did Faith overstep. She erred in trying to force an entry. A patient on the secod floor, fretful and impatient, could benefit by a dose of tranquillity. "Why not use use your religion?" Faith suggested gently.

There was an instant retort, "No! It may interest you to know there's no one here who believes more in psychosomatic medicine than I do, but religion and health are something apart. Don't try to mix them. It won't work! Believe me!"

Faith made no rejoinder. There was nothing one could say without seeming to argue, and truth cannot be argued. It demonstrates. It proves by its workings. Faith could have rejoined that at one time in civilization the priests were also doctors and that they are again synchronizing, realizing afresh man is a whole

307

being—not a body with a brain and some emotions. She could have reminded about the instance of Jesus' admonition 'be thou healed; go forth and sin no more . . .' She could have used the story of Don and her Rh negative factor. She could have said Mari's delivery—and blood were miraculous. In Mari's delivery Faith was able to work completely in spirit and body. Thinking of the doctor's comment on the fifth day she smiled to herself. "Your daughter's okay, Mrs. Wells. We can't understand it when the whole history says she shouldn't be. But we've done blood tests every day and she's fine." Faith had just smiled and thanked him. He would have thought her a crackpot had she furnished her spiritual recipe.

But before this patient's closed mental door Faith's lips were sealed. She yearned to tell of the personal miracles she experienced since first reading Fox's *Sermon on the Mount,* followed by her sincere catharsis. Why, her "ticker" had troubled her several years after the miscarriage between Rob's and Doug's births. She wasn't even supposed to have Doug—to say anything of Don and Mari! Doc had advised her heart condition would be something she'd just have to learn to live with.

That blessed, haunting recurrent dream which led to Fox's magic interpretation. What a stinker she'd been on the 'inside of her cup,' her attitude toward her fellow man. She grinned to herself remembering how Doc shook his stethoscope after examining her heart when she was pregnant with Don, re-examined her, sat back and looked hard, then said, "What have you done? Your heart is better than it was in your first pregnancy." Sure it was! It was no longer loaded with hatred and resentment!

Lately too she'd noticed the hanging moles at the base of her throat were disappearing. And she no longer had corns or calluses on her feet. As a girl her complexion was quite sallow. It didn't seem to be now. How was it old friends commented she looked younger with the passage of the years, and the other day she overheard a patient say to his roommate, 'I defy you to guess her age. This one has an ageless quality.'

Well, she reflected, we all come to the degree of truth we can comprehend and work with in the right time. Where doors open I'll use the opportunity to plant Your truthseeds, Lord. Perhaps it's also like the sheep . . . a measure of confidence before they will heed my voice.

Slowly it occurred to Faith this was a test period—even as they thought their farm project a proving ground for truth principles. This is my challenge, she thought. I must learn to remain positive with God although in the midst of negatives and man's false acceptances. Although seeing appearances and effects with physical eyes, I must behold the truth in my heart. This will be my perennial conflict so long as I am a nurse, bridging the gap in writing nurse reports and commenting on appearances while decreeing the spiritual truth—that God is perfect life and health, freeing man from all limitations just so soon as the individual will accept the priceless gifts. Nurses are trained to look for symptoms. My metaphysical training has taught me to repudiate the appearances and affirm instant, constant perfection.

It's the old conflict. Sometimes they didn't understand the Master when He taught from the Son-of-God side. For centuries they believed He broke the laws of divinity rather than that He worked with those laws, employing the patient's faith plus His Divine love and imagination. If there were no law of instant healing, blood would not coagulate immediately, nor would there be any other miraculous demonstration of perfection in man's body temple. It seems self-evident! But I must not condemn or wonder at their slowness to comprehend. It had to be pointed out to me also.

So it was that time and thoughts passed. The ice and snow and sleet of winter produced washboard country roads, relinquished seasonal rights to pea-soupers and rolling mists of early spring. Many of those nights Faith straddled the road's white line all the way up the mountain to The San. The big dipper moved further to the southwest, from the top of the hill to just over the English Pavilion.

By the time the crocus thrust eager fingers to the light it was established routine for Faith to limit sleep, report at eleven for Mrs. Hunkin's report, pray and study between rounds until the pre-dawn, flip on the light switches at the ends of the halls, awaken the patients for temps and pulse counts. Not always did she remain on the mountaintop in consciousness. Sometimes, bolt upright in the chair during the meditation periods, she slipped into a doze, lulled by the quietness of the hours, drugged by her body demands. To counteract the physical numbing she held her meditation period walking the corridors, physical activity generating the power to remain awake.

During these weeks she marvelled how God works everything together for the highest good: The practical nursing career that furnished experience to qualify for this position, plus status for the establishment of the Farm Summer Home. The backyard metaphysical groups which came to her, for now there were two groups, both organized by Alice Starr. She loved the teaching programs. Unlike Henry Clay—or was it Daniel Webster—she didn't have to practice lecturing chickens. She could expound and dramatize to people! Receive encouragement through that wondrous chemistry known as empathy. Where educators taught principles by which man could earn a living, Faith could teach God's principles by which man could *be more*—establish his life as rich—rich in mind, soul, body, and affairs!

Truly she was constant witness to the power of prayer. Genuine, unselfish prayer! In her life with their children on the farm, with Pal—that little mongrel with the sense of humor, they had proved conclusively the workability of esoteric Christianity beyond any shade of doubt! She could shout from the mountaintop "there's no such thing as unanswered prayer! You don't do the work! Your prayers are to change yourself, bring yourself into tune with the Infinite One. And gloriously God works through you!"

Humbly Faith learned the truth that one must work with what one has, work in love, praising and being thankful. This concept did not come as a sweeping, overwhelming conviction. Aura didn't whisper or scream it. It came as a gradual perception. In its afterglow John and Faith constantly discovered big and little ways to work with God. Their wonderful Partner!

Just that week Faith found another opportunity. Putting her exhausted frame on the bed Friday night for the two-hour nap before duty, she breathed her prayer. "Dear God, give me the quality of eight hours' sleep in two. . . . Thank You." She couldn't recall the precise moment she slipped over the border between consciousness and sleep. She woke up to the ringing of the alarm, thoroughly refreshed. She realized too that she received that quality of sleep only when she remembered to ask for it.

Mulling the experience in the dimly lit corridors she wondered when all men would understand they could use God in their bodies, prayerfully, specifically. As Jed had said, now is the time for the integration of all spiritual truth and teaching. Not another

310

cult or church. Not another science or study. Rather the combination of all channels of God—religion, education, medicine, psychiatry, sociology, nutrition, chemistry, arts—literally all the departments and facets of God expression.

"The millennium," whispered Aura.

"I behold it," Faith answered, half aloud. All over the world man is renewing friendship with his Creator whether he calls him God, the Cosmic, Divine Mind, or by some Eastern name. Schweitzer, Laubach, Gandhi, Buchman, Unity, Divine Science— all the occult or metaphysical schools—each is an outer manifestation for the universal second coming of Christ. This second coming is already in the hearts of millions. It will antidote all the A-bombs and H-bombs, all the darkness of Communism and anarchy.

One Thursday night Mrs. Hunkin finished her report with, "That Joe Quelquhomme I mentioned is in the private room on the west side." She arose to get her coat from the back of the door. "He says he knows you." Faith was shaking her head. "You live in Red Mill, don't you?"

"Yes, but I don't know anyone by that name."

"Maybe you'll recognize him when you see him," buttoning her coat. "I'd take you down and introduce you, but he's sleeping at last. He's a bed patient. Did I mention? You don't mind introducing yourself?" her voice lifting in slight questioning tone.

Faith grinned impishly, "Since my nursing home experience I can meet any man, any time."

Hunky looked startled, but whatever Faith meant it was none of her business. She had a teenage boy to get out on a milk route in a couple of hours and she wanted home! Cautioningly, "You'd better open his door and look in on him whenever you make rounds."

Opening Joe's door noiselessly each rounds time, Faith verified his sleeping comfortably. Beaming the flashlight on the ceiling she could hardly tell what he looked like. The night was quiet. It always was. Faith walked the corridors, consulted the stars from time to time, wished she knew astronomy, fleetingly recalled Kessler's ejaculation, "Oh, God, I thank thee for thinking Thy great thoughts through me"—later used it for her meditation period.

These early spring nights she could smell the blossoms of the trees and shrubs, their fragrances increasing with the dews. Morn-

311

ings the birds greeted the dawn with her. Truly she was privileged to be atop a mountain for each dawn, watch the daylight creep into the lower places. Sometimes deer came out of the nearby woods, fed with rabbits on the clover in the spacious lawn before the English Pavilion. Surely, surely God makes a beautiful universe!

Finished with the men that morning Faith knocked on Joe's door and entered. He got the same lilting 'good morning; time to greet the happy dawn.'

A long, slender figure, he lay quietly under the covers, dark eyes surveying her every movement. She counted his pulse, recorded it. No, she'd never seen him. She was positive. What in the world had she collided with in the atmosphere of his room! It was almost a physical impact she'd met in the doorway that morning!

She flecked Joe's temp stick, wiped off the alcohol flavor, inserted it between his lips. She procured his wash basin, set up the morning equipment.

The thermometer removed, Joe mildly protested, "You shouldn't need to wash me. I can take care of myself."

Soaping the washcloth, she answered lightly, "Oh, I'm used to scrubbing dirty necks and ears of little boys."

"But I'm not a little boy."

A pixie note in her voice, "Most of us have second childhood ahead." Metaphysically it was a horrible thing to say. She did not believe in old age, therefore, 'second childhood' too should be scrapped.

Joe watched her minutely, enjoying the lights of laughter in her eyes, the lines of joy in her face.

"You have the hands of an artist," she commented, soaping his long, sensitive hands.

"You are so young. How do you know so much?"

"Faces can fib occasionally but hands always tell the truth, don't they?" she persisted. She was very serious, inwardly admiring those masculine yet sensitive hands. (Why was this man so familiar to her?)

"How do you know that?" His turn to be persistent.

Lightly, her face radiant, "I listen to the music of the spheres."

Moving into his private bathroom, she emptied the little basin

312

of its soapy water, hummed while she filled a waterglass. She picked up his toothbrush, emesis basin, and paste.

"I never heard anyone talk like you. Are you always so happy?" eyes wistfully on her countenance.

"Yes, I am. I hope it's contagious!"

Yearningly, "So do I."

While he did his teeth she fetched a glass of ice water from the cooler in the hall, placed it on his stand, began elevating his bed. When he finished his teeth, she adjusted his pillows, rolled his table in place for the breakfast tray.

"How long are you here?"

"Since the last night of the old year," returning the toothbrush and other equipment to his bathroom.

"One would think at least fourteen or fifteen years."

She brushed away the implied compliment. "I had a year's experience in a nursing home, week-end relief."

"Magnolia?"

"Yes." She surveyed the room and the patient, her habit before leaving.

He detained her at the doorway, "Do you come on tonight?"

"Yes, I just had my weekend."

"Will you come in and talk to me? I like to hear you talk."

"I have to check on you during the night," smiling.

"Wake me when you come on."

"No. Sleep is God's restorative. Better than pills or injections. Second only to food and joy. Have a good day!"

And she was gone to the third floor to check on the children before writing the night report.

Casual enough beginning, this friendship with Joe. Magnificent empathy developed between them, sometimes manifesting when he answered her unspoken questions. His very attitude brought forth the harmony in her soul, filled his with poetry. They inspired each other and their conversations were lofty, occasional bits of humor here and there.

One morning as Faith emptied his soapy water she remarked, facetiously, "There's a huge ant on your sink. Want me to kill it?"

From the bed his instant resonant answer, "No. I cannot give life, therefore I have not the right to take it."

For a split second she remembered Hunky's gossip that Joe and his wife deeply wanted children. None came. In the next flash she recalled Schweitzer's phrase 'reverence for life.' Whatever had prompted Joe's words Faith loved him for them! Standing again at his bedside she looked at him with new vision. Prosaic enough looking. Dark eyes. Olive complexion. Had what John would humorously dub 'holy hair, running from temple to temple.' But a peculiar opaqueness about his eyes, an impenetrability. She could not always know his thoughts. His emotions she heard perfectly.

Joe talked about the household of wasps living near his hobby shop at home, how he fed them banana—or at least left it for them. When he told his co-workers, they scoffed at him, warned he would be stung. "You know," he finished, "I think some of them felt a little miffed I wasn't stung."

"You wouldn't be. Anything you sincerely love can never harm you. Universal love. It's the cure for the world! They say there's a thirty mile radius around Albert Schweitzer's location in the African jungle. It's as though there's a distinct circle of divine light protecting him and all his hospital, for no dangerous animal has ever crossed the invisible line."

One night during her prayer period a vision came to Faith. Enswathed in white, she carried Joe horizontally in her arms through the lighted corridor to an altar at the far end on which she placed him. She interpreted this to be her divine assignment, her direction to exert special effort in raising Joe's consciousness for God's good.

So Faith began to offer packages of quotations and little family stories, all designed to assist Joe in a speedy recovery and for whatever divine purposes God had in Mind for Joe. Once, to his complaint about his heart (he had been admitted as a cardiac), Faith explained he could go down into his body mentally, speak to an organ, command it to perform perfectly. It was deep metaphysics quite beyond his comprehension. He lay there looking bug-eyed. She had tried too much too soon, although she also knew the validity of what she presented.

The next evening to reinforce that teaching she presented Dr. Alexis Carrel's quotation, "Joe, did you know that a famous doctor said, 'Except for a brain and a nervous system man could live forever.' Don't you see this means man is misusing his brain? The nervous system is merely the telephone lines from the brain."

Another time she presented Jed's quotation of the physicist . . .

314

"Joe, did you ever hear of Sir James Jeans? He said, oh, something like this, 'It may well be that the power of our thinking controls the universe around us.' Those might not be the precise words but it's the gist of what he said. The other night I gave you a medical doctor's viewpoint. This man was a scientist. Don't you see, Joe, they are saying the same thing! Man must learn to think constructively. *Constructively.* Then no one will ever be ill or lack any good, and all men will live in harmony everywhere."

She spoke a new language. Joe was fascinated, intrigued by the beauty of her ideals. He reached those long, sensitive fingers of his up to her face, slightly turning or tilting it as though for better lighting, scrutinizing her coloring. None of this was dangerous. Faith felt she knew all the dangerous approaches since her nursing home experience—or Andy down the hall who bid aloud for her attentions with a noisy, "If you were my wife, I'd never let you out of my sight!" Andy, not only with his noise but also his thoughts, made Faith feel unclothed. With Joe she felt safe.

Aura gave Faith no warnings, unless it were through the persistent conviction she knew Joe from somewhere, sometime.

So she peppered Joe, sounding casual enough with her evening or morning inspiration, "Joe, did you ever stop to think how fabulous the human body is? How it is continuously rebuilding itself? With every mouthful you eat, with every breath you breathe, your body and every cell, atom, and tissue is being renewed, sustained, rebuilt. Just think! With every thought you think—with every prayer from your heart or your lips—you are rebuilding not only your body but also your soul and affairs.

"I'll bet you don't know that by the end of six weeks you won't have one drop of your present blood supply. A whole new vital supply, this is such a continuous process. And blood is symbolical of life because there is no part of your body doesn't bleed if cut, and there is no part of you without life—or at least you should tingle all over with life " She laughed slightly. "Sometimes we walk as though we're half dead."

Her lessons continued, sandwiched with the morning care of soap and water, toothpaste and bed elevations, decorated with her quick smile and wit, permeated with her joy of living.

"Psychology says that whatever one thinks about frequently appears," she began another time. "Teddy Roosevelt thought and dreamed health, worked at it too, and from a puny body grew to a vital, dynamic, strong man. Religion says it poetically, 'as a man thinketh in his heart, so is he' and 'heart' is the ancient way of saying 'subconscious mind.' But our subconscious mind can't reason. It is a vast and terrific power house. With our thinking mind we have to direct that power. This makes it like the nine-tenths of the iceberg that sea captains of long ago feared, for the size and shape invisible under water is more dangerous than the visible part.

"So, Joe, it's simple. With your thinking, conscious mind you plant good suggestions of health, harmony. If you will do this with prayer—rather than the personal will, you know—you accelerate the engines. I'm mixing the metaphor a bit. But you must always be unselfish. You can't use this power to impose your will on someone else. Unselfishness. How the world needs to develop a universal consciousness."

But while Joe was entranced and fascinated, he did not always comprehend. Rather he thought of intriguing ways to capture this woman. The morning she funningly named him Sir Galahad he made the most of it. "Let me have your hand," commandingly, extending his. He had often examined her hand while she bathed or shaved him. Easily and trustingly she obeyed. He raised it to his lips. Kissed it. No passion. Mere tenderness. "You called me 'Sir Galahad,' you know," freeing her hand.

No business about being lonesome or misunderstood or her being strong.

Faith smiled trustingly, reflecting how all people need love and attention and joy. How they respond to it! People of any age! It's wondrous therapy in healing.

Knowing she loved him but misunderstanding the kind of love, he dared further, "Would you kiss me when you go?"

She grinned heartily, "They don't pay me to go around kissing all the boys."

"I didn't ask you to kiss all the boys. Just me. In fact, I wouldn't want you kissing all the boys."

She laughed him off, but he was gentle. And persistent. "Will you awaken me when you come on tonight?"

"No," firmly. "You are here to sleep as much as possible, and rest all the time."

"You said yourself my heart is strong. The other day when you did my pulse. Remember? And yesterday when the doctor made rounds he confirmed it."

The inner woman reflected, 'there goes the power of the spoken word again!' The outer woman shook her head slowly, definitely.

"Then I'll stay awake until you come. If you don't come to see me, I'll read all night."

Faith laughed aloud. Actually he took the orders. Not gave them. He counted heavily on Faith's compassion. Lying quietly, his dark eyes surveyed her minutely, calculatingly. Faith understood it all as being a happy kind of therapy, their conversations—other than her 'packages' designed to raise his consciousness—which flowed about beauty in nature and colors and poetry. The artist in each soul responded.

But the morning after kissing her hand, he wished her eyes upon departure for the day. "What for? Like someone in *Midsummer Night's Dream,* I've forgotten who. . . ." Faith's voice trailed off. Aura was screaming at her!

"Rather so you behold only beauty this day."

There, see, she retorted to Aura. It's all quite harmless. There's no need for you to get so excited. He's a pure being. No dark subtleties at all.

Then why do you acknowledge that certain quality of opaqueness about his eyes? Aura shot back.

Conversation was in order right now. Faith jousted verbally. In that routine lay safety. "I wish I knew why I feel as though I know you since the beginning of time when it's only a few weeks. Do you believe in reincarnation?"

"No. When you die, that's the end." He scrutinized her expression. He did not always comprehend her words but her voice and manner commanded his attention, awakened a quality he construed to be a clarion call to any Romeo.

"No one can prove it either way, of course," she admitted. "But I believe Life has a purposefulness and for Life to be one brief flash in what man calls time—well, enough of us don't achieve the highest spirituality in that flash. . . . And there are many things one can't explain except through acceptance of reincarnation. . . . Neither could I believe my God is a God of Love and Justice without such acceptance because of the seeming inequalities of birth in body, mind, or circumstance."

Definite and clear her words scintillated in the morning quiet of his room. She walked to the foot of his bed, leaned casually on the rolling table. "I only know I kept having unaccountable experiences until I said to myself, 'Okay, I accept this. This is the logic of the universe. God doesn't punish us. We punish ourselves . . . the eye for an eye, tooth for a tooth bit . . . we make our own junk.' From that moment on I never had peculiar experiences."

"What kind of experiences?"

"I remember standing on a small bridge looking down at the rush of water below me, feeling that once before, long ago, I stood exactly there with the same person. The personality part of me had never been there before that day. The other person later became my husband. We have a wonderful life together, a tremendous understanding. . . . I wonder if such a union could happen in one lifetime. . . .

"I believe nothing in life is willingly. I believe there is no such thing as coincidence, but that everything moves through law. The law of love—or its opposite, hate—which science calls gravity and man calls attraction. The law of order whether you think of it as keeping stars in their orbits or evolution. The law of creation, whether sowing and reaping in the fields or creativity that manifests as art, inventions or whatever."

Joe shrugged, offered no comment.

She saw that he was as Esau, the physical man who lived to eat, rather than as Jacob, who contemplated God and all His works. But from her vision in the night she was impelled to carry Joe to the distant altar.

It was time to leave. She moved toward the door.

"You are not going without my kiss."

With a rushing impulse she leaned over, kissed his forehead, impersonally but warmly. Then she was gone.

During her normal day at home, caring for the children, the stock, and the household, she pondered her actions. What in the world had propelled her to do that. What were these feelings she had toward Joe? And why? She never behaved like this in her whole life! Throwing herself at a guy. Before John came into her life, she was always able to maintain friendly relations with her dates, keeping the boys at arms' length skillfully and without too much frost. Even John she had dated a long time before she permitted kisses. She'd shared fellows' dreams and plans for rebuilding the world.

Furthermore and most important, she was happily married to John!

He was still her ideal guy, and surely she wasn't bored with life. Heavens, she had no time for boredom.

Also, according to Hunky, Joe was happily married. His wife visited him every day. She, Faith, had no desire to hang his heart on her belt. She'd never been promiscuous in all her life.

Then, what prompted her action? Surely receiving a vision to carry a man to an altar didn't require kissing him, not even his forehead.

She could not fathom her behavior. Neither could she account for the atmosphere in his room that first morning. Nor the opaque quality about his eyes. Intuitively she felt the opaqueness had something to do with his aura, that it was dark and not full of light as she sensed hers to be. Quietly her Aura agreed, cautioned too. Faith repudiated the idea of caution. Given the vision there could be no danger to her.

While Faith did not dread the night, knowing Joe would be awake to greet her, he haunted her thoughts all day. She who had practised mental self-discipline, deliberately choosing the thoughts she would entertain, now found herself enmeshed in thoughts of one Joseph Quelquhomme! She knew she was a receiving set of his thoughts.

Only John had awakened the flower of love in Faith. Oddly, John's way of awakening it was the same manner, gentleness and beauty. Lovely conversations about nature. Fragrances of flowers. Colors. Books. The sound of rain and the elements. With John it was walks in the rain too, coming in soppy and exhilarated from the joy of the elements. She did not remember that Joe once asked about her romance with John, wording his question deftly as to whether it were a romance of sudden, flaming passion, or slow, quiet growth.

She planned to say something to Joe that night. She would be definite but kind. There would be no further nonsense.

But Joe met the offensive campaign with artful defensive strategy. "Tell me, were you angry with me all day?" his opening question.

"No, I wasn't angry. I did the kissing. . . . Only confused. I have never thrown myself at anyone in my whole life. I am not behaving normally."

He ignored her confession. "One thing more bothers me. Did

you kiss me because you pity me?" His eyes scrutinized every flicker of expression.

"No, compassion perhaps. Not pity," then her eyes twinkled and a spontaneous smile swept over her face. "Besides you aren't sick to me. I behold the divinity in you—always completely well, in harmony and in prosperity."

They were a world apart in consciousness. Although he had no idea what Faith meant he was satisfied in a personal sense. His immediate questions were answered and they pleased him.

"Talk to me," his next command.

"You are supposed to be sleeping."

"Yes. I know, Honey, but I like to hear you talk. Your voice—I could listen to it forever. You are a strange woman."

Drily, "Thanks, and I hate to admit it but I'd prefer being called a girl."

"You are very young."

She smiled, rejected his bait. She knew his age from the charts.

"Ever read Maeterlinck's *Blue Bird?*" He shook his head. She had chosen it for its beautifully presented metaphysics. "Then I'll tell you the story, briefly, and you turn over to sleep. I have rounds to make." And for the next fifteen minutes she held Joe's attention, painting with words on the atmosphere rather than upon a canvas.

He had a wonderful night's sleep, his first without a sedative. Listening to his quiet, rhythmic breathing each round's time, she was pleased with her therapy. But in the morning when she finished his bedcare and was ready to depart, there was another kiss. No passion. But on the lips.

At home that day she was sufficiently disturbed to take her problem to the Lord. Accepting her mission so sweepingly she assumed she could dispense with step-by-step prayer. She had been intrigued by the psychic elements, the 'stuff' with which she collided in the atmosphere of Joe's room that first morning.

From the moment of return to Him for guidance, she attained mastery of the whole situation.

Reporting that night, Hunky commented, "Joe's waiting to say 'hi,'" and flipped the report book shut. In Faith's heart there was neither trepidation nor eagerness. Joe had never sent a message, so to speak, via Hunky before. Now Faith had an inner poise, the first degree of situation mastery. After donning her uniform, she walked the corridor with a new sureness of step. No specific thoughts, words or pictures came to her, nor had any come during her whole day at home. Somehow she had an increased understanding and she was more acutely aware she was being used—divinely guided and used—in the whole situation. She had had this assurance before, this wondrous feeling of divine channelship. Whenever she had this feeling she also wore the mantle of divine protection.

Joe stretched his hand to her as she opened his door. "Hello, Hon," eager words concealing a hollowness.

"How was your day?" A routine question. She already knew from Hunky's report. He had seemed low and out of sorts all day. 'Typical cardiac behavior,' Hunky had added.

"Depressed," he admitted.

"Why?"

"I don't know. Just was. . . . It is good to see you. Talk to me. Last night you told me the story of a bluebird."

"And a bluebird represents happiness . . . and happiness comes from within. . . . You should sleep," gently. "Remember—sleep is God's restorative."

"I want to hear your voice. I could listen to you forever. I've never heard a voice like yours. Nor thoughts like yours."

She remained silent. She wished to soothe him, but she must act in divine wisdom. She must not be enmeshed. She must maintain the objective attitude of the metaphysician.

Commanding from the bed, "Talk, please."

Firmly but gently, "No. Turn over now and rest." She made a movement to the door.

"You're not going that way!" He found her hand, put his lips to it.

Now what she planned to say the preceding night rolled forth. Words came in a detached fashion as though being said through her, Spirit using her as a vehicle of expression. "Yes, Joe. It is time for brakes. Time to pull up the tiny weed lest it grow into a tree— or dam the trickle lest it become a torrent."

"Honey!" His word stabbed the air.

Faith's pause was only momentary. With the same firm evenness in her tones, "Yes, it is. We are both sensitive and emotional. You and I are each happy in our marriages. Mine is a made-in-heaven variety. . . . If I were to meet Isabelle I want to be able

321

to look her right in the eye, not require forgiveness. We have said these kisses have nothing in them, that they are pure. But even pure love must be tempered with wisdom."

Joe did not touch her hand or arm again with his lips. He lay his cheek against her palm, and there was strength in his gentleness. His reply came in a whisper, "You are right. Must you always be? You are so young, yet you speak with the loftiness of the ages. 'Love tempered with wisdom.'"

"Good night. Joe. Have a good rest."

She stepped into the corridor. Outside, making rounds through the stillness of the night, only the starched swishing of her uniform interrupting the monotonous quiet, she pondered. Pondered his reported depression, pondered her opinion he was not a cardiac case for his pulse was strong and even. Slow perhaps. But strong. Pondered the manner in which her words came forth, those things she contemplated saying the preceding night had rolled forth effortlessly this night.

Briefly, in an outer sense, she was frightened. Who was she to opine whether or not Joe was a cardiac! This was not only a man's soul in her hands but also his body!

But greater than the flurry of doubt was the welling up within, the steady spiritual assurance she was being divinely employed as a channel of enlightenment, that only good could ensue from the whole episode. Good for Joe. Surely not harm either to his physical body.

During her prayer period another vision came, a slowly opening door. It was little better than merely ajar. And it was exceedingly dark beyond the doorway. She did not fully understand. If her action were divinely guided the room beyond should be full of light!

Checking every hour she found Joe awake. He greeted her each time she noiselessly opened his door. She was confounded. He couldn't afford a sleepless night, and she disliked resorting to sedatives. If her kiss acted like a sedative, why not bestow it? But she wasn't a giddy kid, and neither was he. One doesn't go around kissing a man to woo sleep for him. Not even if one walks into psychic stuff in his room!

Why that unshakable conviction she knew Joe from somewhere? Sometime? Why? Why, God!

Always her voice sang as she performed the morning wake-up

routine. It was her way to awaken the men, her joy and happiness she could so easily bring to this almost-sinecure. That morning she was full of questionings. The song did not bubble in her voice, would not effervesce.

Joe noticed the absence of the lilt in her voice, but neither made direct reference to the preceding night's conversation. Faith asked if he would like her to 'cook up some reason for the girl on third to do his morning care.'

"No. I've known you a long time, Honey. I've driven past your place just to see you. I will still have to, I guess. . . ." Dreamily, "The first time I saw you was when you were crossing the road with a ewe and two lambs."

She could find no comment. Inwardly she winced at sight of the purple-black circles under his eyes. In an effort at being kind, "Now it is clean between us, Joe. Now you and your Isabelle can visit us any time."

Aura screamed again. She didn't have to go that far as a divine channel of light! Leave him at the altar. Carry him there. But leave him.

"I haven't the strength."

"I have strength for two," she affirmed. His dark eyes surveyed her, nourished themselves on her radiance. She sought to turn the whole thing toward spiritual channels. "Isn't it wonderful how each experience in life expedites one's understanding and compassion? I never thought two people, happily married, could . . . could get rolling." She had floundered for an instant. But the next words rang with definite assurance. "We shall receive great spiritual strength from rising above this thing. Your healing will be hastened."

"If you say so I believe you."

It was a strange answer. He knew nothing of her metaphysical work, of the power of the spoken word, or of her divine assignment. She had chosen words carefully, seeking to quicken his consciousness as well as because words have miraculous power, because they are 'spirit and life.'

She had thought of their first meeting many times, of the collision with the atmosphere of his room. At first she had believed it to be 'soul stuff.' Later she thought it psychic stuff. Now, in light of his comments about seeing her cross the road with some of the stock, the whole thing was cast into a different design. Might it be that his intense desire projected his illness? Generally people do not see a connection between cause and effect, that their ardent wishes produce fulfillments.

Slowly she moved to the foot of his bed, raised her foot to the comfortable place between the bed spokes. It was an unprofessional position but Faith's concept of herself in this position was as a growing metaphysician rather than a practical nurse.

"I know we have acted in divine wisdom," she said distinctly. "You don't know me, nor why I am here. I have work to do and I must be clean for that work."

Joe made no comment.

She felt guided to continue. There was much to say, not only for inspirational value but also for therapy. "I had quite a struggle with my conscience when I first came. I never had a sinecure before. This is almost one. I am only a glorified sitter." That, of course, was the outer aspect of the situation, she reminded herself.

"I have always given full measure. Long ago, when I was a secretary, I left a position and they had to split the work between two girls. I do not say that to brag but I am efficient and accurate. Nursing was new to me until a short time ago, but I went forth in high consciousness and learned faster than if I had gone in mortal or personality desire."

Joe was silent, outwardly receptive to her words.

"Spiritual law demands one give full measure. . . . Also," she continued quietly, "it is not only a matter of earning so much per day. It is a deep awareness of my divine assignment."

Did he comprehend at all what she was saying? His face was completely impassive, although she surely had his undivided attention. His fathomless eyes penetrated every nuance of her expressions.

"When I first came I thought I was not giving full measure. I had only to rearrange my sleeping, then sit up for eight hours, making rounds periodically, and during the last of the eight hours poke thermometers in people's mouths, record their pulses, write a report. . . . Yet I know if I were to leave, someone else would fill the place. She grinned a little. "So I am taking a sabbatical. The family mending is nicely up to date all the time. I read voluminously. I've begun to dab at painting. . . . And to give a fuller measure I began a prayer pledge for the patients. . . . This position has become a spiritual fulfillment."

Still no comment from Joe.

"The first night of my prayer vigil God showed me a vision of myself walking in a huge, rectangular garden. Gorgeous! Filled with flowers of all kinds, from roses to daisies. The whole thing was a magnificent bloom festival ablaze with color. The vision was so vivid I could smell the flowers, delicate fragrances as well as more forceful ones. Everything was in bloom, even flowers and shrubs that normally do not blossom simultaneously. Lilacs and roses. Tulips and zinnias. I walked toward the far end and began climbing a white, marble stairway. Then the vision faded." Her voice dropped and the next words were almost a whisper. "Last night I had a sequel. The doorway at the top of those stairs opened."

She did not mention the blackness of the room beyond. Now, repeating the mystery to Joe, she knew its significance. It spelled the same thing as the opaque quality around Joe's eyes, his non-receptivity.

Joe shifted his glance from her face to his hands, unable to meet her radiance. Since full comprehension was beyond him, he brought the conversation to his level, "Did you start painting?"

She grasped the morsel with enthusiasm. "Yes! And forevermore the world holds more color for me. I saw countless shades of gray in a catbird this morning. Never did I see all those shades. Mine isn't talent or genius, you know. I only paint by numbers." She grinned readily, knowing the category a real artist would put this phase.

"There are sixteen to eighteen shades of gray in a catbird," Joe commented seriously.

His breakfast tray arrived.

So April fused into May and as Faith sandwiched many metaphysical stories with his morning care, divine love and understanding spoke through her. He was fascinated and entranced and each day he quietly treasured her thought, eagerly awaited her coming at night. Occasionally she shared family tidbits, home scenes just for their humorous quality, like the episode about Rob's birthday present from Doug.

"Eight-year-old Doug greeted me at the car, said he had gathered together all his worldly wealth for Rob's birthday—his favorite comic, a turtle, and thirty-eight cents." They laughed together. "Well, he'd put it all loose into a large carton, tied an enormous blue ribbon around it and presented it to Rob at breakfast. Rob put on a dramatic facial expression. He's eleven, and I suspect he was making a try at sophistication.

"Rob took out the turtle, said nothing. Then the comic. Said nothing. Breathing hot down his neck, Doug prompted him about the money. Rob fished out the quarter. Doug prodded again, 'There's more, Robbie.' Rob gathered unto his bosom, as the novelists put it, the nickels and three pennies. Then he looked questioningly at me, for we've been teaching them about what we call 'the Lord's pot.' I nodded to him. 'How much?' says he. 'Four cents.' 'There's only three pennies,' he commented and before I could speak Doug bursts out with an enthusiastic, 'Go ahead, Robbie, he's a big shot! Give the Lord a whole nickel!' "

"Kids!" laughed Joe heartily, wagging his head.

His enthusiastic response encouraged Faith to tell another episode, knowing the therapy of laughter. "Our kids must be psychic. . . . We have a little mongrel, probably some dachshund in it. Recently she came into the way of female dogs and I had the bigger lads put her in the battery house until the matter would be finished." Faith paused, wrinkled up her face remorsefully. "Well, while the boys were in school Princess decided in favor of the romantic life. I had her back by the time they got home. Says Rob to me while I'm peeling potatoes, 'I think Princess is going to have pups.' I grimaced but I surely wondered how he knew!

"At dinner the same night Doug announced—no question but rather a statement, 'Princess is going to have pups. Who do you think did it, ma?' So with his definite attack I calculated the time for evasion was finished. I answered 'Shep.' (Shep is a collie someone gave us this spring).

" 'Shep!' says he. 'Shep! That isn't fair. Look how long Kim has lived here!' "

Joe's uproarious laughter well repaid her efforts.

Many days had passed since she first told him about commanding the organs of his body. She wondered if he had practised it. She wished he would volunteer the information. She waited a few moments. Sometimes he answered her unspoken questions. It didn't seem he would this time. Gently, "Are you taking over the dominion of your body?"

He glanced up uncomprehendingly.

It is not wise to teach via the negatives. Neither would it be wise to have him hopeful there was one iota of the personal in her attitude. She was following through on her divine assignment but she must be positive he understood her attitude to be entirely impersonal-personal. Things had settled nicely since she mastered the situations—but she well knew his hopes were not completely dashed.

"Bless your body and all its works," she clarified. "Think and tell yourself that you are in harmony with God and all His children, that all the food you eat is in harmony with you and you with it. Man has been given dominion—or at least the potentiality of it—over his body and all his affairs."

Joe looked stupefied!

"You can do it," she encouraged. "I've done it. Not immediately, but unless you start sometime you never get anywhere. It takes practise. Neither did you walk the first time you stood up. You crawled and pulled yourself up on everything, lifting chubby little legs often. You stepped around furniture for many miles before you were strong enough to walk."

She reflected it would be permissible to stretch the facts a bit, It would be like annointing him spiritually. "You have a great name, Joe . . . Joseph of the coat of many colors. He was a dreamer and he lived close to God, learned to read dream symbols. The name means 'receptivity to God.'"

So Joe Quelquhomme rapidly improved. Surgery would not be required. He would be discharged shortly. When he knew his hospitalization would soon end, he intensified his personal tactics, accelerating his pace as the sands emptied from the top of the hour-glass. Although he no longer teased openly for kisses, she sensed he was using the metaphysics selfishly. Once, facetiously, she almost called him Svengali and Aura shouted. So long as Faith kept attuned to indwelling Spirit she would be perfectly protected.

The little warnings of Joe's lustful ideas seemed inconsequential. If she omitted lipstick he asked the reason in hopeful tones. When she used toilet water on warm evenings he snidely urged. One stormy Friday night Faith felt the impact of Joe's criticism of John, a seemingly casual question, "Tell me, did your husband bring you tonight? The storm is very bad."

Her eyebrows shot up in surprise, momently blinded to his thinking, "Of course not!"

327

Possessively, "*I* wouldn't let you go alone!" Faith heard the echo of Andy's shout before the men's ward.

"He should leave four children alone to bring me!—Besides I am under divine guidance and protection."

"Yes, I know. In visions."

"More than that," softly. She couldn't tell him about Aura. He would not comprehend how one can listen to the little voice within and be perfectly led. As an artist it could well be his guidance might come through visions too. So she answered, "Sometimes in the symbols of the night. Occasionally He talks to me in thoughts. When it is through dreams I can tell which dreams are from Superconsciousness. They are full of light, often in technicolor, like the full blooming flower garden I told you about. Sometimes the light is almost blinding. But if for purposes of symbol the vision is dark, then I am always aware of my Invisible Guide. When my dreams are from subconsciousness, they are to show me what needs cleansing. Many times my dreams are prophetic."

Joe followed her words but now that she stopped speaking he lay mentally berating John. Faith was keenly aware of his thoughts. Joe simply didn't understand about divine assignments. John did! John gave her spiritual-mental freedom to fulfill it too. And John was living up to his highest understandings as well. Bless that fabulous guy at home! She wished to exonerate John. He was too noble for anyone to think ill of him—even someone like Joe who mattered not one whit in a personal sense, perhaps had not the capacity to understand how and why she and John were dovetailing their divine assignments. A little laugh began deep within herself, for at home she and John quipped either of them could do the same things—interchangeably—except have a baby.

She was silent several minutes.

Joe sought to spark something. Fiercely, "He'd better be home when I call!"

She was startled by the thunder in his voice. That night, several days or weeks ago, Joe could have been a cad. He had remained a gentleman. She respected him for that. Loved him too. Impersonally, of course—but always the overtones of that personal, undownable feeling she knew him from aeons ago. Well, his morals were not for her to judge. She was required to live by the vision she had been given carrying him down the lighted corridor to the altar. His heated comment about John's being home gave her the right cue. She could finish the soul cleansing now. Softly, but firmly, she began, "So long as our friendship remains platonic, Joe. John and I shall be glad to have you visit any time, although my working a night shift keeps our social life pretty limited. I have many responsibilities—besides the family ones. I have a personal covenant with God to work with Him. Teach also. And one teaches best by example."

She couldn't tell Joe about her horizon, the glimpses she had of a divine plan and her place in it. She couldn't tell him about the prayer-study group nor the high purpose for the Farm Summer Home. The grapevine had informed him about a summer boarding arrangement they had for children, but the neighbors did not guess its higher purpose. If she were to cleanse Joe of lustful thoughts she must do it then, and completely—from all levels.

"This is a mental world, Joe. Unless we keep our friendship clean and pure, John and Isabelle would know. Every time you shave you'd wonder if she knew—or how soon. Every time I put my hair up I would hate myself for deceptions.—And I have four children. Four of them."

"I never think of you as a mother," he interjected.

She knew that. His thoughts about her were on the romantic level, although once he had intoned some whimsey about 'I don't desire your body; just you.'

Faith's outer answer did not come quickly. It came with many spaces between the phrasing. "Perhaps because you have no children . . . I could not do as the Buddha. He felt the divine call and left his very young child and beautiful wife . . . I co-begot all four of ours. Wanted them. Planned for them. . . . Have you ever seen the bewilderment in the face and manner of a child from a broken home? Or a home filed with distrust and dissention? . . . In a sense I was such a child. My mother committed suicide when I was ten and a half. It took me many, many years to learn she had not rejected me personally—just life in general, perhaps. John helped me see that, helped me by just being normal and undramatic about the incident.

"I love John. It is a profound love, and a spiritual one. We understand each other. Want the same things *of* life. Are willing to give the same things *to* life. It was never a love of passion.

It goes to the depths of Being itself—and in spite of four children there is no passion in me . . ."

"Everyone has passions," he interrupted.

Faith shook her head, distinctly, firmly, with finality. Greater than any spiritual surgery she was hoping to inspire Joe away from the plane of selfishness and lust. From her lofty mountain-top she taught beyond his immediate comprehension. Thinking now of her John, her eyes were soft and luminous, and she smiled gently with her next words. "John gives me freedom too."

She was reflecting on John's unpossessiveness regarding her, of his never forcing his ardor, of his freedom regarding the tithe commitment. John behaved as though any divine assignment of hers was also his! Of course, now she was out working to help get things in the clear financially, reestablish themselves as well as working out this divine assignment. The whole plan was not merely a Wells' plan. This was their co-work with their Partner!

While Faith was thinking of freedom in a spiritual sense, Joe thought of it in a moral sense. As she moved to the door Joe suggested huskily, "Come to me after rounds. I'll be awake." Intensity in his eyes, he grabbed for her hand.

Surely he didn't mean what he implied!

"No. Good night."

The closed door behind her she stood momently in the corridor. A pucker appeared between her eyebrows. She had told him she must stay pure and clean, that she had a divine assignment! Perhaps she hadn't used that phrase, but surely she'd tried to clear up the matter. Could it be he thought all those words mere verbiage! She had spoken from the mountaintops of understanding, had poured out her soul.

She was not frightened. There were no tempestuous or milling thought-people bombarding her. As she ruminated over some of their conversations during the past weeks the name Svengali came again to her, and it was a clue. Whenever she had difficulty at the nursing home with the old men and their sexy ideas, she mentally told them 'man is a spiritual being.' Usually it worked so well their suggestive remarks about her strength or their open invitations to their beds ceased. In all but one instance it worked well from the silence.

Making rounds that night she seeded the corridors with the words, "Man is a spiritual being, not a creature of lusts and materiality."

It was as though she were weaving a protective cape about herself, and she experienced the sensation of increased security, greater dominion.

Saturday night Joe was not sleeping when she made the second rounds. Noiselessly opening his door, beaming the flashlight on the ceiling, he extended his hand to her. Trustingly she accepted, "Aren't you sleeping?"

He rolled over, facing her, put his lips to her hand. "No, Honey. I can't sleep."

"Pain anywhere?"

"No."

His lips travelled up her arm, gently, persuasively. Slowly, firmly, he pulled her to him until she was hard against the bed. He was not rough. But exceedingly strong.

Faith was not frightened. She did not guess his intentions. Aura warned. Faith remained unafraid, for Aura's indications were a reminder of divine protection rather than alarm. In a miraculous way Faith felt peculiarly master of the whole situation. Hard against Joe's bed she stood straight, unyielding, stronger than he, fortified by spiritual strength. Low and evenly, "Joe, stop."

It was the voice of one expecting to be obeyed.

"Don't I arouse anything in you?" His voice filled with warmth, reluctant to lose any possible gains.

"There is no passion in me. Deep affection. No passion."

"Everyone has passion," his lips placing gentle tokens.

She was silent. Her heart requested release.

Joe's grasp remained firm, but sensitively he knew his maneuvers to be unsuccessful. He tried another tact, "Once I told you I don't want your body—here I am trying to get it."

In silence lay her power.

"When I was younger the girls pestered me . . ." He paused for a reply, some indication of relaxation on her part. "Don't I awaken you?"

Victory was hers. Now she could answer, "I must keep clean. I am becoming a metaphysician. I have work to do that I know to be my divine assignment. How could I teach about God's laws and love and how to live unless I live it!"

He released her instantly, his grasp springing open as his jaw clamped shut and his eyes squeezed together. Immediately Faith withdrew from his room, leaned against the wall praising God for His protection. Used for His purposes she was not required to be a temple prostitute! Through her God was managing the whole situation. The way was essentially clear to her. A new melody sang in her heart.

In his small private room Joe lay awake all night. In the morning she was ashen, violet circles under his eyes extending to midcheeks. As Faith administered morning care he apologized fiercely, "Forgive me! I don't know what the hell is wrong with me! I can't leave you alone! Always, I could control myself!" His eyes flashed, little lightning bolts in them amid the darkness. "If I'd got you last night, you'd never be on duty this morning!"

Calmly Faith received his apology. Wonderful, really! she communed with Aura. I've never been placed in a situation beyond my understanding. Last night I was not frightened. I *knew* spiritual strength is greater than physical.

The only time I was scared was when Hunky told me Sandy was on the verge of a hemorrhage. Then as part of me quailed with fear, wondering how I should manage, You told me You are the power. All I had to do was remain calm and unafraid, and declare the constancy and continuity of Life, that You are Life . . . and I stood looking down at Sandy later he was so white and scared too. And We stayed at his bedside, You and I, until I could arrive at a feeling of great calm and could see the golden light of healing all around him and about his bed. It was like the Alice Starr thing only that time I was not there physically. Next rounds time Sandy had a beautiful smiling expression on his face as he slept, and the next morning he bounced up with 'Gosh, I had a fabulous sleep,' as though affirming how well You worked. God bless You, God! You are with me all the way! Forgive any moment I ever doubted or waivered—and with all my heart, thank You!

"Will you forgive me?" Joe was asking.

"Yes," quietly. "Last night is finished. Do not lacerate yourself about it. I understand. You are lonely, and Isabelle is far off at home. I trust you."

"That's because you are wonderful and there is no condemnation in you."

Metaphysically it is good for him to cleanse himself, she thought. She was acutely aware of his intensity and she recognized something new in him. She couldn't quite name it. Intuitively she felt it was there, at least the beginnings of a nameless thing. She was thankful for the spiritual strength that overcame his physical stamina. In her heart she admitted some of this was her error too. Didn't she teach her prayer-study group there is always a mental correspondent, that nothing happens by coincidence? Furthermore, she should never have made the gesture to his forehead even! How long ago? Days or weeks? The whole Joe chapter was a blur.

Mental correspondent, she mulled. Of course! One can't run from a situation. Instead of remaining to dissolve lustful appetites of old men in a nursing home she had fled. Fled to another position, a stronger situation with younger men and fiercer sex drives. She could hardly condemn Joe for something still part of herself.

"Well, I had a helluva night!" Joe's comment brought her back abruptly.

She was carrying his basin into the bathroom, emptying it into the sink. "Want the girl on third to do you?" casually.

"I don't blame you after last night. No!"

"I didn't mean that. Perhaps I bother you."

"There's nothing in you bothers me . . . but I seem to be acting like a kid."

She converted it to a witticism. "You are merely following the Biblical injunction 'to become as a little child.'" Washing his face, she pretended to bathe him spiritually. Now she set the water for his teeth. Softly she added, seriously, "You must forgive yourself, then 'go forth and sin no more.'" Her eyes smiled on him.

"You're a rock," he admired. "I never knew anyone so unyielding."

She hoped the episode finished the chapter. But during the nights and mornings of that week Joe vacillated between determination to break her unyieldingness and admiration of it. As time slipped along his determination increased correspondingly with the ardor of his seduction. A constant flow of hints and invitations.

"Put out the light and kiss me. . . ."

"Come to me after rounds. . . . Why won't you? . . . You're afraid . . . Come to me tonight? . . .

"You know you do things to a man he can't control. . . ."

333

And for the most part Faith met his insistence with silence and her silent affirmation. "Joe, you are spiritual being, not a creature of lust." When his insistence required an outer answer she had a new one.

"Not tonight—or any night. . . .

"Six reasons . . . John and four children and Isabelle.

"Don't you see? If John gives me freedom I must merit it, not betray that trust."

She was thinking only of her divine assignment and as spiritual freedom. He cringed before her answer. She thought it would settle his desire entirely!

It didn't.

"How can I merit business with children? My own or other people's.

"I kept clean for John before marriage. That doesn't absolve me from remaining clean during marriage."

One night he appealed to her vanity and pity. "You are very beautiful. If I were younger you wouldn't refuse me." The merriment in her eyes was insuppressible. "Why are you laughing?"

"There's a Puerto Rican boy on the other side. In spite of high school Spanish I can't understand him—nor he me. But we try. The other day he was ready for breakfast, walking the corridor as I came downstairs in my own clothes, no uniform, and he shouted, 'You are boo-si-full' I understood him perfectly." Faith laughed aloud.

Joe only smiled, reached her, pulling her close. "You are. I love you."

"You don't love me, Joe. You merely love the ideals I represent to you."

Ignoring her reasoning, "Do you love me?"

Quietly, "I love your soul, Joe."

Through Joe's hospital stay the shrubs of May bloomed and the world splashed itself with many new colors, earth's renewal established, darker greens in the background proving it. Standing in the open doorway, the night, the twinkling stars, and the mellowness of the season warmed her. She wondered why the milky way seemed so unusually light.

Her thoughts returned to Joe as the big dipper slipped below the western horizon. Although she no longer puzzled about his room atmosphere of the first morning, her persistent affirmations of man's spirituality didn't seem to be "taking." Shortly he would be leaving. She was relieved, weary of parrying answers.

She communed with her Lord, too, saw a new perspective on her divine assignments. Where before she believed she was at Kipp only because of the patients, she now recognized the need to be active—silently or otherwise—with the co-workers. Smiling to herself in the quietness, she recalled Nina, the little substitute on third. How she had run on and on about the illnesses and operations her little family sustained! It seemed interminable! Quietly Faith said during Nina's pause for breath, "Now that I've heard all the negatives, tell me how well God keeps you most of the time. Consider how health is normal. Instantly something is amiss in the body temple, a corrective commences. Is there a fever? The body is burning up the germ, killing it." Nina had caught her breath, ejaculated an, "Oh, we're healthy all right," and fled to third, returning no more that night.

How people enjoy their maladies! Perhaps it's because they are so starved for love and attention. Being ill gives them a legitimate and socially acceptable way to gain attention. If man only knew that each thought and word goes forth and "does not return unto him void!"

How was it the seamstress put it, when Faith went for her uniforms? Something like "they hug their TB to them and they do not know God."

She thought of Jed and his parable to the children about gardens and the atmosphere in which we live being as the soil, our thoughts the seed. Peculiar if they didn't hear more frequently from Jed. She wondered if Jed knew about their Farm Summer Home. It was beginning to pay its way. The scope was more modest than they had hoped, but it was a solid foundation, with her heavy schedule about all she could manage. Even Henry Ford began his manufacturing on a small scale. And Heinz began his industry in an old shed, peddling the products after cooking and bottling them. Well, she thanked the good Lord the Wells' success ensued divinely and in perfect order! The dead horses of debt were covering up more rapidly now!

Time to awaken the men, do Joe's morning care, check on the children, write the reports, head for home so that John could have the car. Busy with many thoughts and thanksgiving to God she picked a flower from the lawn for Joe.

Joe ignored the flower. Greeted her with, "I go home soon. Will you miss me?"

She hardly knew how to answer. If she answered affirmatively, he would be encouraged. Only a few days ago Aura shouted at her when Joe asked, quite casually, how often John traveled for his company. And a negative answer would wound those sensitive feelings of his.

"Will you?" persistently.

She settled for the indirect method. "We've known each other only six weeks, yet our empathy is most unusual. Frequently you have answered my unspoken questions."

Joe shrugged.

"I like to know the cause behind every effect. Once our Doug said—he was not even five—'Don't you want to know everything in the whole world!' My mind works that way too."

He wouldn't give up. He would use her pearls to rend her. Although she felt like a lamb destined for slaughter in the outer sense, beneath that surface was the mighty fortress, the abiding conviction of divine protection. A thought occurred to her. Sometimes just our being meek and willing to go through fire is sufficient—and the fire is extinguished.

So that night he resumed with his desires. It was almost as though his morning's sentences hung in the air and when the night came he pulled them down, and added to their persuasions. "Don't you want me?" in honeyed tones.

Resolutely she shook her head. "I told you long ago our friendship has to remain pure and clean. It wasn't honest for a while—but it has stayed pure."

"Don't you want to belong to me?"

She didn't answer aloud. This strange friendship! We've quarreled and vied with each other, held the loftiest of visions and poetry. I don't understand the reason completely, but perhaps that isn't necessary right now.

Seeing she would not surrender, he answered for her. "We each belong to someone else. Is that it?"

Bantering was a safety device. "Look me up in another incarnation. With luck I'll be wearing red hair—my own."

The personal part of her dreaded Joe's last night, not because she feared divine protection would take a holiday. That protection had been with her from the very inception, before she held

336

the mastery of the friendship, even the night Joe's intentions could have spelled rape. While he never again degenerated that low, she had been thoroughly aware of his subtlety, his open hints, pulsations as he endeavored to press against her, hopeful of arousing the passions he thought resident in every human being.

To the very depths of her being she was weary of the cat-and-mouse game, of being on guard verbally, of evading those roving hands of his. Persistent? She'd never met such persistency in her entire life!

Faith couldn't sleep before duty on Joe's last night of hospitalization. Trying to rest, mindful of the many demands on her at home the following day, she felt she would give anything to avoid this last night. Practically anything! Aura brought a quotation to sustain her, to treasure in prayerful silence, to keep alive in her heart. Over and over she fondled the words. They soothed her, refreshed her. The alarm clicked. It was time to arise, prepare for duty.

John had coffee ready. As she appeared in the kitchen he was assembling things for her two o'clock snack. He read the meditation from *daily word* as their grace. They had coffee.

They were silent together. Sipping her coffee Faith reflected this whole Joe episode was a forty-days-in-the-wilderness thing. She had not told John any of it. Some day she would. In the beginning she did not want to empower the situation, she was rolling with it too much. When she achieved control of herself and the situation, she felt it would worry him needlessly, and that perhaps his worry would whittle away at her controls. He'd probably say, "Baby, you are beautiful. If I were those guys lying in bed and nothing to do all day I'd make a play for pretty nurses too."

But John wouldn't. Wonderful John!

In all our years of togetherness he has never forced himself on me. Always he has been kind and considerate, practically let me establish the rhythm of our sex life. Our marriage is a balanced one, erected on the foundation of spiritual understanding and love with the blessed ingredients of mental camaraderie and physical attraction. God, John is wonderful!

They had not spoken. Reluctantly she arose to go. John thought from the slowless of her movements she was very tired, and the necessity of her having to work stabbed him. Tenderly he brought

337

her to himself, kissed her gently. He subtracted nothing from the act by words.

Driving to The San, Faith whispered Aura's quotation over and over, let it run through her heart like a melody. It refreshed and lightened her heart, lifted up her courage.

'Father, remove this cup from me. Nevertheless not as I will but as Thou wilt.'

Faith walked from the car with firm, quick step to the nurses' office. Hunky gave the report, finishing with, "Joe goes home tomorrow. He's waiting to say 'hi.'" Faith smiled acknowledgment and Hunky left. In charge, Faith performed the preliminary duties, donned her uniform, Aura's quotation reiterating and calming her. She moved quietly and efficiently, finishing the rounds.

Noiselessly opening Joe's door he was sound asleep. Breathing like a babe! Silently she closed the door, leaned against the outer wall. Her innate reaction was to laugh and cry. Greater than the momentary hysteria rose feelings of reverence, humility, and awe.

"Thank You, Father! Thank You! Such a simple 'out.' Truly You are wonderful and You never fail me. Would that I never fail Thee! Such a simple, easy victory for Us, You and me!"

The night was still. At dawn Faith picked a couple white petunias bobbing in the slight breeze among the red geraniums clustered around the sundial on the front lawn. The petunias were unusually fragrant, the dew drenching their whiteness. On her last rounds she surreptitiously opened Joe's door, popped them into his drinking water. They were tangible messengers. They were to tell Joe 'man is a spiritual being, and my love for you and everyone is spiritual and pure, part of Divinity itself.'

At six, she flipped on the light switches at the end of the corridors, assembled her temperature book and wiping papers for the temp sticks. The usual foolery with the men, then into Joe's room with a purposeful, "Good morning. Let this be a happy day for you!"

"Where were you last night?" before she could place the thermometer between his lips. No demand in his tone. Just as casual. . . .

Lord, there's no end to Your miracles, Faith marvelled silently. Always he had sounded possessive or suspicious. Aloud she answered, "You were sleeping when I came on." As she recorded his temperature and pulse rate Joe sat up, swung his legs out of bed.

338

"No basins. I am able to be up."

"Okay," grinning easily.

Suddenly he was shy. "I don't know what to say." Possibly he was thinking of the almost-night as well as the other nights he was dark subtlety and seduction itself.

She made it easy for him, offering a handshake. "So long. It's nice to have known you."

Joe was very different this morning. Surely shyness had not been part of his composition before. Perhaps there was a touch of reverence in his manner and voice too, like the morning he had intoned, 'I cannot make life, therefore I have not the right to take it.' He seemed to want to talk. Faith waited. He studied his hands, then lifted his gaze to her face. "Honey, you've taught me a lot. I can't exactly explain it yet—and maybe it doesn't show—but I've got it here," pointing to his heart. "I guess I sound corny—I only know I am a different man—from even last night."

Thank You, God, for using me, Faith prayed within. This is the altar, my vision in the night.

"You are made of wonderful material. Much better than I. There were times we talked from different levels."

With a teasing grin, "Oh, Joe, there's a little bitchiness in all of us and a great deal of divinity." She chose the word 'bitchiness' deliberately, recalling an occasion she had once employed it and he reproved her. 'How shall I say it? That word does not belong in the same mouth with the other words. Do not use it, please, Honey.' Now she reused it to assert her freedom. He made no comment.

He drew her close, pressed her lips with his, released her and promised, "I shall remember you always."

"Yes," she agreed, "but it is transmuted. And if it be divine, our paths will cross again. So long, Joe. Best of luck to you and Isabelle—always. Tell her that her eyes are lovely, that she is beautiful, that her voice thrills you. Tell her she's a good cook too."

Faith was going to stop there, but Aura prompted her further. It was good to give a person something to grow toward, like one reads Shakespeare to children. "You're a wonderful guy, Joe, but you never quite found yourself. You have stayed amid the throngs too much. One has to be alone in the woods or on a mountain top

339

now and then. When one finds himself, then he comes down amid the crowd to do the work of his divine assignment. . . . And always there must be periodic returns to the mountaintop for renewal and refreshment, and the increase of Spirit."

Their eyes held briefly. Faith walked quickly from his room.

Equinox

So it was that in rhythmic procession seasons slipped along before the appearance of the equinox in Faith Wells. The equinox, that perfect balance and blend of day and night, activity and rest, true dominion of all thoughts and feelings.

Along the way were many indications of the real spiritual equinox. In the new tone of Faith's teachings to the expanding backyard prayer-study groups, certainly in the increase of her inner radiance. I, Jean Carter, knew well of the years spent plugging away in the outer sense at the mountainous debts—not that she mentioned it, of course. How can I describe the depths of poise and trust and courage that emanated from her? Perhaps to say there was so much of her heart and sincerity in her teachings we all knew the principles she set forth were not theory but recipes, scientifically tested formulae.

Some of us sensed the new horizon in her. It evidenced as a kind of prodding us along, each to his own fulfillment. She taught through a kindly humor with underlying seriousness. . . . "You are all metaphysicians, you know," her first gentle prod. As weeks slipped along there were other hints, finally the announcement.

Jed had contacted them a couple years after their "winter" manifested. From time to time he wrote, telling of his healing center somewhere in the Great Smokies. It seemed foreordained that he would write ultimately, invite them to join him, John for business administration abilities, Faith for her special talents. For this they were divinely prepared! Each of us in the prayer-study groups knew it.

"It is good for you that I go away," Faith added after her initial announcement. "If I were to remain with you, you would be content to lean on my access to God's door, forgetting or neglecting that each of you must make his own at-one-ment. God is always ready for you. Your at-one-ment must be individually effected."

Yes, Faith was a new woman these days. The part of herself she whimsically called Aura had grown in wisdom and in stature. Often I witnessed the luminosity about her as she walked and

341

worked. During silent time or prayer time, her face was incandescent with a wondrous glow. Even the newest among us would comment she looked as though she swallowed a klieg light.

Once I commented on the glorious texture of her skin. She teased, "Do you want my short lecture on physiology wherein I prove how the human body is constantly rebuilding and improving itself, responding to right thoughts? Or—shall I say I am spiritualizing my body temple?" Her voice and eyes were so full of laughter we both joined in merriment. I never returned to the subject. I knew she was prodding me to a do-it-yourself project.

Last year their Farm Summer Home had eight children besides the Wells' foursome, preponderance of ages pre-teen. Faith maintained her full schedule, including laundry and cooking, all the extras—around the larger groups! True, she employed a woman to tidy up in the morning, make beds for the younger children while she napped two hours. But she was up to cook the luncheon, manage story hour and recreation demands of the afternoon. The challenge of new personalities and backgrounds seemed nonexistent. When any of us in the prayer-study groups remarked about the tremendous harmony among the large group of assorted children, she used it as her proof.

"God does all things through us—all things—channeling life and health and prosperity as well as love and strength to do laundry, whisk a delicious dinner together or clean house.

"As for harmony, isn't it the basic of ALL? A body in harmony is health. Affairs in harmony are prosperity. A personality in harmony conflicts with no one. Neither is it a wishywashy drab thing of no color! None of us would classify Jesus as lacking in courage. Imagine the courage of convictions demonstrated in the temple scene! His daring to rebel against established customs. Overturning money tables! Setting doves and lambs free!

"You must *use* God! Use Him in the glorious sense of *working with* Him and His laws. Do it constantly. In the little affairs of life—even in your business deals and your social life. Then you know Him very well for events of larger magnitude. Nothing is yours unless you use it. Merely to collect theories or quotations is of no merit. Use the truth you know. As you do, your understanding grows. More truth clarifies for you. The law of use and appreciation is always at work. No holidays. Just like gravity. What you refuse to use atrophies or wastes. This is a spiritual truth applicable in the mental, physical, and material world. Use—or lose!

"A graduate, content with his diploma and no application of his education, loses his mental brilliance and sharpness. Unused muscles atrophy. An unused house falls apart. Moses demonstrated this law, the materialized manna 'stunk' when hoarded. Jesus taught this truth in the parable of the talents, emphasized it by His declaration that 'every tree that beareth not is cast into the fire.' "

So it manifested that Faith prepared to leave the community as well as The San. Her last night on-duty was filled with prayer and self-appraisal. In a vast sense she was part of this beautiful sanatorium. She had come to give so much, so much more than helping free the family of cloying debts. She had come to give the jewel of truth. Inspire. Teach the way of working with truth to expedite the healing of mind, soul, body, and affairs. Hushing the clamor of her body for rest, compelling awakeness during the prayer vigils, working with zeal and humility, she had used her own vitality and her spiritual understanding. Sometimes that impish grin of hers appeared in her eyes as well as on her lips and she declared she 'worked with white magic while on a sabbatical.'

Awaiting the first light in the east and the orchestration of the birds, she took inventory as she looked to the vast stretch of mountains. There had not been many receivers of the whole jewel. Here a thought. There an idea. Some few the whole gem. Joe received something, perhaps not what Faith proffered but that which he could comprehend. Like snow balling down the mountainside, Joe's comprehension would gather more unto itself at the right time for Joe.

Mitch was Faith's pride and joy! A shining example! Possibly Mitch alone made all the nights she walked to keep awake worthwhile, treading miles of corridors until mortal demands were conquered and she achieved the spiritual mountaintop.

Mitch would never 'break down'—that haunting fear most TB'ers live with. Faith smiled to herself, remembering Mitch's first morning under her care. Witnessing the luminosity around him she half giggled to herself, the seeming contradiction that so black a face could be so full of light. Funny, mostly she had a way with the colored people. They were so easy to reach, had that innate simplicity—not stupidity—of soul. Maybe simplicity con-

343

tains the basic ingredient of humility. No, she didn't believe God wanted her to join Albert Schweitzer. Surely Jed though!

She could see a whole divine pattern now: their finding the farm and getting to know Jed. Even Jed's leaving the vicinity and not contacting them for a couple of years. During that time she and John were forced to plumb their depths, know God face-to-face, their individual at-one-ments. Wasn't this the same pitch she was giving her prayer-study groups! Even the Master said something like 'I go away . . . but if I were not to go away you would not grow as readily' . . . something like that. Wasn't it in the sad, sad chapters of St. John, the thirteenth or the fourteenth. She must look it up later.

Very true too, she reflected. My, how John had grown when he stopped riding her prayer kites. That time the company board of directors pitched the profitless product to his management. They had wanted to drop it and John pled so sincerely for its retention they gave him its management plus the deadline of six months. Being new to this prayer discipline, John experienced tremendous vacillation of hope and confidence, felt he was a yo-yo. All she'd said when he told her was, "God and you are a fabulous team."

How the Lord had worked out that challenge! Everything fell properly into place. It was a case of miracle and wonder following one another, almost tumbling into place in a profusion of goodies. They got bargains on paper needs for the promotion gimmicks. Deadlines were not only met—they were bettered. The product became established in a foreign country through a Chicago visitor raving about it! It was as though God's wind blew John's prayer seeds through all the world.

All these years since knowing Jed, working with God and His principles—John still in the cities and Faith in the nursing home and in The San—and of course their beginnings of the Farm Summer Home, and the prayer-study groups, all was His glorious preparation. The sheep . . . Pal . . . Jane Allis . . . everything had worked together to prepare them for this bigger divine assignment. Working with Jed. Jed's wonderful way of demonstrating truths of Being.

Divine assignment!

How right her Lord had been that dark day of the overwhelming corn crop failure. 'Get a job,' He said. Humbly she looked again at her memory. The failures were cosmic prods. Nothing opened to them. Even Pete had come! In the combination of desperation and humility she went forth.

She smiled gently. Bless God!

How truly wondrous and parent-like. In spite of her temper He guided to the right places, and all the little pieces of her life's divine assignment, her personal jigsaw puzzle, fell into place. John's and her schedules dovetailed. The children were unharmed by Faith's need to work. And all around them, in their personal lives as well as their family life, their desires and ambitions—everything—moved forward to greater good.

Her thoughts returned again to Mitch. God prettied up the world through Mitch. Most of the colored men were modest pressers or laborers. Mitch was an interior decorator. Was?

Is!

At their initial meeting Mitch and Faith experienced unusual rapport. They communicated without speaking. The relationship remained warm but that rare blend of impersonal-personal. (No more wildernesses for her!) To Mitch she could pitch prayers or thoughts or books. He caught them all. Only one fumble. After surgery. He came back looking better, but in a few weeks seemed to slip. Hunky briefed Faith one night that Mitch was moved to the other side of the building, "his sputum positive again, the operation unsuccessful."

Three days at least Mitch lay facing the wall. Not wanting to force an entry Faith patiently waited for him to reopen the door. But remembering old Minnie in the nursing home she could not let him wallow in despondency. (The Minnie episode came back to her with full force: Almost ready to be discharged from the Magnolia Nursing Home, the five sons trooped in and presented a legal document for signature. When they left Minnie said 'I never thought my boys would do this to me.' She turned to the wall, refused food and attention. Three days later she was dead. Faith knew even Minnie's action of facing the wall was an indication of her inner rejection of life itself).

So a Tuesday morning before her weekend, Faith gently knocked on Mitch's mental door, jambed it with a soft, "What's the matter, Friend?"

No light in Mitch's face when he turned. Only darkness, eyes dull and listless, voice timberless, ". . . so I guess it is God's will for me to be sick."

"Nonsense!" Her tone slapped him.

"God's will indeed! If His will were for anyone to be ill, then every doctor, nurse, scientist, is distinctly violating that will in trying to achieve health . . . for you or anyone! God needs you as much as you need Him! Your place in His plans is interior decoration. How many things can you pretty up lying here!

"God is Spirit, Mitch! Not a powerful Santa Claus who gives only if a child of His is good! God expresses and fulfills through each of us. All the time. This is what makes progress. He is ideas and beauty as well as life and health. His will is always the highest—'the bestest for the mostest'." She ceased speaking, grinned disarmingly. Although her tones were low there were lightning jabs of truth bolting through each word.

Startled, Mitch answered, "I guess I had that coming to me, Mrs. Wells. I wasn't thinking clearly, and everyone kept telling me you got to expect most anything with TB."

She shrugged lightly, as though not to argue with these who prefer bondage and negation to freedom. Mildly, "You merely accepted the false for a while. . . . You know Principle, Mitch. Work with it. All the way. Like the hymn, 'All the way with Jesus.' Every thought you let occupy your mind and heart manifests. Now transmute every thought to be positive with Good. Good is God. Let your mental company be thought-people of health and wholeness, beauty and joy. Remember St. Paul's 'whatsoevers'?"

Mitch turned a puzzled expression to her.

"Remember?" Quoting softly and slowly,

" 'Whatsoever things are true,
Whatsoever things are honorable,
Whatsoever things are just,
Whatsoever things are pure,
Whatsoever things are lovely,
Whatsoever things are of good report;
If there be any virtue and if there be any praise,
Think on these things.' "

She paused a moment for his absorption. "That's an early version of psychology, Mitch.

"God's very first law is healing. All His forces rush to cleanse a cut by the initial flow of blood. He heals from within outward, and all healings—whether through pills, injections, surgery, or pure spirit—are from within outward. They can be permanent. Perhaps," thoughtfully, "This is the biggest proof of psychosomatic ills. Until the inside is free of the corroding thoughts or emotions, the outside manifestation of illness appears. But I suppose we have to be mature and admit there is something icky in our thoughts or attitudes. It is so much easier to blame germs—or God—or contagion . . ."

Yes, had her mission been only Mitch, he alone made the covenant worthwhile.

Oh, this Christyoke of Truth makes life so simple! Not easy perhaps, but simple!

So wondrously simple! No matter if one calls it Christyoke of Truth or self-psychology or metaphysics. It works! It frees from all bondages of lack and limit!

If she could just stack Truth thoughts in her hands, give them out with temp sticks in the morning. Or if she could just put visible seeds in their hearts and minds the way one can inject penicillin! No, she giggled to herself in the lonely corridor, penicillin is always inserted in the fanny and truth seeds must go into the hands and feet. But that's the point, really. Truth is abstract and visible only to the eyes of faith and understanding . . . yet how huge the harvest when one waters the seeds of communion with the Lord's ideas and teachings.

If she could just coax, cajole, coerce, implore, inspire, *love* them all into trying it, proving it . . .

Abruptly she stopped the tumult of thoughts. All the persuasion in the world would not work as perfectly as keeping her inner light shining! Each one who caught the intangible truth opened his door to her with questions about her happiness. Or health. Or radiance.

And probably most of us come to Truth because of the loaves and fishes. Even me.

"You have brought us a long way, dear God. A l-o-n-g way!

"Surely not as we planned or hoped, but surely Your way. Now, of course, we wouldn't have it otherwise. Had the investment produced the huge harvest or had John's salary increased by geometric proportions or had we found the right lender of

347

sufficient funds to really commence the Farm Summer Home we would still be idling our motors, using Your laws only for the family and our smaller world.

"You made us mindful of the whole world. You have prepared John through his business experience, his personal use of Your principles. Surely John knows You intimately. Personally.

"Me? . . . You've driven me to the right books and the right people—and the right experiences to prove the workability of this . . . this magic! Sheer magic! You've sent me places the lesser part of myself would have never ventured. You have proved Yourself. You have stretched my horizons and grown my dedication through Itchy, sheep, Pal, Jane Allis . . . our children and other people's. I no longer want to see bigger and better hospitals. I have a dedication for the preventive kind of medicine, but my accepted 'cure' comes not from serums or shots. I now know—personally—divine love perking on the inside of one's heart is the panacea. Christ Jesus said it once, the bit about the cleansing of the inside of the cup and the platter, for He meant the inner thoughts, emotions, and attitudes.

"So, Blessed Father, I know You 'face-to-face.' You aren't just church-on-Sunday to me. You aren't the yearning within me that is a bit vague and warm. We are Partners. You are real to me . . . and I hope I am growing the way You want me to. You've given me—us—a vision of the universe and all the people in it. You have taught us the joy of fulfillment and selflessness. Thank You."

It was good to take inventory. Possibly a banker wouldn't be fantastically impressed by the size of their opportunity fund. Doctors would attribute their family health to 'luck' or 'excellent resistance' or 'fine heredity'. Neighbors would satisfy themselves about the appearance of the sheep as further good fortune. Yet—oddly—even those who ran through life occasionally saw something—like the time her uncle stared peculiarly at her upon learning of their Fresh Air program, mumbling something like 'some of us merely amass fortunes and others live their ideals.' Faith thought she detected self-disappointment envelop his words.

In the outer sense they had done little in Red Mill they set out to do. They didn't establish themselves in the chicken business. There wasn't a chicken on the farm. They had not built up the sheep population to three or five hundred. The present census was one hundred forty, and they were being sold that day, so that they could join Jed at his healing center.

Seemingly they had bogged down with Itchy problems, dry wells, taxes, mortgages. So forth and so on. When all the sheep but four ewes twinned and the corn crop was fantastic, farm prices not only dropped, they plunged!

It was as though the Lord shut all the small doors to force them toward the big door. Forced them to walk with Him. Work with Him. Prove Him. Cosmic prods.

So?

So they swapped a small dream for a huge vision.

A huge vision!

Jed's center, a retreat and study place as well as healing center for the body physical! A combination of all the things they were practising. Fantastic. Utterly fabulous. That's what God is, blessing and blessing all people, all contacts, in an ever widening circle. Truly this is the parable of the talents . . . use that which you have and more is given.

How restless we mortals become when we cannot see the immediate goal.

Wondrous too that through all the days and nights—whenever John travelled away from the farm in the early days of their residence, Faith was never alone. Always He guided, led, encouraged. Always there were minor miracles, His hand with them, as though to surely see they weren't too engulfed. The perfect Parent who prepares the child for being more, living to his highest potential. Then when it was necessary for Faith to get a job, John didn't have to travel so much. Truly their careers dovetailed in time and talents!

The cleansing period had to be, she honestly admitted to herself, the letting go of jewelry, insurance, bonds so that they would be completely dependent on Him! She saw herself as a slim teenager, carefully explaining to her friends she really didn't like the diamonds; they were too ostentatious but she wore them to please her dad. Eventually her lack of appreciation removed the diamonds—although by that time she enjoyed them. Even as a judge in man's court says 'ignorance of the law is no excuse' so it seems to be in the spiritual realm . . . like the 'windfall' thing the day of the hurricane.

Surely, all these years of working hand-in-hand with Him was

349

preparation for the greater vista. How does the quote go? 'To give the light one must have the light.'

How beautifully God taught through the sheep! And how wonderful to have the backyard study groups to practice on! She thought of Alice Starr, the organizer of the first group, smiled to herself seeing Alice that Saturday morning in the nursing home reach for her hand and say, "Honey, whatever it is you have, I *want* it!"

Great humility and awe enveloped Faith. Surely she was a witness to the practicality and the workability of this modern spiritual science, God's blessed leadings, patiently bringing them to the higher purposes of living, teaching, channeling.

Many of us wondered how Faith could contemplate leaving Red Mill after pouring their love and sweat into the very soil. Faith, and John too, knew this whole farm project was His preparation, their proving ground. God pruned them, developed greater depths and heights of consciousness. Now they could give the light for they comprehended the light—while even greater light beckoned.

No special fanfare the last morning at The San. Most of the men were indifferent, at low ebb, on awakening. Those who caught the special something from Faith quickly healed and moved out. So the census was a thing of flux. Performing her wake-up program Faith felt she might as well have worked merely for the paycheck rather than building-the-cathedral-invisible thing! Only a few recognized the divine love she channeled.

No wonder Jesus deplored Jerusalem. He had come to 'gather it to Himself as a mother hen her chicks' and they had preferred the familiarity of struggle, sweat, taxes. . . .

She must not condemn. Nor mourn. That would be as Peter slipping into the wetness of the waves rather than walking them to Christ. Each one unfolds according to his own divine pattern. Nothing—surely not truth—is lost. And—who but God can evaluate? Perhaps each accepted as much truth as he could individually digest . . .

Impulsively she flung her arms upward, "O, God, let it be that man everywhere is increasingly receptive to Thee in soul, mind, body, and affairs. Amen!"

Moving from ward to ward with her buoyant good morning,

she deliberately imagined each temperature stick to be immersed in the magic of 'with God there is nothing impossible . . . here and now, through your indwelling divinity, you are healed.'

The west hall finished, she returned to each bedside, recording pulse rates and temperatures. In each ward doorway a casual 'so long.' Her heart's silent prayer lingered as she proceeded to the east hall, then to the children on the third. A few minutes after seven, the report finished, she strode from the Pavilion to her car on the hillside.

Early morning summer freshness greeted her. Dew drenched blossoms trickled their perfume, the mountain top seemed drenched with the aroma of wild honeysuckle. Another day of fulfillment ahead.

The last day of the prayer-study groups the lesson would be about Law and Love, for recently a newcomer asked if she thought of God mostly as Principle or as Love. "Law—or Principle—and Love are two aspects of the same truth," she had answered. "He taught it simply, 'Love God and your neighbor as your self. On this hangeth all the law and the prophets.'"

She would base the secondary teaching on 'Ye tithe mint and anise and cummin and omit the weightier matters of the law— justice and faith and mercy. These ye should do without neglecting the other.'" (She wondered if they knew cummin belongs to the carrot family). But the important thing, the qualities of justice, faith and mercy, they are the components of the Love-Law. She must be sure to remind them His law is not hard and binding like the stone tablets Moses chiseled on. Rather the law lived and taught by Jesus is full of joy and light. Working with it in mind and heart brings joy and freedom—and wondrous power to do great good. It is the difference between His hand over yours while you paddle life's canoe perfectly through rapids—or being tossed and churned by those waters, tumbled about on the rocks, wedged on sandbars or splintered at the foot of the falls . . . the cosmic prods to return to Him in consciousness.

This curiously wonderful mixture of karma or boomerang and free will . . . that when we elect to merge with Him the karma is minimized . . . and gradually we really want to do His will. . . .

And she must clarify that Law is a trinity. First, there's the big sweeping universal law of love that holds the planets in their

351

places, manifests as order and harmony, recurrent seasons, gravity, attraction-repulsion, spiritual economy, and synthesis.

Secondly there are society's laws—patterned after Moses' teachings. Traffic regulations and rights among nations and men. Some day courtesy would not have to be enforced but would well up within each heart, spill over into affairs, and every man 'would have God on His hands as he touched his brother.'

Thirdly there are the laws each of us sets in motion for himself, usually in ignorance or superstition. The modern false gods. Like expecting cycles of depression. Saving for rainy days. Knowing the right people becomes the sesame to success. Unintentionally we set up these limitations, like the woman who knew she would heal if 'she but touched the hem of His garment' . . . the laws we set in motion by our silly chatter . . . 'it's too good to be true' . . . all that jazz. Even herself as a teenager talking away the family diamonds!

'Grumble rumbles' she'd dub them.

"Grumble rumbles are the fears, criticisms and complaints the mortal part of us spouts forth," she would teach them. The fears, the petty resentments and minor irritations we hold so closely to ourselves and enjoy fussing over. "Karma, like gravity, never takes a holiday," she would teach. "Every thought in your garden of mind is harvest seed. Watch your thoughts. Watch the inner reflections of your heart. Learn to sit in self-judgment of your thoughts and meditations. Your attitudes. The Hawaiians say all religion boils down to harmlessness . . . kindness to others . . . Law is Love and Love is Law. . . . What you hate you bind to yourself inseverably until you will love it and let it go. . . . You *must* love."

These things she would teach the last day with her group.

She must remember to tell them the gem from Fischer's book about Gandhi. Lest they treat this lightly—this power of the spoken word. The little scene where Gandhi greets Fischer with 'I am a spent bullet.' In a few weeks the assassin's bullet completed its mission.

Faith wondered if Gandhi used those words deliberately as Jesus sought the crucifixion for all its wealth of symbolism and the opportunity to prove His 'power to lay the body down and to lift it up.' To say nothing of His demonstration of continuous life!

She must reread Fischer's wording so that she could word-paint with colors rather than sketch in shadings.

Faith parked in the driveway as John came across the side porch. He had awakened the children, readied their breakfasts and his own, prepared himself for the day. How well God designed their lives, dovetailing and complementing their individualities and personalities as well as their responsibilities, all in preparation for His larger divine assignment!

They kissed, and chatted briefly. John slipped into the seat. Faith watched until she heard the rumble from the little wooden bridge, the echo fading as the car climbed the northside of the mountain and the echo reverberation faded downstream.

She entered the house and greeted the children around the breakfast table.

Author's Note

Life *need not* be drudgery or dreary plodding.

Life can be a glorious, exciting, mystical adventure for you as it is for John and Faith Wells. Though these are not their real names, they are actual people who lived these experiences.

All other characters are also clothed with fictional names for their privacy.

Jed is composite biography.

Perhaps you can see something of yourself in any of them.

So—this is my little store in various cities. May its advertisement—and gift—bless you! If you desire to learn more about these ideas, may I suggest any of the following channels of light which I know personally, although there must be many others equally sincere and dedicated. To put them alphabetically:

Astara Foundation, Los Angeles, California

Dr. Norman Vincent Peale, Minister of Marble Collegiate Church, New York City

Rosicrucian Fellowship, Oceanside, California

Dr. Ervin Seale, Minister of Church of the Truth, New York City, affiliated with International New Thought Alliance

Unity School of Christianity, Lee's Summit, Missouri

Dr. Helen Zagat, Minister of Church of Divine Unity, New York City, affiliated with Divine Science Federation International

Emmet Fox gave his gifts to the world until 1951, and his wealth of books is available in many libraries.